PAUL JONES;
THE
PIRATE.

PAUL JONES SHOOTING HIS LIEUTENANT FOR STRIKING THE AMERICAN FLAG.

PAUL JONES;

BY

THE AUTHOR OF "ROBIN HOOD," "WAT TYLER," &c.,

I have a tale to tell—'tis of the sea,
Filled with wild wonders, blood, and mystery.

CHAPTER I.

" A sullen languor still the skies opprest,
And held the unwilling ship in strong arrest."
FALCONER.

' The greatest danger here was from a shark.
BYRON.

" I saw him beat the surges under him,
And ride upon their backs ; he trod the water
Whose enmity he flung aside, and breasted
The surge most swoln that met him ; hisbold head
'Bove the contentions he kept and oar'd
Himself with his good arms in lusty stroke."
SHAKSPERE.

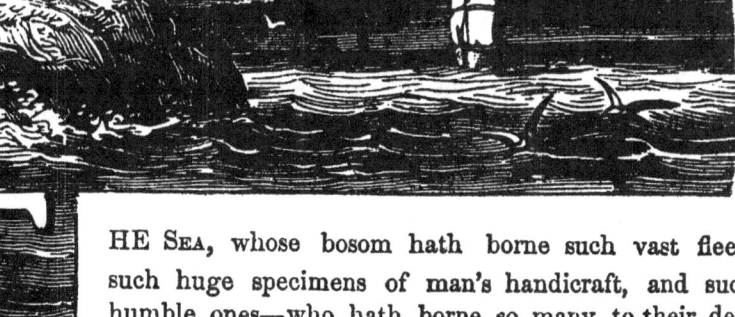

THE SEA, whose bosom hath borne such vast fleets
such huge specimens of man's handicraft, and such
humble ones—who hath borne so many to their destination safely, and swallowed others so remorselessly ;
who hath in its slumber smiled, and seemed so gentle
and placid to those whom a few short hours sub-
sequently it has filled with horror at his wrath, lashed in its fury and en-
gulped unsparingly, so that they may never more glad with their presence

the eyes of those who hold them treasured in their memories, and who, with hearts that deferred hope makes sick, are waiting anxiously for their arrival at home.

Whose surface, now unruffled, now whirling in fretful disorder, makes the spirit that trusts to its support, while he is borne to distant isles, alternately bound with gratified senses, and raised high by pleasant hopes—cast down with despair and filled with the fear of death, from which escape is hopeless; of perishing, so that none may know how, when, or where—know only that they never reached their port, or return to the spot they quitted. Whose broad expanse, whose trackless and pathless waste, abounding as it does with strange varieties, gives but small indications of the wonders, the mysteries, which are hidden in its depths; its palaces of coral, its rocky caves, its boundless wealth, or its numberless strange inhabitants—wild, and singular, and fearful, yet beautiful.

Whose depths are unfathomable; over whom thousands of miles may be traversed, and no land glad the eye: whose chronicles are filled with tales of horror, of mysteries, of deeds of high daring, and wondrous enthusiams; of blood, of crime, of glory, of riches, of honour, of monstrosities, and death; who hath its regions of sunshine, of skies cloudless and windless, and of ice, of dreariness, and darkness; its climes of the sunny south, where the creatures that live in its blue waters glow and shine, and are clothed with the most beautiful, most gorgeous hues: its gloomy northern ones, with its cold keen blasts, abounding in huge monsters, leviathans of the deep, and creatures of form and character to make human beings, shudder in gazing on. The dream of the boy enthusiast, the blight of many a fond heart, the home alike of the noblest, the bravest, the villain, and murderer, the honoured and the outcast, and the grave of the fair and lovely, the brave and good, the ruffian and heartless.

The SEA—the theme of the poet, and the writers of prose over the world—the subject of many a pleasant history, and many a terrible one—lay stretched out in calm repose, one wide expanse of undisturbed surface, as a frigate, bearing the English flag, was making her passage homeward, after cruising in the West Indies: there was not a breath of air to move the pendant from clinging to its haliards; the top-sails and top-gallant sails, hung unruffled in the clue lines, and the vessel herself remained stationary, save her slight roll as she heaved and fell over the swell of the sea, which seemed like the slow beating of the pulse of this sleeping mass. The crew were lounging idly about in he forecastle and waist, and the officers were lolling on the quarter-deck, listening to long yarns of a questionable character, which each in turn regaled the others. There were a few boys, and a number of marines; but all seemed overcome by the listlessness which the sultry air shed over them, and were mixed together in little groups, amusing themselves in various fashions, as their inclination led them, provided they did not trench upon their discipline or duty. The captain was in his cabin indulging in a siesta, in which the vessel itself seemed to join, for she lay upon the waters, nor advanced an inch though she had almost all her canvas spread to catch the slightest breeze.

She was a fine frigate of English build; she carried fourteen ports on a side

was of unusual length; her hull was low for a vessel of her calibre, but had a very clean run from her bows to her counter; her spars were tall and thin, and raked almost as much as those of a schooner or brigantine, and as she lay there with her clean white duck spread out, she looked like a swan upon the waters.

Among those on board who were engaged in conversation, there were two young men in the forcastle; one of them was leaning lazily on the bitts, and the other was seated upon the deck with his shoulder reclining against the bitts, and was to all intents and purposes as idle as his companion; the former was the elder of the two, and bore evidence of many years' exposure to the air, and hard work; his features were open and frank, his skin almost the colour of copper—his eyes were dark and very bright; his hair was nearly black, was long, and confined behind in the form of a long-tail, while at his temples it hung down in ringlets; his height was about five feet eight, his shoulders were broad, his figure sturdy, and his hands large, and, with his labour, as hard as iron. There was an honest, ingenuous look about him, that told his heart was of the true material; his companion was evidently much younger, but was quite as tall, almost as brown, and nearly as robust, save that in all his limbs there was a character of a higher order than those of the elder—it was the difference between the racer and the hunter, the greyhound and foxhound; his feature were regular and manly, decidedly handsome, and not the less so for the quick glances of a brilliant black eye, or the impatient curl of his upper lip; his hands and feet were small for his statue, and his bearing altogether, albeit he reclined so carelessly, was that of one who was more fitted to command than be commanded. He was listening to his elder companion, who was trying to impress something on his mind, with the impatient gestures of one who hears matter he will not suffer his mind to be weak enough to credit.

"I tell ye, John," said the elder, after receiving a short laugh of disbelief in reply to something he had just advanced, "there is one in this ship doomed —you may laugh, and shake your head like a top-sail sheet block in a gale; but I tell you 'tis as I say—there is one abroad here who'll be over the side, and never find the bottom."

"If he did he'd be a cleaverer fellow than any on board," replied the young man, with a laugh; "we sounded here yesterday, for the want of something better to do, with ninety fathom of line, and the lead never grounded; why, I'll give him a week, and then he won't touch the bottom."

"He'll never be permitted to try it, for there has been one awaiting a good many watches for him, and he won't go till he has him," returned the elder.

"You mean the devil, I suppose," cried John, "and the purser is the one he is keeping such a bright look-out for."

"Not I, John—no! Not but what I believe the old one is in his wake," returned his companion, "and will hook on his grappling irons as soon as he has dropped his peak, seeing that he has been running to leeward of honesty all his life; but what I mean to say is, that there's one of the crew of this crack frigate, whose grog 'll be stopped afore a breeze makes her walk through the water; I tell ye, John, no shirk ever followed a craft without taking one of her crew. I've stepped in plenty of crafts; I've been upon blue water all my life—was entered on a ship's books before I was half as tall as a handspike; ah! when I was no taller than a mainstay block. I have sailed east, west, north, and south, and never clapped eyes on a shirk that left a vessel it had followed more than a day without having a taste of human flesh, and here's a big fellow been hanging on to us for a week. Them creturs, John, knows, as well as you do, that there's somebody's life-lines unreeving when they hold on so hard, and that blue-nosed cannibal, that's backing and filling about us, knows well that there'll be one of us slip our wind before long."

"Is he or you prophet enough to tell which it will be?" asked John.

"Why, no, that's hard to say," replied his comrade; "I've been trying to think—there's nobody on the doctor's list, nor is there any foremastman or petty officer hanging on to the hallards of the yellow flag—there is only the first lieutenant that I know of, at all likely."

"And why him?" inquired John.

"Why, I'll tell you; did you never hear how he came to smell salt water?"

"No; he was third lieutenant when I first came on board; he was made second lieutenant when Lieutenant Addison was shot in our affair with the pirates, and now he's first lieutenant, because our first lieutenant died of the yellow fever—that's all I know about him."

"Well, I'll tell you a little more; you see he belongs to a family that carry a high peak in London, but haven't much shot in their locker, and it seems that at some grand party he fell in with a little schooner—the prettiest bit of craft he ever clapped his eyes on; he ranged alongside of her, and. I fancy, in their first engagement with their eyes, she boarded his heart, and carried it in the smoke, so that he hauled down his colours to her, and followed in her wake. Well, you see, as I take it, the cut of his jib being very ship shape, she hauled her wind, hove too, and would have no objection for him to rub her name out and put his own there, but her owners wouldn't consent, because his lockers were low. Well, there was the devil to pay, and no pitch hot; she vowed she'd carry no colours but his, and he swore he would command no vessel but her, and he would have her in spite of old Nick himself; but somehow they laid hands on her, and run her into some latitude that he couldn't overhaul, and his father got him rated a midshipman—then, by some mystification, before he half knew a backstay from a forestay, he was drafted to this saucy Wildfire, as third lieutenant, just before you were pressed on board her, so he's been taking on ever since; he looks as white as a new bolt of duck in an old topsail, and fights like a devil when there's any to do, just as if he was in a hurry to get over the standing part of the main-sheet; he has been as dull as an empty grog-can these last few days, and I've seen him eye the shirk, and the shirk eye him, as much as to say, they would join company soon."

"Pshaw," cried John, with a contemptuous laugh; "I've eyed the shark, and the shark has eyed me, and yet I have no intention to join company with him: the creature has had a few things thrown overboard to him, and he follows for what he can get—from a lump of junk to a cocked hat, nothing comes amiss to him."

"No, they've been known to swallow bottles and swords, and articles that other creturs finds not easy to digest, without feeling any inconvenience from the snack," said his companion, "why, I've seen 'em shove their teeth in the blade of an oar, and snap it in half—and they'd make a grip at a jib-boom, or, for the matter o' that, a main to'-gallant mast, if they were very hard up for for food—being a long time on short allowance, say a fortnight, without anything to eat; but I tell you, John, you are out o' your latitude when you talk so lightly of shirks; I tell you the cretur that's whistling and rolling over and over, like a nigger in good luck, scents death on board this vessel; and how do you know it mayn't be you he's waiting for."

"Me!" exclaimed John, almost with a start, for the other spoke with considerable earnestness; in a moment after he laughed, and said, "No, no, Gasket—my time is not so near at hand:" and then speaking with singular energy, continued—"I have too much to do in the world yet; I feel that I have some stirring course tracked out for me before I am sewn up in my hammock and hosted over the side. I can tell you, Gasket, I have a strange impression that before very long I shall make one among the men of whom the world speak loudly—I feel it here, Gasket," he added, striking his breast forcibly "it haunts me as that shark has haunted this frigate; do what I will, thing what I will, it is always present. I have not mentioned this before to a soul—I have tried not to think about it, but I cannot shake it off; it clings to me whether alow or aloft, whether laying out on a yard or lying in my hammock; whether in the mess, or in the tops; taking my spell at the wheel, or during watch, it is all the same—there's the same thought always before me."

"Why, it must stick to ye closer than a barnacle to a ship's copper, exclaimed Gasket, somewhat mystified: "what's it like?"

"What is it like?" echoed John; "do you know what ambition is, Gasket?"

"Ambition!" iterated Gasket, looking up to the truck, as if he expected to see his reply written up there; "why, I think I do, it's what makes a foremast man the first on deck and the last to leave it—wear the cleanest shirt, and go cleanest shaved—be the smartest hand to shake out a reef, or hand a sail—the nimblest to lay out on a yard, or to give the truest heave of the lead so that you know your water to an inch—never got rated as an idler, or have his grog stopped for being last up the main hatchway; it's what makes an officer love to command the sweetest bit of craft a shipwright can build—keep her like a king's parlour—work her and fight her as nothing on salt water can come near—that's what I take ambition to be."

"You're right to a certain extent," replied John; "but you have only mentioned the workings of ambition, not its motive."

"Your learning, John, makes you get the weather gage of me," exclaimed Gasket; "I don't know exactly what you mean, if what I have described is not ambition."

"It is easily explained," replied John; "what makes the foremast man try to be the smartest man in the ship?—is it not with the hope of being a petty officer, and so on, hand over hand, until he becomes a master? What makes the captain desire and endeavour to make his vessel the most perfect piece of wood and iron that ever ploughed salt water? Is it not with the hope of becoming an admiral? That hope, that motive, is ambition, Gasket, but there is an ambition beyond this, which out-sails all thoughts of mere personal aggrandisement—it is the desire to have your name spoken of with wonder and praise—to have your fame in men's mouths after your death, and be held up to future generations as a model of bravery, of honour, and worth—that is ambition—that is mine; that is the desire, the craving, that incessantly fills my mind, so that I can think of nought else."

"You are a strange fellow, Johnny Paul," exclaimed Gasket, "there's no man in this frigate like you—you're accounted the smartest hand on board, though you are a pressed man; you are captain of the main-top, and are not likely to stop at that; you're always called aft when the captain wants the best hand in the ship, and though the youngest in the mess deck, save the boys, are looked up to by all hands, and more deference paid to your words than to the bo'sen's when a yarn is being spun, and anybody wants to lay out an anchor to windward of our senses. There's not one of the crew—and we've some rough 'uns too, that would be all the better for being run up to the yard arm—that dares top the sea officer over you; one fellow tried it, and as you flattened his jib-sheet in less time than a middy could hail the tops, nobody else followed in his wake. I like you, Johnny Paul, because there's the true stuff about you—on every tack you are the same, and that's what I like. I know well, that if I did not suit your log you wouldn't make me such a constant mate, and as I know on every point you are fair and above aboard, why I know you mean it; and I'll stick to you while a timber of me holds together; but though I know you are above us all in bearing, and all seamanlike qualities, I think it only making sail in chase of a Cape flyaway to expect that you should become an Admiral Drake, or like the Dutchman, carry a broom at your mast head to shew that you sweep the seas; no, no, John, you might as well try to beat up to windward under bare poles as expect such promotion as that, unless you were under the lee of his majesty, or had some shipmates at court that could get commissions as easy as a purser makes money. Why, look at our first lieutenant, he had friends at home to give him a cant for'ard, and luck has given him pretty fairish head-way, but you'll see that when he reaches England, and gets regularly entered on the books of the Admiralty—for he's as yet little more than half a luff tackle— he'll wait and wait ere he's made commander, and then, unless he gets another cant from his friends, he'll be a long while ere he's posted."

"How came you to know his history—none of the ship's company know anything about him, but that he is a smart officer with a good and gallant heart, interrupted John Paul.

"What I've told you is nothing to what I know," replied Gasket, sinking his voice suddenly to a whisper, "there's more that's caused his pale face and dull eye than what I have told you; I came athwart him before he ever trod the decks of the Wildfire."

"You did?" exclaimed John, with surprise.

"Aye, it's a wild and singular story," replied Gasket, "and though you may laugh at my speculations about the shirk, I have good cause to think that the creature is waiting for nobody else on board but him, and he knows it. When his eye first caught sight of it, he started as if he'd been brought up suddenly in the wind's eye, and then he shook off his quiver with a laugh that sounded not over and above merry—"

"Sail ho!" suddenly shouted the look-out from the fore-topmast head.

"A man overboard!" was the next moment vociferated, and in an instant the whole scene was changed from the greatest listlessness and quietness, to one of great bustle and activity. As the last cry, uttered with startling clearness, rung in the ears of the two speakers, they sprung to their feet, and Gasket laid hold of John's arm, and said—

"I told you truth, you see, Johnny, there's some poor fellow's log made up, and the shirk has not kept us company for nothing."

But John Paul, paying little heed to what he said, sprung to the side, and saw a poor fellow closely pursued by the shark Gasket had spoken of, struggling and striving with all his strength—shouting for help—to get towards the bows of the ship; he glanced his eyes aft, and saw the first lieutenant leap off the taffrail into the sea, while a dozen hands were busy in lowering the jolly boat from the davits abaft; disengaging his clasp knife from his

No. 2.

waistband, and opening it, he plunged into the sea, almost at the same moment as the Lieutenant, and swam direct to the shark, who was but a short distance from the poor fellow that was striving so desperately to escape from him.

The Lieutenant in the meanwhile made towards the man, who could swim but very little and who, overcome by fear of the shark, was unable to use that little, and sank two or three times. When the Lieutenant reached him, he caught a firm hold of him, and sustained him until a rope was flung to him by Gasket. He grasped it tightly, and was, with his perserver, soon hauled on board. All eyes were now turned upon Paul, who swam resolutely up to the shark, which, when it saw him coming, opened its tremendous jaws and displayed its many rows of terrible teeth, as if anticipating a dainty morsel. His progress after the man who had fallen overboard had been exceedingly swift: but seeing Paul making deliberately towards him, almost swimming into his mouth, he abandoned his first object of pursuit, and made a dart at him, which would have cost Paul his life, had he not instantly dived under the ravenous monster. As he sunk beneath him he, plunged his large knife into him up to the hilt twice, and then swam away hard and swift. He had barely reached the surface of the water, ere he saw the shark within five feet of him, rushing at him with the speed of lightning, his murderous jaws distended ready to receive him the moment he reached him. Again Paul dived, and again he plunged his knife desperately into the body of the fierce fish; and this time, with great strength, drew it down at least half a yard. The shark gave a loud whistle, almost like a shriek, lashed the water with its tail until it flew around in showers, and again made at Paul, who dived deeply down, and swam swiftly away, preparing for another attack.

During this conflict the sides of the frigate were thronged with gazers. The cry of "A man overboard!" had aroused all the crew. It was speedily known that the first Lieutenant had gone over after him, and brought him safe on board. Gasket was not long in making it known also that John Paul was foolhardy enough to battle with the shirk, which was unusually large, and the whole crew, officers and all, crowded to the side to witness the fight. It appeared terrible to behold to those on board the frigate. The sea, for some distance, was dyed with blood, and from the rapidity of motions of both Paul and the shark, it was impossible to tell which had the best of the conflict. In the excitement which this affair caused, the communication of the man in the fore-topmast head passed unheeded; indeed, had a vessel came athwart the the frigate's bows, she would at that moment have scarce been noticed. The look-out himself, attracted by the shouts of the men below, cast his eyes on the scene that was going forward, and, for a time, in watching the affray thought no more of the strange sail.

Gasket could scarcely be kept from leaping overboard to join Paul, and stood watching with intense interest the result of his daring. When the Lieutenant and the seaman had been hauled in at the bows, the men who were lowering the jolly boat were made acquainted with it; they immediately held on, and then hoisted her again to her former situation, and all of them crowded to the quarter and looked on the terrible combat between Paul and the shark with eager and anxious eyes. The perseverance, the strength and activity of Paul, encumbered as he was with his clothes, surprised them all. Every now and then they lost sight of him as he disappeared under the water, just as if it was thought, he was imbedded in the jaws of the monster. Each time this occurred the loud whistle from the shark told them the knife was doing its work; and the extraordinary increase of blood in the water shewed that it was doing it effectually. The men gave a loud cheer as Paul again arose apparently untouched, and as fresh as ever, and faced the terrible monster, it was noticed he always faced him the moment he appeared, and then dived directly under him, making a tremendous incision with his knife. From the repeated stabs—and deep ones they were—it seemed wonderful that the shark could retrain its powers, apparently but little impaired, and still lash the water so fiercely, and dart so swiftly at its gallant enemy. The sea around was, if such an expression might be used, deluged with its blood; and it bore in its body several tremendous wounds, and yet it kept on its efforts to seize Paul with the same vigour as at first. It was not to be supposed that Paul could continue this combat much longer successfully, unless his antagonist began to exhibit great weakness; and as he had not made any such display, the fear became general on board that Paul would be bit in half ere he had slain the shark. Once this appeared to be realised; the sea had become so thickened with blood by the mad and desperate plunges of the monster, that Paul could not use his eyes beneath the water. He had continued, after a dive, rather longer than usual under water, and rose immediately after the shark, instead of proceeding him, as he had hitherto done. His back was towards him also; and the shark, with the swiftness of lightning darted at him, seizing him, as everybody on board could have sworn, with its terrific jaws. A strong shudder ran through them all, and a shout of horror arose. The next instant Gasket leaped over the side into the sea, and the first Lieutenant's voice was heard, shouting with a loudness that startled every one into instant action—

All hands out, boat, there!"

The boatswain instantly, although completely wrapped up in watching Paul—such is the effect of discipline—piped, and with his hoarse voice, which had been cultivated by a thousand sea fogs, shouted—

" All hands out, boat! jolly boat, boys, away!"

" Jolly boat, boys, away," the boatswain's mate; " bear a hand there."

The words had scarcely left his lips ere twenty men sprung to the davits abaft; half a dozen stout fellows, accompanied by the first Lieutenant, who had watched Paul's conflict with the shark with singular attention and anxiety, jumped into the jolly-boat, and were lowered swiftly until the boat swam upon the sea; she was unhooked—the oars were immediately in the rollocks, and the men bending to their task, had in a second good way upon her, and pulled swiftly to the scene of action.

CHAPTER II.

" And in the warm hedge grew lush eglantine,
Green cow-bind, and the moonlight coloured May;
And cherry blossoms, and white cups, whose wine
Was the bright dew yet drained not by the day;
And wild roses and ivy serpentine,
With its dark buds, and leaves wandering astray;
And flowers azure, black, and streaked with gold,
Fairer than any wakened eyes behold.

SHELLEY.

"I love thee, by my life I do;
I swear by that which I will lose for thee,
To prove him false that says I love thee not."
* * * * * *
What can you do me greater harm than hate?
Hate me! wherefore?"

SHAKSPERE.

" And have you mercy too! I never did
Offend you in my life."
" Help! help! oh, help!"

IBID.

Upon the same evening that the foregoing event was transpiring, a young maiden—tempted by the beauty of a clear sky and a sweet cool air that was playing gently around after the sun had been trying his hardest all day to persuade the inhabitants of England that the little Northern Island could be made as hot as Africa—strolled down a narrow lane contiguous to the sweet little village, Grasmere, in Westmoreland. The lane was a kind of lovers' walk; it was lined on either side with hedges, or rather banks, which were profusely decked with shrubs and wild flowers; the hawthorn trees were in close companionship with nut trees, and a blackberry bush would ever and anon claim acquaintance with both, and with a perseverance not to be denied, would thrust its thin straggling arms among the stems and leaves of both, probably anticipating to be eventually upraised and shine out at the top as tall and well-looking as the best; young sprigs of oak, too, would fight for a place, and put forth their green leaves, looking fresh, and strong, and healthy, as though there was no mistake about their intention to become fine trees in that particular spot, without caring who or what they displaced; the holly, too, with its dark, shining, " crankled" leaves, containing at every sixteenth of an inch a sharp thorn, which seemed placed there like pins in a young girl's waistband, as a sort of gentle hint that they were not to be too freely handled, put in its claim for an abiding place, and even at the expense of being locked in the embraces of a nut, a hawthorn, and wild rose, resolved to remain and grow there, although it looked upon all around with a gloomy, solemn look, indicative of not liking its company; never, on any occasion, looking pleased until nearly everything else was dead, and then it put on its scarlet ornaments, and shone alone in its glory, proud and haughtily. In some parts, the elderberry, as the elder is familiarly termed, and elbowed its way into notice, and had been like the nuts, pretty successful in getting a good place, after having squeesed some nearly to death, displaced others, and out-grown most, acting like a tall man in a crowd, who puts everybody on one side, lurches and jostles here and there, getting before this one, shoving aside that, and chuckling all the while to himself, that whoever can't see, thanks to his long carcase, his rudeness, and his selfishness, he can. The wild rose, which was very modest and very pretty, pleasant to the eye and grateful to the nostrils, seemed to have the goodwill of all, and did not appear to suffer so much from intrusion as most of them; if it did 'twas done more lovingly, and it put forth its simple, but beautiful flowers as though it was glad it had the power of making some return for the kindness it received. But there was one plant which was welcomed by all, and as it appeared twining here, and nodding there, with its graceful red-yellow blossom, it seemed that the various green things were ready to cry 'lean on me;' and its fragrance made the air faint, and whenever human eyes were cast upon it, the gazer cried 'how beautiful is that honey-suckle.' Then came the wanton bine weed which made love to everything near—never could anything be so fond of embracing as the bine weed; it could not live without caressing something—its affection was most comprehensive—a coquette, with a hundred lovers, was nothing to it: it threw its arms around whatever it could reach; it twined all over the nut trees, it curled around the hawthorn, it gave the blackberry bush a share of its favours, and did its utmost to entrap some broad dock leaves. Its desires were most inordinate; it deemed nothing too proud or too humble, too high or too insignificant, to lavish its caresses upon. Wherever it found an object to embrace, it twined round, and put forth its little light green-pointed leaves as if in delight and gladness, but it stretched its long arms, leafless, until it reached something to curl round, and then, when it had a good stout swain, such as a full hawthorn bush, or a thickly grown elder, it poured forth leaves innumerable; embellishing its green drapery with white bell-shaped cups, whose hue would lend a whiteness to the most snowy marble ever raised from the earth, and was so profuse in his gifts of leaves and buds, as to bid fair to smother and kill with kindness the tree it loved so much. It had a companion in the ivy, but the latter was gloomier, looked not so fresh and fair, and was a thought more chary of its embraces. And underneath this entanglement of green things was a luxuriance of wild flowers—some were bold and flaunting, others very modest; the foxglove not caring who saw it, in fact rather preferring to be looked upon than otherwise, and the little pale blue bells and yellow-eyed flowers, shrinking beneath broad green leaves in all humility, taking pattern by the violets which had been the first to show, with their small, but fragrant blossoms, that the cold winds and bitter frost would soon give place to warmth and sunshine. Here were briars, a perfect forest of thorns—no more to be touched with impunity, than a porcupine— scratching their way among some ragged robins, with their pink starlike blossoms, and hosts of other plants that bore no thorns, nor had a thought that way; and above all these grew the thin stems of sapling oaks, beech, ash, elm, and sycamore, some with their sturdy branches and stems, others with their thin graceful arms and light tracery of leaves, quite elegancies of nature; and there were added to all these many other beauties, which would occupy too much space to narrate, but no less captivating to the eye or sense. It was surprising to see, but delightful to hear, the numerous birds that had taken up their abode in this charming land, each warbling its notes with its best ability, as if in rivalry of his neighbour, or else to show how excessive was the happiness heaven had granted it.

To her who walked slowly down this pleasant path, every beauty had its distinct charm, from the tallest tree to the smallest flower; she would frequently pause to regard the green-leaved, bright-blossomed plants, with a gratified gaze, or listen to the notes of some little unseen chorister pouring forth his melody

"In profuse strains of unpremeditated art,"

with the keenest sense of its sweetness; yet was she thoughtful and sad in her demeanour, and when she plucked a flower and gazed upon it, it seemed as though there were other thoughts in her mind than those which the small plant might have raised: she was pale, and would sigh even while listening to the warbling of a sweet-noted bird, as if she wanted some of its gladness; ere it ceased she wandered on, and appeared to have so sunk into abstraction as to have no more remembered that she was surrounded by these things of beauty; again the utterance of a deep drawn sigh would rouse her from her reverie, and once more the flowers, and trees, and birds, would claim her attention for a short period, and again lost in some recollection which could not be other than sorrowful, from the melancholy expression with which it was entertained. While indulging in one of these musing fits, which a close observer might have seen had brought tears, she was startled by the sudden appearance of a man, who quitted the hedge in which he had concealed himself, and stood before her. So rapid and noiselessly had he accomplished this feat, that he laid his hands upon her arm ere she was aware of his presence; she uttered a faint scream, and drew back hastily as though she would have fled; but anticipating her purpose, he stopped her, and said—

"You needn't be afraid—it's only I."

The maiden cowered beneath his bright gaze, but did not speak. He was a young man, about three and twenty, tall, and rather strongly than well formed, for his arms and legs appeared somewhat too long to be in proportion with his body. He had large black eyes, whose expression was more fierce than amiable, more wild than soft, quick, impatient, and restless in their demeanour, but were the best of a set of features which, if physiognomy be a true science, would have induced his fellow creatures not to have placed a superabundance of faith in him—dark straggling hair, of which he had, according to the costume of the period, a great profusion; and in his hands he bore a stout blackthorn cudgel. He regarded the maiden with a gloomy gaze, and finding that she did not speak he exclaimed—

"Have I frightened the tongue out of your head? Well, I didn't think neither, that I was quite so repulsive as all that, even to *you*." He laid great stress on the last word.

"You came upon me so suddenly, Jasper," she replied, shrinking with fear and speaking timidly, "that you alarmed me; I did not think there was anybody in the lane but myself, and seeing you so unexpectedly, naturally made me for the moment startled."

"Seeing me unexpectedly?" he replied; "why, yes, I dare say it was unexpected to you, because you never think about me, or if you do, only to discard me from your thoughts as something hateful, and despicable."

"I despise you not," she said gently.

"You hate me, which is as bad," he exclaimed roughly.

"I hate no one!" was her meek reply.

"But you don't love me, and so its all the same to me as if you hated me," he cried; " you shrink from my touch as if I was a reptile that would poison or sting you; you avoid my presence as though you loathed the sight of me; I have seen you in the midst of a smile grow serious and pale when your eye has lighted on me, as though I was a pestilence whose breath would wither you, and yet you tell me you do not despise me, and hate no one. You do not curse me with words—you do not turn your back on me disdainfully—your eyes do not flash haughtily and offendedly at me, it is true, but your hatred of me is no less bitter, your dislike to me no less powerful. Why is this? I love you, Florence; oh, my God!" he cried with vehemence, "how dearly, how madly I love you—I, the rough unbendable Jasper, that nought living could move, you might lead as a child. You! a thing I could crush life out as easily as I grind this worm to powder now crawling beneath my feet; yet I would be your slave—I would sooner bow down to you and worship you, than Him who says none but himself shall be worshipped. I could be to you a very spaniel, that would crawl and lick your feet, and yet stand before a king though the block were the price of my insubmission. I have never bent leg to human being, yet could I fall upon my knees to you, and pray you to love me as I love you—yet you could never do that—but only to love me, only to tell me that you love me, and act as if you did, and I will do your will as humbly as if I was a slave, an hundred times more abject than the black wretches that toil beneath a burning sun without knowing what freedom means. Come, Florence, what say you; will you throw off your dislike of me, and walk with me? If I am rough and rude to others, I will be kind and gentle to you; I'll teach my tongue to say soft words, and my brow to wear a woman's smoothness. I have knocked about, here and there, all my life—slave to nothing but my passions and my will. My nature is not so uncouth and harsh as it seems—you can curb its wildness, you can tame it to your liking, for there is not a pursuit I love, however reckless or pleasant to my feelings, that others may deem daring and wild, which I will not give up if you wish it. You don't give me any answer," he said, after a pause, " but stand shivering and trembling as if you were a lamb in the jaws of a wolf: mark, me, Florence, I can be a wolf even to you, or as tractable as a well-trained colt; it will depend upon yourself, you c in make me what you please. Have me, and there's not a village or town in England shall turn out a man whose deeds are more to your wishes than mine shall be—reject and scorn my offer, and you had better raised the worst devil in hell against you. Stay! you leave me not without an answer," he cried, seizing her by the waist as she turned away from him to retrace her steps homeward, " you shall tell me now yes or nay."

"Unhand me, Jasper!" said Florence, "you terrify me,"

"You shall give me an answer!" he exclaimed.

"Let me go, I entreat you," she cried; "some other time I will speak to you—not now, not now."

"Now or never, Florence," said he sternly. "I am not of a nature to be put off day by day, and then have some smiling, trimfaced hound bear you off while I am waiting for your answer. No, no. I am not to be gulled by any such trick; mine you shall be or no one's; no man shall laugh, and cry he bore off the prize that was out of the reach of Jasper Chough. No! no! This is a very good time and an exceeding good place for an answer; there is none here to interrupt, and none to bias you, if you feel inclined to say yea. Come, pretty Florence, can you not form your own pretty lips to say yea—do you love me?"

"Do not stay me, Jasper—suffer me to depart," said Florence, appealingly; 'what you may have to ask me, I will answer at your father's not here."

"Why not here?" demanded Jasper, with a sullen brow. "Look you, Florence—your inverted face and cowering frame tells me you shrink from me as some hideous monster, and yet to me you are dearer that any object in life: even as it seems you hate me, do I love you. I will not stay to question why I, who always returned hate for hate, scorn for scorn, blow for blow, with all—even my own father!—should return you affection for loathing; but whether you love or hate me, you shall be mine. I laugh to scorn all ties of blood or honour where my will is concerned; I set at defiance all laws, when my mind is set upon any object; and I have the means of carrying out my will securely when it is once formed. Give me your promise, nay oath—for one such as you would be bound by that to any sacrifice—that you will wed with me, and you shall at once leave me and return to my father's. We will be married when you will, and you shall find that Jasper Chough can be as mild and gentle as the best gallant that ever stepped: if you say nay, you go with me now to a spot where none can find you, known only to myself, and there you shall learn to love him you now despise. In that lone spot, with no companion, no living thing near you, save a wandering eagle, which in its search for food may wheel past you, you will be glad to bestow the smiles you now withhold upon the only human being you will there see. The place is wild and cheerless, I can tell you, and has its horrors, but it is very secure. I have not roamed the hills, a roving, restless boy, for nothing. You will find it not so pleasant as your own chamber at the hall, but it will be of your own choosing, and you must bear with it. You have seen enough of me I think, Florence, to know I am not addicted to romancing; in giving this alternative, I mean that you shall accept one or the other—either be my wife by your own consent, or my mistress by compulsion. I am prepared for either. Answer me, girl—you had better accept my first proposition."

"I cannot do either," murmured Florence, evidently suffering under considerable apprehension and agitation.

"I do not intend to give you the opportunity of refusing both," he said, with a laugh; "you must say which you'll do: say that you will not marry me, and

that instant I seize you and carry you off, and sooner than you should be rescued from me, I would plunge my knife into your heart."

"Jasper, you cannot seriously mean me this wrong?" cried Florence earnestly; "you are only doing this in one of your wild humours to terrify and make sport of me; but pray do not continue it, for indeed you frighten me I am not used to jests of this nature; let me return to the hall."

"Jests of this nature!" echoed Jasper, with a hollow laugh of scorn. "Jests, perhaps you think my love for thee a jest? perhaps you deem the burning flame in my head and heart, since I have seen you, a jest? You may think it a jest that I, who was reckless of all, had no thought or care for any living thing save myself, have passed sleepless nights and days which knew no peaceful hour since I have known thee. It may possibly be a jest to you that I have watched beneath thy window the long night through, when the wind howled and the rain came down in floods; and again when the moon shone so bright that the hounds bayed affrightedly at it. It may be a jest that I have struggled with my feelings as never man wrestled with himself before, ere I would acknowledge, even to you, that any living being had dominion over me. All this may be a pleasant jest and food for mirth for you, but it has been worse than death to me. Mark me, Florence, I do not trifle with you; you shall be my wife by your own assent, or, by the living God! I bear you this hour away where mortal, save myself, never shall behold you more."

No. 3,

"Jasper, Jasper," cried the terrified girl, bursting into tears, "remember I have been placed in thy father's care, beneath his roof; he has pledged his faith for my safety—you dare not so violate his honour as to wrong me in this terrible manner."

"Have I not told you," he replied, "I hold in scorn all ties of blood where my will is concerned? I heed not my father's honour, or his word, no more than if he lived not. I know of no earthly consideration to stay me; nothing but my own death shall step between me and thee. I could see my father upon his bare knees to turn me in my purpose, unmoved; I could bear to see my mother, who has most influence over me, shed tears of blood in appeals in thy behalf, and reply to her with a laugh of scorn. I own no power but my will, save thy beauty, and that is a power to which I bow; but yet only in so much that I still will hold the rein and guide it my own path. Come! Florence, time is waning, decide quickly—"

"Have mercy, Jasper!" cried Florence, clasping her hands, and addressing him with an air of passionate entreaty; "you have the attributes of a man; you would strike to the earth him who would doubt your courage; you would think it base in you to strike a weak boy, who had not strength or power to resist you; and were one of great might to tell you, over such only did you dare to exercise your bravery and strength, you would peril your life to teach him different—"

"To what tends all this?" interrupted Jasper, impatiently.

"That I am alone here with you," she replied, "a weak, defenceless girl—powerless to aid myself against your superior strength; one so timid and strengthless, that exercised against me, your strength and courage would be base cowardice and unmanliness; even your rough companions would laugh contemptuously at him who exerted his might against one so poor in power as I. Oh! Jasper, take me not at this disadvantage—force not a reply to your question from me, while death stares me in the face; ask me when there are others by, that I may reply to thee—"

"With scorn and derision," retorted Jasper, interrupting her again, "No, Florence, I am not such a fool! Here I can get a reply that if I like not I can put aside as easily as move a briar out of my path; here you are as free to choose as in your father's house, and as free to reply, but if you disdain the offer of my hand and heart, you have only youself to blame for the consequences that will as certainly ensue as that I stand here. For the last time, I ask you, will you have me?"

"What, if I answer no? You say I am free to choose," said Florence, eagerly."

"And so you are," he replied, with a coarse laugh; "whether you will dwell as my wife in happiness and every luxury in my father's hall, or whether you will prefer to be my mistress in an abiding place where only the eagle comes."

"Oh, Jasper!" cried she, wringing her hands bitterly, "do not be so merciless. You tell me that you love me—you! would wish me to love you—are these the means to gain my affection?"

"I have no chance of any other," he returned, sternly. "Were I to resort to the common mode of making myself agreeable in your eyes, I should still be a dangler, still have a negative from you for every prayer to be mine ; you would show no mercy to me—you would make no sacrifice to become mine— why should I then sacrifice my feelings that you should become another's ? Loving forms a little part of my nature. I would not Love you if I could help it—I would rather hate you; but that, it seems, is a power over which I have no control ; I must love you in spite of myself—and since fate orders it so, it shall ordain that you shall be mine. I wait no longer ; all appeals are vain : the spray of the sea should sooner dissolve a rock of adamant than your most passionate entreaties have the smallest effect upon me. Will you be mine ?'

" I cannot," she cried, with intense agitation, " I am sworn to another."

" To another !" he shouted fiercely ; " it is my brother."

" No !" she cried, striving to escape from the powerful grasp with which he had seized her. " No, no, it is not ; release me, Jasper, let me return ; do not harm me. If you have pity, let me go."

" Let you go! what to the arms of him to whom you are sworn?" he cried. No, weak fool, you come to the arms of him who has sworn to have you."

He passsed his arm on the instant round her waist, and hurried her a few yards ; she screamed violently, and he tried to force his hand over her mouth, to drown her cries. Close to the spot where they had stood was a small stile, and just as he was passing it, a youth, seemingly about twenty years of age, leaped lightly over it, and stood before him.

" How now ?" he cried. " What means all this, Jasper? Why are you laying your hands thus roughly on Florence ? "

" Oh, Frank, Frank," she screamed, " protect me, protect me ! "

" Protect thee !" he uttered, with surprise. " I hope there is no need, and Jasper here ! "

" Frank," exclaimed Jasper, sternly, " take my advice ; if you wish not to come to harm you will wend your way homeward, or any way but the path I am taking."

" I don't understand you," he replied, looking on each with astonishment.

" Understand this," cried Jasper, through his teeth, "' your presence here is an interruption to what you cannot prevent. Away with you, you know I brook no meddling with whatever my mood may lead me to do. You know it's dangerous to step between me and my will : do not you attempt it, or you will not be safer from my rage than a stranger."

" Frank, Frank !" shrieked Florence, still struggling with Jasper, " do not leave me, for mercy's sake do not—Jasper has vowed to inflict the most terrible fate upon me—I shall be safe while you are by. Take me away, and let me return to the hall."

" Do not be alarmed, Florence," said Frank, soothingly, " it is only a wild freak of Jasper's—he will not harm you. Jasper, if you must indulge in these mad humours," he added, turning to him, " why do you not seek one better fitted to bear them than this gentle girl ? Take your hands from her, and cease your rough jesting ; had you any consideration you would not have been so foolish. Can you not see how terrified she is ? Unhand her.

Jasper's breath seemed quite taken away by this speech ; he uttered a laugh, more like a howl, of intense scorn; he knitted his brows until they almost covered his eyes, and then, with a malicious grin, he cried,

"Brat! how long is't since you dare talk to me in this fashion? Idiot! dost thou know to whom thou talkest?"

"I have not that to learn;" replied Frank, looking on him with cool steadfastness, unaffected by the scowl with which Jasper regarded him.

"Then mark me, Frank, were you a thousand times my brother," roared Jasper, "I would strike you senseless to my feet, even if the blow beat out your brains, if you attempted to thwart me! Take yourself off, therefore, while you are yet unhurt, and bandy no more words with me."

"I shall take Florence with me," said Frank, firmly.

"You'll take nothing but your life," cried Jasper, and not that if you bait me still. Begone, fool!"

"It is not your wish to remain with him?" said he, appealing to Florence.

"Oh, no, no!" she replied, weeping. "Oh, Frank, he vows I shall consent to be his wife, or he will tear me away and carry me up the mountain, where no one will ever see me more."

"And mine you shall be, though all the angels in heaven and demons in hell said me nay," cried Jasper. "Look you, Frank!" he added, fiercely, "quit the lane at once, and if you dog my steps, or look which path I take, or say one word at home that you know aught of Florence's absence, nothing shall spare you from my fury. I'll bring you down as surely as I ever shot a heron.

"I care not for your fury," replied Frank, coolly; "I never did. You lorded it over everybody—never over me. If you gained your wish when it ran counter to mine, it was only because your greater size and strength obtained by force what my spirit never yielded; but I am no longer a weak boy—I fear not you nor any man; and while I have strength you shall not offer insult or wrong to one who, independent of being a defenceless maiden, is a guest of our house, and who by right calls for protection and respect from us all. I tell you again, Jasper, I go not without Florence; that if you attempt to perpetrate the villany you intend, I'll hunt you as I would a wild boar to its lair. I'll never leave you, and treat you as the deadliest foe man can have among his fellows. Not tell what I know of her absence?—foh! Take your hand from about her waist, and no longer disgrace your manhood or your family in this brute fashion."

"To hell with the family!" roared Jasper. "Fool! do you seek your death? Stand aside, or your blood be upon your own head."

"I'll not budge an inch," cried Frank, his eyes glittering with excitement; "and if you do not at once unhand Florence, I swear by the Almighty, I'll fasten on you, and compel you."

"Jasper, Jasper, have mercy!" almost shrieked Florence; "let me depart, let me not be the cause of your quarreling in this dreadful manner. Let me depart, I entreat you; for heaven's sake let me free."

"Swear to be mine, or I'll strike him dead where he stands, I swear by the same God he has invoked."

"Heed him not, Florence!" uttered Frank, loudly and earnestly; "I fear him not for one instant. He shall set thee free."

"Frank, will you stand aside?" shouted Jasper, grasping his blackthorn cudgel and compressing his teeth.

"Set Florence at liberty," replied Frank, with a determined look, and standing firmly, ready either to spring upon his brother, or to receive his attack.

"Not though a battery of twenty-four pounders opened fire upon me," roared his brother. "Away with you, or I'll beat your brains out: my blood is up, Frank, and if you persist, your mother's grey hairs could not save you."

"My blood is up too!" cried Frank, his face flushed to scarlet; "unhand Florence—I care not for your threats a straw—I, too, have a devil in my spirit Let go your hold of Florence—will you take your hands from her?" he added with teeth and hands clenched, and speaking in his throat.

"No! fool!" shouted Jasper, making a tremendous blow at him with his stick; Frank avoided it, and instantly sprang upon him—seized him by the throat, and cried, in tones of furious determination—

"By heaven you shall! or fulfil your threat on me."

The struggle was tremendous. Frank was a fine looking young fellow, and very strong; but Jasper was in height and strength his superior—however, he found it no easy matter to keep himself from being throttled, incommoded as he was by Florence, of whom he kept firm hold, although she struggled and shrieked—and by his stick, which, in these close quarters he found of little use; he, therefore, threw it to the ground, and seizing his brother by the neckcloth, strove to hold him off. Florence, as might be expected, overcome by fright, fainted away—as soon as Jasper found she was a dead weight, he let go his hold of her, suffering her to fall to the ground, and turned his whole force and strength with the ferocity of a tiger against his brother. Neither uttered a word, but the struggle was fierce and deadly; each put out his best strength, and Jasper, who was endowed with enormous power, found that his brother was almost his match; they swayed to and fro, each striving to throw the other, and once Jasper succeeded in flinging Frank off in an effort to regain his stick; his face was deadly white, and Frank could read his death warrant there if he was not able to to get the better of the contest; but he regarded it not, and before Jasper could recover his weapon, he fastened on to him again. They gripped, and held each other with the tenacity of a couple of bull dogs—they strained every nerve and muscle to obtain the superiority, until the large drops of perspiration rolled off of them like huge pearls; at length, in one of these evolutions Jasper got a more favourable hold than he had yet obtained—he made sure of it, and then said between his teeth—

"Will you take your life—agree to my terms, and away!"

"No!" replied Frank, "I would rather die."

"Then to hell with you!" roared Jasper, and making a tremendous exertion of strength he lifted his brother from his feet, and hurled him with frightful force upon the ground; he uttered a loud groan as his head came in violent contact with the earth, but Jasper heeded it not; he gained his stick and beat him in the fiercest manner about the head, until he felt sure that life was extinct, he then threw the stick into the hedge, seized the senseless body of

Florence, flinging it over his shoulder, and hurried, at the top of his speed, from the spot—once only, looking over his shoulder at the bleeding body of his brother.

CHAPTER III.

" And Jonah was in the belly of the fish three days and three nights."
                                                                        JONAH, Chap., I.

"Now while on high the fresh'ning gale she feels,
The ship beneath her lofty pressure reels ;
Th' auxiliar sails that court a gentle breeze,
From their high stations sink by slow degrees.
*   *   *   *   *
                    The winds arise,
And the dark scud in quick succession flies ;
While the swoln canvas bends the masts on high,
Down in the wave the leeward cannon lie.
The sailors now to give the ship relief,
Reduce the topsails by a single reef.
*   *   *   *   *
Here perseverance, with each help of art,
Must join the boldest efforts of the heart."
                                                        FALCONER.

Before the jolly boat could reach the spot where John Paul and the shark had disappeared, John Paul again appeared, and this time without displaying the remarkably dexterous manner he had previously exhibited; he gave a cheer, and swam leisurely towards the boat, and the next minute the white belly of the shark was seen rising slowly to the surface of the water. John Paul had proved victorious: the shark was dead.

All the men in the boat instantly gave a loud hurrah, which was immediately responded to by those crowding the side of the frigate, who saw Paul hauled into the boat unhurt, and the shark appear dead upon the waters. Gasket was immediately afterwards picked up, and stretching out his hand to Paul, he exclaimed with much interest and anxiety—

"How is it with thee, Johnny? the shirk did not get thee in his grinders, did he?"

"Not he," replied Paul, shaking him warmly and heartily by the hand; "I carried too much sail for him."

"You've turned him up handsomely," replied Gasket, with a laugh.

"It was a mad trick, Paul," said the first lieutenant. "What induced you to peril your life with such recklessness?"

"I did it, Sir, to cure my messmate, Gasket, of a foolish superstition he, in common with blue jackets, holds."

"And what is that?" asked the lieutenant with a smile.

"He believed, Sir, because the shark followed in our wake, that there would be a spare berth before he parted company with us; vowed there was a doomed man in the crew, and when I jumped over after Tom Oakham, and found that you had picked him up, it struck me that I would try and disprove the superstition. There lies the shark dead; and now, Gasket," he added, turning with a laugh to his friend. "what becomes of your 'one aboard who will be hove over the side, and never find the bottom?'"

Gasket shook his head, squeezed some of the water out of his hair, and then said with some emphasis—

"I don't know how it is, but you always get to windward of me; I try to battle the watch with your arguments, but I am always obliged to strike my colours, raked fore and aft."

"Have you any spare line in the boat?" suddenly asked the lieutenant to one of the men in the bow."

"Ay, ay, Sir," was the reply.

"Take a turn round the shark. tow him to the side, and let him be hauled on board," he added.

"Ay, ay, Sir," replied the man, touching his hair, for he had no hat on, and proceeded to obey the order.

"Paul," continued the lieutenant, "when you have changed your wet clothes, come aft; I wish to speak a few words to you."

"Ay, ay, Sir," replied Paul, respectfully.

The boat now reached the ship, the lieutenant went on board, followed by Paul, Gasket, and the crew, save two, who stayed to hook on the boat, preparatory to its being hauled up to the davits. The lieutenant sought his cabin to rid himself of his wet garments, and most of the crew gathered in a crowd round Paul and Gasket, to learn all the particulars of the adventure. Paul, however, replied very briefly to their numerous queries, and followed the lieutenant's example, in descending to his berth to change his clothes. Gasket, who was less taciturn, was besieged on all sides, by topmen, idlers, marines, mates, and mates' ministers, all eager to know whether Johnny Paul had not dived down the shirk's main hatchway, and cut himself out; one of the main-top men, named Stretch-out Dick, from his propensity to get the weather gage of possibility in a yarn, suggested this feat, and was instantly greeted with a loud shout of laughter from all around.

"Ah!" cried Stretch-out Dick, when the laugh subsided, " you needn't open your ports and grin like a lot of niggers over a rum keg; the thing ain't unpossible, seeing we have scripter to tell us of one who did a trick which leaves what Johnny Paul's done a long way to leeward."

" What's that?" asked Gasket, quickly, not thinking there lived, or ever did live the man that could accomplish such a feat.

" What's that!" repeated Dick, with great contempt. " Upon what water have you been sailing, that you don't know that? Did you ever read the scripter?"

" I can read bunting, but not books," replied Gasket, coolly; " I can hand, reef, and steer; I can make a short or a long splice, haul taut, or belay with any hand in the ship, tho' I say it; I can work a ship's reckoning after my own fashion, and work it true, but I was never put to pot-hooks and hangers. Now John Paul can overhaul the best book ever launched, whether in large or small print, ah! and sail away as he reads, at a faster rate than a vessel runnning large before the wind, no backing or filling, no bringing up for a hard word, or lying-to to fathom the meaning, unless I hoist a signal of ignorance, and then he makes the matter all as clear to me as blue water in a calm. Then he stands dead on again, not hoisting in a skysail or any flying kite, until he has run into port with the last leaf; you ask Johnny Paul whether he has read the scriptures, and see what he'll say to you."

" Yes; but I ask you whether you've read the scripters, and not him," replied Dick, when a murmur of applause from the listeners followed Gasket's speech, which had come home to them, had ceased : " but I see that you haven't, if you had, you'd have known how a taut seaman, one Jonah, was hove overboard because he'd run athwart hawse where he should have steered clear, disobeyed orders, as we are all apt to do some time or other."

" Hove overboard!" cried Gasket; " what, made to walk the plank?"

"Why, something of the same bearing; you see what he had done didn't please the Lord no how, and he knew it, and so he thought he'd up stick and run for some other port, until the affair had blown over; but, you see, the Lord carried too many guns for him, and tho' he stole away in the smoke, he was discovered, and just to show him that he was overhauled, a gale was sent, hard enough to blow the devil's horns off. There was a tremendous sea running, and the ship would neither stay, nor wear, nor lie-to, nor scud; she shipped heavy seas, and trembled at every shock, like a doctor's mate that's seized up to have two dozen; well, all this while this Jonah was turned in."

" Turned in!" cried several of the crew.

" Ay, snug in his berth, snoring like a porpoise afore a gale, and all hands

were turned up to the pumps, for there was almost three feet water in the hold; well, he snored so loud, that he was heard above the roaring of the wind and rattling blocks, and the master not being able to understand what it was, asked the first mate, and he said it was the lower deck going to blow up with the water that had filled the lower hold."

"What, him snore make dat noise?" rather incredulously asked a black, who was cook, and who, with extended eyes and mouth, was listening to Stretch-out Dick's tale.

"To be sure," replied Dick, "do you think some men can't snore as if they had a speaking trumpet to their nose?"

"No, but him tink dis Jonah hab dam large nose, dat all," and he showed his white teeth, in a satisfied grin at his own wit; a roar of laughter from the men accompanied this sally, which Dick seemed by no means to enjoy, he gave his quid a turn, and regarding the black with a look of intense contempt, he said—

"Why, you black lump of a monkey, what are you grinning and jibbering at, like a smutty Chester cat? D'ye think because your woolly figure-head is as flat as a mainstay block, that nobody could have a nose of a decent size. Why, there was a man, I've heard say, down westward of the parts I came from, whose nose was so long that he was obliged to keep a man to brush off

No. 4

the flies, that were fond of settling on the tip of it; and, although there was a heir born to some property he expected to get, his nose was too long to be put out ajoint by it; it took you two hours afore you could see to the end of it—there, put that in your cheek with your quid, and see how 't chaws."

"Ah, 'em berry long noses, and berry long yarns were you come from, Masser Dick," replied the Negro, drawing another laugh at Dick's expense from the bystanders.

"Well, but what became of Jonah," asked Gasket, seeing that Dick was about to have another fly at the Negro's gullibility.

"Why, you see," said Dick, returning instantly to the original subject, "the master was not quite satisfied that the first mate judged right, because the noise had more tune and less rumble, and he resolved to see himself, and he went below and soon found Jonah snug in his hammock, paying away his music like a marine at his drum. Well, the captain was taken quite aback, as you may suppose, to find how comfortably he was taking the weather, so he roused him up; he stood two or three calls before he opened his eyes, and then the master talked to him in King's English, with the bight of a rope's-end, which quickly started him upon deck; when he got there he was over-hauled, and he was quite boxed up to find it blowing a heavy gale, and he knew nothing of it; seeing that it blew so hard all hands were obliged to hold on to their teeth to prevent them being blown out of their heads."

"I think you might take in a reef there," said one of the topmen, with a laugh.

"Not I," replied Dick; "you see this took place in old ancient times, when it blowed much harder than ever it does now."

"So I should think; but what about this Jonah, that did more than Johnny Paul did just now?" said Gasket, impatiently.

"Why, ain't I making all sail to the point," returned Dick; "you understand that he didn't belong to the ship, and I believe wasn't entered at all on the ship's books. He'd come on board as they cleared out, and no questions were asked at the time; but now when they found out how he'd skulked, they wanted to know who and what he was, where he came from, and where he was going to. Well, he ups and tells 'em, like a true tar, that hates lying and deceiving, and all sorts of sailing under false colours, and, to their admiration and wonder, begs 'em to heave him overboard, and they would see that the wind would drop, and they might proceed on their voyage with a fair breeze.

Well, they didn't exactly like to do this, and, perhaps, thought he was mad, as any reasonable Christians would; but the gale increased, they expected the masts to go by the board, and they thought they'd try his advice; so they took him up and put him over the side, and immediately the sea went down, and their vessel lay like a duck on a pond."

"That was in old ancient times," said Gasket, with a laugh.

"I told you so just now," replied Dick.

"Em berry odd it nebber do dat now," ejaculated the nigger with a grin, in which the hearers joined.

"Do you suppose, darky—" began Stretch-out Dick, intending to say something so severe that the black would never recover it, but he was stopped by Gasket, who pertinaciously kept to the main story.

"What did Jonah do when he got into the water?" he inquired.

Dick contented himself with a look at the negro that he fully believed would make him small enough to lie in a nutshell, but it didn't; so wondering at his thickness of penetration and hardness of belief, he continued—

"Jonah struck out and dived through some seas, and was lifted over others. Presently he saw a monster of a fish, crowding sail towards him, as that shirk did after Tom Oakum when he fell over the side."

"Was it a shirk?" asked Gasket.

"No," replied Dick, "it must have been larger than that; our chaplain says it was a whale."

"A whale!" returned Gasket; "why in what latitude did this affair take place, in the North or in the South Seas?"

"I can't exactly say, but I think it must ha' been in the North Sea; and werry likely it was a whale, because, you see, it was above two hundred and fifty feet long, and had a mouth larger than the main hatchway of a hundred and twenty gun ship."

"Dam large whales in ol' anshun times," said the negro.

"And with rows of teeth that would beat any line of battle ship in the service," continued Dick, not heeding the cook's remark, beyond troubling him with a scornful glance.

"Then it couldn't ha' been a whale," said the topman, who had spoken before.

"And why not?" asked Dick, sharply.

"Because whales have no teeth," he replied.

"Aha!" shouted Stretch-out Dick, with a laugh of derision, "no teeth! why, what's in a shirk's jaws is nothing to 'em. How should you know they have teeth or no?"

"Ah!" said the negro, addressing the topman, "dat dam good too; whale no teeth! Do you tink if Jonah, hab such a berr large nose, dis whale would hab no teeth?"

"I dont care for Jonah's nose," cried the topman, "but I've been several voyages whale fishing, and seen more whales than you could count in a day. I never saw any whales with teeth, nor mouths as large as a first rate's main hatchway, or longer than sixty feet."

"Oh, but dis in ol' anshun times," cried the negro, and there was another roar of laughter.

"I'd advise you to keep a bright look out, Master Sambo," cried Dick, indig-nantly, "for if I don't clap a stopper on you in a way you don't like, my name's not Dick Thompson."

"Him forget, it Stretch-out," replied the negro with great glee.

Another roar of laughter followed this speech.

"You black-muzzled, bow-shanked, jury-rigged, binnacle-eyed, shahk-heeled nigger, I'll make your inky mug as scarlet as the figure-head of the Red Lion sloop of war if you don't spring your luff. Avast, you pitch skinned—"

Gasket stept between him and the negro, who rolled his white-looking eyeballs round, half in glee, half in fright, for fear Dick should keep his promise and, checking his ire, said—

"My lower stanchions want a pair of dry cases, and unless you bring your yarn to anchor, I shall sheer off. Did this Jonah, out knife and whip it into the gills of the whale, as John Paul did into the shirk?"

"No," replied Dick, smoothing his ruffled visage; "no, he looked down his throat as he bore down upon him, and saw there was plenty of stowage room for his gullet was as large as a captain's cabin; well, it struck him, mind ye, that if he dived into the hold, he might lie there coiled up snug enough, until it got fair weather, and then he might get out just as some ship was passing, and be picked up, and work his passage home. So when the fish was right up to him, just athwart his bows, he makes a clean spring, and into the belly of this lump of a fish he goes, and there he found it rayther warm, and strong fishy smelling, but, howsomdever, werry comfortable, to battling with a sea that was running mountains high, And there he stayed for three days and three nights—"

"What, in a fish belly?" asked the negro, in undisguised astonishment.

"In the belly, you unbelieving heathen!" cried Dick, with a fierce aspect.

"An' what him do for him dinner all dis while?" inquired the Negro.

"You be ——;" what Dick was going to say is lost to the world, for Gasket again checked him with a laugh, and said—

"Why, Johnny Paul was no such fool, or he could have been snug enough in the shirk's belly long ago.

"Ah, but Jonah lived there—lived as jolly as a tar when a ship's paid off, and there's lots of prize money to share," responded Dick; "I don't say he had beef and biscuit, and grog, but he had plenty of small fish and such like, to make him comfortable, and at the sunrise on the fourth morning, the fish, I suppose, feeling a little disarranged in the stowage, a little sick at stomach, makes for shore, and opening its mouth when close in to the surf, Jonah, all a-taunt-o, because he smelt—over and above the strong smell of his berth—land quite fresh, leaped out, and beating through the surf, got safe to land again; now I take that as something more than Johnny Paul did.,'

"Rather," replied Gasket, emphatically, "that same Jonah was a clever fellow."

"Iss," cried the black, "him clebberer dan Johnny Paul, but den him lib in ol' anshun times, you know."

"It's not a bad story for the marines, but it won't do for the blue jackets," said Gasket, with a laugh; "if you'd told me he'd battled with a shirk in this fashion, I'd perhaps ha' believed you,"

"Don't you believe it?" cried Dick, with indignation displayed in his broad red features.

"I can't say exactly I can hoist it in," replied Gasket.

"No," cried the topman, with a laugh, "it would carry away half a hundred luff tackles to hoist it in."

"Iss, but tings different in ol' anshun times," cried the Negro, grinning, "it carry away no luff tackle to hoist anyting in 'bout dem."

His sally was, as usual, rewarded with a roar of laughter, and Dick's brow waxed red and wrath.

"The chaplain will tell you that this yarn is all true, for it's in the scripture," he exclaimed," and he told it to me ; besides, it's in a little book, and he says, there is wonders and strange things about the deep, and God's power, that seamen can't fathom, and what I've told you isn't half so strange as other things he can tell."

"Ah, he was laying out an anchor to windward of you," said Gasket.

"Not he," replied Dick, " its all gospel in the good book, and he told me other wonderful things."

" 'Bout ol' anshun time," said the negro, " cos mus believe anything in ol' anshun time."

Dick's patience was exhausted at the laugh that resounded once more, and he sprung at the negro to give him a thrashing, but the black was too nimble for him, and escaped to the waist, while dick's messmates interfered to prevent him following, and restored him speedily to good humour.

The shark was placed on deck in the waist, and waited but the captain's leave to be cut open and its contents laid bare, and a group of men stood round, speculating what they would be. John Paul had obeyed the order of the first lieutenant, and having shifted his wet and bloody clothes, attended him in his cabin. For near an hour he was left alone with him, and when he returned to his place in the forecastle, his brow wore an expression of thoughtfulness and gravity which he had not shown before the interview had taken place. The lieutenant came upon deck at the same time, and soon after he seized a speaking trumpet and hailed the tops.

"Sir," cried the man.

"Did you not report a sail a short time ago?" he asked.

"Ay! ay! sir!"

" Where away?"

"On the weather beam, sir."

"Do you see her now?"

"No, sir, her trucks dipped five minutes since."

" What did you make her out?"

" A merchant brig, she looked like, sir, but she rose so little before she dipped again, I could scarcely make out her rig. I think she's felt a breeze that's coming up on the weather beam ; I can see the change in the water, sir, and before the sun rises in the morning we thall have a cap full."

The first lieutenant made no reply, but obtained a glass and looked long and earnestly in the direction the man had stated the appearance to be, and saw a dark blue line extending along that part of the horizon to which the man had pointed. His experience enabled him to tell that the man's judgment was correct. He regarded it for some time in silence, and perceived it gradually extend until it became visible to the naked eye; and the colloquy having been overheard, the men crowded to the side to watch for it, for having been becalmed more than a week, and being homeward bound, they looked forward for a breeze with the greatest anxiety. A number of them began to whistle with great earnestness, in the fond hope that they should by such means hasten the breeze, and as the line widened and widened, they whistled with fresh vigour; presently one of them sung out—

" Hurrah !" there's a cat's paw !"

Alluding to a light breath of wind that just disturbed the surface of the sea into a tremble, and then vanished, to be succeeded by others. These were soon seen and pointed out to each other, and the whistlers increased in numbers and in hope. While the breeze thus anxiously expected was drawing nearer and nearer, Gasket appeared on deck, having donned dry garments, and having approached John Paul, he whispered—

" You have been aft with the first lieutenant; if it's no offence, what did he want with you ? "

" I will tell you by-and-bye," replied John Paul, " this is not a time; you can keep the middle watch with me, and shall hear all. What you told me about him is true, I have found, but I have heard that which hath made me wonder; but I see there are ears as open as port-holes round us: I must brace up and haul aft—you shall know more by-and-bye."

" Well, Johnny Paul," cried a captain of the top, laying his hand familiarly, upon his shoulder, " you cut adrift the life lines of the shirk, without leaving him a strand to hold on by. By the blue oakum stuff under Neptune's bowsprit ! I have seen Guinea men, and other darkys, along the coast Afriky, work their ship for sich an engagement as your's; but if they wern't snapped in half like a light spar in a strong sow-wester, they never sheered off without losing one of their timbers. Lord ! them shirks is woracious creturs, as one of our lieutenants that I sailed with in the Lightning, eighteen gun sloop, said, when he saw a brace of John Chaney men swallow a pig that had died of some bad disease, and had been hove out of some dirty merchant brig a fortnight afore."

" Them Chaney-men are not over particklar in their eating," said one of the crew.

" No," replied the captain of the top, " not where pork is concerned. Lord bless you ! them fellows knows when any vessel, king's ship or merchantman, have any pigs on board that's on the doctor's list. Ah ! as well as the unclean creturs themselves. You see they come on board all day to chop and trade, and so on; and at night—because they are such nat'ral born thieves, they'd steal a man's teeth out of his jaws afore his face if he didn't keep a bright look out—they're made to go aboard their junks, which are the queerest craft that ever swam on any water, and have as many cabin windows as a shirk has teeth, or Dick Stretchout's marine's yarns. Well, you see, they makes these John Chaney-men keep a wide berth, because they would lay their thievish paws on whatever was near them—no matter whose, and no matter what. Well, as soon as these fellows knows as a pig, or for that matter a sheep, but pigs is their glory and delight, is dropping his peak, they sing out 'Hi ya, hi ya, hi ya,' and then they clap on all eyes; and when the dead cretur is thrown overboard, then you should see the boxhauling and scrambling, the screaming and chattering, like a mess of monkies over their rations; and when the lucky one grabs him, he holds on like grim death, and the others crowd sail round him, paying away their tongues as a bundle of wenches of the Point would read the articles of war to any-body who ran foul of 'em, and wanted to luff up and bear away, without serving out some grog,　Well, all their shots and small arms ain't of no use, for whoever gets him keeps him ; because, tho' they pull each other about like great gals, there isn't one as will stand fire, without dropping his colours and making a clean run for it—a single lurch of a man-o'war's-man would shake a dozen of 'em to oakum ; but that's neither here nor there.　Well, when they gets the pig aboard, they waits but a little time to cook it afore they stretch along the eating haliards, and then huzza in the bow. They never bring up until the decks are cleared."

"Why, they're worse than cannibals," exclaimed a young seaman, who had listened attentively to the foregoing story; "for your cannibal does mess on fresh meat.　Why, they'd like soup made of bilge water, and lunch on the live stock that's beat out of a two-year-old biscuit."

" I was going to say, afore them Chaney-men and the pigs come athwart my mind, John Paul," exclaimed the captain of the top, "that I, and for the matter o' that, all the crew, thought you had gone into the shirk's lower hold, as a hungry youngster tumbles down the main hatchway when the hands are piped to dinner; and Dick Stretchout here says you did, and you cut your way out of his belly.　Now, for the benefit of any poor devil who may have the misfortune to run foul of a shirk in one of his voyages, and be boxed up, so that he must do that, or part with some of his timbers, mayhap you'll tell us whether the thing is to be done, and in what fashion a man is to set about it."

" Dick Stretchout's imagination is like a Cape fly-away," replied John Paul, with a laugh, " if he makes sail upon it, it will run him out of his reck-oning in a very little while.　No, I did nothing but rip the shark up, and any man with a strong arm, a good knife, great agility, and plenty of resolution, can do the same ; but enough of this," he added, " your yarns and idlings will have a stopper, for here comes a breeze which will make many of you topmen wear a wet jacket, and keep a long watch to-night."

The men turned their eyes in the direction in which he pointed, and saw the wind, which they had seen rippling the sea on their weather beam, and had been flying in patches on the surface, had now reached the skysails or flying kites, as the sailors call them, and was gently bellying them out from the light spar to which they were appended ; presently they felt a slight mo-tion in the vessel, and the man at the wheel sung out that the vessel felt her helm, and in less than ten minutes she had way upon her ; soon all became bustle and activity, and the men prepared, at their respective stations, to be called into action for the performance of duties which their own knowledge told them would be required.

The captain now appeared on deck, and returned the salutations of the officers, he stood for a minute or two gazing to windward, regarding in silence the approach of the breeze. He was a hard featured, stern-looking man, stood about five feet seven, and looked rather thin and bony, yet, as it appeared, rather the aspect of a strong, wiry frame than a deficiency of muscular power. He was compactly made, and there was an air of command about him that appeared to awe even those who were next in dignity to him. He did not change his posture, save to raise his hand to his brow, and then he fixed h is eye intently upon the horizon and remained immovable; at length he said hastily to the first lieutenant—

"Mr. Prior, lend me your glass, if you please."

The lieutenant handed him his telescope. and taking it with a slight bow, he put it to his eye and bent it to the spot on which he had been so earnestly gazing, and after looking for some time, he said—

"Take the glass, Mr. Prior, and tell me whether you see aught on the weather-beam beyond a light cloud or so, which the breeze is bringing up?"

The lieutenant took 'the glass, and surveying the portion of the horizon pointed out to him, said in a moment—

"I can see the spars of a ship rising up fast,"

"Sail ho!" shouted the look-out from the mast-head.

The captain now hailed the tops, and inquired of the man stationed there, whether he had seen her before; the man replied in the affirmative, stating that he had reported her to the first-lieutenant, and the captain turned to Mr. Prior, who replied—

"The vessel reported previously was a merchant brig, and had dropped below the water line as you appeared. This is not the same vessel; she carries taller spars and looks like a ship of size, but as she is still hull down, it is scarcely possible, to tell what she is. These West Indian gentry are so fond of carrying tall spars and trim cut royals, that they are not easily made out until you see their courses."

"She appears bearing towards us!"

"She does; ten or twelve minutes with the breeze she seems to have, will show us her hull."

"If this should be her," muttered the Captain, almost inaudibly, "she shall not this time escape me," and then he watched anxiously the vessel, which now became quite distinguishable to the naked eye. The man at the wheel was bade to keep the helm steady, and, as the breeze had barely reached them, they drew through the water at a very slow pace, while the approaching vessel still bore on, until her hull rose out of the sea. When this took place the Captain surveyed her again with his glass, and then turning round to the lieutenant, he said—

"What do you make her out now, Mr. Prior?"

Mr. Prior took the glass and exclaimed—

"She has the rig and build of a slaver, but there is a smartness in the cut of her sails and in her trim, that shows, if she is one, she has, at least, a smart captain. She is handled in a very seaman like manner, and her commander, I should say, was a man who never crawled into his vessel in the cabin windows. Ah!" he exclaimed, suddenly, "by heaven, she is altering her course. What is she frightened at? She has gone right about."

"What?" exclaimed the commander, hastily.

The lieutenant handed him the glass, which he scarcely needed, and his

practiced eye saw at once that he had spoken the truth. He shouted suddenly, in a loud startling tone, which was heard by every one on board—

"Three points fall off, and haul on the weather braces."

The command was repeated from mouth to mouth, and the command was
instantly obeyed. The effect of this manœuvre was to place the vessel in the
same course as the stranger had suddenly and unexpectedly taken; but as
they felt but little wind, their vessel obeyed but tardily. However, in a little
time the sails began to draw more decidedly, and the ship to gather more way,
and then the lieutenant gave the necessary orders to the men to see that
everything was home. This done, the men awaited in silence the next command, and were wondering what sudden motive could have induced the
captain to stand after the strange sail, which they could see had a light pair
of heels, and enjoying the benefit of the wind, was making way three feet to
their one, leaving them fast, and in all probability with every chance of
escaping them completely: for with the wind light clouds had sprung up
and were succeeded by heavier masses. The sun had dipped into the sea ere
they had moved an inch; and the moon, which would be rather late ere it
gave its light, made the night appear to have set in with darkness. The wind
freshened every minute, and it soon became necessary to take in the lighter

No. 5

sails, which was speedily done.   The vessel, with such a cloud of canvass as she had previously borne, had begun to fly through the water at a very swif rate, and now that she had still her top-gallant sails set, she went bounding through the sea with a velocity that compared strangely with her previou dead immovability upon the water.   A troop of porpoises now went rolling past, and scarce a seaman but what instantly augured that he would be a lucky fellow who kept no watch that night.   The wind had come from the eastward, and until the present moment, had shown a clear light streak of sky, but this now had vanished, and was covered by large dark masses of clouds that came angrily up, and gave "dreadful note" of the gale that was brewing.   To the westward the light still continued, and gave somewhat of an unearthliness to the scene, that made it seem lonely and desolate.   The wind increased rapidly, and the ship flew swiftly through the waters; the captain still carried a large quantity of canvass, urging the ship in the direction the stranger had taken, and whom he could still see.   Presently the curling heads of the sea to windward seemed to be fading in a mist, and then the captain suddenly cried—

"In with the studding sails fore and aft.   Tell the boatswain to see the men do not go to sleep over it."

Mr. Prior repeated the order in a loud voice, and then the boatswain in a hoarse voice shouted the command, continuing—

"Clap on to the top-gallant clew lines, clew up and clew down; pull together cheerily; pull with a will, men."

Soon after this, top-gallant masts were sent down, and the ship was close-hauled; the topsails in turn were reefed, and ultimately were close-furled. The wind had now reached a gale, and blew with fearful violence. The ship would no longer bear her courses, and the topmen were turned up to hand them, and the daring fellows scrambling up the rigging.   The courses were hauled up, and the vessel was now urging her rapid course through the sea, which was one succession of sweeping waves.   She behaved admirably, and in the various manœuvres necessary to keep her to the wind she answered her helm to perfection.   The seamen, who noted everything with keen eyes, felt proud to observe this, and Gasket, seizing John Paul by the arm, said—

"John, I have been in many a heavy gale, and this is as hard weather as I ever saw, but never did wood and iron perform its duty so truly as this Wild-fire has to-night.   The gale has not half blown itself out yet, and you'll see that when the sun shines bright again, and the water has a smooth face, there'll be scarce a spar or seam strained in the Wildfire."

"We shall see," replied Paul, briefly.   "The ship must be first cousin to the Flying Dutchman that will outlive such a night as this without parting a stay or lanyard, or opening a seam.   I hope none of us will part company to nigl t; but if this weather holds I have strange misgivings."

H had hardly uttered the words, when by some accident, the parrel which confined one of the topsail-yards to its mast gave way; it tore the lifts from their fastenings, but not being quite free of the braces it dashed against the topmast with immense force, and two or three hands were sent up to cut it adrift ; they accomplished their feat ; and at the same moment a tremendous sea struck the ship, and one of the poor fellows was shaken from his hold and precipitated into the sea. The cry of a man overboard was scarcely heard in the roar of the gale, and in the confusion which ensued from the heavy sea the vessel had shipped; but Gasket, who had made a contrivance for any such accident, and brought it on deck, heard the cry, and with the aid of two or three of his messmates, hove his "light buoy," as he called it, into the sea; it consisted of a water cask, made air tight, three or four case shot fastened on the bottom to keep that part under water, and on the top a lantern with a blue light in it, which would burn long enough for a seaman to obtain a hold of it, and cling to until he was picked up. They watched it as it was borne from them, half buried in the foam of the huge waves, and offered up a prayer that their poor messmate might, through its instrumentality, be saved.

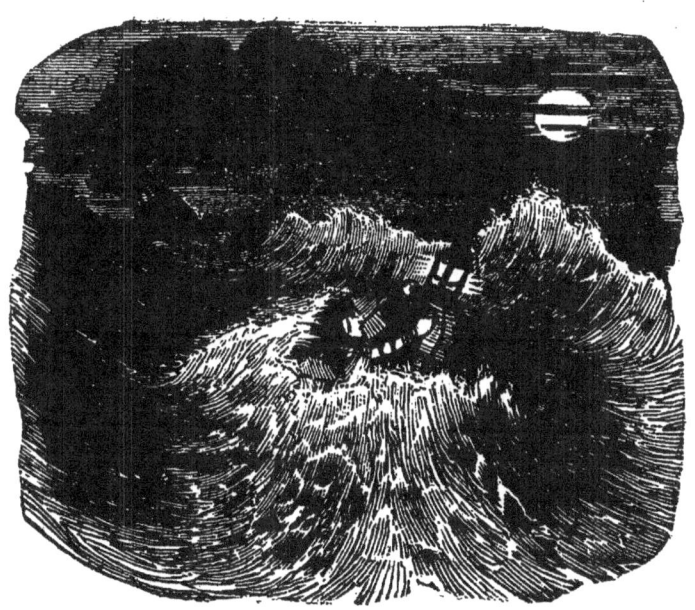

CHAPTER IV.

"Light thickens, and the crow
Makes wing to the rooky wood;
Good things of day begin to droop and drowse,
While night's black agents to their preys do rouse."
                                        MACBETH.

"O night and shades!
How are ye join'd with hell in triple knot
Against the unarm'd weakness of one virgin,
Alone and helpless!"
                                        MILTON.

Jasper Chough, with his senseless burden, took his way down the lane at his swiftest pace; he seemed but slightly incommoded by the weight he bore, and flew along as if sensible of nothing but the fear of pursuit. The narrow lane seemed to grow narrower still as he advanced down it; the foliage, thick as it had been, was in greater profusion than ever, and as the sun was fast declining, the place began to wear a lonely aspect, in the place of one simple and enchanting. The trees, so green and fair in their hue, were beginning to assume deep tints, and their light graceful forms to merge into large and solid masses: the light, feeble and waning, had no longer strength to penetrate the interstices of the branches and leaves, and the previously scarce perceptible shadows were now flung with a depth of hue that made the path gloomy, dark, and wild. The flowers, recently so distinguishable in their " scarlet and purple suit," were now lost in one grim body of leaves, and the place which but a short hour since had been sweet and pleasant for the gentle and timid to wander in, was fast becoming one which they would have shuddered with fear to have been left in alone. The way grew lonelier and gloomier, as though the act Jasper had committed had made him fly from the clear light of heaven to plunge in the dark desolate passages which dwell in the regions of sin and crime; the aspect of the coming darkness had little effect on him, save that of gladness, for it gave him so many more chances of escaping undetected: he had turned his head anxiously several times as he left the spot where his brother lay, a bleeding ghastly evidence of his villany, and could see no prying eye or intruding form appear while he was in sight. As he darted round the bend of the lane which hid the body from his sight, and him from any one who might reach it immediately after he had turned the corner, he could scarce refrain from uttering the laugh of exultation that went through him at his success thus far. His only care was not to be seen with Florence in his possession, and the path he had determined upon taking was so secret, known, he believed, to none but himself, that he scarce feared to be detected or followed.

He dashed on, regardless of every impediment. The maiden he bore still exhibited no signs of life, and her weight was as nothing to his powerful frame.

He occasionally turned his eyes upon her face, which hung back on her shoulders with so lifeless a character that once or twice he thought the scene she had witnessed, and, perhaps, her fall when he had suffered her to drop on discovering she had fainted, might, perhaps, have killed her ; and, on the impulse of the surmise he once or twice stopped short : but there was a warmth about her heart, and a pulsation, though very feeble, which told him she had not passed the " bourne from which no traveller returns." He, therefore, hurried on, and by increasing his pace strove to make up for the time he had lost in stopping. As he reached the end of the lane, he remembered that there was a small stream that wound across it, over which was thrown a iltle wooden bridge to enable persons to cross it, and as he emerged from the lane and gained it, a light from an opening in the trees made him again turn his eyes to Florence's face : he started to see how white it looked. It might have been the effect of the lurid twilight upon her delicate skin ; but, whatever it was, she looked so spectrally white, that he little less than shuddered. Water was at hand, and its refreshing coolness might revive her—might prevent her from dying.

He knew little of women, save that they were weak, trembling things, and he could not tell but their fright at such a situation as that in which Florence was placed was not sufficient to kill the strongest among them. He had known such things as men who were wounded desperately, grow every moment, after receiving their hurt, fainter and fainter, until they died—never rallying although, perhaps, they had survived three or four days. How was he to know that the frail and delicate creature he bore was not in the condition of a wounded man, and sinking under the shock she had received, grow every instant feebler and weaker until her life ceased altogether. This speculation ran like wildfire through his brain, and made him fear that he should lose his prize altogether ; that he should have committed fratricide, and have violently outraged the feelings of one he passionately loved, involving her death also, to have the object for which he had done this torn from his grasp, and he stand a murderer of two beings—one near, and the other dear to him, and gain nothing by the dreadful act. In the moment of his apprehensive doubts, he could have cursed his precipitancy, which had not permitted him to wait until his plan was more matured ; but the impetuosity of his feelings were not to be controlled by any consideration ; and the first moment he had, as he thought, the chance of gaining his purpose, he seized it, without considering whether it was the time or not to ensure success. The consequences which had followed, taught him that villany needed much watchfulness, much art, and circumspection, ere it could be practised with the success it was necessary it should be attended with, to prevent discovery and punishment.

He crossed the bridge as he arrived at this conclusion, and laying Florence gently upon the bank which skirted the little stream, he descended to the water's-edge, and gathering some in the hollow of his hand, he returned and bathed her temples with it; the coldness of the water, which was that of a clear spring, had the effect of showing him she was not dead, for she moaned and raised her hand towards her face, and then muttered a few words. This display of returning animation was sufficient for him, and once more he raised her in his arms, and proceeded on his intricate path; he wound his way swiftly towards the uplands to fulfil his promise of placing his prize where she should have no companion but himself, or see aught living but the eagle.   As he went on crashing among leaves and foliage, which he could not in the fast increasing darkness see clearly enough to avoid, he suddenly imagined he heard footsteps following his own; they might be but the echo of his, and he kept the on in belief that they were, discarding all idea that they could be the sound of other than his own; but he was startlingly awakened from this delusion, by hearing them crush some dry twigs and leaves, while he was moving swiftly over a patch of soft grass, which suffered his feet to make no sound. There was, then, some one following him, tracking his steps so that they might pounce upon him when they pleased, and wrest from him the treasure it had cost him so dear a price to obtain; a moment's reflection told him this must be prevented; the spy must be detected and silenced, at whatever cost. Florence was still in a state of unconsciousness, and he had no fear of her escaping, if for a minute he placed her upon the ground and turned back to discover the intruder. He was armed with a brace of pistols; he was never without them, and he resolved to make use of them on the person of the prying fellow that hung upon his heels.   Not that he would be guilty of such great imprudence as to fire one, and let the report in the stillness of the night be heard for miles round; but the butt-end would serve his purpose as effectually, and what was better, silently.   There was no time for further reflection—the necessity of the case was imperative; he stopped and placed Florence upon the green turf, and while yet stooping over her, laying her carefully down, he was startled by hearing a voice almost close to his ear, exclaim, with a coarse laugh, which grated strangely in his ear—

"How now, brother, what be'est doing with a youn glass in this drear place at this hour."

He turned with the swiftness of thought, and exclaimed, fiercely—

"The foul fiend! who speaks?"

Not a sound replied; he drew forth his pistol, and hastily setting the spring which should prevent its discharging, he grasped the muzzle in his hand and sprung to the spot from whence the sound proceeded, but found no one.   It was too dark to see—the sun had quite sunk; the moon had not yet risen, and large sweeping masses of clouds were gathering up; the spot, too, was so shrouded with overhanging trees, that the darkness was unnaturally increased, so as to prevent anything from being visible.   Jasper swore a fearful oath at being disappointed in seeing the speaker, and groped about the hollow places with a rapidity which did his speed and knowledge of the spot credit; he, however, did not succeed in discovering who had addressed him, and though he even for a few minutes stopped, held his breath, and stood motionless, he could not detect by the rustle of a leaf, the cracking of a twig, or even the sound of a man's breathing, that any other than himself and the maiden were near the spot; he strained his powers of listening to the very utmost, and stood in an agony of suspense and wild speculation respecting this mysterious occurrence.   He was, however, aroused to his senses by a low long moan from Florence, and saw that he could spare no longer time in making efforts to discover the stranger; he at once, therefore, resolved to run all hazards, and if he caught a glipmse of him while continuing his progress, to discharge a pistol at him, no matter what echoes it waked, and, if possible, send a bullet through his brain.

"I can bring down a heron on the wing," he muttered unconsciously aloud, "and it shall go hard if I spoil not this hound's prying for ever."

A laugh followed his utterance of these words, but it rang so suddenly and so loudly, that it was impossible to tell the precise spot from which it emanated : once again he made a swift search all around, listening attentively for the slightest sound of a retiring footstep, but in vain—and once more he was compelled to give up the task as hopeless; he had no weakness of nature to complain of, but his brother's blood was yet wet on his hands, and reckless, brutal as he was, it would tug at his heart, and be present to his brain constantly. He was not superstitious, nor of a nature to be so—but the scorn with which he had always treated the doctrine,that murder "would speak with most miraculous organ," might be without foundation, and this occurrence be an evidence of it; then he shook it hastily away, and said in a loud voice—

"Whoever you be that has dogged my footsteps, beware how you continue it, for if I catch a glimps of you, you shall have a bullet crashing through your brain, ere you can cry God help me !"

No answer was returned to this speech, and he made to the side of Florence, who partially recovered, had half raised herself up, but was not sufficiently restored to understand her situation; he lifted her up in his arms, and then she seemed to remember her position, for she screamed aloud. Jasper's hand was in a moment placed over her mouth, and the same instant a vivid flash of lightning illuminated the spot, and was almost immediately followed by a loud peal of thunder, which seemed to shake the earth and stun them. Jasper heeded it not—he had seen the storm brewing, and it was no more than he expected, although it had burst rather suddenly. He did not check his speed, but continued until he reached the road, and then a steep ridge called the pass of Dunmail Raise; up this he wound, although the forked lightning flashed fearfully, and the thunder rolled in long peals, making the rocks echo its solemn sound; untireingly he held on his way, and felt that his victim in this wild scene of elemental violence was incapable of resistance. Her fright at the thunder and lightning equalled her horror of him, and she shrunk and cowered as flash succeeded flash, and the thunder roared like tremendous discharges of canon, even burying her face in his neck and clinging to him in the wildest terror; he laughed to himself to see her fear of a matter he scorned, and feeling himself secure in her possession, he turned his head at every vivid flash of lightning, in order to see whether there was still a follower of his footsteps—but with all his earnestness of gaze, he could discover nought, save the trees and huge masses of rock he left behind him. After pursuing his way for some time longer, he suddenly turned from the beaten track and struck across the hill, over knowls and patches of vegetation, then diverging among a thick mass of stunted bushes, he stopped suddenly short, pulled them aside, and where it might least have been expected, displayed the entrance to a narrow passage cut in the rock; here he for the first time suffered the maiden to regain her feet, and then he whispered to her—

" You must enter here with me: do this quietly, and I will not lay a finger upon you, I swear; but resist, and you may welcome death with prayers of gladness. All escape is hopeless, your fate certain, without help—therefore hesitate not, but enter, I will leave you for to-night, in the morning you may see fit to regard me with a more complaisant eye. This will be your resting place for to-night, to-morrow it will depend upon yourself whether you have a better or not. The place is dark, but comfortable," he added, as she suffered herself to be moved passively forward along a winding passage, until he stopped, and, by the echo which attended his speech, she judged she was in a spacious apartment, but it was so intensely dark she could see nothing. " It is dark, but dry—I cannot spare you a light; there are chairs of stone, and for one night you must not mind sleeping in one. You need not attempt to escape, because you will be locked in, and there is no other outlet but the one which I shall securely fasten. Good night; in the morning I trust you will be better prepared to regard me as your future husband."

She returned him no reply, and he quitted her. As she heard his retiring footsteps die away, she sunk on one of the stone seats he had led her to, and, burying her face in her hands, she burst into a passion of tears, and exclaimed—

" Oh, Eustace! Eustace! had you been near I should not now be in this frightful situation."

Jasper, when he had left her, had the intention of making for the lane where he had left his brother senseless, for the purpose of burying him, of recovering his own hat, which he had left behind in the struggle and hasty flight, and removing, in fact, all trace of the murder. He hurried along with extraordinary speed, quite insensible to the fatigue he had already endured in bearing Florence such a distance; and although the length of the way was considerable, in a very short space of time he stood again upon the spot where his brother had fallen by his hand. The moon by this time had risen, and though a swift scud flew over it, still there was sufficient light to trace distinctly every object present. He looked hastily for the body of his brother, but it was gone; his hat, even the stick which he had flung into the hedge, for which he searched on missing the rest, had also vanished; he could not himself, with all his desire for concealment, have more effectually removed every trace of what had transpired. Everything was gone; but how, or by whom taken, it was impossible to surmise; he searched all round the spot, but nothing remained, and with an anxiety which tortured him miserably, he sought his home, fearing to find the body there, and be at once challenged with the murder. At first he resolved not to return home, but without being conscious of where his feet were bearing him, he drew nearer and nearer to it, until he stood before it; he started to find himself there, and gazed earnestly for some token which should show him that they had discovered his vilainy; but no—a solitary light burned in one of the windows, and all seemed peaceful and still. Mustering a stern resolution, he determined to enter, and know to a certainty what he had to fear; he put his

resolve into execution, and on his entrance was greeted by an old servant, who, elevating the light, and looking at him, said hastily—

"I thought it was young Master Frank and Miss Florence. Master Frank followed Miss Florence out, and neither have returned."

"They have, no doubt, taken shelter from the storm somewhere," replied Jasper, hastily, "and will soon return. Give me a light; I will to bed."

"Bless me, how pale you look—are you not well?" asked the old man, suddenly.

Jasper started at the question, but replied hastily in the affirmative, and went at once to his chamber, and he threw himself upon his couch and slept; but in his sleep he fought the fearful fight with his brother over and over again, until he woke with the horrid feeling of being suffocated in the warm blood of him he had murdered. A figure was standing by his side as his eyes opened, on whom the clear moon was shining, and with a shout of horror he sprung from his bed, but the next moment he discovered it to be the old porter; he told him that neither Master Frank nor Miss Florence had returned, and having conveyed that intelligence to his father and mother they feared some accident, and begged Jasper to go and seek them. He speedily recovered his self-possession, and with a grin of exultation, which, however,

No. 6

he took care not to let the old man see, he consented, and dressing himself hastily he quitted the house; it was just day-break, and the cool fresh morning air came gratefully to his hot brow, but he took little heed of it, and hastened to the spot in which he had confined Florence. He found her weeping, and almost worn out with fright and fatigue. Again he made his hateful proposition to her to become his; she refused though death were her portion, and then he dragged her in a violent rage from the place, swearing she should be his under the most humiliating terms. When in the open air she screamed franticly, and in his passion he struck her a violent blow upon the forehead that felled her to the ground, and rendered her insensible. Once more he threw her across his shoulder, and pursued his way up the crags, until he arrived at the cave in which he had sworn she should pass the remainder of her days.

CHAPTER V.

" With sloping masts and dripping prow,
As who pursued with yell and blow
Still treads the shadow of his foe,
And forward bends his head,
The ship drove fast, loud roared the blast,
And southward aye we fled.
  *   *   *   *   *
All in a hot and copper sky
The bloody sun at noon
Right up above the mast did stand,
No bigger than the moon."

COLERIDGE.

All night did the Wildfire urge a mad career through the raging waters, without displaying a rag of canvass. The wind blew a perfect hurricane, making the vessel fly with a swiftness that surprised the oldest hands on board; she had been put directly before the wind, and leaped over the waves, which ran in the same direction as herself, as if trying to vie with her in a race, with a lightness that seemed to laugh their efforts to catch her to scorn, and thus they dashed along, the wind roaring and howling through the rigging, and passing through it with a violence that appeared as if it would scatter it before it. The light, which had been affixed to the cask, and lowered for the support of the poor fellow who had fallen overboard, at a time when any attempt to clear away a boat to his rescue would have been madness, was soon lost to sight; and as the gale blew furiously all night unceasingly, the poor seaman was quite given over as lost. The day broke very early, and the wind in no degree abated; the vessel, however, had so nobly done its duty, that violent as was the storm, there were few fears entertained that she would not see it out without considerable damage; as it grew lighter, the vessel pursued, or one uncommonly like it, was observed on the edge of the horizon, dancing like a cork; all eyes were turned upon it, and it seemed that she took notice of them as quickly as they did of her, for she was observed to spread a sail upon her foremast, and thus increase the swiftness of her course, which had been, as the Wildfire's, scudding directly before the wind under bare poles.

Immediately this was discovered the captain's voice was heard commanding the fore-sail to be set, and but little time was lost in accomplishing it, although it was both a difficult and dangerous matter in such a gale to perform ; its effect was to increase the speed of the vessel amazingly, and all eyes were turned anxiously on the strained canvass and bending mast, expecting to see it every moment carried away. The vessel they were pursuing still kept the same distance, and though it appeared impossible for any other vessel to go so fast as they were sweeping through the waters, yet they were not able to diminish the distance between them. The hands were piped to breakfast, and no change had taken place, but towards noon the experienced and practised eye of the sailors told them the gale would soon drop into a fresh breeze, and it was soon seen the chase was as well aware of the fact as themselves, for they began to hoist their top-sails as well as spread their courses, to take advantage of what little wind they had left; and their manœuvre was speedily imitated by the crew of the Wildfire, and sail after sail was set while yet it was blowing a gale, and the vessel plunged through the water at' a frightful pace, scarcely able to bear the press of canvas heaped upon her. Still the stranger kept his old distance a-head, and the captain of the Wildfire seemed growing dreadfully impatient in finding that the speed at which he urged his vessel was attended by no better results. Presently he ordered the maintack aboard, and the top-gallant sail to be set, which was done, and the top-mast bent like a piece of whalebone ; he, however, heeded it not, and fretted as though the vessel crawled instead of flew through the waters. It was soon evident that the gale was fast abating, both by the lessened strain on the canvas and by the diminishing turbulence of the sea. The worst of it was that the chase would have the benefit of a stiff breeze, while their sails were flapping against the mast ; and to meet this disadvantage, royals were set, studding-sails, everything that could be packed upon the ship to urge her in her desperate course, until the oldest hand shook his head, and hinted it would be as well to keep a wide berth of her bows, for if the vessel's head was not shoved under water, it would not be the captain's fault. The groaning and and creaking cordage, as it strained and quivered with extreme tension before the heavy pressure of the wind, seemed also to bid fair to send the whole fabric tumbling down ; but notwithstanding the extraordinary force it had still to resist, it did its duty admirably. The chase had been strictly and closely watched, and the captain of the Wildfire had the mortification to perceive that he had served as a barometer to the pursued ; they had taken all his movements for a guide, and were now covered with canvass from truck to hull. The Wildfire was buried to her bobstays, she had the reputation of being a rattling scudder when going large before the wind, and now she had it direct over her taffrail, with every stitch of canvas she could set without carrying all her top-masts by the board, and yet was unable to lift the hull of the chase. The men stood in little clusters waiting the orders of their superiors, doing nothing but having an occasional pull at the sheets, and obeying the impatient order which ever and anon burst from the captain's lips, to see that everything drew and was home; they amused themselves by criticising the merits of their own vessel and that of the chase.

"I've sailed in many a crack craft," said the captain of the top, who had enlightened his messmates respecting the love of the Chinese for pork; "your regular fliers and clippers, from a sloop, or a' Merican coaster, to a voyage in a phantom ship, a sort of flying Dutchman, which I had in a dream after turning in on a double allowance of beef, in which voyage I sat on the tops, and went faster than the wind, which is to say, I was going through the water ten knots and a half an hour faster than we have in this gale, and I could see the the wind blowing as heavy as the devil could make it, coming roaring aft. but could never overhaul us; and there were the caps of leaping waves in our wake, which, with all their jumping, could never overtake us, and all this time I was in smooth water—"

"Steady!" exclaimed a topman, with a laugh—"don't top Dick Stretch-out over us."

"What about Dick Stretch-out?" cried that worthy, suddenly advancing.

"Nothing particklar," exclaimed the topman, winking to his messmates; "I was only saying you was such an out-and-out clipper of a messmate, that it is a pity you ain't run up to the arm of the main-yard, to be turned in for a jewel-block, that the ship's company may have a better sight of the ornament of the berth-deck of the Wildfire."

"A pretty jewel for an ear-ring he'd make!" said John Paul, wittily.

"You carry tops above your lower-mast heads, I think," cried Dick to the topman, rather restively, not quite forgetting the laugh at his expense which the Black had caused, and eyeing the topman with a look that ranged from his toe to his hair.

"We always do in king's ships," replied the topman; "that is, if they're cutters, and such like—then, Dick, we carry cross-trees; howsomdever, don't hoist the red flag, because a tar gets the weather roll of you, when you've clapped on the jawing tackle."

"He wants to haul his wind and keep away," said Gasket, with a desire to bring Dick out again; "don't you let him go about in that fashion, Dick; he said your yarns were not half so long as a fore top bow line, and sailed so dead on to truth, that they never got within hail of the marines."

"No," cried the Black, with a grin; "'em 'bliged to hoist signals to know when 'em lie to come."

A roar of laughter followed this sally; Dick was about to utter an anathema, when the captain of the top stopped him.

"Avast!" he cried; "I was pitching a yarn, and while my line is running out, here come three or four of you and take a severe turn, as if I wasn't commissioned as well as any of you, to read a page from my log."

"Well, heave a-head," said Dick.

"What I've to say, is this!" he responded; "I've been in many a fast-going craft, but never in one that could scud like the Wildfire has done this morning; nor for that matter do I believe there's a blue jacket in the service as has;

but there's the chase a-head, which, whether under bare poles, or under every stitch of canvas from truck to hull, has never let us draw on her an inch—nor, to my thinking, it is not in the nature of real wood and iron to be able to do it, and if that chase isn't one of the devil's babies, I should like to know what it is. You see we've skimmed like a seagull, and there's not another craft could have kept us in their wake, but one—the old gentleman's, which, to my thinking the chase is—it reminds me that when I was off the coast of Norway, I was shown a woman as sold wind to weather-bound seamen; now you see she was a hag-looking old anshent—"

"Hold on, Master Toppinglift," cried the Black, suddenly; "'em send for de marines, all old anshun stories for dem."

A shout of laughter was the consequence of this remark, and instantly the first lieutenant's voice was heard crying loudly—

"Silence in the waist there;" and then added, "forward there, send the captain to the main-top, John Paul, on the poop."

John Paul instantly obeyed the summons, and stood before the captain, who eyed him attentively for a moment, and then said—

"You have a sharp and quick eye; take the glass, and tell me what you make of the chase."

"I make her out a privateer; she is the same rover we gave chase to in the Leeward isles a month since," said Paul.

"You are sure of that?" said the Captain, eagerly.

"I am!" replied Paul; "we gave her a shot which went through her mizen top sail when last we chased her, and I can see the new cloth they have repaired it with."

"Are we likely to overhaul her, if the winds hold at all?" asked the captain·

"A stern chase is a long chase," replied Paul; "I suspect she is too light-heeled to be overhauled, running large; we might stand a better chance on a bow-line, but as long as she can run before the wind, we shall see no more of her taffrail than we do now."

"Sail ho!" shouted a man from the tops; it was reported on the quarter, and as a complete wreck; a signal of distress was flying, and it appeared that the chase had passed it, neither shortening sail, or taking any heed of it. The captain took his glass again, and looked in the direction of the reported vessel, and discovered its hull with a jury-rigged mast lying like a log upon the waters. The captain turned his eyes again on the chase—it was still flying along, and he knew that if he bore up for the wreck he should lose his chase entirely; his first impulse was to keep on and pass the wreck the same as the rover, but a few words from the first lieutenant made the cause of humanity prevail, and the orders were given to shorten the sail, and lay the vessel aboard of the wreck.

The seamen quickly obeyed the command, and in a few minutes were alongside of it. It proved to be a merchant brig with all her masts cut away, and with only three persons on board her—a female and two men, one a sailor, who was not far removed from a skeleton; and the other, an elderly man, whose dress betokened him to be a landsman. The female was young, and had features which would have been beautiful, but like the sailor, she was almost a skeleton, and so reduced by freight and exhaustion, as to be, according to the doctor's statement, very near death. The elderly man had received a hurt from a falling spar, and was also in a dangerous condition, but the sailor seemed only to suffer from want of food, and was placed in the berth of the poor fellow who had fallen overboard. The wreck was searched for whatever was valuable, and all they discovered was transferred to the Wildfire, but not much time was allowed them for this, for the ship had sprung a leak, and was settling fast. As soon as the Wildfire's crew were again on board their own vessel, the yards were squared, the reduced sails again resumed their station, and once more they stood on in the direction the chase had taken, and which had now disappeared below the horizon, but it was in vain that every thing was hoisted the vessel could carry. The night passed away, and the morning appeared, without their catching a glimpse of the pursued.

In the meantime, every attention was paid to those rescued from the wreck; the captain had a side cabin prepared for the female, and the doctor was incessant in his attentions to her; the elderly man, too, was carefully tended, and the crew vied with each other in doing their utmost to restore the sailor to health. As all he required was food and rest, he soon began to get strong; and two days after this event he was summoned into the captain's cabin; a glass of grog was presented to him, and he was asked to detail a history of the young lady and himself, and after a few preliminary touches of respect and deference, he commenced :—

"I was first mate of a West Indy brig, bound from Port Rico to London, the Pen-ne-lopee was her name, and a good vessel she was as ever was turned out of a shipwright's hands : we were laden with sugar and spices, and a general cargo, because there was a good stock of merchandise belonging to an old gentleman who was going to settle in England, and had sent all his property by us, but was going to make the voyage by another vessel. Well, we were secure in blue water before we were boarded in the middle watch by one of those damned thieving rovers as are always lying about there, like shirks, to swallow all that comes within hail. Greater part of the men were killed and hove overboard before they were awake; howsomdever, I managed to get on deck, and I saw the young lady, Lord love her sweet face and gentle heart! struggling and screaming in the arms of a black-muzzled thief. I got aft where he was, and picked up a capstan-bar which was near me, and dropped it on to his skull, and it dropped him on the deck. Most of his messmates were roaming over the ship, murdering Captain and crew, and plundering, and when I spoilt the shape of his figure-head there happened to be nobody near; it turned out afterwards he was the Captain of these devils, for you see when he fell I took from his belt a brace of barkers half as long as a handspik—young muskets—and a wheezer of a hanger, and then I lifted him up and dropped him quietly over the side. Well, I had hardly done this, before a dozen vagabonds were upon me, and would have cut me down, but they didn't like chopping on the pistols! and so, when I'd breathing time, I told 'em I had promised to join 'em, and I was left in care of the young lady, and if any laid a finger on her, I was to stop their wind with a bullet. When they saw I had their captain's pistols and hanger, they thought I spoke the truth, and left me to get the valuables on board their own craft; they did their work neatly and quickly, and then scuttled the Pen-ne-lopee, and set fire to her as well. Well, you see, their first lieutenant directed all their movements, and a pretty devil's 'chick he was; and as their captain wasn't missed, for though a clipper to fight, he didn't like work, so they thought he had gone aboard his own vessel, when he had done fighting in ours, and turned into his berth to sleep the rest of the watch out. Well, I was removed with the young lady, and two of our men—rough devils, who agreed to join them, rather than be sent to Davy Jones, on board their craft, and as the Pen-ne-lopee was blazing like fury, they sheered off, and we stood away. We soon saw the burning ship go down, and as we stood southerly, the little breeze we had began to drop, until it quite left us; and it came on a dead calm. One of the men from the Pen-ne-lopee hold brought the yellow jack with him, and it spread dreadfully. The captain was searched for the morning after we left our ship, but when they couldn't find him they asked me a few questions about him, which I did not exactly answer according to truth; but they didn't say much about it, which, I look upon it, was through the first lieutenant, who became captain. Well, the men died wery fast, and were hove over the side as soon as their jaws dropped, until there were not hands enough left to work the vessel if a breeze had sprung up. It didn't touch me nor yet the young lady, who you must know hadn't been harmed, for you see the first lieutenant was a man who loved money better than women, and I told him her friends would give him a chest full of gold if he returned her to them as safe as when she left. He had some thoughts of making her his lady, but this yarn of mine slewed him round, and so he was very polite to her. Well, he took the fever and was thrown overboard, and then and there was only four men left and the lady. All this while there wasn't a breath to lift a pennant, and the sun burnt and fried like a galley fire of a first-rate. Well, somehow or another, the pirate sprung a leak, and there was six foot water in the hold before we discovered it. Working at the pumps wasn't to be thought of, so we set to work, and made a raft, and when it was made we slung it by the yard stay-tackles, and lowered it into the sea; then we put a cask of provision, some bedding, the young lady's chest, and a few things, and then got on it, and shoved off from the sinking pirate.

" She had only two boats with her : the one on the booms was too heavy for us to move, and the other had been scuttled by some of the men who had the fever, because it was proposed, in order to stop it, to put all that had the yellow jack in and send 'em adrift. We didn't make much way; the vessel had filled so fast, that we hadn't much time to knock up the raft, and so couldn't rig a sail or use sweeps. We saw the pirate go down before we were very far from her, and there we were, nothing in sight but the sea, sky, and sun, just as if we were anchored, and were broiling in the heat ready to die. In two days, my three companions died, and I heaved e'm into the deep, and then I and the young lady were left alone. The sun went down and the broad moon came up and watched us all night, until the sun took the watch— and, lord bless your honour, it was terrible to bear the suffocating heat and

not to be able to get under the lee of anything for shade or cool ; here we were,
day after day, our provision getting very low, and our water, of which we had
a cask, drying up almost as fast as we drank it.   I had borne it very well at
first, but at last it got the weathergage of me, and I began to feel uncommon
down.   I saw no hope or help ; I felt as if my life lines were unreeving, and
I must soon die.   I confess I had a devilish thought or two respecting the
young lady, but she talked so kind and pleasant, and smiled, and tried to
cheer me—her good friend, as she called me, that I hadn't the heart to turn
villain.   Well, our water was out, our biscuit and beef was but enough to last
us a day, and we were still as it seemed in the same place.   I felt very faint,
for I had eaten very little, to make the food last out, and when the moon came
up one night, I laid my head over a water cask, for I hadn't strength to set
up, and I begged the lady to pray for me, which she did, and then I dropped
off senseless, and dreamed I was dead."

CHAPTER VI.

" Thou sure and firm set earth,
    Hear not my steps, which way they walk, for fear
    The very stones prate of my whereabout,
    And take the present horror from the time,
    Which now suits with it."
                                        SHAKSPERE.

" If I stand here I saw him.
    Fy, for shame !"
                                        IBID.

The cave to which Jasper Chough had carried Florence was a natural
formation, and so situate that it was not likely to be discovered, nor easy of
access to any but a daring adventurer.   It was at a great height, and it was
not without much fatigue that he gained it ; but in a matter on which he had
set his heart, mere bodily labour was of little consideration ; the energy of his
mind, added to the excitement of the circumstances, prevented him feeling
the fatigue which might in an undertaking, the success of which was indifferent to him, have caused him to desist.   The opening to the cave was
marked by the presence of a tree and led by a long narrow fissure into a somewhat spacious cell ; into this place he carried Florence, and depositing her
upon a rude couch of stone, but covered with a large cloak, he stretched his
arms to shake off the stiffness her weight had occasioned, and then proceeded
to use means for her recovery.   He had once already found water an efficaci-
ous remedy, and he went to a pitcher which stood in a corner, and filled a
small vessel ; he returned to the maiden and bathed her temples and lips ; it
was with feelings of shame to his manhood that he observed a bruise upon
her fair forehead, where his rude hand had dealt her the blow which had
felled her to the earth.   He felt the hot blood tingle his cheeks, and he mut-

tered a curse upon his own hastiness; he even looked around as though he feared the presence of a witness of his brutality, but there was no one in that lone spot to meet his rapid gaze, and he turned to renew his attempts to restore Florence to life. While thus engaged he fancied he heard a stealthy footstep, and rushed out to discover the intruder, but could discover no one; the sound had appeared so clear and decided to him, that it was not without the strictest and most minute investigation that he could satisfy himself there was not a third person hidden somewhere. His search, however, failed to discover one, and after at least a quarter of an hour thus occupied, he believed himself to have been deceived, and returned to Florence. He started back on entering the cave, almost with terror, at finding her seated upright, her pale face directed towards him, and looking in the dim light, which penetrated through an opening above, like a spectre. He recovered himself in a minute, and approaching her, he took her passive hand, and pressing it, asked her, for want of knowing what to say, if she knew whither she had been brought. She made no reply, and it took him but little closeness of inspection to perceive that she was not conscious of anything, but seemed as if in a dream. He did not heed this much, because there were several things which he proposed doing before he again attempted to persuade her to love him.

In anticipation of having to bring Florence to this cave, he had from time to time furnished it with many articles essential for her support and convenience; he had yet others to bring, and under the circumstances of his brother's mur-

7

der and Florence's abduction, it was his policy to be as much at home as possible, to prevent suspicion falling upon him, not that he was much afraid that it would, for though he was known to be wild and reckless, yet he had always appeared friendly with his brother, and few, if any, suspected that he was passionately in love with Florence ; thus, whatever the conjecture, it was not likely, unless he had been seen, that he would be dragged into it. He therefore resolved to return to the Hall, and after reporting that he had not been able to trace anything of the youth or the maiden, to hint that they had fled together, and on pretence of tracking them, supply himself with whatever he still wanted, and at nightfall return to the cave. On finding that he could gain no answer from Florence, and that her eyes wandered listlessly and mechanically from him round the cell, he dropped her hand, and placing a small flask of wine and some provisions near her, he quitted her, and fastening a rude door formed of branches of trees roughly nailed together, but very strong, he wound through the passage, and swiftly, but cautiously descended the crags, taking a very circuitous route to avoid detection, and slackened not his pace until he entered his father's house.

He was encountered at the door by the old porter, who cried, eagerly—

" What news, master Jasper?"

" None," he replied, gruffly. " Have they returned ?"

" Heaven bless us, no," returned the old man, and added in a quivering voice, " what can have come to them? Lord! lord! thy good mother is distraught with fear; she has wept ever since they have been missed, and is full of thoughts of evil, and the worst that can have happened."

" Has there been any one beside myself in search of them—any meddling villager, or prying, inquisitive dog been sent to discover them?" asked Jasper, rather earnestly.

" How oddly you talk, master Jasper,," returned the old man; " but to be sure, you always did! I remember, when you were a boy, you used to—"

" Answer my question !" roared Jasper, fiercely, making the old man recoil several steps. " I want none of your garrulity now. Tell me, has my father sent any one beside myself to find out what has become of Frank and Florence ?,'

" You have such a very rough way of speaking, that really—"

The old man's words were stopped by Jasper seizing him by the collar, and saying passionately—

" I'll shake every morsel of breath out of your body, you old fool, if you do not answer me without any more equivocations. Who has gone in search of my brother and the maiden ?"

" Half the village ! half the village !" cried the the old man, terrified, and speaking quickly, " your father has himself been into the village, and offered a rich reward to anybody who will discover the slightest trace of them."

" Damnation !" cried Jasper, flinging the old man from him; he quitted the room, quickly, and then returned again, and said—

" Has any one of them returned ?"

" No, no," replied the old man, quickly—rubbing his shoulders ruefully, from the effects of his fall, and speaking quickly, for fear of being once more flung down ; but Jasper, to his satisfaction, left him, and went into the chamber which contained his parents. He flung wide the door, and entered with a rough swagger, and threw himself heavily, as if much fatigued, on one of the chairs. His mother in an instant rose and went hastily towards him.

" Have you seen aught of them, Jasper; have you found them ?" she asked in hurried tones."

" No !" he replied, sullenly.

"Could you discover no sign, nor learn anything of them ?" asked his father, with eagerness.

"No !" he replied; " they managed matters too well for that; they got too much the start of us, to either find the road they have taken, or overtake them if we had."

" What mean you ?" exclaimed his father, sternly.

" What should I mean ?" he replied, with a scornful laugh; " but that they have gone off together by premeditation, and in all probability by this time you will have a daughter-in-law, or your son a mistress, if the lady is not over particular."

" Oh, Jasper, speak not thus of your brother or Florence !" exclaimed his mother, weeping; " you are wrong, nay, wicked in making such surmises, for there is not any truth in it."

" How should you know ?" he asked roughly, " Frank was not such a fool as to tell you all his secrets."

" Nor you, Jasper !" replied his mother, evidently hurt by his manner of speaking to her: " or you would have known he did not love Florence."

" What !" he cried, eagerly.

" That he honoured and esteemed her, but did not love her; for his heart was elsewhere bestowed !" rejoined his mother.

Nor was her heart his," exclaimed his father; " of that I am well satisfied, and that I believe is sufficient to disprove your surmise."

Jasper sprung from his chair, and said, with an interest he did not think of concealing—

" Tell me how you came to know this, by what means could this have come to your knowledge ?"

" By such as I mean to keep to myself," replied his father, coolly ; but in what way can it interest you to know? you care little for either, and therefore can be but little affected in knowing whom they love."

Jasper knew not what to reply. If this were true, he had indeed overreached himself, for he might have spared himself his brother's blood and laid some well-invented plan, which would have removed him from all chances of detection. While this was running through his mind, a man was ushered into the room—a young, strong built fellow. He had been searching all the morning, he said, to discover the missing pair, but had not succeeded in finding them.

" But perhaps Master Jasper has been more fortunate," he added.

" Why ?" asked Jasper, fixing his eye steadfastly upon him.

" Why, you were last in Miss Florence's company."

" I !" exclaimed Jasper; " what do you mean, booby.?"

"Only that I saw you last night talking to Miss Florence."

"Where?" he cried, quickly.

"In a green lane that leads to Dunmail Raise; she screamed, and you stopped her, and said, 'you needn't be afraid, it's only I.' I saw Master Frank advancing, and I thought he might fancy that I was eaves-dropping, so I went away."

"You were dreaming, fool," exclaimed Jasper, knitting his brow, "I was not there last night, nor near the place."

"Then I am not here," returned the young fellow, positively. "I both saw and heard you, and if I ain't much mistaken, before I got a very long way off I heard—"

"I tell thee, dog, I was not near the spot," cried Jasper, interrupting him, and speaking fiercely; "away with you—you have been drinking."

"Water, if anything," said the man; "you may deny it if you like, but I will take my oath—"

"To a lie," roared Jasper. "Insolent scoundrel, begone!"

"I didn't come to wait on you," replied the young man with a lowering look, "and if your honoured father tells me to go I will, but not till then; and since you have treated me so roughly I shall lose some of my respect for you; I tell you again, I saw you there, and I believe you know more of their absence than you choose to tell."

"Lying hound!" shouted Jasper, and struck him a violent blow on the forehead, which sent him flying to the ground; the young fellow soon recovered his feet, and would have rushed at Jasper, but the latter's parents interfered and kept them apart, while Jasper's mother begged of the villager for the love of heaven to depart. He suffered himself to be persuaded, and even in his rage respected her, but he turned to Jasper as he left the room, and shaking his fist menacingly at him, said, with marked and fierce emphasis of tone—

"You know why, and where Miss Florence and Master Frank have disappeared. Now, mark me, beware of me, for I'll be revenged upon you for that blow, when and where you least expect; thrice tenfold I will, so God judge me."

Jasper's lips curled with a contemptuous smile, and with a look of deadly hatred the villager quitted the room. When he was gone, Jasper's father advanced to him, and looking on him with a fixed look, beneath which his eyes cowered, said, "Were the words which that man spoke, truth?"

"No," he replied, sullenly; "I saw neither Florence nor Frank since yesterday morning."

"Will you give me your oath of that?" asked his father, looking at him as if he would read him through.

"Not I," returned Jasper, with a harsh laugh. "If you will not take my word, you shall not have my oath."

"My dear Jasper, have you seen aught of them?—I entreat you to tell me," exclaimed his mother, throwing herself upon his neck, with a passionate burst of tears. "You have always been rude and rough to all, but you have been gentle to me, Jasper; remember, I am your mother—the mother who brought you forth and reared you, in pain, who spared no trouble or labour to raise you when you were helpless and sickly. I am your mother, Jasper, who, when you needed gentle words and kind looks, never denied them to you—whose arms and heart were ever open to receive you and shelter you; tell me, Jasper, did that man speak the truth? do you, as you stand before God, and I, who have brought you into the world, know more of Florence and Frank than you have told us."

As she concluded her speech, she raised her head from his neck, and fixed her eye, which looked bright and clear, upon him; he could not met her gaze—his eyes dropped, and he felt her words upon his heart like bolts of fire, but he had taken too far a step in villany, that he could not now retract; he made a great effort, and gently removing his mother from about him, he said, coolly—

"I have told you all I know, and these are all the thanks I get for tiring myself to death in searching for them; you may look for them yourself in future—for if I am to have no better return for my labour than to be sus·pected of, I don't know what not, nor you either, I'll not move an inch further in the matter," and muttering an oath, he flung himself out of the room, and retiring to his own, he locked himself in, and gathered together all he proposed taking to the cave. Waiting until night had set in, he lowered his parcel, not a small one, out of the window; armed himself with a brace of pistols and a sword, and then sauntered slowly out of the hall door; the old man was not there, and he flattered himself no one saw him depart. He went to the spot where he had deposited his bundle, and lifting it upon his shoulder, he made straight for the mountain; he wound quickly up it—and as he hurried on with all the swiftness he could, he accidentally stumbled and fell. Just as he was raising himself up, he distinctly heard footsteps again following him; there was no mistake—no delusion, they sounded loud and clear, as swift as his own had been, and were certainly not the echo of his, for he was not moving when he heard them. To throw down his burden and rush to meet his pursuer was but the work of a minute, and he ran swiftly along, turning his eyes right and left, and peering into the darkness intently, to unkennel the stranger—but no, he was hidden from his sight, and kept so. It was in vain that he searched every spot—he could not discover any one, and listen as attentively as he would, he could not again hear the sound of a foot-fall in any direction; he was compelled at length to give up the search, and raging with fury and ap·prehension, he returned to the spot where he had thrown his bundle, but it was some time before he could discover it; he, however, succeeded eventually, and shouldered it, went on towards the cave, stopping every now and then to listen to a following footstep, or see if his eyes could light upon a spy; but, although he strained every sense to its utmost limits, he could not detect a form or sound. He was agitated by a thousand wild speculations and fears, but could not arrive at any elucidation of the mystery, but he resolved, whatever it was, that he would not be the victim of it, if cunning would counteract it, and determined not to go to the cave until the morning dawned, and then he should be able certainly to see if he was watched, for his road commanded the whole distance left behind, and should he find there was a tracker of his footsteps on his path, he swore never to leave him until he put it out of his power to relate what he had seen.

The morning dawned freshly and beautifully; he waited only until its grey light spread itself around, and then with an eagle's eye on the road he left behind him, he wended his way to the cave; he reached it without seeing any one on his path, and entered it very gently, and found Florence sleeping; he looked at the flask and the provisions, and was glad to find they had been partaken of, and he prepared a rude breakfast for her, and sat by her side until she awoke. She started and shudderd when her eyes lighted upon him, but she did not utter a word. He addressed himself several times, but she made no answer; she steadily refused his offer of food, and sat motionless.

" I will cure this moody fit by-and-bye," he muttered, and commenced eating the meal he had provided for her; he finished, after doing justice to it, and then said, "this place is close and hot; I don't wish to injure your beauty by hurting your health, so you shall have a little fresh air; but remember, a scream or cry uttered above a whisper, shall bring at once the fate upon you I know you live in dread of. Come, if you won't talk, you can walk."

He took her hand—it was like marble; he pressed it, but the pressure was unreturned; he led her forth, and guided her to a ridge higher than the cave; she went unresistingly, and when he stopped she stopped also, and seated herself by his desire, looking, as she sat, the embodiment of hopeless misery. He sat by her side, and talked to her, but obtained no response; and he, tired of talking without a reply, turned from her, and scanned the scene below him. Suddenly he started, and drawing a pistol from his belt, he crawled to the very brow of the ridge, and looking anxiously and earnestly down, beheld a man fast approaching the spot where he was stationed, bearing upon his shoulders a musket, and ever and anon gazing with intense inquisitiveness about him.

CHAPTER VII.

" And when I woke, it rained,
My lips were wet—my throat was cold,
My garments all were dank,
Sure I had drunken in my dreams,
And still my body drank."   COLERIDGE.

" And my heart beat loud,
How fast she nears and nears.
Are those her sails that glance in the sun,
Like restless gossamers ?"   IBID.

" I can't tell you honour," continued the seaman, who was relating his hietory to the captain of the Wildfire, " how long I laid in this dead sleep, and, for my part, I believe nobody but the Lord himself can ; but howsomdever, after dreaming I was made Admiral of a fleet, which will never happen, seeing I am no ways fitted for such a berth—and believing, too, I took all the ships of every enemy in every sea, after a good deal of hard fiwhting, and then was lashed to the back of a tiger in Africa, under a burning sun, making all the headway he could, and then of a sudden found myself on a iceberg, drifting in the North Sea, without a rag on, and lay coiled up small to get a little warm, then I woke. It was quite dark, and it was raining ; the rain came down very slow and gentle, and was cool, and made my breath come and go easy, when before I found it a hard matter to pump out any. I looked 'fore and 'aft, but I could not see anything, and I waited a little while to make a reckoning as to whereabouts I was, and how I got there ; for you see, your honour, I was not quite sure I wasn't still on the iceberg. I stretched my hand out, and I felt the wet dress of the young lady, and then, all of a sudden, like the flash of a four-and-twenty-pounder, I remembered everything. My heart tossed up and down like a brig's boom in a calm, and I was very anxious to know what had taken place while I had been asleep. I found we were still on the raft, and I could tell we had drifted a long away ; but whether any vessel had seen or passed us, or whether we were both dead, and were sailing into the other world in this fashion, I couldn't tell—for you see, your honour, I've heard old hands say that when a seaman slips his wind he goes through the duty of a regular voyage before he gets to Heaven, which is the port he is bound to, or the other place, as it may happen, according as his log is clean or foul ; and first he has a bit of a fair breeze—light winds for light duck to—"

" Keep to your story, my man !" interrupted the Captain, " you found yourself still on the raft with the young lady."

" Ay ! ay ! your honour," said the seaman, touching his hair, " and after a little turning the matter over in my mind, and changing my quid, which, do you see, wasn't over fresh by this time, I thought it would be best to hail my fair little mite : well, I tried, but either she was deaf, or my voice was sunk low for want of eating, that I couldn't get it up ; for I couldn't make a sound. I tried to rise up, but I was too weak. I stretched out my hand again and felt her shoulder ; I shook her, but she didn't answer ; I tried again to sing out, but it wasn't to be done ; and so, after a little while, when I found she didn't move nor answer any signal I made, I found she had made a spare berth, and only waited for me to heave her over the side, and then I should be alone. Somehow or other, I can't tell why, perhaps your honour can—for the captain of a man-of-war, if he's a true seaman, knows the trim of a man as well as he does of a ship—perhaps your honour can tell me ; when I thought the soul of that kind-hearted young lady was gone aloft, I felt as if I had swallowed a two-and-thirty pound shot, gun and all. It wasn't that I was left alone, though that was something ; but it was as if—as if—as if—it's that I can't overhaul, your honour. I could have flung myself overboard ; I could have, its no use sailing under false colours, your honour, I'll tell the truth, I don't believe you will think me any the worse topman, or a blue jacket that don't know how to do his duty, when I tell you I laid my head upon my knees and piped my eye like a loblolly boy rope's-ended for stealing the steward's sugar. Had your honour seen the water run out of my scuppers, you'd a thought there had been six feet water in the hold and all hands at the pumps. I tried to say a prayer for her, as she had for me, but I couldn't think of anything but the Lord's prayer, which my mother taught me when I was a little how-dacious youngster that could have hid myself under the lee of a rope-yarn ; but I thought, if I said it with a will, the Almighty wouldn't mind letting it be put down in the log in her favour, and then just as I said " deliver us from evil, for thine is the power," I felt the raft go bump against something. I heard the ripple of water ; we wasn't ashore—we were in too deep water for that, and it was too dark to see what it was, for the rain, which still came down, covered us with clouds like a tarpauling over a skylight. Howsomdever I looked straight up aloft, and then brought my eye as near as I could within range of what we had run foul of, and then I could see a great, dark looking object close under my bows. At first I thought it might be Davy Jones come to press me, but then, as he didn't hail and I couldn't, I thought I might have made a false reckoning ; and then I thought it might be the hull of a wreck, and the rippling I heard might be the water against her side—

" Did you find out what it was ?" asked the Captain, a little impatiently.

" I did, your honour," he replied.

" Then tell me ; and for the future don't yaw about so much in your yarn."

" Your honour shall have it all plain sailing," replied the seaman, respect-fully ; and continued—" but if I keep too good a full, I am afeard I—"

" No matter—go on !" said the Captain, impatiently, seeing very well that if he attempted to make him tell the story more briefly he would, as he was about to say himself, " get jammed," and then he would have some trouble to get on fair again.

" Well, your hononr," continued the seaman, " I thought it might have been a vessel waterlogged, and left by her people. I thought a good many

^things, but I didn't hit on the true mark. We waited until daylight, for it held us fast; and then I found it was a rock standing bolt up, as if placed there for vessels to run foul of. But it was a welcome sight to me, and I thought it should go hard but I made it a landing place for I and the young lady, until we spoke some ship. With the daylight the rain cleared off, and the sun began to show he was tumbling up the main hatchway, and, as if the Lord sent it as a special providence, a great bird—something of the fashion of a gull, but every way bigger—came and perched on my knee, and began to clap on to my eyes with his bill, as if all my line had run out. It's strange what canibal propensities them wild things has. He seemed hungry, and was about to make his breakfast off me; but I wasn't prepared to be made dead meat of, so I stretched out my fingers gently and caught him by the neck, and held on like grim death. But, Lord help me, I soon discovered that it was stronger than I was, and it flapped and screamed, and beat its wings, until I thought he'd have staved in my bows; but, your honour, I was hungrier than he, too hungry to let him go, and using all the power I had, I contrived to get him under me, and settled down on him until I felt by his keeping quiet that he had dropped his peak. Then I brought him up, and out knife, I cut him open and sucked his blood, it was rayther salt; and when I think of it now, I wonder how I thought it so good, but I was as thin as a pennant haliard, and uncommon hungry. I thought of the lady, but I knew she wouldn't have a pull at the blood, and so I didn't ask her; but I was not so partickler,

No. 8

and I warnt very long before I finished the bird, for I plucked out his feathers with my teeth, and eat his flesh.   Well, I laid a little while and found I was getting stronger, and on trying my voice, I could speak.   I hailed the young lady, but she didn't answer me, and I tried to raise myself up, and I was able; Lord, I could have cried for joy.   Well, I turned round to look at her: her head had fallen back upon the chest, and she was as white as new duck; I tried to wake her up, but I couldn't.   Somehow I didn't think her dead, yet she looked uncommon like it; well, I crawled by her side, I rubbed her hands, they were quite cold, and her dress, too, was wet through; so I overhauled some of the things on the raft, and in some of the bedding which had not been touched, I discovered a kit full of biscuit, a bottle of wine, a bottle of rum, a powder flask, some bullets and small shot, a lump of beef as big as my head and as hard, and many other useful things, which had been stowed in, I suppose, by some of the messmates that I had put overboard.   I had a pull at the rum and the wine, just to see if I was right, for I didn't know but my nose might have deceived me, and when I found that there was no mistake, I poured some of the rum into my hand, and rubbed her temples with it, and her hands, and behind her ears, and after a little while, her lips moved, and I washed them with the wine, and when she opened her mouth, I poured a little down her throat, but that nearly choked her, and I broke out into a sweat, for I feared in trying to bring her to life, I was very likely to kill her; but she got over that, and I laid her head on my breast, because I was warmer than her, and the sun soon came up, and he was not long in showing us he was warmer than either.   The Lord is good and bountiful, your honour, for while setting with my precious cargo in my arms, I happened to cast my eyes into the barrel, and saw it was half full of water; it was tinned inside for some service or other, but we had stowed the provision in without thinking or caring about that, and I had taken the last crumb of bread out of it before I fell into my sleep; so here was life for us some little time longer.   Well, with the rum, and wine, and sun, the young lady came to life again, and I began to feel much stronger; I tried all I could say to cheer up her spirits, and talked, and looked as if I was walking the deck of the smartest craft in the service, and was homeward bound.   I had a bite at the beef, and then I felt strong enough to climb the rock.   I did it, your honour, and found it easier than a youngster making his first trip aloft.   It was a nice pleasant place at the top, not very large, but it was nearly flat, and covered with green stuff; well, to make a short story of it, I carried the young lady up, for she was too weak to walk, and I had no great deal of strength to be sure, but I managed to lift her up and set her on the top; then I brought up the water, and the provision, and the bedding, and the musket, to which we lashed a sword and a piece of duck, and made fast to the young lady's chest by way of signal of distress, and then I emptied the young lady's chest and brought that up, and all the things I had taken out I carried up afterwards, and—"

" You cleared the raft," interrupted the captain, impatiently.

"No, your honour, not quite, we—"

" Well, what did you on the rock?" said the captain, rather weary of these minute details.   "How long were you there before you were picked up?"

" Oh, your honour shall hear," replied the seaman.

The Captain gave a sigh, almost a groan, helping himself to a glass of wine, and made himself up to hear all with desperate resignation.

" The first day," continued the seaman, " we eat the beef and buiscuit, and she had a little wine, and I a little rum : the next there were lots of birds flying about, and I thought if I could bring one down it would be pleasanter eating than the beef, which, though I cut it thin, was very hard, and kept our teeth going as if we were munching old shoes. I tried and one of the fellows, more impudent than the rest, setting close to me, I loaded the gun, and firing at him, hit him; well, I picked his bones, and then got a timber of the raft, which I cut, and made a fire, and so roasted it, and we eat it and enjoyed it very much. Well, we went on this way, and never a ship hove in sight. All our beef went, and nearly all our biscuit, and still I never saw the spars of a vessel lift up from the horizon; our water lasted us but a short time, and yet we were very sparing of it, and every day we eat less and less to make it last the longer. The birds began to grow shy, and I couldn't get at 'em before they were so far off that if I hit them they would drop into the sea, where I couldn't get at 'em : at last it became the same thing over again—the young lady, bless her dear heart, starved herself to let me have something to eat, though for that matter I had got one of her shoes, which I chewed to make myself fancy I was eating. Every scrap and crumb of biscuit and beef was gone again, and though I could chew the shoe, the young lady couldn't; she grew weak and faint again. I wrapped her all round in a large boat-cloak we had with us, that, as she must die, she might slip her anchor as comfortably as she could. Well, your honour, as if those damned cannibals of birds— saving your honour's presence—knew death was ranging alongside of us, they began a awful screeching, and wheeled and whirled about us like Mother Carey's Chicken's in a gale; one saucy beggar perched his ugly carcases within a boom's length of me; my gun was loaded, and before he could spring his luff I stopped his grog, and then thinks I here's something for another day. I spoke to the young lady, but she lay back just as if her log was made up, and her sweet spirit was ready to go aloft. I was about to make a fire and try to cook the bird I had shot, and get her to eat some, when I turned my eyes mechanically to the water line, and lord! lord! your honour, my heart shot up into my mouth like a piece of bunting running up the signal haliards before its shook out—I saw the top-gallant masts of a ship rising up. She soon came up—aye, your honour, her hull lifted till I could see her ports."

" Was she a ship of war?" exclaimed the captain, quickly.

" She was, your honour," returned the man ; " I waved a piece of duck, but her look-out didn't see us. I had about two charges of powder left; I determined to fire the gun. It struck me at the moment if I failed to make them see me, that I should not be able to bring another bird down, and then we should starve entirely; for though the shoe kept my jaws at work it put nothing in my stowage; but it was worth the hazard. I had thrown my gun down when I saw them first, but I picked it up and loaded it with as full a charge as the powder would divide into two, and I put in a ball, and then fired towards them; but they still kept on—I was not seen. I loaded the gun with the last charge—I leaped on to the chest, I fired it again, praying at the same time to God to make them hear me. The Almighty didn't desert us then, your honour, for immediately after I saw them back their topsails and lie-to, and then I saw a boat lowered from the taffrail. Lord love your honour! a man at them times feels strange and queer. If I'd been seized up to the grating and had two dozen, you wouldn't have seen a tear in my eye; but how I laughed and cried, and almost screamed—in truth, your honour, I don't know what I did. I took hold of one of the young lady's hands, and sat on the chest, waving the duck, until the boat's mast touched the rock. The third lieutenant of the frigate, for such the vessel whose boat's crew picked us up, was, your honour, was in the stern sheets of the boat; a good, kind man he was, too, and thoughtful. He had brought some rum and tobacco with him, and climbed up the rock with the men, leaving one man boat-keeper; well, your honour, I was top-heavy with joy, and nearly fell into the sea when I tried to follow the young lady down, for, you see, three hands carried her between them, as light and as tenderly as if she'd been a baby, and I thinking myself stronger than I was, tried to go down after her in ship-shape and Bristol fashion; but there was too little grub in me for that. I missed my hold, and should have gone down like a double-headed shot, but one of the boat's crew caught me in his arms and passed me into the boat; and then they brought the chest and the rest of the things, and once more we had the deck of a good ship beneath our feet; but the frigate was bound for a long station in the Indies——"

"What was her name?" inquired the captain.

"The Andrew Mackay," replied the seaman.

"The Andromache," exclaimed the captain; "we spoke her a week since.'

"Very likely, your honour," returned the seaman, "but as she was going to a foreign station, and the young lady was going to England, after showing her all the care and kindness they could, and the same in the berth deck with me, your honour, we were put on board a homeward-bound merchant brig, and we had only been in her a few days when the gale came on which wrecked us. The masts were cut away, nearly all the cargo was thrown overboard, and when it was discovered she had sprung a leek, the people took to the boats and deserted her. They had as many as the boats could bear, and as we were last comers, and were none of the ship's company, they left us aboard. I asked 'em to take the young lady, but they wouldn't, and pushed off from the side, leaving us once more with the chance of being sent to Davy Jones. The passenger who lies ill in his berth, was hit on the head by a top-sail-yard, and they thought he couldn't live; besides, he was a passenger, and when you take to the boats, it's ship's crew before passengers. Howsomedever, before they had left the ship's side a minute they were both swamped by a tremendous sea, and every soul perished. By God's good will, your honour, we were once more saved, and that's all, your honour; only, I've this much to say—I should like, when I've seen the young lady safe home, to enter this ship as a topman, for I can see it is a clean-going craft, with kind officers, and a real true-hearted crew for messmates; therefore, if you have a spare berth, perhaps your honour will be kind enough to enter on the ship's books one John Andrew."

"There's a spare berth now; one of the people fell overboard a few days since—you may take his berth when the doctor gives you a clean bill."

"Your honour is very kind," replied John Andrew, "and I thank you kindly."

"But you have told me very little of the young lady now," said the captain, "you have not said who or what she is."

"I know very little more than I told your honour," replied John Andrew; "I knew nothing of her afore she came on board the Pen-ne-lopee."

"You know her name?"

"Yes, your honour, it is Alice Manners, and, the Lord bless her! sweet manners she has too!" replied Andrew.

"Know you aught of her family?" inquired the captain.

"Only a little that she herself told me, your honour," replied Andrew, when we sat on the rock one night, watching the stars looking on us so bright, like the binnacle on a dark night, and as the young lady said, seemed put there by the Almighty to make us hope for help on the morrow."

"And what was her story?" inquired the captain.

"She said," he replied, "that she had travelled very much; that she was born in Scotland, and her family was noble, but poor; that she had left her native place when she was about fourteen, and had been to Spain, and traveled a good deal there, they left Lisbon for the West Indies. Well, it seems her father is a very stern man, one who was always, as I could take it, bringing her upon the quarter deck to hear the articles of war, which he read very often, because she would remember a friend she'd left in Scotland when she went away."

"Remember a friend!—how do you mean?" inquired the captain.

"Those were her words," replied John Andrew, "which I suppose means that she had clapped into her log the name of the youth, as she explained it, which her father wanted her to scratch out, but she swore stock and fluke she would not, and though her father, she says, tried to frown her out of her senses, she would not be spliced to an old factor with sacks full of joes. Well, while all this beating to windward was going on, who should heave in sight but this friend. The father comes athwart his hawse and promises to make a clean run with him to the yard-arm, and the Lord knows what; the friend laughs at him, and sees the young lady. Well, true to her colours, she receives him very kindly, but having promised her father never to read a page out of Hamilton Moore with him, unless by his consent, begs of the friend to 'bout ship and steer for some other latitude, until the weather is fair for them to sail in company. Well, he consents, and to oblige her, springs his luff, thof he's loath to do it. When her old commander finds the coast clear, up he brings the old merchant ship again, but, although he tried all his best manœuvres, backing and filling, and working his ship in the best manner he could, yet she wouldn't haul down her colours; and so, in a towering rage, her father ships her off to England by herself, pretending that though he is mighty fierce, and looms very large with her, that he will not compel her to consort with a man she hates ; but when this young lady tells me the name of the merhant—why, who should it turn out to be but the very man who shipped his goods in the Pen-ne-lopee to settle in England, while he made the passage in another, in order to make her think he was at anchor in Port Rico ; so, although he thought he was making a good stretch towards getting the weather-gage of her, he will find himself brought up right out of his reckoning. That's all I know about her, your honour, but the captain of the main-top knows her very well—that is, better than I do."

" Who ?" exclaimed the captain, with surprise.

" The captain of the main-top, John Paul !" replied Andrew ; " he changed colours like a dying dolphin when he clapped eyes on her, and overhauled my log, until he knew every word in it about her. He told me he knew her family and all about her."

" It is singular," muttered the captain, musingly ; I may not be mistaken after all—I will search it out. Upon deck, there !" he cried in a loud voice.

" Sir," said a quarter-master, in reply.

" Pass the word forward for John Paul," he exclaimed ; " let him instantly attend me in my cabin."

" Ay, ay !" replied the man, and in a minute or two, John Paul was ushered into his presence.

CHAPTER VIII.

" And darest thou, then,
To beard the lion in his den,
The Douglas in his hall ?"   SIR W. SCOTT.

" Round he spun, and down he fell ;
A flash like fire within his eyes
Blazed."   BYRON.

For a few minutes Jasper Chough watched the motions of the stranger he saw approaching the spot which contained himself and Florence. His breast was torn with a variety of emotions, and his brain was filled with a thousand contending suggestions of what course to adopt to avoid detection or confront the stranger that was approaching ; he was not certain whether or not he had been seen—if he could be certain he had not, he would have at once retired into the cave and trusted to chance to have saved him being unkennelled. The man was fast approaching, and by the facility with which he climbed the mountain, it was evident that he was no stranger to the art or place. Jasper tried to see his face, but save the first moment that his eye had lighted upon him he was unable to get a fair gaze at his features ; he could not believe that the man had any other motive in climbing the mountain than coming in search of him ; and bent as he was in keeping Florence in his possession, he made up his mind, whatever the issue of the discovery, that he would sacrifice the lives of all three rather than she should escape from him. The man did not slacken his pace in the smallest degree, and the opportunity that Jasper might have had to have led Florence unseen into the cave was past, for the man was now within a hundred yards of him ; he, however, seized Florence by the wrist, and muttering in her ear—

" Someone approaches ; retire with me to the entrance of the cave ; whatever takes place, come not forth, unless you would have me imbrue my hands in the blood of him who comes, perhaps, also, in yours."

" Have you no mercy ?" said Florence, in a feeble voice.

" If to part with you be mercy, I have none !" he replied emphatically. " I have gone too far to retract—you shall be mine—or no man's. I've not spilled the blood of him nearest to me, to suffer you through any weak consideration to depart ; come, we have not a moment—utter not a cry or a word— you will only bring blood and death, perhaps shame upon you if you do. Away—do not even attempt to look back ; the prying fool at our heels only approaches his doom every step he takes."

Without another word he led her down the ridge to the cave, and she had barely entered before he received a slap upon the shoulder, and heard a rough voice exclaim—

" How now, brother ! do you find this good roosting for young birds ?"

Jasper started as if a ghost had seized him ; he did not expect the stranger to have been at his side so soon. For a moment he could not speak ; and the man, uttering a loud laugh, continued—

" What ! thou didst not think a friend was so close to thy elbow."

" No !" he replied ; nor a stranger. I know thee not, nor seek to know thee ; which ever way your path lies, take it—you tarry not here."

" Do I not !" replied the man with surprise ; " perhaps you are king of the mountain—even Dunmail himself, who is said to walk this part of the mountain where Edmund defeated him. Whoever you are, you talk mighty lordly ; but whether Dunmail or the devil himself, I shall not move from hence untl it is my pleasure to do so, if it be till doomsday."

" I seek not to resort to any means of violence or conflict," exclaimed Jasper, with a sudden frown ; " let me advise you, therefore, to depart. I am determined you shall not stay here, and if you attempt it, it will be at your peril."

" With all my heart," returned the stranger ; " and yet I shall stay here, even though there be such a mighty scowl upon your handsome countenance." he added, with a laugh ; and then continued sternly—" I am not a boy, nor was yesterday the hour of my birth, that I should look upon you with an eye of alarm, and pay obedience to your wish in whatever fantastic form it may exhibit itself ; perhaps I interfere between you and the damsel you have hid so snugly in yon recess—so much the better ; it is my whim to do so, and you cannot, aye, shall not say me nay. You see, I can talk as big as you."

" You are a fool," cried Jasper, in a rage ; " a brainless fool—that on the verge of a precipice know not how near death you stand. You yet breath—

be satisfied with that and depart; a minute's delay may make you wish you had never sought this path."

"Or attempted to thwart you," cried the stranger, with a derisive laugh. "I fancied but now I was in England, in one of her choicest spots," he said, giving a half glance at the beautiful view beneath him; "but to hear your words would make me swear I was in some despotic land, where slavery was at its highest point; however, I do not think I am your slave—I do not think I am likely to be; and this I know, I care not for your commands a grain of powder, and to show you I do not, I shall not leave you for the remainder of the day—so the sooner you introduce me to the damsel the better. You see I have a greater fancy for your company than you for mine."

"You will not go?" cried Jasper, trembling with passion.

"Most positively, no!" replied the man, coolly, deliberately cocking his gun as he saw Jasper's fingers clutch his pistol, which he had replaced in his belt when he led Florence to the cave, and placing it upon his arm, ready to put to his shoulder at a moment's notice.

"Tell me," cried Jasper "what was your purpose in coming up the mountain?"

"Oh!" said the man, with a laugh, "you wish to know something about me before you drive me away with a bullet?"

"Was it to dog my footsteps—was it to search for me?" asked Jasper, grinding his teeth.

"If it was, I have found you, and don't mean to leave you," returned the man; "come, bring forth the girl—I long to see what sort of bird you catch in these high places."

"Dog!" shouted Jasper, drawing his pistol; "if you do not quit the spot, I'll blow your brains out."

"Shot for shot!" cried the man, bringing his gun to his shoulder, and presenting it at him; "mark me, if you attempt to level your pistol at me, I send this bullet through your head on the instant. The smallest attempt to raise your hand will bring your death upon you. I can make certain of my aim, and then, my saucy fellow, the pretty bird will be mine. Drop your pistol, or I fire."

"Fire, and be d——d!" roared Jasper, suddenly discharging his pistol at him; at the same instant the man pulled his trigger, but both missed their intended victims. Jasper's shot went through the stranger's hat and twirled it off his head; and the stranger's bullet cut a passage through Jasper's hair, making a cut in the skin of his skull, as if it had been gashed with a knife, but not sufficiently to hurt him much; it made his ears sing, and nearly stunned him—but he shook it off, and drawing the other pistol, was just about to fire it, when the hand containing it was seized and forced up with such a sudden jerk, that the pistol went off in the air, and at the same time, his throat was gripped with such strength, he felt as if nothing could prevent him being throttled. He struggled violently, but he was held firmly, and as every effort he made to free himself added to the sensation of strangulation, he was rendered powerless. He felt himself growing black in the face—there was such a rush of blood at his temples, he fancied

they would burst, but the pain having reached its utmost height, began to cease, and he at the same time was growing unconscious; everything faded from his sight and memory, when suddenly he was forced to the ground, and then his throat was released from the iron grip of the stranger, and being ena bled to breathe freely, he was in less than five minutes restored to his senses. He was still in the power of the stranger, and, to his rage, found himself bound by the arms to the gun, which having been passed along the middle of his back, crossed the bend of his arm, and effectually prevented him from being able to liberate himself. The stranger stood over him, and said with much coolness—

"You know the old adage, 'Never play with edge tools' if you had known me better, you would have been a little more circumspect, and used persuasion rather than force. I have not to thank you for life at this moment, though you have me, or you would, instead of sitting, lie there throttled. As you were bent upon making me an enemy, you shall have your wish. For may I be hanged, and that's an elevation I have not the smallest ambition to attain, if I be a friend. Ah! come forth my fair damsel; do not eb alarmed, I will not harm you," he cried, suddenly catching a glimpse of Florence's white face peeping round the edge of the rock, "I saw you peeping while we struggled," he added, "and your white and frightened face made me take my hands from about your swain's throat, when I was marvellously inclined to send him into the other world. Come hither,

No. 9

you need not be terrified; you have only to say the word, and I will cut this tame youth's bonds, and leave you once more to yourselves."

Florence, moved by his words to believe that he would assist her, advanced towards him, although she did it timidly, and said, as she clasped her hands earnestly—

"May I trust you as a friend?"

"You may," replied he, approaching her and taking her hand; "I will be a friend to you—but excuse me if I do not extend the same grace to your companion. Why, good God! maiden, you look very wan and wretched; your pretty face seems the picture of despair and misery: what sad circumstances have caused this to come to pass?"

"Will you take me from here?" she said, appealingly.

"Ah, that will I right cheerfully; trust me, this is not a spot to be alone with a youth of this graceless fellow's nature; even though he may have beguiled you to love him dearly. You look gentle and modest; it is strange that you should have forgotten your most beautiful attribute, and come into this wild place alone with him."

"Indeed, indeed, I did not come of my own free will," exclaimed Florence, bursting into tears.

"Beware what you utter," cried Jasper, suddenly, his eyes almost hidden by his eyebrows; "a silent tongue will save you from a fearful fate."

"Heed not the hound," cried the stranger, with startling earnestness. "Heed him not, maiden, he shall do thee no harm. What! has the ruffian dragged thee hither by violence?"

"He has!" replied Florence, burying her face in her hands.

"The scoundrel!" muttered the stranger, with flashing eyes. "Tell me, maiden, that he has inflicted on thee a worse outrage than carrying thee hither by force, and by the God who made me! I'll send him to death with a bullet from his own weapon."

"No, no," replied Florence, speaking quickly; "he has done ME no greater wrong than tearing me from my friends, from beneath his own father's roof, and threatening me with the worst wrong he could do me if I did not become his; but although he brought me hither, he has not been so wicked, or so heartlessly cruel, as to put his threat into execution—therefore do not take his life, although—"

"Beware, Florence," cried Jasper, interrupting her; "beware what you say. Keep silence on all that has transpired, if you would not have my bitter curse—for to make it so, I would not hesitate to fling myself from this height, cling to you like a robe of fire, to you and to all who come in contact with you, to all who touch thee in kindness or in love, all whom thou would'st desire to wear in thy heart, to—"

"Peace! you babbling villain," cried the stranger; "think you, because you happen to be an immeasureable scoundrel, who can pour forth curses as a a gun will scatter shot, that God will suffer them to take effect. Pah! say what thou hast to tell, maiden," he added, turning to her, "and fear not any evil words from his mouth. Why did you lay such stress on the word

ME, when you said he did you no greater wrong than tear you from your friends ?"

" Ay," said Jasper, " tell all and make broken hearts at home."

" Oh, Jasper," said Florence, bitterly, " if you had thought of them you would not have acted thus."

" But I had not—at least, I cared nothing about them," said Jasper ; " when you return you will have a tale to tell—look how you word it ; my mother is weak-minded, and not over strong bodied—a full relation, may put her in her coffin, and make my father put a bullet through his head ; then I doubt not that you will feel happy in having had your revenge of Jasper—but you will deceive yourself, it will not affect me. I never from a boy cared when I parted from them, whether I should see them again or not, and neither do I now. It is, perhaps, in your power to have me swung from a gibbet ; I don't care if you do ; but if its in the power of a spirit to come back to the world, I'll haunt you to your grave, and if it is not, I shall go out of the world quite sure that you will be eaten up by misery in knowing you have been the cause of the destruction of a whole family."

" I have seen many ruffians, to be sure," said Florence's deliverer, in a tone of disgust, " but it never was my lot to meet with such a cold-blooded monster as you. God help me ! I am none of the best, but I feel myself an angel of goodness compared with you. I am sorry I took my hands from your throat until the devil had you ; and yet, upon second consideration, I am glad I did, for the slaying of such a rogue who deserves no better death than the gallows, would have hung heavy upon me."

" Pray, let us depart from here," said Florence ; " I am faint and ill—I have been very much terrified, and am weary-hearted until I am once more safe at Chough Hall."

" Chough Hall !" reiterated the stranger ; " what down in the vale of Grasmere ?"

" Yes," replied Florence, " let us hasten thither."

" So you are Jasper Chough?" said the stranger, addressing Jasper.

" I am—what of it ?" replied Jasper.

" You shall know hereafter," returned the stranger ; " perhaps, in a way which may not be altogether pleasant. Will you accompany me, or remain here ?"

" Neither," said Jasper, gruffly.

" Oh, yes—you will do one," observed his conqueror ; " perhaps, it will be as well that you remain here. There is an inlet or something, where you was hidden, I believe, fair maiden, is there not ?"

" There is a cave, where I was to have been confined until I consented to become his wife," answered Florence.

" Scoundrel as he is, his taste in this instance is unimpeachable," said he, gallantly ; but, as if he felt it was no time for compliment, he changed his tone instantly, and said to Jasper, " you will remain in this cave until my ret un

" Not I," said Jasper, with an oath.

" I think you will," said the stranger ; " that is, I will do my best that you shall; and so far as tight binding goes, I'll take care to have you pretty secure, my fine fellow. I'll just see how the land lies, and then for your abiding place until my return."

So saying, he quitted them and entered the cave. The moment his back was turned, Jasper said, eagerly—

"Florence, you see what your obstinacy and hardness of heart has caused. I have my brother's blood on my head—for which crime I shall, if you appear against me, be hung; my mother will die at once of a broken heart, and my father will destroy himself. I know this as certainly as if the events had already happened. It rests with you to prevent all this misery—be mine, fly with me—we can seek some foreign land, where we may yet be happy. I love you very dearly, nay, madly; you cannot doubt it, for I have hazarded my soul for your sake: only be mine, and fly with me, and no savage ever worshipped his idol more devoutly than I will you, so help me God! Say the word that will save my mother from a broken heart, and my father from self-slaughter. I ask you not to think of me, but to spare them—say it, Florence, say it as you hope for God's mercy."

Jasper, I could bear every evil or ill under heaven rather than on any terms be your wife," said Florence, firmly; "your touch, your look, fills me with horror, but for your mother's sake I will not disclose to her that it was you who bore me away—you who murdered—"

"Hush, hush, hush," whispered Jasper, rapidly, for the stranger re-appeared. The latter saw that he had stopped Florence speaking, and said quickly—

"Let me not interrupt you—say on; unless you wish me, I will not repeat it, or will retire until you have finished your colloquy."

"No, do not leave me," said Florence, afraid to be left alone with Jasper, even though his arms were bound; and then continued her speech to Jasper, saying, "I will spare her the pain of knowing from me what you have done, for to none will I ever disclose what has occurred until there is no danger of her being a sufferer by it; but seek not to appear before me again—I will not then answer for what the horror of your presence may cause; I can bear any evil, even death, rather than look upon you with any other feeling than loathing."

"That's rather severe, but seems to me very just," said the stranger.

"Florence! Florence," cried Jasper, "the curse of whatever may happen hereafter be upon you, and blight every happi—"

"Silence, you ill-conditioned wolf," said the stranger, "and into your lair."

"I'll not move," roared Jasper, fiercely, trying to gain his feet; but the stranger seized his shoulder firmly, and held him down, as he said—

"I think you will move, and that speedily, if you go not of your own accord. Must I drag you hence as I would the carcase of a slain beast?"

Jasper ground his teeth audibly, and his eyes rolled wildly, as if he was mad. His whole frame shook convulsively, but the stranger took no heed of it, and taking some rope which he had found in the cave, which Jasper had brought there, he tied his arms, not without some hard struggling, firmly to the gun, and then seizing him with both hands, by the neckpiece of his coat, he dragged him into the cave; he then passed the end of the rope, which was more than enough to keep his arms fast, through a ring which was affixed to the side of the cave, and made it fast.

"There," said he, when he had finished—"I think, although you do not, that you will stop here till I come back. This cave's a discovery, I must make some further note of it; it's a little mysterious, and may contain something worth looking for. Farwell, Jasper Chough; if you are not partial to ghosts, keep your eyes shut, for I fancy much villany has been done here, and the spirits of the victims haunt it unmercifully."

He quitted the place as he uttered the last word, and taking Florence's hand, he began slowly to descend the hill; she was very weak, and was compelled to lean on him for support, but he treated her very gently and kindly, and spoke of the beauties of the scene as they descended; but she was too weak and agitated to reply, and scarcely uttered a word until they reached Chough Hall.

Without waiting for the appearance of one of the inmates of the Hall, the stranger pressed the hands of Florence, and said hastily—

"My pretty damsel, I heard you promise the rascal who behaved so ill to you, and from whose fangs I was lucky enough to rescue you, that you would not tell more than was necessary to account for your absence, without wringing the hearts of his parents. Now, though he deserves to be well punished for what he has done, they do not, and, therefore, I will lend no hand to make them; but as I made him no promise to hold my tongue, and as I do not fell disposed to be very friendly towards him, it strikes me as being more than probable that, if they asked me anything about the matter, I should tell them all I know—showing them what a beauty of a son they have, which, by the bye, I dare say they have found out long 'ago, and be putting them on the high road to be very miserable, and God knows there is not much need of that; for though this may be a happy world, I should like to discover how— for I never found it too much that way, and very few others, I believe. So, my fair maiden, your friends will see nothing of me, at least for the present; but you and I shall meet, and that not long hence—until then, adieu; be under no alarm from 'Jasper Chough—he will be provided for in such a mannan that he will not be likely to trouble you, or any one else in this quarter, again, for a long while to come; so cheer up your spirits, and think of him who is far away. Nay, never start—I know more than you think I do, and more than I intend to tell at present. Some one comes. For the future rest here without fear; there will always be a friend watching over you until your destiny changes, and causes your removal. Farewell."

"Stay," cried Florence, quickly; "what name shall I remember in my prayers, when I thank heaven for my deliverance."

"A friend," he uttered hastily, and waving his hand, instantly disappeared. At the same moment, the old porter hearing voices, made his appearance, and immediately his eye lighted upon Florence, he uttered a cry of surprise, staggered back a few steps as if he had seen a spectre, and then recovering himself, hurried forward. "Lord love us," he cried energetically, "here's a joyful sight—Miss Florence back 'again! Heaven be praised. Welcome home, Miss—welcome home. Oh, we have been in such a sad taking for you and Master Frank, bless his noble heart. We have had such mournful hearts, aye, and weeping eyes, for we could gain no tidings of you. Master Jasper has been on the search for you, but could not discover you. He has gone again—at least, we suppose so, for he went out in the night; but he's a strange youth, and does things as nobody else thinks of doing. My master and mistress are in the drawing-room, Miss: how happy they will be to set eyes on thee again, to be sure. But where's Master Frank: where does he stay? I thought I heard—"

"Lead me to the drawing-room, David," exclaimed Florence, interrupting him, speaking in a faint tone. The old man observed it, and said hastily—

"Bless me, how very white you look. You seem very ill—lean on me, my dear young lady, you need not mind me, I am an old man, and a faithful servant. Dear heart, you look wond'rous ghost-like, in truth."

"I am not well, David," said Florence, hoping to stop the old man's loquacity, and induce him, without further delay, to lead her to the room which contained Squire Chough and his lady, She felt very feeble and hysterical and was in no condition for an interview which would require so much judgment to manage, in order that all the occurrences which had transpired might not be related; but she knew that it must take place, and the sooner it was over the better. She could not tell how she should get through it, for she felt each minute as if she should swoon, but was anxious therefore to get where she knew she should receive assistance in case her senses left her. Her reply to David, however, had not exactly the effect she wished, for he was desirous to hear what had occasioned her absence, that he might be Sir Oracle of the kitchen for the time being; but not being well skilled in the art of drawing from any one desired intelligence without direct inquiry, and not daring to put the question plump, he was likely to be some time beating about the bush before he could get at the bird he was after.

"Well, Miss," he returned, in reply to her remark—"not well! Indeed, Miss, I believe you, for I never, and I am sure no one else ever saw you look so ill. I dare say you have had a great deal of trouble and fright, and fatigue too into the bargain, I'll be bound—have you not, Miss."

"I have indeed, David," she replied, and then continued, urgently—"lend me your arm, and lead me at once to your kind mistress—I feel very faint—"

"Lord bless us—don't faint, Miss," said the old man. "Cheer up, my dear young lady—you are at home again, and safely. Shall I call Master Frank."

"No, no," murmured Florence, "lead me at once to the sitting-room—I am very weak and very cold."

"Dear heart—yes, Miss," cried the old man, but not offering to move: "it was a terrible storm, and must have frightened—Hollo, eh, good Lord—look up, Miss. Here, Dorothy, Martha, Robin, Judas—help," roared the old man, for Florence, overcome by exhaustion, had sunk upon his shoulder, and her white face and closed eyes made him fancy she had fainted. He exerted his lungs to some purpose, for nearly all of whom he had named came running to his aid, and there was no little surprise manifested on discovering who it was that needed assistance.

"Miss Florence, Miss Florence," was passed from mouth to mouth, and Martha, one of the maids, a pretty girl between sixteen and seventeen, the moment she cast eyes upon her, burst into tears.

"Dear, sweet Miss Florence, look up to us and talk—will ye? don't die away so, don'tee," she sobbed; "we've been crying our eyes out for'ee," haven't we? Ay, that we have.''

Florence had not fainted, but was so dreadfully feeble from the effects of what she had undergone, that she had barely power to move. Roused, however, by the appeal of the sobbing girl, she opened her eyes and tried to smile, but the effort was so apparent that it made the poor maid redouble her tears.

"Oh dear, Miss," she cried, "wher'st thou been to come home half dead like this."

"She wants to go to Missus," said the old porter, beginning to think it would have been quite as well if he had led her to her when she first asked him. He did not, however, give utterance to his thoughts, but merely advised what he knew was Florence's wish.

"Ay, to be sure, to be sure," cried Martha; "here, David, I'll carry her, poor dear—poor dear, she's worn and hagged to skin and bone, I wish I had in my claws those who've made her like this; their own mother and father should not know them when I had done with them."

With many more such remarks, uttered between sobs, the simple girl lifted her young mistress from the ground and bore her tenderly, but as lightly as if she was a child in her arms, followed by the rest of the servants, all of whom had at a minute's notice congregated. She soon gained the apartment in which Squire Chough and his wife were seated, sorrowfully pondering on the strange absence of Frank and Florence, and so absorbed in their grief, that they heard or heeded not the hubbub which Florence's arrival had occasioned. A sudden knock was given by one of the servants at the door, and before the permission to enter was given, it was flung wide open, and Martha and her burden were in the centre of the room in an instant.

"Here's Miss Florence, madam!" cried Martha, with an hysteric laugh.

The old lady screamed, started from the chair in which she had been sitting and ran to the side of Florence.

"My dear child my beloved girl! where have you been?—oh, you have nearly broken our hearts. Speak, love—what made you leave us so suddenly, and frighten us out of our lives?"

Florence tried to speak, but her tongue clave to the roof of her mouth; her bosom heaved convulsively, she stretched forth her arms to the old lady, who opened them to receive her, and murmering a few words inandibly, she sunk upon her shoulder in a swoon. The old lady screamed with fright; she sent every one of the servants for remedies; she wept bitterly, and was herself so excessively agitated, that it seemed almost certain that she would follow the example of Florence, and faint too—but with much exertion, aided by the entreaties of her husband to be calm, she succeeded in preserving her faculties; and as the servants returned, one with smelling salts, another with cold water, a third with a piece of burning linen rag, and so on, each with some favourite recipe, she took advantage of the presence of the restoratives to keep her senses from leaving her, and lent her assistance in restoring Florence. After much perseverance, she was brought to, but soon again relapsed, to be again recovered, again to swoon. The village practitioner, for whom one of the servants had been despatched, now arrived, and he was not long in recovering her, but she immediately went into hysterics of the most violent description, and the doctor, perceiving how exhausted her frame was already, ordered her instantly to be carried to bed, which was done; in the meantime he went himself to his house, and compounding some soothing medicines, returned with them, and administering a composing draught, waited by her side until she, overcome by the excessive fatigue, mental and bodily, which she had undergone, aided by the medicine, sank into a deep slumber. The medical man then gave very strict orders respecting her, commanding that nothing should be suffered to disturb or agitate her in her present weak condition, or he would not answer for the consequences. He promised to call again in a few hours, and departed after repeating his injunction. She was too much beloved by every one in the Hall for them not most punctually to obey them; and though the old lady was in an agony of suspense and doubt respecting Frank, she would not disobey the orders of the doctor, by putting a single question to Florence.

When the doctor returned she was still in a deep sleep; her face was flushed, she breathed heavily, and by her restlessness and occasional moans, it was evident her dreams were painful. The doctor feared a violent fever would ensue, and provided against it to the best of his skill, which, though but a village practitioner, was of no mean kind; in fact, he had studied in London, when young, had taken all his degrees, and bid fair, from the talent he evinced, to become a first-rate physician. He was possessed of a moderate income through his father's death, but one, which, if it did not enable him to live splendidly, furnished him with every comfort; he was, however, on the high road to realize a fortune, and was about to be married to a very beautiful girl. As they were proceeding to the church to be married, in an open carriage, a boy fired a squib, which, when he threw it from his hand, alighted upon one of the horses, and got entangled in the harness. The horses instantly took fright, dashing along with tremendous rapidity; the coachman was flung from his seat and severely injured, and the horses without control flew madly along, and when the squib exploded, almost leaped out of the harness with terror. Upon reaching the corner of the street, they got upon the pavement, the wheels caught with terrific force in some iron railings—the carriage was shivered to atoms, the bride was thrown out, fell upon her head in the area of the house, and was killed upon the spot. Two friends were also dreadfully hurt, and the doctor was flung into the street; he was picked up senseless, with a broken arm, and a fractured skull; he, however, recovered after a long illness, but instantly quitted London, and came down to Grasmere, where he attended patients, more for the sake of passing away the long dreary hours than for any remuneration. His skill and success, coupled with his kindness and attention, made him beloved by every one in the village, and if any one was afflicted

by illness he or she resigned themselves to his care, with a perfect assurance that, if it was in the power of medicine to cure them, they would beneath his care, be restored to health.

He sat by the side of Florence, and watched her hour after hour unremittingly—he gazed upon her countenance anxiously, and perused every lineament with the air of one who saw traces there which called upon his memory for features he had known in other scenes and other times, and the more he regarded her, the more eager and astonished his face appeared; at length, as if unable to restrain his curiosity farther, he turned to Mrs. Chough, who was seated by the bedside, and said—

" You will not deem me impertinent, my dear madam, if I ask you a few questions respecting my gentle patient here ?"

" Most certainly not, doctor," replied the old lady, expecting him to refer to the circumstances which had thown her into this weak condition. " Whatever you desire to know I shall be happy to answer, as far as I know."

The doctor bowed, and then said—

" She lies in a very precarious state, I am sorry to say, and much care will be required to restore her; because her indisposition, as far as I can at present judge, appears more mental than bodily. The difference of treatment required under such circumstances must be evident; but unless I in some

No. 10.

degree know by what the mind is influenced, my efforts will, to a certain extent, be unavailing. I have occasionally met her previous to this, but my notice of her never exceeded a glance, and I gathered nothing but that she appeared unusually pensive for a maiden of her age. But there must have been some frightful excitement to have thrown her into the state she is now in, and perhaps you will favour me by putting in my possession some of the circumstances which have led to this. Understand me my dear madam, I do not ask this out of impertinent curiosity, or desire to know more than you may deem it necessary to tell, but I think it essential to know a little; for though," he added, with a slight smile, "our immortal poet doubts the possibility of administering to a mind diseased, yet it is to be done, so as to restore the body to comparative health—that is, aleviated; but, I confess, not relieved effectually—not effectually," he concluded, with a deep-drawn sigh.

"Did you not hear of her being missed the evening before last?" inquired the old lady, with some surprise.

"Missed!" reiterated the doctor, with astonishment—"missed!" he repeated. "No, my dear madam, the fact is," he added, "I was summoned three days since to a lady who lies in a very dangerous state a few miles off, and did not return until an hour previous to the arrival of your servant; I have, therefore, heard nothing of what has transpired in the village during my absence."

Oh dear, doctor! we have been in such bitter trouble and anxiety," exclaimed the old lady. "Florence went out on Tuesday night, for a walk—you know what a lovely evening it was, and she is fond of strolling in the lanes and fields in the cool of the evening—we therefore thought nothing of it. Frank, my dear son—you know my Frank, doctor?"

"Indeed I do, madam!—a fine noble fellow—a son of whom you may justly be proud," replied the doctor.

"And I am—I am," repeated the old lady. "Heaven knows he has always given me cause to do so until now."

"Pray proceed, madam," said the doctor, anxiously.

"Well, doctor, he followed Florence," continued the old lady, " after she had left a short time, and soon afterwards that frightful thunder-storm came on; from that time until half an hour previous to your arrival we heard nothing of either of them. And then Florence returned in the terrible state in which you first saw her; but Frank—my blessed Frank—I have had no tidings of whatever," added the old lady, bursting into a paroxysm of tears.

"Have you no clue to this strange proceeding?" said the doctor, after a pause.

"None whatever," replied Mrs. Chough. "Florence was fainting when she returned, and there has been no opportunity of putting one word to her since."

"It is very singular," observed the doctor, thoughtfully. "Where was your son Jasper?" he asked, a little earnestly.

"He was away at the time, and knew nothing of the matter," replied she. "He returned late at night, and retired immediately to rest; David, however, roused him from his sleep, and he went in search of them, but returned in the middle of the day, yesterday, without having been successful."

"Where is he now?" he inquired.

"I do not know," she replied. "David tells me he quitted here before day-break this morning."

"To search for them?" inquired he.

"I cannot say," she returned; "he has very singular ways, and will not brook much interference with his humours, whatever they may be. He was much ruffled, because one of the villagers who went in search of them, told him they saw him speaking to Florence, and saw also Frank approaching them."

"And what said Jasper to this?" asked the doctor, quickly.

"Denied it," replied the old lady, "and even struck the youth because he persisted in the story."

"Ha!" muttered the doctor. "there is some mystery in all this; we must wait till our patient recovers, to hear what she will say of the matter."

He paused for a little while, and then said—

"Have you any reason to believe your son Frank to be in love with this young lady?"

"No," she replied; "for his heart was already bestowed ere he saw her; nor does she love him, for she was sent down from London to our care, to be kept from the clutches of one, who, as we are told, is a profligate, poverty-stricken wretch; one who has succeeded in gaining her affections by the basest artifices, and would induce her to wed with him if he knew where to find her upon his return from sea."

"He is a sailor, then?" observed the doctor.

"Yes: the lieutenant of a frigate," replied the old lady, "and although of, I believe, good family, yet so miserably poor, and withal so dissolute, that her friends have resolved she shall not sacrifice herself by wedding him."

"I know enough to guide my proceedings," said the doctor; "she must be kept very quiet, and everything done to soothe her feelings; there is such an infinite sympathy between the mind and body, that unless we relieve one, we cannot hope to cure the other. Pray, madam," he added, "do not be offended with me if I prosecute my inquiries so far as to ask her name."

"Her real name, doctor, must be kept a secret," said Mrs. Chough; "she is with us under the name of Ranklyn, and believes me to be an aunt, whom she never saw until her arrival here."

"I would not have put the question, my dear, madam," said the doctor, hastily, "had I not perceived in her an extraordinary resemblance to one with whom some of the most painful circumstances of my life were connected; but believe me, I will intrude my curiosity no farther. Ha! my patient is awaking, and I fancy I perceive favourable symptoms appearing—let us hope that it may be so."

"Most fervently—most fervently!" ejaculated Mrs. Chough.

Florence opened her eyes after sighing heavily several times, and then stared wildly around her. Her eyes roamed from one to another restlessly;

she did not appear either to recognise who was near her, or where she was. Mrs. Chough approached her, and leaning over her, said gently—

"Florence, my love, do you not know me?"

She gazed earnestly at her for a minute or so, and then suddenly flung her arms round her with a cry of joy, and said rapidly—

"Thank God! my dear aunt, it is you. Oh, I thought I was still in that dreadful place, and he by my side, threatening me with horrors worse than death."

"Do not ask her any questions now, my dear madam," interposed the doctor, "she must not talk, nor hear a voice or footfall, until I again see her."

The doctor then administered some medicine to her, gave directions for all that was to be done during his absence, and quitted. It was a hard matter for the old lady to keep silence respecting Frank, but as the doctor had said the smallest agitation or excitement might prove fatal, she refrained from speaking to her. Every care was displayed towards the invalid, every order of the doctor religiously fulfilled, and at the expiration of two days he pronounced her so far recovered as to sit up and bear the desired conversation. She was dressed and seated by a fire, although it was summer time, and then Mrs. Chough, with a beating heart, wound her arm round the attenuated waist of Florence, and pillowed the weak maiden's head upon her shoulder, and after a few preliminary hems, she commenced—

"We have suffered dreadfully from your absence, my love."

"You must, indeed, my dear aunt," replied Florence, in a low voice, dropping her eyes.

"We thought you had taken shelter from the storm somewhere," continued the old lady; "we knew Frank had followed you; we thought he was with you, and I knew he would take every care of you, and were therefore not alarmed at your absense, until we had suffered hour after hour to pass away and midnight approached—then we grew anxious, and as morning drew near, we became frightened, and despatched David to Jasper's room, for he had returned home."

Florence shuddered as his name was mentioned, and Mrs. Chough noticed it; she asked her if she was cold, but she shook her head negatively, and Mrs. Chough resumed her speech.

"Jasper went in search of you, but returned without finding you, as did many others. Pray, my love, what caused your extraordinary absence?"

Florence did not reply, and Mrs. Chough, after waiting a little while for a reply, found she was weeping. At this moment the squire entered the room; he inquired kindly after her health, and then put the same question to her as his wife had; she still replied not, and the squire, on finding she remained silent, said—

Why do you hesitate to reply—do you fear any unkindness or harshness frow us, Florence?"

"Oh, no—oh, no," she replied, quickly.

"Then why are you silent upon a question whose solution is of the greatest interest to us? Your absence was not voluntary?"

"No, indeed, it was not," she returned.

"Then it was by compulsion," he said.

She remained silent; he waited a moment, and then continued—

"There is much mystery in all this, lorence. Although I fear that I can unravel it, still I would rather hear its confirmation from your lips in relating the reason of your absence, and the miserable state of exhaustion in which you returned, before I utter my surmises."

A pause ensued—she then muttered—

"It was by compulsion."

"Who was the villain who dared commit so base an act?" he asked, earnestly, speaking through his teeth. Florence was again silent, and in undisguised anger, he said "Think not, by your silence, you will screen Frank from my resentment."

"Oh no, no; you mistake," cried Florence, energetically; "it was not Frank, indeed it was not; it was—"

"Who?" asked the squire; for she stopped short just as the name of Jasper was slipping from her tongue.

"I cannot, dare not tell," she exclaimed, clasping her hands.

"I knew it could not be Frank, my darling Frank," cried his mother, with fondness, and continued in a kind tone to Florence—"where is Frank, what has become of him?"

A strong shudder like a spasm passed through Florence's frame, and the tears poured in torrents from her eyes, but she made no reply.

"You alarm me," cried the old lady; "indeed, my love, you terrify me; you surely saw Frank upon the night you left us?"

"I did," she replied, sobbing.

"And what became of him?" she inquired.

"I—I—do not know," she answered.

"Not know!" reiterated the squire, looking fixedly at her; "you DO know, Florence, and you keep it disguised from us; your excessive agitation and grief assures me that there is the worst to apprehend. Answer me, my dear, dear girl, as you would wish to see our aching hearts relieved—where is Frank?"

The poor girl sobbed violently, and then suddenly sinking upon her knees before Mrs. Chough, and clasping her hands appealingly to her, she cried, almost franticly—

"Do not ask me—for mercy's sake do not ask me; I cannot answer; indeed I dare not—I dare not."

"Florence!" exclaimed the squire, solemnly, "answer me as you hope for mercy from Heaven hereafter. Has any villain vilely wronged you?—has any scoundrel inflicted upon you, by violence, an injury which nothing can replace?"

"No, uncle, no, as I hope for heaven," she cried.

"Then, my dear child, why this grief when Frank's name is mentioned?" asked he. "You may have been carried off, and be unconscious of ought that occurred to him, but if so, why this agitation? I am sure there is much you dread to tell, and it seems odd indeed that the victim of an outrage, you should, when you must know that you are beneath a roof where you are quite safe, be afraid to relate what has transpired, unless you know that your story will much afflict us, because you will touch us nearly—tell me, Florence, and car not I shall shrink to hear it.   Has Jasper—"

"My dear uncle," cried Florence, turning to him, ready to faint from weakness and agitation, " I will tell you as much as I dare;" and then speaking very rapidly, she said—"I was accosted by a person in the lane leading to the pass of Dunmail Raise, who professed love to me, and threatened, unless I consented to accept him as a husband, to bear me up the mountain, and keep me there in horror and misery.   In the midst of my fright and terror, while endeavouring to get away, Frank came up.   I appealed to him for protection—a struggled ensued—" Here she shuddered violently—" what followed heaven knows," she continued.   "I remember nothing further until I found myself being carried swiftly along, in the midst of a frightful storm of thunder and lightning.   I was so terrified by the vivid flashes, which nearly blinded me, and by the thunder, which roared so loud as to nearly stun me, that I could not utter a word.   I was borne to a cave in the mountain, in which I was confined the whole night.   In the morning I was liberated by my jailor, and again was pressed to save myself from the worst fate and consent to be his. I refused firmly, and was dragged forth ; I screamed for help when in the open air, but in vain, and a blow took away my senses."

"Did he strike you ?" cried the squire.

"He did," replied Florence.

"Execrable villain !" exclaimed he.   "If he crosses my path, he shall not escape his just due."

" I was then borne up the mountain higher still, and was again left for the whole day and night. I was still sleeping when he came again and when I awoke he was seated by my side, watching me.   He spoke, but I did not answer ; I only thought that the hour of my death was near at hand, for if he had dared to lay his rude hand upon me, I should have destroyed myself. I had secreted a knife, which he left with some provisions, for the purpose.   He led me forth for some fresh air, and we had been seated but a short time when he observed a stranger approaching ; he led me into the cave, and even while speaking to me the stranger was by his side.   A few angry words passed between them, shots were fired at each other, and a deadly struggle ensued, which ended in the stranger binding my enemy, and proving himself a friend indeed, led me safely hither."

"Why came he not with you ?" asked the squire.

"He would not.   He disappeared immediately after I arrived here."

" And his name ?"

"He gave no other than ' a friend,' " she returned.

"Your tale is singular," mused the squire. " Know you the name of him who carried you off ?"

Florence did not reply ; her sudden silence made her interrogator scrutinize her features earnestly, and presently, he said—

"Heard you my question, Florence ?"

She turned from him and flung her arms round the neck of her aunt, and again burst into a flood of tears.

"Ask her no further questions, my dear," said the kind-hearted old lady "you see how you distress her; she is not strong enough yet to bear it. Come, Florence, my dear, do not cry so; if you see fit not to answer the question it shall not be pressed."

Florence, however, heard her not—the excitement had been too much for her, and she lay senseless; the bell was instantly rung for assistance, and the squire quitted the room. As he went out he clenched his hands together, turning his head upwards, exclaimed, bitterly—

"Oh God! why did you afflict me with such a son as Jasper?—he is the villain—my heart too truly tells me that; every item of the gentle girl's story agrees with the time of his appearance here, and his absence from here; but she, fearful of wringing our hearts, bears the outrage his brutality has visited upon her, without disclosing the ruffian's name; but he shall not escape so lightly. Frank! my God! what may not have happened to him! My heart sickens—I fear the worst. The lane leading to the pass of Dunmail Raise. By heaven I'll search it! God help me! I hope it will not be to find his body. He seized his hat from where it hung, and hurried out, white with extreme agitation.

During the time these scenes were occurring at the hall, Jasper, the author of all this misery, was seated where the stranger had bound him, the prey to feelings of baffled rage and despair. He had endeavoured to work upon the timid and gentle nature of Florence to prevent her disclosing his villany. But what guarantee had he that she would not? He had everything to fear; it was scarcely probable that in the relation she would have to make of what had taken place, she could help mentioning his name. He knew of old, for he had been in circumstances which had taught him the lesson, how one word will bring out another; and as he had done more than enough to make her hate him, what likelihood was there she would screen him; None! he knew his father's stern nature well, and had not a second thought of escape if it should reach his ears that Frank had fallen by his hand: he writhed again, as each successive thought came strongly across his mind. There was this fellow, too, who had interfered; he was under no influence to prevent him telling; besides, he had threatened, on learning his name, to tell him something he would not like. What could that be? it could not be about Frank—a cold tremor seized him—was this he who had dogged his steps? was this the hidden stranger who had addressed him while bearing Florence to the mountain?

He wearied himself with speculations of this nature—was a prey to the agonies of suspense, almost of terror; for strong-minded as he was, he could not forget that his brother's blood was upon his soul, nor could he forget, nor think without fearful perplexity of the extraordinary disappearance of the body, the hat, stick, every vestige of the conflict. There was as much food for fear and the most agonised doubt in that as in any other part, and, in fact, turn which way he would, there was matter for the bitterest apprehension; and he had placed himself thus, too, for a girl who hated him. He cursed himself a thousand times for his folly, for his madness, and tortured himself with most dismal forebodings; the day passed away, and the night came: it was a long, dismal, horrible night to him; he could not divest himself of the belief that his brother, with a face of ghastly hue, was sitting down before him and gibbering in his face; he nearly went mad with horror and despair, and the morning came and found him exhausted with the frightful strain upon his feelings. He was faint, too, with hunger, but the sun came up and no sound of footstep met his ear; he began to have miserable apprehensions that he should be left there to starve to death, and his heart sickened at the thoughts of such a terrible lingering death : as hour after hour passed away, he became satisfied that such would be his fate, and from howling and raving with anguish he sunk into sullen despair. Towards the afternoon he heard an approaching footstep; he stretched forward—it drew nearer and nearer—at length he heard the door of the cave open—it was thrown wide; a minute elapsed, and then he saw the shadow of a man holding a gun thrown upon the wall. He waited a moment, hesitating whether to call or be discovered it might be some one who knew nothing of what had occurred, and found out the cave by accident, one who would release him, and no sooner did the thought strike him than he called out lustily—

"Help! help!"

The shadow instantly disappeared, as if he who cast it was suddenly alarmed presently it came again cautiously, and the head of a young man appeared round the corner of the rock. Jasper instantly recognised him as a foolish good-natured youth—a farmer's son who lived in the vale of Grasmere, he therefore immediately called him by name, at the same time communicating his own.

"Jasper Chough," cried the youth; "why, lor, how came you here? well to be sure."

"Don't stand wondering and staring there, but come and release me, my good fellow," cried Jasper, in an eager, but conciliating tone.

"What, be ye bound there? Well, that is mortal strange!" exclaimed he, proceeding at once to unbind Jasper. "Why, how came ye bound here?" he inquired, as he released him.

Jasper was no sooner free than he leaped to his feet, uttered a loud laugh of exultation, stretched forth his arms, which were nearly powerless from being bound so long in one position, and, in a paroxysm of delight, shook his deliverer heartily by the hand. The youth repeated his question, and Jasper replied—

"I'll tell you by and bye. I have not been so glad to see any one for many a day as I am you now."

"That I'll wager," was the reply.

"It was a lucky chance that brought you so high up the mountain," said Jasper. "I never knew you were so ardent a sportsman to follow your game to this height, and across, too, the most unfrequent and rugged part of it."

"Why, you see," returned the youth, "that Miss Flor—but, of course, you know all about the queer going off of Miss Florence and Master Frank, your brother, which has made such goings on at the hall, and you—"

"Has not Florence returned?" inquired Jasper, hastily.

"Why, that's a matter I can't exactly say much about, seeing I don't know," returned the youth; "but I rather think not."

"But are you not sure?" demanded Jasper.

"Why, no; because when I first heard your brother and the you lady were missing, I learned at the same time that there was a round sum offered for any news of 'em, so I started off in search, along with Harry Markham—you know Harry Markham, but I know you do, for he told me you knocked him down at your father's."

"Hum," growled Jasper, with a short laugh; "he knows me too; he will be less ready, in future, to tell lies."

"He swears it's truth," said the youth, "and calls all the saints in heaven and all the devils in ——, the other place, to witness that he will be revenged on you for it. Now, I know Harry Markham's a wild desperate fellow, and when he says he'll do anything, he'll do it; and if he says he'll be revenged upon you, he'll be revenged; so you take my advice and keep out of his way."

"Pshaw!" cried Jasper, impatiently, "I have no second thought to waste on such a shock-headed cub; tell me, without any more circumlocution, what brought you up here?"

"That word means circumbendibus, I suppose," said the young fellow, with a stupid stare at Jasper."

No. 11

"It means that if you don't at once answer my question, without telling me anything about your friends, I'll pitch you headlong from the mouth of the cave to the ridge below," said Jasper, grinding his teeth.

"It means a good deal in a little, then," said the youth, with a grin; but observing a slight indication on the part of Jasper, to do much towards putting his threat into execution, he continued, hastily, "Why, I'll tell you all in ten words."

"In six, if you can, and more than a dozen if you dare," answered Jasper, sternly.

"Harry Markham returned from your house, said they wasn't found, I came up here in search, found out this spot by accident, heard your voice calling out, came in—you know the rest," said the youth, speaking rapidly, endeavouring, if he could not repeat his communication in a dozen words, to utter it in the time.

"Then you have heard nothing from the Hall since Markham's return?" asked Jasper, anxiously.

"No," replied the youth; "not a word."

"I wish you had," muttered Jasper; and then added, "but no matter, I must take my chance; tell me," he added, speaking loudly, "and, mark me, no evasion—is Harry Markham near this spot?"

"I don't know," he returned.

"Look ye, Mat Meadows," said Jasper, speaking with strong emphasis, "I believe you have no desire to go down the mountain upon your head?"

"None in life," returned Mat, instantly.

"But you most certainly will, if I discover you to have told me a lie." exclaimed Jasper; "answer me truly, as you wish to reach home in a whole skin, did he accompany you hither?"

"No, indeed," replied Mat, earnestly, pressing his hands together adjuringly. "When he told me about you knocking him down, he left me, and I have never seen him since."

"That is true?" said Jasper, interrogatively.

"It is," he replied, "as I am here."

"Very well, I believe you," returned Jasper; "but if I find you have told me a lie, woe to you—you know me very well, you have not to learn that if I promise any one a beating I am scrupulous in not breaking my word."

"Perhaps it was some recollection of a former thrashing which made Mat Meadows put his hand instinctively to his shoulders, and give an unequivocal nod of assent, and say readily, "Oh yes, I know."

"Well, if Harry Markham, should be prowling about and dog my footsteps, you shall pay the penalty of it."

"But I can't help his following you, if by accident he is here," cried Mat, in a tremulous voice.

"His being here is no accident, if he is here, and you shall receive the punishment if he follows me, you must therefore prevent him. One other thing I have to demand of you, which is, that you say not a word to a soul breathing that you have seen me."

"But suppose somebody—your father, for instance—should ask me?" inquired Mat, with an alarmed countenance.

"Well, fool! do you suppose you are obliged to tell everything because somebody asks you," said Jasper, with a bitter sneer;" whoever asks you about me, profess entire ignorance; say, too, that you have been anywhere but here this morning, and, to every interrogatory, say you know nothing. If you do not—if you tell any one that you have set eyes on me, even your own father or mother—or whisper it to yourself, so that it reaches other ears than your own, I'll try the depth of the lake with your carcase."

The youth shuddered, and cowered beneath the stern glance of Jasper.

"I'll not breath a word to a living creature," he murmured.

"Look you do not," continued Jasper; "nor come from this spot to the mouth to see which path I take for at least twenty minutes or half an hour after I am gone, as you wish to avoid the effect of my anger."

"I'll do all that you wish me," exclaimed Mat, with an anxious glance round the cave, as much as to shew that he thought half-an-hour's sojourn in that lonely place by himself not at all refreshing; he did not, however, dare to express an objection, and Jasper, shaking his forefinger, menacingly at him, said, after taking up the gun to which his late opponent had bound his arms—

"Remember, Mat Meadows, that if in thought even you break your promise to me, I will most positively keep mine to you."

He turned to quit the cave, and had nearly reached the mouth, when Mat called to him; he stopped, and returning, said—

"What now?"

"You could not take me with you, could you," exclaimed Mat in tones very much like entreaty. Jasper, laughed scornfully.

, "Do you take me for a fool?" he asked.

"Oh, no!" returned Mat, quickly; "not at all; but if you would let me accompany you a little way—only to leave the place together, you taking one road, and I the other, you have no idea how much you would oblige me."

"I have not the smallest desire to know," uttered Jasper, with a frown; and adding, "keep where you are and do what I have bid you, or beware of me," he walked hastily from the spot.

Upon reaching the outside of the cave, he looked round him, far and near, but he could not see a human being; he paused a few minutes, and looked with the minutest scrutiny in every direction, but saw no living thing, save birds, wheeling and flying about; he then commenced his descent, and although weak from long fasting, and his limbs stiffened by remaining so long in one position, he accomplished his progress with a tolerable speed. His object was to gain the place to which he had first borne Florence and remain there until night, and then to concoct some plan for the future, which he would immediately put into operation. As he advanced, having left the cave some two hundred yards behind, he was startled by the sudden report of a gun, and hearing at the same moment a bullet whiz past his ear so close as to almost make him fancy he had been struck, he gave a leap in the first moment of alarm, and the next instant turned to see from whence it came; but although, he saw the white smoke from the explosion of the powder rising slowly up, he could not perceive the least sign of the person who had discharged the gun. He cursed and blasphemed at this inability, and on the spur of the moment would have crouched down and played at hide-and-seek too; but a second thought urged him to proceed, as he deemed it the wiser plan to gain possession of a retreat, which was so well hidden that a few minutes' start of a pursuer would enable him to enter it without its being discovered but with considerable difficulty where he had taken refuge; he therefore ran on, every now and then looking over his shoulder to see if he was followed, but he had the satisfaction of gaining the secret place without perceiving a pursuer.

———

CHAPTER IX.

" By your gracious patience
I will a round unvarnished tale deliver,
Of my whole course."
SHAKSPERE.

After John Paul made the customary obeisance to the Captain on entering the principal cabin of the Wildfire, he stood waiting to hear the purpose for which he had been summoned. The Captain seemed at a loss how to commence a series of questions which he had made up his mind to put to John Paul; he hemmed and moved uneasily upon his seat, and then suddenly said, "How's the wind?"

"It has shifted half a point," returned John Paul, with a look of surprise, not expecting such a question.

"What is it now?" inquired the Captain.

"Sou west and by west," replied Paul.

"Sit down, my man," said the Captain, motioning him to a seat.

Paul looked at the Captain, John Andrew, and then at the seat he was shown, and could easily perceive that his presence had been required for some other purpose than to tell in what quarter the wind was; however, he appeared to take no notice, but seated himself, and looked towards the Captain with an air of respect which is nowhere shewn from an inferior in station to a superior so much as on board a king's ship. There was a pause for half a minute, and then the Captain asked Paul to take a glass of grog, to which h

e

proffered not the slightest objection; the Captain gave it to him, and he drank it. When he returned the glass to the table, the Captain said—

"Has any report of the chase heaving in sight been made from the tops?"

"No, Sir," replied Paul; "the horizon is clear; she has shewn us a clean pair of heels, and is, I dare say, by this time safely moored in one of the creeks hereaway, and it strikes me that we must have something more than spectacles to find her."

"I believe you're right, Paul," replied the Captain; "we will stand on for a few hours longer, and then if we do not overhaul her, we will about ship and make for the old country."

"The hands will be glad to hear it, Sir," responded Paul.

"Well, I think it very likely they will hear it before long," said the Captain; and then, giving a slight cough, he continued—

"You are a smart man, Paul."

The young seaman, bowed.

"I know the trim of a man the moment I set my eyes upon him," he went on. "I was pleased with you as soon as I saw you; your conduct while you have been in my ship has justified my first impression, and I shall make it my duty, when a vacancy occurs, to shew you my esteem by bestowing it upon you."

Paul bowed again, but made no reply. The Captain proceeded—

"You are a pressed man, I think?"

Paul replied in the affirmative, and then the Captain, clearing his throat with a desperate determination to come to the point at once, said—

"I should be glad to know a little of your history; but I do not wish you to tell if you have any desire to conceal it. I do not ask you as your Captain, but as one who feels an interest in you. You can, therefore, do as you please in the relation. I do not utter this wish as a command, but as a request— simply that I should like to know something of one who has proved himself a good and an intelligent subordinate in my vessel."

John thought the speech and request rather strange; but, at a loss to understand the drift, he could not see a motive to decline complying with it, or feel offended, because it was couched in such courteous terms; he, therefore, after a little hesitation, said—

"I am afraid there is very little in my history to interest you, Sir, but such as it is, you are welcome to it."

The Captain thanked him, and desired him to proceed.

"I am the fifth child of seven," he commenced. "I was born in Scotland, at Arbigland in Kirkcudbright. My father was head gardener to a gentleman of great property there, which stood near the sea coast. As a child, I was extremely fond of the sea. I was never happy but when bathing in it or making little boats to sail upon it, and many an hour stolen from school—and which when discovered, was repaid by repeated applications of birch—was passed in rambling by the sea.side. It was in vain that my master flogged me, my father threatened me, my mother exhorted me, and even the minister, whose frown was death, spoke to me: they could not keep me from it. I loved the sea: it seemed to me to stretch out its wide arms with joy to receive me when I approached it, and to mourn for me when I was away, pent up in school or at home. All the day it was in my sight or thoughts, and at night it was the constant subject of my dreams. I never came across a book that had a word about the sea in it which I did not devour with the greatest avidity; every endeavour to coerce me to a different way of thinking failed. I grew sullen and gloomy. I would keep away for days, wandering among the coves and inlets with which the coast abounded; and although I knew the consequences of this wayward conduct were sound and severe beatings, it had not the effect of curing or checking me. At length, by the advice o friends, my father determined to send me to sea, trusting that short voyages in a coal brig would work a complete change in my opinions. He communicated his intentions to me, and I confess I heard them with no little delight and, at the age of thirteen, by my own desire, and with great reluctance on the part of my father, I was bound apprentice to Mr. Younger, a large ship-owner, at Whitehaven, and eagerly commenced my duties. My first trip was made across the Solway Firth; but, before I reached the end of the voyage, I began to think my father had not been altogether to blame in attempting to keep me from following the sea as a profession. I was knocked about, as all boys are, but not having been used to the rigid discipline of a vessel, I struck again when struck, and succeeded in obtaining twice the punishments and hardships which I should otherwise have had. But I resolved not to suffer the hard treatment to subdue me; I soon got to learn what where the duties I was expected to perform; and a sturdy spirit, one that would not be beat down, enabled me to accomplish them with the promptitude and correctness of the oldest hands in the vessel. I made two or three voyages under these disheartening circumstances, when it happened to come to the owner's ears that I could do the duty of an able seaman; he immediately put me into a vessel which he sent across the Atlantic to Virginia, where a brother of mine was settled upon the Rappahannoc. The vessel to which I had been drafted was a new one, and in every respect well found; she had a small but good crew, a kind captain, one who was as intelligent and well-informed as he was well-disposed: to his good nature and consideration I am much beholden. The change from the collier to a merchant brig, I found very great; the weather was fine, the duties light and easily performed, and my situation altogether was so much improved, that the strong love for a seaman's life, which the hard labour and drudgery in the coal brig had nearly driven out of me, returned with fresh vigour, and I think I may with truth say I was never happier in my life than in that trip across the Atlantic. The chief mate, an elderly man, was a thorough seaman, and from him I learned everything it is requisite for a blue jacket to know: he found me an eager, and, I believe, an apt pupil, and took a pleasure in bestowing upon me the knowledge which, through a long and hard life, he had acquired. I took great delight in navigation, and as he was well grounded in the science, and had a happy mode of communicating his knowledge, I soon became master of ti theoretically, and since that period, I believe, practically."

"You have had a good school education, too, to hear you talk," interrupted the captain ; "your language is not that of a foremast man.'

" In the forecastle, Sir, I speak the lingo of my messmates," replied Paul with a slight smile ; "in the cabin I fit my speech to the station of those in whose presence I stand ; but at home, my father was particular with his children, and restricted any improprieties of speech ; my mother was a very well educated woman ; I was a favourite with her, and received more instruction from her than ever I did from my schoolmaster, although he seconded his lessons with the application of the rod ; he was a harsh man, a stern repulsive man, one totally unfit in temper to bring up young people ; his motto undoubtedly was, that, 'to spare the rod was to spoil the child, and to do him so far justice, he carried out the proverb to the letter ; I have much stubbornness of temper to thank him for ; had he been less severe I should have been less obstinate : but that has nought to do with my history. After a pleasant passage, the weather being moderate, we made our port. I went direct to my brother's dwelling ; he is a planter, and has a pleasant estate upon the Rappahannoc. The chief mate accompanied me ; he took ill, and remained so for some time ; I stopped with him instead of returning to my vessel, and profited by his lessons considerably, until, poor old man, he died ; he had neither kith nor kin in the world, and he had taken a love for me as I was his son ; he died in my arms, and was buried on the banks of the river."

Paul hastily brushed his eyelid, as if to disturb a tear which memory had brought there, and his voice sunk at the moment, but he instantly roused himself, and proceeded in a clear voice.

" The brig in which I had come out had by this time made her second trip across, and was about to return again to Whitehaven : I had made such progress in my studies, that I was made third mate, and in that capacity returned home. I then went a voyage to the West Indies as third mate in a slaver, but it was a trade I found did not suit me, and upon my return I tried to get into another vessel ; but the owners had too good an opinion of my services, and made me first mate of a beautifully built vessel, which also was engaged in the slave trade ; I made my voyage out in her, and while at Porto Rico, I determined in disgust to quit and come home in another vessel, when you being short of hands, and there not being any to be had in the port without impressment, it was my lot to be among the pressed ; and there sir, you have all my story, for you know everything with which I am connected since joining your ship."

The captain coughed, and moved a little restlessly in his chair, as if he had not obtained the information he desired. After being silent a little while, as if boxing about for some fashion in which to shape the questions he intended to put to Paul, he said—

" I could see you were no common man—hem—I say, as soon as I saw you I was sure I had a good hand in my ship. How old are you?

" I am just turned twenty, sir," he replied.

" You look a little older—hem ! You have no reason to be ashamed of your face ; its open and frank. Your face has been your friend, I have no doubt, with the lasses, eh ? "

" Sir," exclaimed Paul, a little haughtily.

The captain coughed, took up his glass of wine, and raising it level with his eye, intently regarded it for a minute and then drank it off; it scarcely, however, covered the confusion which the monosyllable Paul had used created., He was a stern man in his station, and preserved that immeasurable distance between the captain and the common man when in the exercise of his duties, which elevated him almost to a deity, while the sailor was lowered to the humblest slave; but as this is necessary to preserve strict discipline, it is not regarded as a hardship. His present position, however, was new to him, and he was enough of a gentleman to feel that the questions he was about to put to John Paul bordered on what might be deemed impertinent curiosity. He had all his life been used to the utterance of direct commands, and was unacquainted with the art of conducting a conversation in such a manner that he might draw out any required information without appearing distinctly to request it, and his efforts at present seemed not the best calculated to accomplish this feat. He had received one check, but he resolved to try again, and after clearing his throat, he said—

" What I meant to observe was, that when in port your appearance made you many friends among those who are apt to judge with their eyes rather than their reason, as the smart performance of your duties did on board ship. But to come to the point at once, for I am no hand at beating to windward, there is a young lady on board, rescued along with this man from a wreck, as you know, for you were one of the hands who brought her on board; I understand she is not unknown to you, and I have a shrewd suspicion that she is not exactly a stranger, as regards family, to me, although personally I know her not. If she is the person I suspect her to be, it will have a material effect in shortening our voyage, for I should instantly bear away for England. I ask you, therefore, as Andrew here tells me you know her well, what her real name is; she gave it to this man as Alice Manners, but that is not the name by which I can recognise her. Understand me, Paul, I ask you this out of no impertinent motive, but in order to set at rest my doubts upon the subject."

Paul's face, as the captain proceeded, had grown a complete scarlet, he seemed horribly confused, and when the captain paused, he stammered out something which was scarcely audible; the captain looked at his evident embarrassment with some little surprise, and said, almost unconsciously—

" What ails thee, Paul?—you know the young lady, do you not?"

" I do," replied Paul, trying hard to recover himself.

Do you know her as Alice Manners ?" asked the captain.

Paul was silent; the captain waited a moment, and then proceeded—

" Why do you hesitate ?" he inquired; " is there any reason that you should desire to conceal it ?"

Paul made no reply; the captain's brow lowered and reddened.

" I have told you," he said, " it was gratifying no idle curiosity which made me put the questions to you; but as my movements must be guided by my knowledge respecting her, it is important I should know. She is herself in

too weak a condition yet to be spoken to upon the subject, or I should have spared you and myself this trouble."

It was with some haughtiness, which he did not strive to conceal, that he uttered this speech; and when he concluded, Paul, who felt it deeply, was disposed to treat it in the same manner, but that habitual deference to him as his superior made him keep down his feeling of pride, and he made answer to it by saying—

"I am quite ready to give you the information you require, sir, but that I conceive the young lady has some powerful motive for concealing her name, and feel it would ill become me, as one of them she looks on as a friend, to betray what it seems she wishes me to keep secret."

"A friend!" repeated the captain, in evident surprise, "a friend!"

"Ay! sir, a friend," repeated Paul, proudly; "an humble one, perhaps but still a friend."

On the impulse, the captain would have asked his pardon, but he checked himself, and said, hastily—

No. 12

"You will not, therefore, satisfy me, unless you have her consent to reveal it?"

"No," replied Paul, with a bow.

"I could command it," said the captain, eying him steadfastly.

Paul threw up his head haughtily, and his chest swelled, as he replied,

"You could put me in irons, sir, you could run me up to the yard-arm, but you could not make me speak what I have resolved not to utter."

"You speak boldly to your captain," he said, drily.

"I would say the same to my king, were I in the same situation with him, in regard to this affair, as I am to you."

The captain had some such thought too; he paused a little while, regarding Paul with a firm and scrutinising glance, which he returned without wagging an eyelid. John Andrew, who had all this while been seated without uttering a word, looking from one to the other, occasionally draining his glass by way of hinting that he should by no means be disgusted if another glass was offered him, but which failed to produce the desired effect, inasmuch as the captain did not see him, now chimed into the conversation, to the relief of both.

"Whatever the young lady's name may be," he said, "I've only to say that she told it me in a quiet, nat'ral sort of way enough, not a bit as if she was, hoisting false colours; I'll tell you how it was that she told it me. You see when we were on the rock, and sitting there watching the moon and stars, and talking about home and friends as was there, one word brought about another; I got speaking of a sort of a friend—a kind of an acquaintance, your honour—a young woman that I had got alongside of when I was last at home, down in Westmoreland, and I was asking her whether she didn't think Martha a pretty name for a lass that loved a sailor—no, no, your honour, I don't mean that—I mean that it was a good name for a little craft that has as clean a run—"

"What has this to do with the young lady's name?" inquired the captain, abruptly.

"Only this your honour. She told me she liked the name; it was a good quiet name, and was likely to belong to a good and quiet girl, and then I all of a sudden asked her, her name. Alice, says she; my name is Alice, says she, just in that way, your honour, as sweet and soft as the breezes on the line. My name, says she, is Alice Manners, and there didn't seem any false sailing in that, your honour; and if her name is not Alice Manners, she has the prettiest way of telling a howdacious taradiddle of any one I've come athwart on since on blue water I've been, that's all."

"You will have no objection, if I guess the name, to tell me if I am right, I suppose?" said the captain, turning to Paul immediately John Andrews had finished. "You will not be compromising your faithfulness or honour."

Paul hesitated; the captain, who felt almost angry at his reluctance to speak, was about to make some sharp remark, but he checked himself, and laughing, said to him, with an appearance of good humour—

"You were correct in saying that your school master beat obstinacy into you. I think there is no doubt that if he spared the rod a little he would not have spoilt you at least. I am afraid you think my anxiety to learn this young lady's right name is dictated by a feeling of unfriendliness to her, but if you hold such an opinion you are grievously mistaken. I have little or no doubt that she is the person of whom I am in search."

"In search?" interrupted John Paul.

"Aye! in search," repeated the captain : "the story of my friend here and you tallies with some information respecting her which I have received, and there needs but her name to confirm it all, and that is—

He rose from his chair and whispered in Paul's ear. Immediately the latter heard him, a change came over his features, his eyes dropped, and he said in a low tone—

"You are right."

"Then for England, ho !" exclaimed the captain. "And now I will explain to you how far my movements were connected with her. When in Porto Rico lately, I met with the father of this young lady, whom I have known for many years ; in truth we were schoolfellows. We had been seperated for several years, and it was with some pleasure I recognised him one morning as I walked through the town. I stopped him, and spoke to him, he shook me heartily by the hand, and then suddenly burst into tears—he was like a man distracted; he told me he had shipped his daughter to England by a merchant vessel, and intelligence had been brought by a brig that she had been captured by pirates. The people on board the brig had witnessed it, but being short of hands they were afraid to render assistance, and made sail upon their ship, for fear of being themselves served in a like manner. My term of service here had not exactly expired, and I promised him I would cruise in every direction with the endeavour of overhauling the pirate, and with many thanks from him, we parted; he told me he was about to sail for England, and if I met with his child, which he much feared I should not, I was to convey her to England; at the same time he purposed leaving a large reward at Porto Rico for any one who could gain tidings of her, and would forward it to him."

"I heard nothing of this," said Paul, with a mystified air.

"No," replied the captain, "you were pressed previous to the arrival of the intelligence, and were not suffered to go on shore. It was my belief that a pirate I was on the look-out for had done this deed; and as I shrewdly suspected where he was hovering, I made for the place, and found my gentleman there, sure enough. We gave him chase as you remember, but he gave us the slip in the night. I believed that the maiden was on board or had been captured and subjected to a horrible fate by the damned dogs, and I swore if I overhauled them, and found it to be the case, I'd run up every one of them to the yard-arm. When again the rascal hove in sight, I chased him while a rag would hold, but he has slipped through my fingers ; it is, however, of little consequence; since my principal object is gained, and the knaves have been wrongly suspected, why, let them go for a little while—Ned Stanmore in the Andromache will get the weather-gage of them ere long. And now, Paul, I have one more question to ask, or if you like it better, four or five in one. I wish to know, as you call yourself a friend of Miss—Alice Manners," e added, has tily, after passing the word Miss; " in what degree of relation-ship your friendship is, and how you became friends at all—where you met, and whether you met often ?"

" If, Sir, a refusal on my part to comply with your request," said Paul, firmly, " would not be construed into some motive which might compromise the honour of the young lady in question, I should beg to be allowed to de-cline answering ; but as all appearance of mystery and concealment bears with it a suspicion that there is something of which to be ashamed, I shall not for the sake of the lady hesitate in relating to you enough to satisfy you and re-move her above any erroneous opinion which you might otherwise form."

" Such a proceeding is no less straightforward than manly, and no more than I expected from you," observed the captain.

Paul bowed, and then paused a moment as though to collect his thoughts; the casting aside the air of incertitude which his brow wore, and speaking in a clear firm tone, he commenced—

" It is about three years since," he said, " that I returned to Whitehaven, third mate in a slaver. I went to visit my friends, and whilst staying at home I received an invitation from a friend to accompany him and his wife to visit the lakes. I accepted it, and a very pleasant tour we had. On the morning we were viewing Loch Lomond, I observed a small boat which, with a square sail hoisted, was sailing slowly over the bosom of the water, which lay as calm and still as though it were a sheet of glass; as I stood gazing, it struck me that there was some confusion on board the boat, and I fancied I heard a shout. I looked intently and saw a gentleman who appeared to have the management of it, toss out a pair of oars, and commence rowing lustily ; sud-denly he ceased and started up in the boat, and shouted at the top of his voice. His cries were accompanied by the shrill screams of a female, and another glance told me the cause of all this was the settling down of the boat, which as I after-wards found, had sprung a leak and was filling fast, I cast my eyes rapidly along the shore, and perceived that fortunately a small skiff was close at hand, fastened to a short stump; to cast it adrift, spring in it, and pull with all my strength towards them, occup ed me but a short space of time, but they were a considerable distance from me, and before I could get near them the boat went down. I never made a boat pass through water as I did the one I urged on then with my utmost strength ; at last I came up with the gentleman who had clung to one of the oars, and pulled him into the boat; the lady was missing, I could see her no where—but I threw off my jacket, plunged in and dived down in search of her. The water was very clear, and I caught a glimpse of her rising. I seized her, and with much difficulty succeeded in getting her into the boat, and then made for the shore with as much speed as I had left it. With the aid of my friend, and one or two others whom their cries had summoned, we bore the lady and the gentleman to a neighbouring cottage, and after using every remedy for an hour, at least, to restore them, we had the satisfaction of seeing them open their eyes, and hearing them speak ; conveyances were procured, and they were taken to their dwelling, one which I afterwards found was at some distance. A fortnight after this had occurred, I received an invitation to spend a week with the gentleman and the lady whom I had saved from a watery grave. I felt too much interest in both not to accept it, and accordingly I went. As you have doubtless guessed, the young lady was Miss Alice Manners, the gentleman her father, and your friend. I was very warmly welcomed. I received from both the highest protestations of gratitude, and the most evident proofs that they really felt all they professed. My stay was prolonged from a week to two months, and then an accident which I am not at liberty to mention caused my departure. Some time after this, I made several trips to Spain."

" To Spain!" echoed the captain.

" Even so!" replied Paul; " you seem surprised."

"You did not mention this in your narration of your history," said the captain.

" Neither did I the events I am now relating," replied Paul, drily, and then as if checking what he felt might be deemed too great a freedom of speech, he continued quickly, " I thought it of no moment, so did not mention it. My destination was Lisbon—some circumstances led me into the interior to an old fashioned chateau, and by accident I again encountered the lady. I had several interviews with her, but her father had thought fit to quarrel with me for a matter I could not avoid, so God judge me, and sternly forbid me ever to enter his presence again. As I found that Alice was likely to suffer harshness from him if I refused to obey him, I resolved never to be the cause of a pang to her, and quitted, as I believed, never again to see her. I have told you I went from Whitehaven to Porto Rico as first mate in a slaver; while there, certainly to my astonishment, I met once again with Alice. I found that her father had suddenly brought her from Lisbon to the West Indies, upon a visit to some plantations which he possessed there; it was not long ere I encountered him—he appeared thunderstruck on meeting me—had I been the most frightful spectre, he could not have shewn more surprise on seeing me, and when he recovered a little, it was to heap upon me every term of abuse, every vile reproach, and, in truth, language which I would have borne from no other man on earth—language which I call heaven to witness I was wholly undeserving of, but that he was her father I would have felled him to the earth, but I restrained myself. How I mastered my indignation I do not know—I know only, that I did respect him for her sake, and would have done had he even struck me, which in his rage he would, but that the fear of something withheld him. A few hours after this I was pressed on board your vessel, and never saw the lady until she was brought on board the Wild-fire from the wreck."

" It is certainly a singular affair," muttered the captain, when Paul had finished. "In what manner could you have aroused the old gentleman's anger, that he should be so furious against you after you had saved his life?"

" I interfered with a favorite project he had formed," said Paul, evasively; " I cannot disclose more."

"So then," said John Andrew, after performing a long whistle, " you then, are the friend she's got down in her log that all the scrimmage has been about to make her wipe off."

Andrew's speech seemed to have an extraordinary effect upon the captain, for he suddenly struck the table with great force, and said—

"I see it all—I see it all; the old gentleman does not see with the young lady's eyes, and therefore holds quite an opposite opinion to her respecting your merits. Well, whatever is to be the result of all this, time will show; however, Paul, understand this, and understand it as a command, that while the young lady is aboard this ship I shall consider her as peculiarly under my protection, and shall expect you will not seek to hold communication or converse with her while she remains here."

Paul bowed his head as if in obedience to his words, but it might have been seen that his heart was full; the captain saw it, and laying his hand upon his shoulder, he said, in a kind, but low tone.

"My position is an awkward and delicate one; I have a duty to perform, and it must be done; you must not judge harshly of me if you are a sufferer by it, for were you in my place you would act as I feel bound to do."

"I acknowledge your justice, Sir," said Paul respectfully; "and your kindness," he added warmly. "You shall be obeyed strictly."

"Enough," returned the captain; then turning to John Andrew, he said, "accompany Paul forward—when you are strong enough, you can do the duty of the topman who was lost overboard in the gale, and receive pay from the time of your entering this ship."

"Many thanks, your honour," cried Andrew, with a nod of the head, and a scrape of the foot.

The captain waved his hand, and John Paul, making an obeisance, quitted the cabin, followed by Andrew. Upon reaching the forcastle he was encountered by Gasket, who immediately eyed him with a very undoubted expression of curiosity, scanning every feature as if he could discover by an attentive perusal all that had transpired in the cabin. He did not at first speak, but whistled part of a tune with a futile effort to appear unaffected by inquisitiveness. Paul observed it, and smiled, but took no further notice, addressing him upon some indifferent topic, which he answered with equal indifference but rolling his tobacco from side to side in his mouth, and glancing at his messmate impatiently, he said suddenly, with emphasis—

"In some of these new ships with young captains, its becoming a fashion to rig to'gau'nt sails, royals, and sky sails on one spar without the use of a royal mast at all, unless they run up a thin spar through a couple of rings at the to'gau'nt mast head for some dandy sail that the Lord only knows the use on; and I begin to think our captain, who has trod the decks of a man-of-war craft for more than thirty years, is going to try that fashion aboard this ship."

"Why!" asked John Paul, with some surprise, involuntarily glancing his eyes upwards, and scanning the royals and sky scrapers, which were appended to a royal mast.

"It's no use looking up there for my meaning," said Gasket, gravely: "the captain won't alter the rig of the Wildfire while she'll walk through the water as she has this week; no, Johnny, it's among the hands that he's about, to my thinking, to work the new fangled notions I was speaking of."

"Riddle me, riddle me, ree; perhaps you can tell me what this may be," exclaimed Paul, with a laugh; "why, man, what are you boxing about ? speak in plain terms, and then I shall understand you."

"It is not the like of you, John, that couldn't fathom my meaning," returned Gasket, "if so be you had a mind that way—but any way you shall not run to leeward for want of plain words; what I mean is that the captain had better make you second in command at once, instead of rigging the duties of half a dozen people upon you."

"Go on," said Paul, as Gasket paused.

"Go on," reiterated he; "why, ain't you captain of the main top? ain't you put into the chains if a very true heave of the lead is required? ain't you called aft if the captain wants advice and opinions, when there are hands in the ship twice as old and twice as experienced as you; if there's any smart work to be done—if the helm is to be put into the best hands, isn't the order always, send me John Paul aft? Isn't it John Paul this, John Paul the other, John Paul forward, John Paul in the waist, and John Paul on the quarter-deck?"

"What, Gasket," interrupted Paul, with some surprise, "do you grow envious, man—do you think I take your share of favour as well as my own."

"Lord love you, not I," cried he, shaking Paul's hand warmly, "I should be glad if you had ten times as much; I only think this, that if you're made to do six times your work, you ought to have six times your pay—whereas I'd lay my wages, prize money and all, against an old ring bolt that you only get your regular pay when you are giving the captain advice what to do, which of course you are, or what else should he want you for in his cabin."

Here Gasket paused, and looked Paul coolly and steadily in the face; it was not a direct question, but was in effect the same, and was precisely the object at which he was aiming. Paul returned his look with a smile which he could not suppress, and said quietly—

"You are mistaken."

Gasket was about to make a rejoined at being thus defeated in satisfying his curiosity, when the captain made his appearance upon the quarter-deck, and after surveying the horizon with his glass, communicated some orders to the lieutenant. The people were instantly summoned to perform the manoeuvres necessary to alter the course of the ship, which once more was shaped for England, much to the delight of the men, who gave a hearty cheer as soon as they heard the news. Gasket had no opportunity of prosecuting his inquiries of Paul relative to the conversation in the cabin, in consequence of having duties to perform aloft, but baffled though he had been, he determined, if possible, to find out what had taken place. He felt in his own mind that if he had been in Paul's situation he should have told him everything, and could therefore see no reason why he should not be told all. When night came on with a bright clear sky and a pleasant breeze, he took an opportunity, on seeing Paul pacing up and down the forecastle thoughtfully, to walk up to him and say—

"I suppose you are thinking about the old people at home; ah, John, instead of wearing the long phiz as if your grog was stopped, you ought to be as lively as the pennant in a breeze. I'm sure, if I'd any old people at home to go to, I should be."

"Have you not?" asked Paul, with surprise.

"Not I," he replied; "I was picked up at sea off a wreck, when a youngster, too young to know who or what I was, by a man-of-war sloop. I was the only living thing they found. An old boatswain's mate took a fancy to me, and took care of me till I was about five years old, when one day, in a stiff gale, the ship gave a lee lurch; he happened to be in the mizen chains, he fetched away, and was gone before a rope could be heaved to him, or a boat lowered. I remained in the sloop till I was about seven, and then was drafted to another ship, and so on until I was captain of the main-top, in the How-dacious seventy-four; and when she was paid off I came on board the Wild-fire; so you see, Johnny Paul, it does not make much of a matter to me whether I am outward or homeward bound—whether I am on the line or in the North Sea, it's all one to me; turn which point of the compass I will, there's neither father. mother, brother, or sister, kith or kin, in the wide world for me ; I am alone; my home is a stout craft, and my country is blue water. But you, Paul, will have merry faces to greet you—kind voices to hail you—smiles and kisses to welcome you to the land where your were born; while I shall have nothing but to seek a new ship, or make a fresh voyage in the old one; you, therefore, have no cause to be as thoughtful and as gloomy as a ship's company when they're on a six upon four allowance; if any one should hoist signals of distress, it should be me, who, put into what port I will, have no friendly grappling irons to hook on to me."

"You have some friends, Gasket," exclaimed Paul.

"Where?" he asked earnestly.

"Why in me, at least," replied Paul; "if you have not another beside you have one in me, aye— and a stanch one."

"God bless you, John," cried Gasket, squeezing his hand warmly; "I believe you, and there's not one in the world I would so soon have as you."

"You shall go home with me, Gasket," continued John Paul; "you will find my father and mother homely but kind people, and you shall never, after you have once been with them, have to say that you can look round the com-pass without its pointing out to you a home if you required it."

Gasket squeezed Paul's hand hard, but could not speak a word—his kind-ness for a moment having overpowered him; after a few attempts he said, hastily—

"I shan't forget this, Johnny! I shan't forget this—I shall enter this in my log for life, and there's not that under heaven which can rub it out, there ain't—there ain't—I'm damned if there is—" He paused for a few seconds, and then continued—"If ever you should want a helping hand, or a friend to stand by you while a stick will hold, and I don't do it, why, may the Lord send me to the devil faster than a signal rocket flies aloft."

Paul laughed, and laying his hand upon his shoulder, said—

"You've a good friend in Mr. Prior, too, haven't you?"

"Why, to be sure, he's very kind," said Gasket, musingly; "but then he isn't like you; he carries a higher peak in his mizen than you—no offence

John; but his family are all king's cousins, or something of that sort, and too high for him to mate with a sea bird such as me; no, no, he's a kind heart, and is generous and grateful; but he is not a messmate as well as friend.   I look up to him as I would to the captain, but to you I look as I would to a brother."

"And brothers may we be," said Paul, and then added hastily, "you said the first lieutenant was grateful—have you done him any important services?"

"Why, as to important services, I can't say much about that," returned Gasket; "I was able to do him a good turn once, as any one would have done if they had been in the same bearing as myself.   I told you the other day it was a strange matter that made me run athwart him; he was the 'cause of my quitting the Howdacious, and entering foremast-man aboard this frigate."

"He was?" exclaimed Paul, elevating his eyebrows.

"Ay!" uttered Gasket.   "I was going to pay out the whole tale to you, when I was brought up all standing by the cry of a man overboard, I mean

No. 13

the time Tom Oakum nearly had a berth in the shirk's lower hold ; now, if you don't feel inclined to turn in, you shall hear it."

"It is the very thing I was going to ask of you," said Paul, quickly.

"Then here goes for a yarn," said Gasket, replenishing his lower jaw with a choice roll of fresh weed, which he deposited to his satisfaction, and then making a short pause as if to recall the events, he thus commenced :—"You see, John, I am not the fist at palavering that you are; my education has been only ship-shape and Bristol fashion ; I can do a seaman's duty, but I make stern way when I clap on to jawing tackle ; however, you must make allowance, and when I'am jammed hard for lingo, you must get me out of irons as well as you can."

"I shall understand you well enough," said Paul ; "stretch out."

"Ay ! ay !" exclaimed Gasket, "the whole matter is coiled away so snug, that when once I cast off I can pay it out fast enough. It is now hard on the end of the fourth year that the Howdacious was paid off ; Mr. Prior entered her as a middy a year before this, and the way I first got into his notice was, while we were in the Mediterranean, we had a third lieutenant, who was a sour, ill-tempered son of a swab, a know-nothing, damme eyes, you sir, sort of a officer, who was always for starting the men with a rope's-end, when they did the work better than he knew how to give the order ; he was very fond of jeering Mr. Prior, and telling him he crawled on board through the cabin windows, and would set him on duty he could not do himself, and jeer and sneer at him if he didn't know how to do it. I never saw a midshipman do the duty he made Mr. Prior do, and he always did this when he had the watch, and the captain wasn't by, or for that matter any other of the lieutenants. Well, Mr. Prior happened to be liked in the birth deck, uncommon, and the third lieutenant hated ; there wasn't a hand but would show Mr. Prior how to do what he was ordered, if he could get near him, when he was at fault, or who would have stopped to turn their quid if he could have shoved the lieutenant over the side. However, one day he happened to be jeering Mr. Prior about his work, and then he got jeering him about his family ; my dear eyes ! he'd no sooner slipped the words out of his jaws—I was aft at the time, on the mizen rigging, and heard it all—when Mr. Prior ups with his fist, and down's the lieutenant bang upon the deck. If he'd been struck by a twelve-pounder, he couldn't have dropped quicker ; up he jumps again, and down he went again : up he jumped once more, and showed fight, but Lord love you ! Mr. Prior hammered him all over the quarter-deck until he laid down and roared murder and mutiny with all his might ; then up comes the first and second lieutenants, the master, master's mate, doctor, purser, and last of all the captain—and all hands as could get near, looked on to see what the upshot would be. Well, as soon as the captain heard a mid licked a lieutenant, he ordered the mid into irons for stricking a superior officer, and it was said he would be run up to the yard-arm for it. Well, he was to be tried by a court martial when we got to England, and I don't know what besides, but you see Mr. Prior happened to be the captain's nephew, and when the whole of the for and by come to be overhauled, the captain was in a towering rage with the third lieutenant. I was brought before the captain to say what I knew of the matter, and didn't I stretch out when I had the offing clear? I up and told the captain all the tricks he had played on Mr. Prior, making him do top-men and waister's duty, aye, and other things that a boatswain wouldn't have asked an A. B. to do, and I said the ship's company would bear me out in what I said, and then I told all I had heard about the quarrel; I didn't for-get to make known as many of the nasty spiteful jeers the lieutenant had flung out as I could overhaul, and when my yarn was spun out, the lieute-nant said I was in Mr. Prior's pay. Well, the captain said he'd judge for himself about that, and summoned some of the crew aft, but they all stood on the same tack as myself, and then the captain told the lieutenant if he forgot his situation—no, his position—that's it—as a officer, he must expect his subordinates—they're hard words for the jaws of a true tar—he must ex-pect they would not respect him, and so he should settle the business with ordering Mr. Prior into the tops for striking his superior officer. The third lieutenant looked marlin-spikes and cutlasses, and as he made for the deck, whispered to me, 'my man, I'll remember you for this.' 'Thank ye, sir,' says I, with a laugh, and followed him. Well, John, Mr. Prior's irons were cast off, and with a clean pair of heels he went into the tops; soon afterwards it come on to blow very hard, and we were not long getting everything snug alow and aloft. I was in the main-top, and when I had spare time, I said what I could to cheer up Mr. Prior, tor he looked very much as if everything in the shape of happiness for him had gone by the board. In the middle of one of my speeches, he drew a paper parcel from his pocket, and said, 'Gas-ket, you have proved yourself a friend, will you do me one more favour, it's the last I shall ask of you; will you give this to my father?' 'To be sure I will,' said I; 'but who is your father? In what latitude am I to find him?' Well, before I had finished, he jumped by me, was on to the foot rope of the main yard in a minute, sided out until he was at the yard-arm, and then he leaped into the water; mind you, John, there was a heavy sea running at the time, so you see he made up his mind to slip his wind; however, I sprung after him the instant I saw what he was up to, and being more nimble on a foot-rope than him, I was at the yard-arm almost time enough to hook on to him, but I missed the grab I made; overboard he went, and I jumped after him. I knew I could swim like a duck in a pond, and he couldn't, and if I could lay hold of him, I could keep him above water till we were picked up— and if there was too much sea for a boat to live in it, why, we must go to Davy Jones together. I didn't care much about that, seeing there was no-body to pipe their eyes because my life-lines were unrove. As soon as my head was above water, I found myself lifted up by the same sea as Mr. Prior, and with a hard struggle managed to reach him. I seized him by the collar and held on like grim death. The crew had seen us jump from the yard-arm; the ship was laid to, and the jolly-boat was lowered, aye, and very neatly capsized it was, too—but to cut the story short, we were picked up. Mr Prior had no more life in him than there is in Sam Stun'sail's wooden leg, and I'd swallowed enough salt water to float a frigate; however, we soon got on our pins again. I got five guineas from the captain, and Mr. Prior had the articles of war read to him in the shape of a long palaver, which was payed out to him in the captain's cabin. The third lieutenant didn't let me have a very easy berth of it after that; he minded what I had said of him, and he roused me out whenever he had the chance, until one day he called out to me, 'here you sir, start the main-topmen aft to haul in the weather braces. You sir, I don't see the main-topmen coming aft; I shall order the boatswain's mate to start you with a rope's end, if you crawl to your duty in this way.' Now you must know we were hauling in the main brace at the very time he was bellowing out this; the captain happened to be at his elbow, and tapping him on the shoulder, he said to him, 'Don't you know the man's name, Mr. Sheave? If you don't, I'll tell you, it's Gasket', says he, 'Gasket, he's captain of the maintop—it's my practice to know the name of every man in my ship, and his station; if you don't know a man's name, ask it, Mr. Sheave, and don't sing out you sir, here, and you sir, there.' People have names, Mr. Sheave, and will answer to them when called by them, but you must not look for any particular man to do what you command when nobody but yourself can tell who you mean.' The lieutenant shewed as many colours in his face as a book of signals, but he didn't say nothing; he didn't forget to carry a heavy freight of spite for all this—not so much for me as for Mr. Prior, because of the licking he got. He happened to be some relation to the lady whose flag Mr. Prior carried at the fore, and when he got ashore, after being paid off, he made use of it to pitch such lying yarns to her, as to make her shove her boat off when hailed by her true lover."

"I thought you said the young lady's friends had sent her to some place which Mr. Prior could not discover?" interrupted Paul.

"Ay! but that was before he went to sea at all. As soon as he was safe on blue water she was brought home," returned Gasket, "and when our ship was paid off at Portsmouth, Mr. Prior asked me to keep in his wake until I went to sea again, which I agreed to, for somehow I'd taken a fancy to him. Well, I went to his father's house in London with him, and sure enough, it's a grand place, and grand folks they are that live in it. Why the young lady's father and mother wouldn't let Mr. Prior splice with her, I can't overhaul nohow—it gets to windward of me; for if they're richer than him they must live in king's houses; but let that be how it may, Mr. Prior made sail to range up alongside the lady, but she luffed up, bore away, and kept clear —she wouldn't see him, and he was desperately cut up about it; his despatches were sent him back, and he was told the young lady intended to part company with him for ever. Well, you never saw a craft that had parted her rudder in a gale yaw about as he did. I looked out sharp, for I expected he'd cut his life-lines adrift, but he didn't; he tried hard for another ship, to make for any sea or port—to the devil, or any where, so that he didn't stay in England. Well, one morning I was making a stretch from his house to Wapping, for a splice in the main-brace with some messmates, and not being over clear as to the bearings, I run right out of my course and was brought up in a large open landfall with trees, called St. James's Park, lying to the south'erd and west erd, as I take it. Well, while I was trying to find the latitude, I feels a tap on my shoulder, and I looks round, and if ever I saw a angel, John, then was the time. Ah! you may laugh, but I never clapped eyes on such a figure-head before; the Wildfire going large with all her light spars up and dandy duck set, was never half so beautiful—and if that ain't saying she's handsome, just tell me what is; such top lights, such a clean run along the bends, so trim built, such a rig, there never was a clipper, a schooner, or frigate, with such—"

" What did she say?" interrupted Paul.

" Why, in a voice sweeter than the sweetest mermaid that ever piped, she said—'I beg your pardon for stopping you, but I see by your arm you were one of the crew of the Howdacious, sevent-four'—you see I had the name of the ship and crown and anchor worked in gold upon the sleeve of my jacket, for Sundays and saints' days, which was the way she made me out. 'You're right, Miss,' says I; 'the captain of the maintop, at your service.' Well, she overhauled my log as to our voyage and such like, and at last, turning the colour of the inside of a Indyshell, says she—'Did you know a Mr. Prior?' 'Did I,' says I; 'Lord love you, Miss, don't I; a better or kind-hearted youth never trod the deck of a vessel in the service.' 'Does he not drink and swear?' she said, as if she was afeard of the very words. 'Not so much as a man ought to do, Miss,' says I; whenever he had to rouse up the idlers and lazy waisters, or hail a sleepy topman, he never used a word you mightn't find in one Hamilton Moore or the Lord's book—and it isn't every officer that can say that, my lady; and as for his drinking, many's the time I've had his share of grog and my own too.' ' I am glad to hear this,' says she, with a smile like the ripple under the forefoot in a calm; ' but was he not fractious and insubordinate—wasn't he ordered into irons and confined for mutinous and vagabondising conduct?' ' Begging your pardon, Miss,' says I, 'did you ever happen to hear of one Mr. Sheave?' With that she turned the colour of red bunting. 'Yes,' she whispered. 'Then,' says I, saving your presence, 'you have heard of the damn'dest rogue a honest tar ever come athwart-hawse on,' so I up and told her all that I've told you, and when I had run to the end of my line, she said some pretty words to me, gave me a guinea, and said that she had heard a good many stories of Mr. Prior, but now she wouldn't log them, for she was sure my yarn was not for marines to believe, but what any one might hoist in, and asked me if I was likely to see Mr. Prior soon. I told her I should before I turned in that night. 'Then,' she says. ' say to him, that if he will be at the same spot at the same hour, that he visited a month before e went to sea, he will meet with Florence.' Them's the words, for I made her say 'em again and again until I had logged 'em as sure as print in a book, to be payed out whenever you opened it at the place. Well, just as she cast lose her fore-top sail, and was weighing anchor, I asked her to give me the points and bearings for Wapping, but, would you believe it; she didn't know anything about it—although I told her it lay due east—nor knowed nobody that lived there; but she showed me where a long, narrow, dirty-looking street, called the Strand, lay, and told me, if I stood on without tacking until I was brought up by the Bank of England, where they keeps all the money, I should find plenty of landsmen who would shape out my course for me; so we parted company. Soon after I had gathered headway, it struck me this angel might be the very craft Mr.

Prior had hauled down his jack ensign and pennant to. Phew! I was brought[t]
up all standing as soon as the thought laid itself aboard of me, and when I
come to overhaul matters I was certain it must be so.   Well, I'bout ship at
once, stood on the other tack, and made for Mr. Prior's house.   I crowded
sail, and after running a little now and then out of my course, I made it. When
I asked for him, the steward and cook's-mate ministers said he'd gone out of
town, two bells before I reached there, down to a place called Cambridge.   I
soon found there was a craft on four wheels that made the voyage every day,
so I bore away for it, and found it just ready to run out of port.   It was full
upon deck, had it's regular complement, but there was room for one cabin
passenger.   I knew my duty better than to stow myself there, and as there
was room upon deck amid ships, I scrambled up aloft : but before I had made
my anchorage good, a fellow claps on to my leg to haul me down, but I gave
him a lurch with my starboard pin, and down he tumbled into' the mud, Well,
there was a regular row, but after I swore I'd keel-haul whoever laid a grappling iron upon me, they hauled their wind and hoisted a flag of truce by pro-
posing for me to pay the cabin fare for a young woman upon deck, who was
to go in the cabin, and I was to have her berth. This put us all in good trim,
and then four horses, which were made fast to the hull, went of with a smack
of the cat, and we went cracking on at the rate of six knots an hour, until we
got to Cambridge, and dam'me if ever I saw such a set of lubberly Tom Bower's
sort of fellows in my life as I saw there ; for after asking half a hundred of
'em where Mr. Prior was, none of 'em could tell me ; and I knew he was there,
because his father's people told me so, and they ought to have known, I should
think."

"Did they tell you to what house he had gone?" inquired Paul.

"Not they! neither did I ask," returned Gasket, with an expression of
indignant recollection of what he deemed the most unmitigated stupidity of
the townspeople. "I was told he was gone to Cambridge—here I was in
Cambridge, and nobody know'd nothing about him. Suppose I had been in
the Howdacious, and you'd come aboard and asked for Harry Gasket—oh,
says the boatswain's mate, that's the captain of the fore-top, and he'd ha
passed the word forward for me—yet we'd five hundred aboard. Well, I run
foul of half a dozen parson-looking young luffs, with a kind of square shaped
truck rigged on their tops, laid athwart ships, and they'd bent a black
spanker something of the same cut as the chaplain's ; I hailed them, and
thought to show a ship-shape breeding, so I called 'em parsons, and they
began bawling out a lingo I couldn't understand; but I soon found they
were skylarking and up to mischief, for they began to run foul of each other,
and make lurches so as to run athwart of me.   Well, I wasn't going to spoil
sport, so I sided out with a bend, and clearing the decks for action, I let fly at
the nearest fellow's figure-head, and I think I nearly carried away his dolphin
striker. I capsized one of his mates, and laid on to another broadside ; but
his mates all came on to action, and I should have been raked fore and aft
and sink, if two or three youngsters hadn't bore up to my help, then they began to sing out a sort of war-cry—'Town! Town!' and the parsons, 'Gown!
Gown!—by the way, that's what they call the black spanker they had rigged

on. Well, in the midst of a crew of these black-rigged fellows who bore down upon us in answer to the signal, was Mr. Prior, ready to pitch into the young fellows who'd stood to me, so I hailed him, and he luffed up short; both crews drew off by his orders while we spoke, and when I explained all, both sides wore ship and bore away ; then I told Mr. Prior what I'd given chase to him for, and he was like a madman. He made me repeat a hundred times the message which she had given me for him ; he made me describe her build, the bend of her sails, her train, everything, every word she had said, and then wanted to make sail for London at once ; but I begged to turn in first, or at least to make a stretch along the eating haliards, for I had come better than fifty knots without having anything but a little grog; for though they had piped to dinner on the road, afore I could get my grinders into a bit of meat, in comes the skipper as held the tiller lines, and sings out, ' Coach is ready,' so we were obliged to drop knife and fork and get on board and were under weigh in the turning of a glass afterwards, but not until the thieves who kept the grog-shop had made a haul of our money for what we never had. When I represented this to Mr. Prior, he made me bring myself to anchor before enough grub to provision a ship's company, and then to finish the night with his friends, who he said belonged to a first-rate, called the University ; but all I know is, if she's manned by such a crew as I saw she must have an howdacious rum set on board."

" Well, I suppose Mr. Prior was not long in returning to London ?" said Paul.

" No, he never turned in at all, but roused me out by daybreak ; we had been drinking wine all night, and was more than three sheets in the wind, but he soon got all right again, after we were stowed in a vessel which they called a po'shay. There were four horses made fast to this craft, in the hold of which I was berthed along with Mr. Prior ; and two old weather-beaten doctor's mates-looking dogs, what they called ' boys,' rigged out in light blue jackets, and white trucks almost as large as the main-top of a seventy-four, or a frigate, worked the vessel along at a spanking rate, but they jumped up and down like a pump chain in hard work. I expected to see 'em make clean fly over their horses heads' every minute, but they didn't—they held on by short tiller ropes, and made fast their lower stanchions to a foot rope. We made the voyage in about six hours, and then, as Mr. Prior looked white about the gills, and as heavy in the toplights as dirty weather brewing to windward, I persuaded him to turn in for about eight bells, that he might not see the little craft that was riding at anchor for him with the look of one who had been bousing up his jib-stay too taut ; he followed my advice, and when he turned out and had a clean shirt and shave, he looked as lively a young fellow as you'd meet in any craft ; he bent one of my suits of sails, and said it was necessary for him to have a false rig, in case of accident. As the night drew on, he prepared to make for the spot where he was to join company with Miss Florence. He pressed me into his service, and I was glad enough to go, for I wanted to have another look at the pretty little lass. The bell was wrung for eight o'clock, and we set sail ; he piloted the way, and after tacking and half-tacking, backing and filling, scudding, and then on an easy bow-line, until we were a little way in the country, we brought up under the lee of a high wall. The moon wasn't up, though she was making sail for it, so it was rather dark; however, Mr. Prior found a door, and; giving it a push, it went open. 'All right,' says he, 'so far;' we entered into a large garden, and crept beneath the bushes until we made the house, and then wearing ship, we got in front of some windows with a little gallery in front of them, and then we dropped anchor among some bushes, and lay so close that nobody could have made us out unless they run foul of us. Well, there we lay until the moon come up and showed the house and all about it as clear as the sea up the Mediterranean, and after we had been there about two bells, watching the window as close as a shirk watches a ship when one of the hands is to be sewn up in his hammock, we saw the pretty face peep out of the window, and the eyes look about to find us; up jumps Mr. Prior and I together, and nearly frightens her out of her life; she jist screamed like the cry of a Mother Carey's chicken, and then she whispered 'Eustace,' and he sung out, gently, 'Florence, my precious angel,' or something like it, and then said, ' Here, Gasket, give me a lift up to the headrail, and if any footstep draws this way, pipe a call; lay down among the bushes, and don't stir a pin.' I nodded to him, and giving him a hoist on to my shoulder, he scrambled up like a nimble topman up the the to'-gau'nt shrouds until he got over the gallery, and then he took a pull at her lips and talked sentimental. I dare say each of 'em had a great deal down in their logs which they read to each other, for he staid long enough with her. At last, out he comes, and as he came over the gallery and stood with his feet at the outer edge, saying a few things afore he parted company, I hears a footstep coming along very slow and cautious, stepping short, and then standing on again; I piped, and Mr. Prior giving the young lady a parting salute, dropped to the ground; we rattled along for the door as we heard a voice sing out, 'Thieves! thieves!' and bellow away as if he'd a top chain in his throat—if I'd run athwart him, I'd ha' spoilt his music. As we crowded sail, still keeeping under the lee of the bushes, Mr. Prior says, ' You make for the door, and bring up somewhere until I join you: with that he drops beneath the bushes, and I stood on; I got out of the door and made sail down the road until I thought I made a long stretch enough of it, and so I lay to; but there I stopped I don't know how long, until I got tired, so I up stick and bore away for the garden again. When I reached it, all was quiet; Mr. Prior wasn't in sight; I tried the door, but somebody had made it fast; I peeped through the keyhole, but I could see nothing; I put my shoulder to the door, and gave a lurch, but it wouldn't move; I piped, in hopes to hear Mr. Prior answer the signal, but no, nothing stirred; I turned my quid, and wondered were away he'd stowed himself, and at last I began to think he might have been overhauled for a thief, and put in irons. If he had, it was my duty, you know, to be alongside of him, and I gave a fresh lurch at the door to break it open. While I was shoving away as hard as I could, I finds my collar suddenly laid hold of, and a fellow with a drawn cutlass standing over me. "Hollo, my fine fellow,' says he, ' what rig are you up to? I shook off his grappling irons, and bid him be

damned.   'You're a blue jacket,' says he, 'and are waiting for Mr. Prior.'
'Am I?' says I, and found out at the same moment I was talking to Mr. Sheave,
I knew his voice, and altered mine that he mightn't know me.   'Yes,' he
says, 'you are, and you shall tell.'   'Shall I?' says I, 'perhaps I shall, and
perhaps I shan't; I don't think I shall.'   'But I am sure you will,' says he.
'Are you?' says I, 'Yes,' says he, 'I am; I've served out your master, and
I'll serve out you.'   Have you, Sir?' says I, in a mild voice, doubling my fist
tight and hard; 'have you, Sir?' I says, quiet and gentle.   'Yes,' he says,
mocking my voice, 'I have; he's laid by the heels, and so shall you be if
you don't tell all you know.'   'After you,' says I, as I got a clear offing for
my arm, and throwing it out, I sent it bang between his toplights, and down
he went; I threw myself upon him, and twisted his cutlass out of his hand
and threw it away; then I told him to stand up and fight like a man, but he
wouldn't, and was roariug out blue murder; so I roused him up to his feet

No. 14.

and paid him over the head and eyes until I clapped a stopper on his jaw, and he dropped down like a log."

"Good God! Gasket, you didn't kill the man?" cried Paul, hastily.

"No," he replied, with a short chuckle; "no, but I flattened his gib-sheet in handsomely; he sung out like a marine seized up to a grating, and his noise brought up a lot of people, but I sheered off before any one laid me aboard, and hung about a short way off—half a knot, perhaps—hoping to see Mr. Prior; but the sun came up, and he did not heave in sight, so I thought it best to heave ahead for his house. I made it about eight in the morning, and found everybody in a commotion. Mr. Prior had been brought home in the middle of the night, dangerously wounded."

"Dangerously wounded!" echoed Paul.

"Ay! that was he," returned Gasket; "the servants said the doctor was with him, and said he wasn't expected to live; and they wouldn't let me see him, and said he was out of his mind and raving all sorts of things. Well, it struck me this was the work of Mr. Sheave; I remembered what he had said to me, and I thought I'd go and have a look for the cutlass, as perhaps that might help to make my suspicions certain; so, without saying anything to anybody, I went back to the place, and hunting about I picked up the cutlass in the hedge the opposite side to the garden wall. I looked at it, and it was stained with blood all over the blade, now, as I hadn't used it on Mr. Sheave though afterwards I heartily wished I had, he must have laid it about Mr. Prior, so I walks back with it, and as I got into the house, I was told Mr. Prior's father was waiting to speak to me. Well, I goes to him in his room, and he asks me if I went out with his son Eustace, the night before, I told him yes; but though he asked me where, I wouldn't tell, because I thought Mr. Prior wanted it kept snug, but I told him I wasn't with him when he was hurt, nor did I know anything about it until I got back, because we had stood on different tacks in the garden, and I had never seen him since; but says I, 'My lord, I thinks I know who cut Mr. Prior down." 'Who?' says he. 'Why, Mr. Sheave,' says I, 'third lieutenant of the Howdacious, who did Mr. Eustace such a ill turn when he was aboard." 'Why do you think so?' says he, quickly and eagerly. So I told him how I'd licked him, and showed him the cutlass, and told him what he had said about Mr. Prior; and when I had done, he said now he knew where his poor boy had been—which rather slewed me, for I hadn't let it out, being very particular about that—and said he was scarcely surprised at what had taken place; then he drew a square piece of printed paper out of his pocket, and said of course that meant me, and put into my hands; but I told him pot-hooks and hangers had been left out of my education, so perhaps he would pay it out for me; he did, and it said something about some villains having illtreated a officer of his Majesty's Navy, named Hiram Sheave. A reward of a hundred pounds was offered for their capture. I felt as if I had been standing an hour before the galley fire, for I thought the old gentleman was going to give me up and pocket the hundred pounds; but he wasn't going to do anything of the sort; he told me not to tell any one what I had done, and as nobody but Mr. Sheave saw me, and he didn't recognise me, nobody could find me out. He thanked me for what

I done to Mr. Sheave, and popped a guinea into my hand, and then told me to go and get some rest, promising I should see Mr. Prior as soon as the doctᴏ thought it safe. Well, after this Mr. Prior grew worse and worse; he was in a bad fever, and knew nothing nor nobody, but talked of a thousand things which nobody could fathom, and laughed and sung, and then his lee scuppers would overflow, and all within the striking of a bell. I knew somebody must keep watch by him, so I begged hard for 'em to let me have the night watch. Well, they granted it me, and I used to sit by his side until the morning, and then turn in. I used to hear him order as if he was on deck; then he would fancy himself yard-arm and yard-arm with Sheave, and then he would speak so soft and low about Miss Florence—I've felt it hard work, Paul, to keep the well clear. One night I was sitting by his side, he had been rattling away as usual, and had just dropped into a sleep, it was midnight; it had been raining hard all the evening, but the wind, which had been southerly with a little west in it all day, got round more to the westward, and was getting on to blow a gale. I was thinking of my mother and father, wondering who they were, whether I had any brother or sister, if I had, whether I should ever come athwart 'em, or whether all of kin I ever had were lost on the wreck from which I was saved. I was rather down, and sad thoughts came fast upon me, for in thinking of my parents I couldn't forget poor old Tom Lanyard, who brought me up, and was lost in the mizen-chains of the Arethusa. While I was thus overhauling all the black days in my log, the door gently opens, I cast up my eyes, and what do you think I saw, John? Now, on the word of a true seaman, what do you think I saw?"

"How is it possible I can tell?" answered Paul.

"Why, a young woman in white," he replied.

"In white?" said Paul.

"Aye, in white," returned he, "with a figure-head as white as her rigging. She looked steadfastly at me, but I was taken flat aback; I stared at her with top-lights like port-holes, and a mouth like a main hatchway. She didn't speak a word, but advanced towards me; I never heard a footfall—she came on like a schooner with a light breeze, and after staring at me as if she would speak, she turned her head away, and stood by the bed; she clasped her hands and knelt down by the side. After she had been there a little while, she rose again, and leant over the bed and kissed Mr. Prior's forehead, that, with his dark hair, looked as white as spray under the forefoot going large; then she raised her toplights to heaven, while the salt water run out of them like pearls; then she kissed him again, and then she turned to me, pointed to Mr. Prior, pressed her two white fins together, and backed out of the room, keeping her bows towards us. Just as she reached the door, Mr. Prior sprung up in the bed and stared at her, she smiled—ah! John, that was a smile!—and vanished."

"Vanished?" cried Paul, looking wonderingly at Gasket.

"Yes," replied Gasket, with a grave shake of the head, "vanished. Mr. Prior gave a loud cry and fainted; I sung out for help, but I never told any one but you, John—the ghost of Miss Florence came to his bedside."

"Ghost?" said Paul, with a derisive laugh.

"Aye, her ghost," returned Gasket, earnestly—"it was her spirit safe enough, come to give him warning that his log was made up."

"Well, but he did not die," exclaimed Paul.

"No," replied Gasket, "not then, but he will, or my name's not Gasket."

"So shall we all," was Paul's remark.

"When our time comes; but Mr. Prior will go before his time, you'll see," persisted Gasket; "for if ever there was a angel come down from heaven, it was that night, and in the shape of Miss Florence, too."

"Why didn't you speak to her?" inquired Paul.

"I couldn't," replied he, "I was all abroad; besides, where's the use? if she wanted to speak, she would, whether I was able to hail her or no."

"Well, what followed this?" asked Paul.

"Why, when the doctor come next day, he said Mr. Prior was better, would recover, and so he did, but he never told how he got wounded.   As soon as he was well enough to get out, he made for the place where Miss Florence lived. I went with him, but we found the house was let to some other folks, who know'd nothing of Miss Florence and her parents, only that they believed they were gone abroad, but where they couldn't say.   Well, every place he tried, but we couldn't overhaul their whereaway; but we did find out that Mr. Sheave had gone as third lieutenant in a seventy-four upon a five year's station in the East Indies, after he got well.   An old messmate of mine told me this, and said he'd seen him before he sailed, and his figure-head was so altered his friends hardly knew him—ha! ha! ha! I was glad of that too, Well, after knocking about a little longer. Mr. Prior was made a third lieutenant, and put on board the Wildfire; and as she had her complement of petty officers, I could only enter as foremast man, but I should have been captain of the main-top if you hadn't saved the captain's life in our brush with the pirates; but I am as glad you have got it as if it was myself.   Now you know all my part of the story respecting Mr. Prior; and now, John, as I have made a clean log to you, you may as well tell me what Mr. Prior said to you when you went into his berth after giving the shirk his supper."

"He did not tell me a ghost story, though it was something akin to it," replied Paul; "but we shall see by and bye how much faith there is to be placed in it. When I went aft to him, after backing and filling a little, he asked me if I had any faith in dreams. He asked it with a laugh, and yet there was a peculiarity about his manner which told me there was something more than a jest in his motive for putting such a question to me. I replied that I had never had but one to which I attached any importance, and what I had heard I gave little heed to. He followed it up by inquiring the one to which I gave credit, and I told him, Gasket. I told him," continued Paul, with singular energy, "that when a boy, I wandered along the sea shore one summer's day for miles, and wearied with my stroll, late in the afternoon, I entered a cave; advancing some distance up it, and laying down, I went to sleep. While in my sleep, I dreamed I had become a man, and trod the deck of a vessel as its commander. She was a man-of-war frigate, Gasket—a noble-looking vessel. I saw every part of her deck—her guns; the men were at quarters, the courses were hauled up, and the top-sails only were set. Above my head, flying from the peak of the gaff, was a flag which I have never yet seen hoisted for any nation, but I shall never forget it ; it was decorated with stripes and stars on a white ground. It waved proudly above my head, and as my eyes glanced upwards I felt my soul swell with proud glee. I thought I gave the word of command for the men to fire, nd then went through all the evolutions of a sea fight, although at that time, Gasket, I knew nothing of the rig, build or working of a ship more than a boy, who had only been on board a few coasters, could ; I fancied I led on a party of boarders, and after a desperate fight made myself master of the vessel I had been fighting. Once more I turned my eyes upwards, and still was my flag with the stripes flying at the gaff. This vision passed away, and I stood in a palace surrounded by nobles and ladies of the highest rank and distinction—I was before a king. I knelt down at his feet, and around my neck he placed a star, and the voices of men, and music, and cannons roared round me, and I sprung to my feet. Then it all at once vanished, and one whose face was the likeness of her who is dearer to me than all the world, appeared to me, and in a gentle voice, said ' All this shall be thine !' She imprinted a kiss upon my forehead, and then whispering in my ear—' For me shalt thou do this ; and the time is come now for ye to commence your career of daring !'—she disappeared, and I awoke in time to discover the sea at my feet. The tide had set in while I slept, and had rushed up the cave, which, being on a rise to where I lay, which was just at the top, was some twelve or fourteen deep at the mouth. I looked for the moment aghast, but the words still rung in my ears, " The time is come now for you to commence your career of daring," and for ever will these words be impressed upon my memory, as will the dream. I instantly un- dressed myself ; I made my clothes into as small a bundle as I could, and with a belt which I wore round my waist, I m e the clothes fast to the top of my head, and then plunged boldly into the water. I could swim like a cork, but the question was, whether my strength would last me till I could make the shore ; I waded until the water reached my chin, and then I struck out, and was not long in reaching the mouth of the cave ; but the hardest part was to come. I looked around—the sea was flush up to the rocks, which stretched high up, for the distance of two or three miles ; to attempt to gain them was hopeless, and I looked around in despair ; as my eyes gazed eagerly in every direction, I perceived a rock within a quarter of a mile seaward, which rose up the distance of ten or twelve feet above the water, and I fancied if I clambered up it I could sit upon it until I was picked up by a passing boat, or, at least, until the tide went out sufficient to enable me to swim with safety to the shore. I had but little time for doubting or indecision ; it seemed the most feasible plan, and I seized it. I swam towards it, and after a long swim against a tide that was making in, I reached it, quite exhausted, to find the side smooth, with nothing to lay hold of; my heart sunk within me, but I made a struggle, and swam round it, half inclined to let myself go to the bottom, but the remembrance of my dream supported me, and I kept on ! it was a large rock, some distance round, and after persevering until I reached the spot from which I had started, I found a place to clutch hold of. I had hardly strength to draw myself up, but I succeeded at last, and mounting to the top, I unbuckled my clothes, and lay down to recover myself. I was nearly half an hour before I was so far restored as to sit up and put on my clothes; but when I did it was with no pleasant feelings, I found myself within four feet of the water, the tide still rising fast; the shore looking to me at a frightful distance; the sun declining, and the horizon bearing indications of a storm brewing. Still I had faith that I should be saved; there I sat watching in every direction for some sign of succour; every now and then a tide wave came in, which made my position less and less tenable. I was perched on the topmost pinnacle, the water was now within a foot of me; five minutes more, and the rock would be under water; what was then to become of me? I cast my eyes shoreward—no sign of a boat there or to seaward. I made up my mind to have another swim for it, and not die without a struggle to save myself, when I noticed something which appeared previously to me, when I had before observed it, to have been the jutting point of a rock, to have got considerably nearer to me. I watched it earnestly, it certainly had advanced considerably, and upon looking closer, I made it out a boat, keel-upwards, drifting towards me."

"Hurrah!" cried Gasket, taking a long breath, deeply interested in the recital. Paul smiled and continued—

"The water now was washing over my feet. I stood up, and remaining until the sea was above my knees, I plunged into it once more, and swam towards the boat. I soon found that my previous exertions had exhausted my strength, and doubted whether I could reach it: I, however, succeeded, and found my surmises correct, it was a boat belonging, as I afterwards discovered, to a brig which was supposed to have foundered at sea with all her crew. I was glad, you may be sure, to find myself astride the keel and drifting fast to the shore. I had now nothing to fear but the turning of the tide ensuing before I was washed ashore, and carrying me out to sea. However, the tide carried me on towards a headland, the other side of which the sea made a long reach, and the knowledge of that fact had deterred me, in the first instance, swimming to it. As I drew near, a fishing yawl stood towards me; I hailed her, and was picked up; they put me ashore, and having had enough of the sea for one day I went home and went to bed. In the night I dreamed the same female appeared to me, and said—' You have begun well: proceed—your destiny must be fulfilled.' Once more her lips pressed to my forehead, and then she vanished. The remainder of the night was filled with dreams of battle—of glory—of honour, but such a mass, I could not extricate anything in particular; that one portion I have told you stood out alone; I have not, nor shall I ever be able to banish it from my memory, nor prevent its having a strong influence over all my actions."

"It's like what happened to Mr. Prior, though his was no dream, for I saw it with my own top-lights," exclaimed Gasket, observing Paul pause; "I dare say it was your guardian angel, as that was Mr. Prior's, for it's my belief it was, and nothing else, and if I had command of a ship her likeness should be the figure-head. But what said he to it when you told him?" he asked.

"Why, he carried as steady and grave a face as you," returned Paul; "and said since I believed so much in a vision of that sort, he should feel less hesitation in telling me his reason for requesting my presence. He said, as you have told me, he was in love with a young lady, but her friends were averse to their union, and gave me a brief history of all you have told me, saying that when he first came on board the Wildfire his mind dwelled very much upon his separation from the lady, and his anxiety was excessive respecting her fate; his duty being trivial, he had too much leisure to reflect upon the perversity of fortune, and was unable to drive the most distracting conceits from his imagination. As you were crossing the Line one night, he lay in his hammock, worn out with unpleasant recollections; he fell asleep and dreamed that he was in a wild-looking building, very old, and deserted by inhabitants—that while gazing upon the ruins he heard a frightful screaming, and rushing forward he saw the maiden of whom he had spoken being carried by a ruffian at the top of his speed down a flight of steps. He followed instantly, and after keeping in pursuit some time without gaining on the fellow, he at length entered a capacious room, filled with armed men; he was attacked, and about to be cut down, when I stepped in to his rescue."

"You!" interrupted Gasket.

"Aye, me," returned Paul; "so went his dream. I had a band of seamen at my command, and placing the lady in his arms, I quitted him: he awoke. Shortly after this he dreamed he was in a range of mountains somewhere in England; the same description of circumstances took place—again I proved his friend. A week after this he dreamed he was at sea with this maiden, his ship was on fire, and they were the only two left on board. The vessel burnt nearly to the water's edge, when a ship appeared in sight; they were picked up—I was the commander, and again the friend who saved him."

"But he'd never seen you then?" exclaimed Gasket.

"True," replied Paul; "and there lies the singularity of the matter. When I was pressed and brought on board he saw me and recognised me as the person he had seen in his dream, and from that moment he has had a strong conviction that in some way I shall be able to do him a great service in his love affair. He has therefore made a proposition to me that when I reach England, if I will assist him in searching for the young lady, the whole interest of his family shall be exerted to get me promoted."

"And you've agreed to it, haven't you?" said Gasket, hastily.

"I have," replied Paul; "not so much for my sake as his, for I feel that my promotion will not come through him, but through my own exertions; however, he seemed so earnestly to wish my co-operation with him, because of the coincidence of identifying me with the friend in the dream, and to which he attaches much faith, that I could make no excuse for declining, and therefore, when once in England, he will have my best aid."

Gasket was about to pursue the conversation further, when the bell was rung for midnight; the boatswain's mate piped the starboard watch, and Paul expressed his intention of turning in.

"I've the morning watch," he said, "and so good night; we'll finish the yarn to-morrow."

Gasket echoed his good night, and in a few minutes afterwards both of them were swinging in their hammocks sunk into deep slumber.

CHAPTER X.

" Thou shalt feel me with thine eye
As a thing that, though unseen,
Must be near thee, and hath been ;
And when in that secret dread
Thou hast turned around thy head,
Thou shalt marvel I am not
As thy shadow on the spot."

                                                    MANFRED.

" MAN.   Look there !
What dost thou see ?
ABBOT.   Nothing.
MAN.   Look there I say,
And steadfastly ; now tell me what thou see'st
ABBOT.   That which should shake me."

                                                    IBID,

" It was with a feeling of satisfaction approaching glee, that Jasper Chough found himself inside the retreat to which he had hastened on quitting Mat Meadows ; he made the entrance fast, and with no little exultation looked upon himself as freed from a considerable danger, and for the present safe both from pursuit or capture. Upon seeing the door was well secured, he sat himself down upon a rudely carved chair, or rather bench, with a back formed of the slateish stone with which the mountain abounded, and remained motionless for nearly half an hour, [in order to satisfy himself that he had not been traced. He listened attentively ; his sense of hearing marvellously quickened by the expectation of approaching foes, but not a footfall or crack of twig, or rustle of grass, told that his hiding-place had been discovered. The long and continued silence relieved his anxiety, and drawing a deep breath, he muttered—

" It would be hard if, after so many years that this place has remained undiscovered, it should now be found out at the very time its secresy is most needed. No, no ! man or devil be he that has laid on [my track, I think his sharp eyes have failed him here."

He paused a few moments longer, and then the unbroken stillness continuing, he rose from his seat, and groping his way to a part of the cave, he drew forth a torch and materials for kindling it. He then went to a recess and pulled forth some provisions, which by their freshness had evidently been recently deposited there—a flask of brandy was also produced and plentifully partaken of—and then the food, consisting of a meat pie and bread, were almost ravenously devoured. When the meal was completed he extinguished e torch, threw himself in a corner, and was soon in a heavy sleep.

He continued buried in profound slumber for about six hours, and then started suddenly from it, and leaped to his feet with a shout ; he seemed dreadfully agitated, and uttered several strange incoherencies ; he groped about wildly for a few minutes, and then placing his hand upon a portion of

the cave, he stopped, and after a moment's silence, he uttered a few broken sentences, which explained the cause of his singular emotion.

"I know now," he said; "I remember all, 'twas but a dream—curse upon all dreams. Why were we made so weak as to be fooled by them—yet I could have sworn HE had his cold hands about my throat—his bloody face was close to mine, and he was dragging me to hell. Pah! I wish I'd not struck him—I wish he'd not been fool enough to interfere. Pshaw! it's done, so let it go; I'd have served any one else so, and should never have cared about it. I have—and had no thought of it since, and what's a brother more than another man! What's relationship, after all? A mere piece of humbug. He was my brother, not by choice, but by compulsion; so are my father and mother my parents—I had no voice in choosing them—I couldn't help myself. Why should I care about them more than any body else? I wish he hadn't been my brother, though—damnation, this is foolery; to the devil with it all, turn up as it may."

When he had finished his soliloquy he rekindled his torch, and proceeded to the end of the cave, and removing a layer of turf, or rather an imitation

No. 15

of it, formed of worsted, and so well done that in the only light which could be used in that place, it was unlikely to be detected from the rest that grew around, he displayed a trap door, in the centre of which was an iron ring; he seized hold of the latter, and raising the door, descended by a short ladder into a small apartment about six feet deep, and fourteen or fifteen feet square. It contained a large number of small casks, ranged in tiers round the sides, occupying the greater portion of the room, but to none of these was his attention directed. He made to a chest, which he opened, and drawing forth a suit of clothes, he doffed his own and equipped himself in these fresh garments, consisting of a long broad-skirted coat, something of the same cut as the one he had thrown off, but made larger and fuller, and ornamented with great buttons; a crimson waistcoat, the flaps, containing the pockets, reaching to his thighs, which were adorned with buckskin leggings; immense boots were drawn on; and a large three cornered hat was placed on his head. He pulled some of his long hair over his face, which he had reddened with some ochre, and then supplied himself with a brace of pistols, which he loaded carefully. He buckled round his waist a large belt, and then taking a stout stick in his hand he ascended the steps, fastened down the trap door, and replaced his covering; he put the flask of brandy in his pocket, as well as a flask of powder and a small bag of bullets. He then took up his gun and shouldered it, but after a moment's hesitation he murmured—

"No, I won't, either—it 'll only be in the way; my bull-dogs will serve me better if I should want any help of that sort."

He threw it in the corner, and standing a few minutes, as if considering whether he had forgotten anything he wished to remember, he extinguished the light, unfastened the door cautiously, and peered forth. It was night— the sky was covered with thick clouds, but there was no sound save the low moan of the wind as it swept slowly past; he looked cautiously round, but the greatest silence reigned. He fastened the door, glided out of the recess, and crouching almost to his hands and feet, he proceeded swiftly along the side of the mountain until he reached the road leading from Grasmere to Dunmail Raise, instead of descending to the lane, the scene of his late villany. He crossed obliquely, and proceeding onwards, gradually descending until he arrived at a patch of trees; among these he made his way into a narrow opening, too narrow almost to be dignified with the name of a lane, and plentifully garnished with slush, in some parts almost knee-deep. Jasper, however, seemed quite cognisant of his road, for although in comparative darkness he stepped from stone to stone—large lumps placed there for the purpose of saving persons the unpleasant necessity of wading through the mire— with the facility of one who knew their locality well. After progressing some distance he stopped, and was greeted by a low fierce growl from a dog, the depth of whose tone proclaimed him to be of no small size.

"Down, Grinder! down, boy!" exclaimed Jasper in a low tone, and then gave a low whistle. The dog was silent instantly, and he advanced a few steps, until he stood before the low door of a cottage; he waited there a few minutes and then whistled again. No answer was returned; and growing impatient, he muttered—

"Cursed mischance!—if he should be away. Luck's dead against me seemingly; there's not a thing that I set my mind upon I am not thwarted in."

He concluded with an oath, and then knocked gently at the door; he tapped several times, and presently a woman's voice demanded—

"Who's there?—who knocks here?"

Jasper bit his lip, and frowned with evident annoyance; but mastering his feelings, he answered in a low tone—

"Dunmail of the pass—husband to her of the Helm Crag!"

Several fastenings were instantly removed, and a female bearing a light appeared; she motioned him in, and then fastened the door again. There was a good fire blazing on the hearth, although it was summer time, but the marshy nature of the place seemed to render it necessary. Upon a rough table placed near the fire was a bottle, and by its side was a small horn. The strong odour of brandy which prevailed made it more than probable that the fluid was in considerable use. The woman placed a chair for Jasper, and said with some warmth—

"I'm glad to see thee, my Bonnie bo', that am I; it's long since thou'st been here, in troth it's a life time."

Jasper regarded her sternly for a moment without speaking. She was a young woman, of about five or six and twenty, tall, with a face which wanted but a little refinement to make it exceedingly handsome; shining black hair which was divided in front in two broad bands, one on each cheek, descending from the forehead, and passing beneath her ears, and the back hair fastened, into a loose, careless knot; her eyes were a brilliant black, large and well formed but told of a spirit which it was better to coax than to cross; her teeth were white and even, and displayed themselves every time she spoke or laughed, and looked the whiter for their opposition to a dark skin, but which, though brown, was transparently clear; she had something of a gipsy in her appearance, on the first impression, yet there was a character about her which, at a second glance, removed the conception,

"Sit down, bo'," she cried, "sit down, and don't look so sulky now you've come to see me; it's a weary while you've been away; don't pull down your eyebrows now you have come, bo,; sit down by me—here, give me thy hat and stick; come, man, seat thyself, and take a drink off the good stuff."

"I wish you would'nt drink off that good stuff so often, Joan," he said, gruffly, seating himself in the chair opposite to where hers was placed; "I hate to see a woman drunk."

"Drunk who's drunk?" cried she, fiercely, her eyes flashing like fire; "who's drunk?—" then checking a volley of words she was about to pour forth, she smoothed her brow, and coming up to him, she put her arms round his neck and kissed him. "Come, bo', don't be cross; it's the first time you've seen me for better than a month, so look a little pleasant. I always smile and laugh when you come, and try to look happy, so that you may not find it disagreeable to come where there's a long face—I do, bo', when, God knows, my heart's heavy. Come, thou'st not "given me a kiss, not one for your Joan, as many times you've called me, and swore you never liked nor loved anybody in the world but me—come, give me one."

"Well, there's one," he said, kissing her cheek coldly, and removing her arms from his neck; the blood rushed into her face and neck, and her eyes looked as bright as if they were filled with water, but she did not suffer a tear to escape; she made a struggle to compose herself, and folding her arms, stood before him, and said in a slow tone—

"You were not always thus, Geoffrey."

"Perhaps not," he replied, laconically.

"No, you were not, and you know it; and I, too, to my cost," she added, bitterly; "but just because I've taken a little drop of brandy you treat me thus."

"A little drop!" exclaimed Jasper, with a scornful laugh; "a gallon I should think by your breath."

"Don't jeer me," she cried, fiercely, "don't jeer me; If I have had a gallon it's no time to jeer me, and you know THAT, Geoffrey."

It seemed that he did know it, for he looked in her excited face, and then with something of an altered tone, he said—

"This is all d—d stuff; bring your chair over here, Joan, and sit by me, girl."

These few words in a kinder tone had the effect of at once dissipating her anger, and with a laugh of glee, she exclaimed—

"That's a bonny bo'—that's my own bo'," and instantly brought her chair and placed it so close that it touched his; then putting one arm round his waist, and leaning her head upon his shoulder, she looked up in his face, and said, "What's kept thee so long away, bo'—didst thee not think how I longed to see thee?"

"I had too many things to do to come over here," he replied, removing her arm from his waist, and his shoulder from the support of her head. "Where's your father?" he added.

"Why have you put my arm away?" she asked, with some surprise.

"I want to talk," he said, peevishly.

"I remember when you couldn't talk without your arms round my waist, and your mouth to my cheek," she said, emphatically.

"I can now, then," he replied impatiently; "to-day is not yesterday, nor yesterday last week, nor last week last year; what I did a year ago is not what I am obliged to do to-day."

"It may be, Geoffrey," exclaimed she, rising and confronting him; "it may be, but last year you shouldn't have talked to me as if you meant to keep in the same mind all your life; you shouldn't have sworn to me—"

"Let's have no more of this," he growled. "I'm not in the mood for it, Where's your father?"

"He's away on service; I expected him back before this; he'll not be long, I dare say."

"I am glad of it, I want to see him," said Jasper.

"You came here purposely to see him, then," she demanded, rather earnestly.

"I did. Why?" he asked.

"Then it was not to see me?" said she, speaking with emphasis.

"Pshaw!" he cried, "why do you pester me with such stuff?"

"Stuff!" she echoed, stuff! Well, no matter," she added, with a forced calmness, and then eying him with a steadfast gaze, said—

"What do you want to see him for?"

"I want him to do me a service," he replied, turning his eyes from beneath her searching look.

"What service?" she asked.

"A service," he said, evasively.

"What service?" she repeated.

"What's that to you?" he roared passionately.

"It is to me," she replied, firmly. "and I'll know it."

"You! he uttered, scornfully. "Poh."

"Don't raise the devil in me, Geoffrey," she cried, speaking quickly, "don't you do it; for your own sake man, don't do it."

"Pshaw!" cried he, recklessly, "why shouldn't I, what is there in you I should fear?"

"That which I fear myself; that which will bring blood on my hands as it has on your's," she returned, with strong excitement.

"Not blood of mine," he said, with a laugh. ..

Ay! Goeffrey, blood of your's" she cried; "my love for you would not stay me; no, not though I have loved you dearer than life, and have parted with all my happiness here and hereafter for you, aye, and would again if you were kind to me, but though I have sacrificed everything for you, you have not a kind word or look to throw to me."

"What have you sacrificed for me?" he said, sneeringly.

"What! what!" she echoed, looking wildly on him. "WHAT have I sacrificed for you!" she cried, speaking rapidly; "have I not parted with all that a woman holds dear? Have I not given up virtue, honour, conscience, all—all to you? Did I not part with my little babe, the offspring of your guilt and my shame, to your care that you might not have an uneasy thought, nor ever asked you about it, but to know that it was well? Have I not told lies enough to send a soul to hell for that sin alone, to screen you from discovery? Have I not borne jests, taunts, scoffs, and blows, for your sake? Have I not lived a life the most bitter and wretched beneath this roof, bearing all uncomplainingly, that you might not fear to have a finger pointed at you, if when I was away you were afraid I should make known your secret? What have I sacrificed for you!" she added, with bitterness; "what is there I have not?"

"Did you expect I was going to marry you?" he said, sternly.

"Did I ever ask you?" she said, proudly. "Did I ever breathe one word that should make you think so? No, I did not; I would not."

"Would not?" he uttered, hastily.

"Would not," she replied. "I am too proud; my pride is as great as yours, Jasper Chough; I would not have gone into your family to be looked down on by them, even by your servants; I knew I was too humble.   I knew myself the daughter of one whose practices have lost him the name of honesty, and had you begged me, upon your knees, to have wedded you, I would have refused.   My love for you was at least disinterested, and with my heart I gave away everything; but think you I have not the feeling of a woman?   Think you, because I have lived in this hole nearly all my life, hearing villanous schemes planned, that I am lost to all sense of what is right and good?   Think you I do not know I have fallen, and feel it not.   I do feel it like a canker; it gnaws and gnaws me here." she cried, striking her breast with energy, "and I drink that fire," she added, pointing to the brandy, "to drown all recollection of my own shame and misery, and your unkindness."

A pause ensued: Joan buried her face in her hands with an expression of passionate grief, and Jasper cast his eyes gloomily upon the fire; but neither uttered a word for some time.   Joan was the first to break silence; she drew her hands from her face, and looking earnestly at him, said appealingly—

"There's a dreadful change in your conduct to me, Jasper: what have I done to cause it?"

"Nothing," he exclaimed, sullenly.

"Nothing!" she iterated, scornfully; "nothing! and is it nothing which has made you treat me, who have been as a spaniel to you, worse than the veriest cur? have I loved you too much and been overcome too easily, so that you are tired of me, and would be rid of me? Jasper, Jasper!—"

"Don't Jasper me!" roared he; "the walls in this cursed neighbourhood have ears, and I don't want every gaping fool to know I make my company cheap in the hovel of Jack-in-the-Hole."

"Or the co-mate of Joan Churleigh, his daughter," she exclaimed; "yet, Geoffrey Smith, since you will have that name, although your pride was too great for folks to know that you cast an eye on Jack's only child, you could stoop to sneak here, to fondle and flatter, vow and lie—"

"Lie!" echoed Jasper, fiercely.

"Aye, lie!" she returned unflinchingly, unmoved by the ferocious aspect with which he regarded her; "you could wind your arms about me, and use soft words, and pretend a love which you never felt—would to God that I had not; you were mean enough to fawn and cringe, and crawl, snake-like, in the dust at my feet like a reptile—"

"By hell, Joan!" shouted Jasper, starting to his feet, clenching his fist and shaking it menacingly at her; "if you don't stop your jawing, a blow from my fist shall send you flying to the other end of this den and quiet you for some time to come."

"I would advise you not to try it, my brave Geoffrey," cried Joan, sneeringly, yet energetically—seizing hold of an iron bar used for raking the wood embers together, which was standing in the chimney corner. "I would advise you not to try it," she repeated; "It may be dangerous to you. You do not know me when I am roused, though you have seen a little of my temper when it's up; but you do not know what it can be when your baseness works it to its height: you know what my love has been—my hate is as deadly as my love was intense. I can revenge vile ingratitude as deeply as I can reward kindness—of which I have so little, God knows I am at no loss how to value it."

There was a cool steadiness in the delivery of this speech which made it a matter of little doubt that she would use the bar if he gave her occasion for it; that she was firm in her purpose of giving blow for blow; her eye gleamed brightly upon him, encountering his enraged glance without wavering before it in the slightest; it had the effect of cooling him down. After frowning and clenching his teeth, he muttered something which was inaudible, became silent, and threw himself back in his seat heavily. He remained gazing on the glowing brands of wood blazing brightly on the hearth in gloomy thoughtfulness; presently he turned to Joan, and, in a quieter tone of voice, said to her, as she still stood with the iron bar grasped in her hand—

"Put that down and come here. I hate all this infernal recrimination—it does no good with me; you ought to know me well enough to know that you only make a fool of yourself to no purpose." He leaned over towards the bottle containing the brandy, and taking it up he poured a quantity of its contents into the horn and drank it off at one draught; then again turning to Joan, who had covered her eyes with her apron, and was sobbing bitterly, he exclaimed—

"Come, Joan, don't be a fool; take your hands from your eyes—what's the use of your snivelling and whining. Sit down and tell me where your father's gone."

She made no reply, but still wept; Jasper muttered a few oaths, and ground his teeth with rage, he was about to roar out a string of angry words, but a second thought prevented him, and swallowing his ire he assumed a conciliating tone—

"Come, leave off crying, old girl," he said, "sit down here by me, and let's have no more of this. Come, give me a kiss, and let's forget it all."

Joan drew her apron from her eyes, they were red with weeping, for the tears she had shed were bitter and scalding; but now they were dry again. Her face was calm, almost rigid, and as pale as before it had been flushed; her look was cold, but determined. She did not move in answer to his request, but fastened her eye, compressed by a lowering brow, sternly but fixedly upon him. He liked this conduct less than any she had yet shown him; passionate grief, reproaches, and invective he heeded not: it had often been his lot to experience them from her, but in this steadiness of demeanour there was a determination which he felt he should be unable to quell, or by pretended affection to dissipate. His power over her was gone, he feared, and it was not without dread he anticipated what would be in its place. He folded his arms with an affectation of indifference, though he was far from feeling it, and did not repeat his request, but merely said—

"Your father's a long while before he comes."

"You think so," she replied, coolly.

"I do," he answered. "What service has he been on ?"

" Not such service as you require of him !" she returned.

"Such service as I require ?" cried Jasper, with surpise. " How do you know what service I require of him ?" he asked.

She paused for a moment, and then, pointing her finger at him, she said, with a little agitation which she could not repress—

"It is little that you have done lately, Jasper, of which I do not know."

"Hell and furies !"—shouted he.

"Nay, never swear and frown and fume—I know all," she exclaimed firmly, waving her hand repressingly towards him. " Snug and cunning as you have fancied your work has been done, it was not close enough to be kept hidden from me."

" What do you mean," he asked, knitting his brows.

"Just what I say," she replied. " I know enough, and can prove enough to make you, proud as you are, swing from a gibbet, if I choose to put my tongue to a justice's ear, and whisper a few words."

" You know nothing," he exclaimed, with forced calmness, " but what you knew months, nay, years ago."

" You are mistaken, Geoffrey, miserably mistaken, man, if you fancy that," she cried, coolly. " I speak of things scarce a week old ; I speak of matters done in the green lane, and up by the pass—Ah ! you understand me now, I see," she added, with a bitter laugh, as he started to his feet, clenched his fists, and with a face pale and ghastly uttered a tremendous oath. " What punishment does the law award for a brother's blood," she continued ; tell me that, Geoffrey. What has the law in store for him who drags a maiden from her home that he may rob her of her honour. Is it not a death on the gallows. Is it not to be sent to the eternal fire by the common hangman. How will Jasper Chough, of gentle blood—the haughty, proud Jasper—"

" Hell-cat !" he roared, coupling the exclamation with a frightful oath, and trembling with excessive rage ; "if you would not be sent to hell at a minute's notice, hold your tongue ; hold it or I shall not have the power to keep my hands from you. Are you mad, or an idiot, that you rouse my blood in this fashion ? Another sentence like that you have spoken and I scatter your brains on yon wall—I will—I will ?"

He forced the words through his teeth, and glared upon her as a tiger prepared to make his spring : she shrunk not, quailed not, but gave him a contemptuous smile.

"You dare not, Geoffrey," she said, " you dare not ?"

"Do not tempt me, Joan, if you value life in the smallest degree. Do not tempt me," he cried ; " it is dangerous."

" I do not value it a single 'worthless hair," she said, with sad earnestness ; not one poor grain of the earth on which I stand ; yet you dare not kill me, for your own life then would not be worth half-an-hour's purchase."

" Pshaw !" he sneered ; " such a threat is idle."

" You would not find it so," she replied, quickly.

" No matter," he returned, emphatically. " I would never hesitate to sacrifice my life to satisfy my revenge."

" Nor the happiness of another's life to gratify your pleasure," she exclaimed, bitterly.

"Perhaps not," he replied, laconically ; and then, with an expression of determination allied to ferocity, he said—" Let's have no more of this ; for your own sake let this subject drop, talk of what you like but this ! and if you can talk of nothing else hold your tongue ; there is a fiend in my bosom too busy now—if he's not kept down, blood will scarce satisfy him."

"There is a fiend in your bosom, Geoffrey," returned Joan, " a remorseless, merciless fiend : when first you saw me here in this hovel, I was in a miserable situation, it is true ; but my father, vile as he is called, was kind to me ; wretched as his abode is, he furnished it with many comforts for me, and gave me good counsel. Strange men came to talk of matters which I scarce understood, save that they were lawless : but though their plans and plots were discussed before me, when they were about to seperate, no eye was suffered to rest too rudely upon me, no hand to insult me, and he found money to pay for me to be taught, privately of an evening, to read and write and receive the education of a lady. Nay, Jasper, you need not utter that sneering laugh —I speak the truth ; I tell you this to show you how low I am fallen, how deeply I am 'degraded by you ; there is not an accomplishment a sister of

No. 16

yours could have been taught which I did not acquire, and for what? God help me; Look you, Jasper, I knew and felt, as I have often told you, that I had a full sense of the miserable situation in which I lived—but I had still something to look forward to. I did not mix with any females here; I had no companions, not one to cheer the loneliest hour—nothing but books to pass away the long and dreary time. I had no pleasant remembrances to fall back on, for since I can remember, here I have dwelt. My father often brought me rich dresses and ornaments—for what? This was no place to wear them, but I had hopes for the future; I thought it impossible I could always live in this desolate spot, and a strong imagination pictured a time when I could move among the brightest and fairest, and be as happy and as gay as they. Scrupulously, therefore, with these fond thoughts did I hoard up my dresses and jewels, and wait patiently for the time to come. At length you came, you fixed your eye upon me, and marked me for your prey. You, you, Geoffrey," she cried, with wild energy, "came and courted my notice, you sought opportunities when my father was absent to come and twine yourself round my heart; you were kind and gentle, your words were tender, your actions all the most loving could wish; you gained, by your vile arts, my affections—my passionate love. I thought it all true, I thought every word you uttered was clear of all falsehood. Without a friend or companion to advise me, secluded from the world entirely, how was I to detect truth from falsehood, honour from deceit? I believed you, Geoffrey, I trusted you, I gave up my whole heart to you; there was nothing I did not, would not have sacrificed for you, so devoted was my love. You know it well, you knew you held the whole happiness of my life in your hands, and without remorse you wrecked it, utterly blighted. I soon awoke from the dream—God knows you did not let me slumber long—and found every hope, every prospect I had formed so fondly, vanished; all, all was gone—I was sunk so low that I could never rise again—still I had a hope that you would not desert me; to marry me, as I have told you, I knew was hopeless. I would not stoop to ask you to be spurned and rejected, or to be a finger scorn if you should have made half the sacrifice for me which I had for you; and in silence I bore the anxiety, the uncertainty, and sickening doubts which distracted me. Oh, Geoffrey, I suffered enough then to have sent many to their grave; would to God it had me, yet I spoke not a word to you complainingly. I still smiled when you came, and what little happiness I did have, was when by your side. When I found myself about to be a mother, my heart sunk within me; I knew my father's fiery nature; I dreaded his discovery of my situation—not for myself, Geoffrey, not for myself, for my love for you then was so strong, I would have died cheerfully to save you a pang. My fear was for you—"

"For me!" cried Jasper, interested in spite of himself, in details of which, till now, he had been almost ignorant.

"Aye, for you," she exclaimed; "for had my father known you to have been the author of my shame, no power in the world would have stayed him from putting a bullet through your brains, or a knife in your heart. You may tart, Geoffrey, but were I now to breathe a word implicating you, he would hunt you through the world until he had run you down."

"But you will not?" he said, apprehensively.

"I did not," she replied, evasively. "He at last discovered what I so long endeavoured to keep hidden from him: my illness, prior to the birth of the child alarmed him; he fetched Doctor Gray, and to his astonishment, all but madness, the child was born; but for the doctor, in his rage he would have slain both me and the child. The good doctor, however, kept him from me and though since then he has treated me worse than the vilest slave—though he has taunted me, swore fearfully at me, threatened me, struck me, the name of the father of my child never passed my lips."

"Nor will it now; Joan?" said Jasper, hastily.

"Why should I keep it longer?" she asked, scornfully; "in what way have you repaid all that I have suffered, that I should still bear more for you? Have you not blasted my life; and have you not threatened to take it from me, but now? Why should I screen you from the vengeance he has sworn the most fearful oath to inflict on my seducer, when he discovers him?"

"Come, come Joan," said Jasper, deprecatingly, "for your own sake you will not tell. I have been harsh to you; I have been unkind, I know, but I will not again. Let this foolish quarrel pass, and you shall find me all that you first knew me."

"So you have said a hundred times, each time to treat me worse than the last," she said, with no little contempt in her manner.

"But this is the last time," he said, with an attempt at a smile, which came very ill from him. "Come and sit down; I wish to speak to you of your—our child, Joan."

"What of it, Jasper—what of it?" she said, urgently.

He smiled again. This time it was one somewhat of triumph; he felt he had still that which would give him a power over her.

"You will not speak my name to your father as its parent!" he exclaimed, fixing his eye steadfastly upon her. She recoiled a little, but recovering, said hurriedly—"No, no! Tell me of my dear, helpless, friendless child!—would to God I could see it."

"You may do that, perhaps," said Jasper, stretching out his hand to take hers, and drawing her towards him.

"When, Geoffrey—when?" she cried.

He led her to a seat by his side, and placed his arm round her waist. Her brow lowered a little, and her eyelid drooped, but she did not remove his arm; he, however, did not notice it, though it told her love for him had received too severe a shock to be easily restored to its original pinnacle.

"Very soon, Joan," he said, "very soon. When I have managed matters which I have for some time been preparing, then I will take you to see her."

"Take me!" she reiterated, in unfeigned surprise.

"Yes, you would not have me bring the girl here, would you?" he asked hastily.

"Why not?" she said.

"Why not! Would you like to see her buried in the patch of ground behind this hut?" he exclaimed, emphatically.   "Your father would not be long in preparing her for her grave, or preparing a grave for her."

Joan shuddered, and covered her eyes with her hands instinctively; suddenly she raised her head, and said significantly—

"He is not always at home."

"No, but his return is always so uncertain, is it worth hazarding the girl's life?" he replied, almost with a sneer.

"No, no, no—oh, no!" she cried, rapidly; "I would rather die a thousand times than a hair of her dear head should be harmed."

"Very well, then listen to me," he exclaimed.   "In a week or a fortnight hence I will come here and fetch you, when your father is out on service, and lead you to where she is staying; from thence you can, if you will, go to London or to France with me, and live like a lady, be all, and see all that you say you have been so long hankering after."

"What! mix with ladies, and wear all the dresses and things I have hidden so snug in my boxes?" she said, laughing almost with childish simplicity.

"Yes, and have other things finer than you have got, or ever seen," he said.

"And my child—our child, Geoffrey?" she said, her fondness fast returning under these promises of Jasper.

"She shall be with you if you like, or stay where I have placed her," he returned.

"She shall be with me—with me!" she exclaimed earnestly, putting her arm round his neck; "oh, I would not part with her for worlds—for all you have promised me."

"Then you shall accompany me," he said.

"And you, Geoffrey—you?" she asked, looking up in his face affectionately.

"I will be with you, Joan, as often as I can," he said, assuming a kind tone of voice, "and will endeavour to be as affectionate to you as I have been of late harsh; but I have had many things to cross and vex me, and that's the reason—not that I love you the less, Joan."

"Oh, Jasper, if I could but believe you—if I could but believe you," she exclaimed, the tears rushing to her eyes from deep feeling.

"And what's to hinder you?" he asked abruptly; "I'll take an oath, if you will not trust my plain word."

"No, Jasper, no," she replied, thoughtfully.   "I have no opinion of oaths; if your word in a case like this will not bind you to me, no oath will.   Give me your word, and I shall be satisfied."

"Upon the faith and honour of a man, I will perform what I promise," he said, giving her at the same time a kiss upon the cheek.   She heaved a sigh, and looking fondly upon him, said—

"Would that you had been alway thus! I do wish that you had never given me cause to doubt you, Geoffrey; how much happier I should have been under all my father's cruelty than I have been."

"Never heed it now, Joan," he said, "you will soon be out of his reach, and will be happy yet."

"What will he do when I am gone," she exclaimed.

"The best he can, to be sure," cried Jasper, with a laugh; "he will most likely get hold of some termagant who will give him blow for blow, and perhaps rid society of such a savage dog as he is—I hope he may."

"He is my father," said Joan, instantly preparing to defend him though she had been latterly much ill-treated by him.

"I should doubt that," exclaimed Jasper, drily.

"Why" she asked, hurriedly.

"If he was really your father, he would not use you so roughly," he returned, evasively.

"He treats me as I deserve," she ejaculated, thoughtfully; "until my baby was born no father could have treated his child more kindly than he did me, but since that, which was sufficient to rouse his ire, I unfortunately, to rid myself of thoughts that burnt me like fire, made a friend of brandy; he has had cause enough for his ill usage.

"Well, let's talk no more about him," said Jasper, "you will soon be far from him. I will take care that he does not track you; if he should, you know how long it would be before your death and that of the child's would follow."

"I must take my chance," said Joan, clasping her hands; "but if it was not for my child, I would not leave him—I could not—"

"Come, Joan, enough of this; you must, for your own sake, do it," said Jasper; "so make no useless regrets, or would's or could's about the matter; it must be done; we've said enough about it now, we will talk more upon it when the time comes for us to depart. Let's talk of something else."

"Yes we will," she replied, suddenly; "we will; after what you have just proposed and promised me faithfully to fulfil, it would be unkind in me to doubt your love for me, and I will not, Jasper. But tell me what has made you act as you hove done this past week?"

The sudden presence of a black cloud upon a clear sky could not have exhibited a greater change than the features of Jasper underwent as she asked the question; her quick eye detected the alteration in an instant, and a pang of alarm went through her breast.

"What do you know of what I have done? Is it report, or is it your fancy?' he asked, with a gloomy expression.

"Neither," she replied; "it is what I know."

Jasper bit his lips, angrily, but kept his mortification down.

"What do you know?" he inquired.

"I know that you carried off the young lady who is staying at your house—your cousin, I think she is."

"She's no cousin of mine," interrupted Jasper.

"It matters little," she said; "you made love to her, Jasper, and she spurned you—spurned you from her as she would a dog; your brother Frank interfered—you cut him down with your stick, and carried her off; you kept her up in the Pass, hidden in the receiving house there, but she found means to escape. A stronger hand than yours set her free."

"Whose hand was it? do you know THAT?" he asked eagerly.

"Perhaps I do, perhaps I do not ; if I do, I shall not tell you," she replied; "but I want to know, if she had consented to return your love, whether you would not have made her your wife, and cast me off, forgotten me entirely."

This was said quietly and calmly, but there was a fire in her eyes that made him feel how deeply, painfully she was affected by it. He hesitated a moment.

"I want no equivocation, Jasper," she said in the same tone, "no lie, I can hear the truth—I would rather hear it from your own lips than from others."

"You are always doubting me," he cried, affecting a peevishness; "I tell you truly, and you may believe me—I do not care for the girl a straw."

"Then why carry her away by force?" she inquired, hastily.

"That's a secret," he replied.

"But one which you will tell me ere you make me believe different to what I have heard," she exclaimed; "you made love to her, THAT I know, and I will know why you did it, too."

"Will you?" thought he; "do not make too sure of that." Then said in an audible tone, "would you have me betray an oath of secresy."

"You are not too apt to be affected by such a consideration," she said significantly; "but retain your 'secert," she contiuned, "and I will keep my doubts and act upon them also."

"Act upon them!" he echoed; "in what way? what do you mean?"

"It's scarcely likely that I shall tell you when I am to be marked out as a sufferer by your conduct," she returned, derisively.

"Still on the same string," he exclaimed, with a sneer; "well, if you must know all, know that I made love to her for another."

"How mean you?"

"Why, there is one whose high station will prevent him wedding her, but whose fortune will not prevent his placing her at the head of a splendid establishment. I am to be rewarded with an appointment if I succeed in persuading her to accept the offer."

"Does she like this person?" asked Joan, simply.

"No; she's an obstinate fool, and blind to her own interests," he replied.

"And to yours also," said Joan, with a laugh; "you have come therefore, to father to help you to carry her away; so that if she will not consent by fair means she shall by foul."

"You are as good as a witch," he replied, laughing.

"Bad as I am, better than that, I hope," exclaimed Joan. "But you say there is nothing would make her agree quietly to these offers," she said, cross-examining him with some tact; he had not said this, bnt it was so like the tact, he might have fancied he had, and so answered in the affirmative, continuing—

"She refuses everything most obstinately, and I suppose the fool's in love with somebody else; I thought at first it was Frank, but I don't think so now."

"Poor Frank," ejaculated Joan.

"He is well enough by this time, I warrant me," said Jasper, eyeing her steadfastly, hoping to hear something respecting him, for as yet he had learned nothing whatever concerning him. Joan looked him in the eyes, and replied—

"I hope he is."

"I hope so too," returned Jasper, "though in my passion I did hit him harder than might have hurt a thicker head than his."

"It was a cruel, unjustifiable act," exclaimed Joan; "however, it is done, and there is now no help for it; but your determination respecting your cousin is not done, and must not be attempted, Geoffrey."

"Not be attempted! what do you mean?" he asked, with fierce surprise.

"Hear me, Jasper, I know the meaning and the feeling of a blighted life; I know the despair and agony of destroyed hopes, of crushed expectations. I would not doom a dog to suffer them, and you shall not rob this poor girl of all her happiness on earth; so take my advice and give up all thoughts of it."

"You will take my advice and not interfere in this affair at all," said Jasper, sternly.

"I shall not only interfere, but do my best to prevent it," she exclaimed, decisively, and then said entreatingly; "you will not persist in it, I know you will not; you would not wantonly break a young girl's heart who has done you no harm."

"I do not mean to lose a good appointment for any such stuff," cried he, passionately.

"Then upon that point we are enemies again, Geoffrey," she exclaimed, quitting his side, and taking up her station opposite to him.

"You make yourself a cursed idiot," roared Jasper; "don't you meddle in this matter—you cannot stop it, and you will only bring danger about your ears if you interfere."

"I tell you it shall not be done," she said, firmly; "every plan you lay, every scheme you invent, I will counteract: I will hover about you like a spirit, and defeat your intentions as soon as they are formed; I have the means, and I'll use them."

"If you threaten me, Joan," said Jasper, with savage emphasis, "you'll see no more of your brat."

The epithet—the threat it conveyed, went like a knife to her heart; she turned as pale as death, but she altered not her determination.

"My father's bullet or knife would find your heart quicker than your vengeance could fall upon that harmless, unoffending innocent," was her reply.

"If it did, where would you look for your child? no one but myself knows where it is deposited," he cried, jeeringly.

"I would search every county in England but I would find it," she answered.

"Perhaps it is not in England," he exclaimed.

"Still would I find it," she cried, "and make the oath upon your grave Jasper, never to rest until it was accomplished."

She uttered this speech with singular energy, and stretched her hand prophetically towards him as she spoke. He could not withstand the bright gaze she fixed on him, but turned away, and with an undefined sense of dread, which he could not shake off, he felt it better to conciliate than to thwart her.

"I suppose you must have it your way, Joan," he exclaimed, "or you will be jealous for ever if you don't. I have no wish to harm the fool, far from it, for I should place her in the midst of grandeur, and present her with a noble lover into the bargain; however, let it go, and my best prospects with it—for nothing else, it seems, will please you."

"You will be all the happier for this hereafter, Jasper," she said, earnestly "so will she, aye, far more so than if you placed the wealth of worlds in her grasp. When we were first together, and I thought you loved me, I would not have parted with you to have received a kingdom—"

A low growl from the dog without announced the approach of footsteps.

"Here is father," she cried, hurriedly. "Remember, not a plot or a word about Florence: she must not be touched. Do you consent?"

"Ask and have," said he, quickly, "I'll do whatever you wish me, my own dear Joan."

"My bonny, bonny bo'," she cried, throwing both her arms round his neck, and kissing him fervently. "Make any excuse you can think of for being here," she exclaimed, releasing her lips, "and leave me to do my part."

A long low peculiar whistle was answered by her tapping on the inside of the door. A gruff voice without, as soon as she ceased, cried—"Alone!"

She unbarred the door, opened it, and disappeared; but Jasper heard her say—

"Where have you stayed so long?"

"What's that to thee, fool?" replied the voice.

"Only this—there's one of your gang been here this hour."

"Who, girl? who?" she was asked hastily.

"Why, Geoffrey Smith," she replied; "and when you ask any of your tribe to come, don't pick out such a haughty, glumpy, moody, haven't-a-word-to-say-for-himself sort of booby as the fellow in there."

"Better words, fool; better words; what should such as he have to say to a trull like thee? you're only fit company for the hell-hound who made you what you are. Now, before God, if I could but light upon him anywhere, there should be one life less in the world—his or mine."

"You've said enough about that, father," muttered Joan.

"Ay! and you've suffered enough, wench; get thee in, poor wretch—get thee in; you've paid a heavy fine for your misdoing. See how you behave yourself—yon Geoffrey Smith is not what he seems."

"No!" thought Joan; "not he, indeed."

That simple remark had a strong effect upon her ; it made her doubt the truth of Jasper's sudden conformity with her wishes, and resolve to watch him closely, though she would not let him see that she suspected him in the slightest degree. Jasper had overheard all that had passed, and felt but little at his ease ; he was aware on what a precipice he stood if Joan should betray him ; for he knew the man he had to deal with. He saw, therefore, it was his policy to conciliate her, make her believe he still loved her, and cajole her until, safe off with Florence, he could laugh at her threats and despise them. While he was resolving to act more circumspectly, the father and daughter entered.

Jack Churleigh, or Jack-in-the-Hole, as he was nicknamed from his residence, was a tall, raw-boned man, standing at least six foot two or three inches ; his limbs were large, but well knit to his frame ; his shoulders were broad, though from his height he looked gaunt. His head was rather small than otherwise, and his long hair, which had once been black, was now a grisly grey, but still hung in curls upon his shoulders. His features were coarse and strongly marked ; there was little to conciliate, much to alarm,

No. 17.

in them; they were forbidding in their aspect, and though Joan had stated she had received much kindness trom him, the truth of such an assertion could never have been gathered from his looks.   He greeted Jasper with rough friendliness as soon as he set eyes upon him, and his cordiality w as returned by Jasper in somewhat of the same strain.

"How is't, my bold Geoffrey?" he cried.   "Is trade getting b risk, buyer[s] plenty, that I see you in my cottage?"

"Something of that sort," replied Jasper; "how get on our friends in the island?"

"Not quite so well of late," retnrned Churleigh; eyes are more open lately watchers are more numerous, and tell-tales have been at work, but there's more bays than one on the coast, and more keels than two or three to navigate them, a will will generally find a way—it has with us already."

"And for many a thief to the gallows," said Joan, coolly.

"Hold your tongue, jade, and let's have some supper," cried her father, "I'm starving.   I'll wager you never asked Geoffrey Smith to eat all the time he's been here."

"Not I," she said, rather pertly, "he never asked for anything."

"Do you suppose, fool, because he did not ask he did not want any?'" he cried.

"He has scarcely opened his mouth since he's been here," she returned; "who would suppose he could want anything to put in it."

"You're an impudent hussy," cried Jack, half smiling; "come let me have something to put in it now."

Joan busied herself to spread the supper things, and soon placed materials for a substantial meal upon the table. Churleigh and Jasper ate heartily, but she scarcely touched a morsel.   Jasper noticed it.

"You do not eat," he said, looking earnestly at her.

"I do not feel inclined," she replied.   "I am not hungry."

"Eat!" cried Churleigh, " eat, not she—you get your supper, never mind her; she never eats in a day as much as a spider would suck out of a fly she always either snivelling or—or sleeping," he added.   He intended to have said drinking, but he substituted the word he used.   Most men, placed as Jasper was in connection with Joan, would have felt this observation as a cutting reproach; but he did not; he was too selfish to care for the misery he had inflicted upon this poor girl.

When the repast was finished, and she was clearing the eatables away, and left the room for a minute, Jasper whispered to Churleigh that he wished to speak to him in private.

"We are in private here," he returned.   "Joan's tongue never wags when it should be still."

"It is matter for your ear alone," said Jasper, urgently.

"About the child?" exclaimed Churleigh.

"Partly," replied he.

"Very well, I'll manage it presently," said Churleigh.

Joan at this moment returned; her father affected to be in the very middle of a sentence which had no connection with the subject upon which he had just been conversing with Jasper; she, however, was not deceived—her quick ear had detected sufficient to justify suspicion. She had heard the request and reply, and determined to see whether Jasper kept his promise to which he had pledged his honour.

After a short time had passed, occupied principally in placing brandy before them, her father unceremoniously bade her go to bed; she offered no objection to his command, and bidding them both good night she mounted the stairs, and disappeared. When she entered her little sleeping-room she divested herself of her shoes, and with the greatest caution descended the stairs which, as in most cottages, led into the sitting room or kitchen; there was a door at their junction with the wall, which she had taken care to close when she left their presence, and having reached it, she placed her ear to one of the divisions of the boards of which it was formed. She listened attentively with the hope of gathering evidence of Jasper's truth or falsehood, but the voices were so low it was with difficulty she could distinguish a word. At length her father exclaimed in a loud tone—

"Damn it, man, what are you mumbling about? I haven't caught two words of what you have said; and for my part of the understanding of what you have been talking of, you might as well have held your tongue, for I am as much in the dark as ever."

Jasper murmured something which she could only understand by her father's reply, spoken with some asperity.

"In the devil's name," he cried, "what do you fear? Have you ever found me and mine so glib of tongue that any open ear might pick up the crumbs we throw thoughtlessly away. I'd trust my life with the girl. I wish you, Master Geoffrey Smith, may be as true as she is. I speak harshly to her, and treat her harshly at times—for on one point she well nigh broke my heart, tough as it is. She ruined a favorite project I had formed for her happiness hereafter—and perhaps there was a thought of my own comfort too, for I did not intend to live always in this way. I have enough to keep her and I comfortably, and mix with the best in the world; but all hope of that is gone, and nothing is left for us but to jog on in the same way until we drop our peak to death."

Joan pressed her hands to her head, and tears rushed down her cheeks in torrents. She stifled her sobs, and by great exertion so far overcame her emotion as to bend her ear again to the task of listening. Jasper spoke, but his words were lost to her; but her father said—

"'Pshaw!—how cursed suspicious you have grown; don't tell me at all if you are afraid of its going further. I tell you she's by this time safe in bed; if you doubt it, take the light and satisfy yourself."

Jasper's chair moved, and Joan affrightedly flew up the stairs, and gaining her room fastened the door on the inside, threw herself upon the bed, and lay with a beating heart, expecting to hear the approach of Jasper. She was not deceived; his heavy, but cautious footsteps told he was ascending, and on gaining the top he paused at her door; he tried it, but it did not yield; he called her by name—she did not answer; he called again, and then, as if suddenly awakened, she demanded who was there. Jasper replied, and making a trivial excuse, descended the stairs apparently satisfied. She was not long following him, but was much vexed at discovering he had left the staircase door wide open, preventing her from approaching nearer than the wind of the stairs kept her hidden from sight. However, the conversation was carried on in a louder key, and she could distinguish all that was said; but it was upon matters which had frequently been discussed before her, and foreign to what she expected to hear. She was not sorry when she heard the subject drawing to a close, and heard her father say—

"Well, now to your private matters. I am tired, and shall feel all the better for stretching myself on my bed; it's growing late—say your say, and make yourself scarce."

Jasper made a consenting reply, but once more left his seat and approached the stairs to listen. Joan was within a foot of his head, and held her breath for fear of being discovered; but the corner which screened her was shrouded in darkness, and as Jasper never suspected her proximity, he contented himself with listening if she was moving; finding all silent, he closed the door—Churleigh grumbling all the while—and commenced the conversation. "I have a favour to request of you, Churleigh," began Jasper—"one of much importance to me; and I rely much on the honest friendliness you have ever shown me to grant it."

"What is it?" asked Churleigh.

Joan bent her ear most anxiously to catch Jasper's reply.

"I require your assistance in an affair on my hands, which I have set my heart on carrying, but of myself I am unable; now by your help, I shall be certain of success, and name the manner and fashion of your reward—what-it be, if in the compass of a hand and heart like mine, you shall have it."

"A love affair, my bonny Geoffrey, I suppose these fine promises lead to, eh?" cried Churleigh, with a coarse laugh.

"Why, it is something of that sort," replied Jasper, returning the laugh.

Poor Joan's heart throbbed with violence on hearing this, and she grew sick with apprehension of what was to follow.

"With the young lady you carried off the other night, I suppose?" cried Churleigh.

"S'death! do you know this, too?" exclaimed Jasper, with astonishment.

"Know't, I should rather think I did, man," returned Churleigh. "It caused me some fun, I can tell you."

"How?" cried Jasper, "Fun! I do not understand you."

"I'll soon make you understand," exclaimed Churleigh, after indulging in a long, loud peal of laughter. "How now, brother! What be'st doing with a young lass in this drear place, at this hour, eh, do you remember that."

"Oh! so then it was you who dogged my footsteps that night?" cried Jasper, hastily, and with much earnestness.

"Ah! to be sure it was," he replied. "I followed on your heels all the way you went, chuckling to myself to see how you worried yourself, fearing you had the devil or some such gentleman upon your skirts."

"I heard you, and searched every spot. How did you contrive to elude me?" inquired Jasper.

" You did not think of looking for the bird in a tree," laughed Churleigh ; ' I mounted an old oak while you was searching a spot some distance from where I lay hidden."

"But after this did you again follow me ?" asked Jasper, quickly.

"What, that night ?" said Churleigh.

" No, the next," returned Jasper.

" Not I, I was away from here then some miles, on my way to the island," he replied.

" But I was followed the next night, and was as unsuccessful in finding the intruder as I was in discovering you," said Jasper, with anxiety ; " I would give something to discover who it was."

" Pshaw !" cried Churleigh, "it was your own fancy, I'll wager a night's venture ; but whether it was or no, I want to go to bed. Either say what you want to tell at once, or come again to-morrow."

" To-night it must be all arranged," exclaimed Jasper.

" Then out with it," said Churleigh, impatiently.

" You know the girl has got away from me, I suppose ?" commenced Jasper.

" Not I," returned Churleigh, " this is the first time I've been home since I saw you running with the girl up the mountain. I thought then it was a foolish trick to carry her there ; if any of the king's hounds were to scent out the receiving kens, they would soon be in full cry upon them."

" You need not fear that," said Jasper, concealing the fact of the stranger who had rescued Florence having entered the one highest up the mountain. " I have taken good care of that ; the girl is at home again, and as this part of the country is getting a little too ho to hold me, I mean to give it the slip ; but I must have her with me."

" Pshaw, why pester yourself with a girl. You had better make a voyage in the sloop until the country cools a bit, and folks' memories grow dull," said Churleigh.

" No, no, Churleigh," returned Jasper, speaking with considerable energy. " I would rather stay here and run every hazard than go away without her."

" What in the devil's name is the reason of that ?" asked Churleigh.

" Why, I love her, Churleigh, I madly love her," cried Jasper, excitedly, forgetting in his passionate earnestness the caution he had previously used. Every word was distinctly heard by Joan, who, cold as ice, felt every one go to her heart like blows from a poisoned dagger ; she pressed her fist against it to repress the violent and painful pulsation, and listened in an agony of despair to Jasper's acknowledgment of that which proved him a base, faithless villain to her.

. " My life and soul," continued Jasper, " are all bound up in her ; my breast is on fire while I am from her—I feel consumed by flames which rush through my veins instead of blood while any uncertainty exists of her being mine— she must be mine—I have sworn a bitter, fearful oath that she shall be mine and so she shall, if the next instant I am sent headlong to everlasting perdition."

"Wheugh," cried Churleigh, "here's a burst! I never expected this from Geoffrey Smith."

"You never knew what it was to love pasionately, heart and existence being mere trash with her your soul is set upon," cried Jasper.

"How do you know?" cried Churleigh, in a rough voice, which sounded strangly agitated; "how do you know? how should you know? speak for yourself man, not for me; and don't allude to any subject of the sort again, that's all!" he added, fiercely.

Jasper looked at him with surprise, and Churleigh, who had in the excitement of the moment started to his feet, recovered himself as he noticed it, and flinging himself back in his chair, he waved his hand, and said sullenly—

"Go on! go on."

"I want you to aid me in getting her from the Hall?"

"What is she beneath your father's roof?" asked Churleigh.

"Yes, yes," exclaimed Jasper, impatiently; "my plans are laid, and I want you to obtain for me a pony, and the cloak and hat of a dairy-maid or any farm servant; the means which I shall employ to draw her out I will tell you by-and-bye, but I shall want you to be with me at the time, to give any impertinent prying fool a settling for his curiosity, and keep the girl's tongue from wagging too freely till we get safely beyond pursuit; and then the rest I can manage by myself."

"This is a deal of trouble to take for a girl you care as little about as for others you have been following, and fancied you were in love with," said Churleigh, with a sneer.

"I never cared one jot for any woman on earth before," exclaimed Jasper, with emphasis; "there was never one that I dangled after, that I cared one curse about more than just to serve the purpose for which I made love to them; but this girl I have set my whole heart upon, and if ever man loved a woman, I love her, and will peril everything to have her—all the rest may go to the devil for what I care."

Joan felt as if she could have shrieked with the agony his words inflicted upon her; she had surrendered her whole soul to him; he had obtained it with consummate art from her, and to the love he had laboured so hard to raise, and so well succeeded in accomplishing, she sacrificed every other feeling in the world. If he had been kind and true to her, she would have clung to him, forsaken everything in the world for him, would have kept to him in poverty and wretchedness, if such had been their lot, with more faithfulness, with more enduring affection than if he had been surrounded by wealth; unkind words, harsh treatment, blows she would have even borne for him, and while he still preserved a show of kindness, 'she loved him the more'; would have been true to him, kept by his side when all the world fell off, and never have deserted him, however great the changes of worldly circumstances might have been: but now it was all gone, all vanished; the love she had felt for him he had himself wrenched from her heart. A woman's love is most enduring; it will submit to the most painful trials, and still come through the fire pure; it will cling and remain where everything else has faded, even when she has discovered that the man who has seized her heart is a mean abject wretch, even this shock it will stand; but it will not bear the discovery that she has been cajoled out of her affection by one who cared nothing for her—who made her the instrument of the basest passions—who, having blighted her hopes for ever, casts her uncaringly away, and bestows his own heart, the possession of which she once fondly believed she had, upon another. Then comes a fearlul revolution of feelings, she is loath to believe that this frightful discovery can be true, even though she hears the avowal from the lips she would have pledged the salvation of her soul would never have uttered them; but when the conviction comes too painfully home, to admit even of a doubt upon the subject, then hate takes possession of the bosom as strongly, as intensely, as the love that once reigned there paramount.

Joan felt the loathing, the disgust, the revengeful feelings of bitter hatred steal over her for the scoundrel she had once so passionately loved; but it yet remained to receive the consummation which should utterly preclude its changing. In the fearful emotions which had raged in her breast, a considerable portion of the conservation, subsequent to Jasper's last speech, had passed her unheard; her own miserable feelings had required too powerful an exertion to repress, so that the outbreak they were near making might not cause her discovery, to enable her to pay sufficient attention to what was passing; and it was not until she heard her father speak of her child, that she could recall her scattered senses to hear further.

"I don't doubt your honesty to me, Geoffrey," she heard Churleigh exclaim, "because you are a Chough, and money is not much of an object to you, but I should like to know more than you have told me about the disposal of the baby, and the money I gave you for it."

"Have you told Joan you gave it to my care?" inquired Jasper.

"Not I," replied Churleigh, "I was not such a fool; you would have been pestered to death with her questions every time you came. No; I told her it was safe, and gave her my word that it was, and she seemed to be more easily satisfied than I thought she would."

He did not know Joan was aware it had been entrusted to the care of Jasper; and in the full confidence of affection, she believed it would be taken every care of, because it was his own child, and looked forward to the day when it would be restored to her with delight. Her feelings may be but faintly imagined, much less described, on hearing what followed.

"She is safe enough, you may rest satisfied," said Jasper with a laugh which grated in the ears of Joan like that of a fiend. "When you first gave it me, a puling and sickly thing, I had strong thoughts of hurling it into the Rydal or the Rothay; but as its body, if found, might have caused inquiries, I took second thoughts, and took it to the woman I told you of, five or six months since."

"You were always damned mysterious about the child and the woman," exclaimed Churleigh, abruptly; "here's two years nearly passed away, and

I've heard little or nothing about it; you've had above fifty guineas in gold from me, which I hardly know what you've done with."

"Well, now, I'll tell you once for all," exclaimed Jasper, "and shall claim your thanks when I have finished."

"They shan't be held back if you deserve them," said Churleigh.

"You had no great love for the brat, I believe?" began Jasper.

"Perhaps not," said Churleigh, with a little surprise.

"So I concluded," continued Jasper; "and therefore was sure you cared little what became of it."

"Don't be too sure of that," exclaimed Churleigh.

"Nonsense, man! I know you would rather have it out of the world than in it; it is no joke to have the brat of a daughter running about, and the priest no hand in making its mother a wife."

"It's no jeering matter, Geoffrey," cried Churleigh, fiercely, "and very dangerous work to try it with a man like me. I wouldn't answer for your brains keeping in your head if you play such jests upon me."

"I meant nothing," said Jasper, rather disconcerted; "but as you are so rusty, I'll tell my story without any comments.

"Do," said Churleigh, laconically.

"Well, I kept the child at the house of a woman at Ulverstone."

"You told me, Ripon," cried Churleigh.

"I know I did," said Jasper, "and I took it to Ripon first, but I thought it too near inquisitive people, and having to make a visit to Man, I took Ulverstone in my way, and left it there until my return, and then I fell in with a fellow who was not over particular as to what he did, and having twenty guineas of your money by me, I added ten of my own, and the fellow for that sum took the brat out in his boat one night, made some distance in the Irish Sea, and then dropped her where she would be some time finding the bottom.

A smothered shriek startled both of them at this moment, and they simultaneously rushed to the stairs, from whence the sound appeared to proceed. Jasper opened the door and darted his eyes up the stairs, but there was no one stirring; he seized a light, and followed by Churleigh, ran up the stairs. No one was visible—they tried Joan's chamber door—it was fast. Churleigh applied his ear to the keyhole.

"She sleeps," he said in a low voice; "it wasn't her. I can hear her breathe. She is in a sound sleep. It must have been an owl, or a bat, or a rat. No matter what it was, it wasn't her.

He descended the stairs, followed by Jasper. The staircase door was again closed, and then Churleigh, with an expression of countenance Jasper by no means felt satisfied to observe, said to him—

"Don't you think yourself a damned hard-hearted son of a gentleman?"— The last words were uttered with a contemptuous sneer. "I'm not over particular; I wouldn't hesitate to bring a man down if he affronted me. I'd cut your throat, or beat your brains out if you gave me cause, as coolly as I would shake your hand if I cared nothing for or against you; but I wouldn't have the murder of a little child upon me—no, not for the sa-

tisfaction of the greatest revenge I ever tried to obtain.   You have been too fast in this matter, Master Jasper or Geoffrey; there's only you and I here and her aboye—she's all I care about in the world," he said, energetically, pointing upwards; " it's her child you have murdered, and used my money to do it with, when I particularly told you to be careful of it.   Now, Jasper Chough, before you quit this cottage you must explain why you were so interested in putting the child out of the way, for I don't understand your being so damned ready to do what you wer'n't told."

Jasper did not like his position.   He felt he had been too premature in telling this piece of villany without being sure it would be well received.   He felt completely in the power of a man whom, as he had boasted, he knew would note hesitate to murder him if he saw occasion, and he glanced his eyes right and left, as if seeking some outlet to escape.   Churleigh's eyes followed his; he burst out in a laugh, which, in its tone, was too harsh to indicate anything but savage glee.

" You've no chance of escape, Geoffrey," he cried, " even though yon door," he said, pointing to the entrance, " stood wide open, and you had ten yards start of me; there's Grinder without, he would stop you at a word, and pin you to the ground as tightly as if you were nailed there."

No. 18.

"I do not mean to attempt it," cried Jasper, with a haughty toss of the head. "If I thought you meant to play me foul, I would trust to this," he concluded, producing one of his loaded pistols from his pocket.

Churleigh started, his sharp eye glittering like a diamond.

"I have a voice that would speak as quickly as yours, and more surely," he exclaimed, producing suddenly from a corner by the chimney, a very long pistol, magnificently mounted; "I can sight it as I fire, and never miss. An attempt to raise your pistol to an aim would find you with a hole in your carcase big enough to let out your life; so beware what you do."

"This is the return I get for doing you a service," said Jasper, after a moment's pause, resolving to defeat Churleigh, if possible, by sophistical argument.

"Doing me a service," cried Churleigh, with a bitter laugh.

"Yes," said Jasper, warmly. "You had everything in the shape of peace and anxiety to lose while the child lived, everything to gain in its death; who now is to know what has happened to Joan? Who can tell when you quit this place and move among the respectable citizens of some town, whether she was ever a mother, or whether she had a husband who died at sea, or anywhere else it might be convenient to mention? Who could know anything about her if you chose to keep your own secret?"

In this strain he went on, and found that Churleigh lent an attentive ear and seemed half convinced that he had acted for the best; he, therefore, pursued his advantage, painted the degradation of Joan's condition in the most exaggerated colours, and the security now there was against scandal of any sort, until at last Churleigh met all his views, and acknowledged that he considered the murder of the poor little child a good service, and even shook hands with Jasper. As he thanked him, Jasper laughed exultingly.

"I knew, when you understood the matter rightly, you would be glad," he said.

"So I am," said Churleigh; "but there's one thing I looked forward to, which was that she might grow up like her father, that I might see his face in hers and get a clue to him; and if I did, I would hunt him like a famished wolf until I had glutted myself with his blood." He growled out his bitterness with such vehemence that Jasper could have no mistake about the fate in store for him if Churleigh once discovered him to be the seducer of Joan, and, with a feeling approaching dread, he asked—

"Did Joan never disclose anything which could afford you the slightest clue to—to—the father of her child?" He hesitated in what form to put the last words.

"Not any," replied Churleigh. "She comes of a true breed, Jasper," he continued; "she would be torn piecemeal rather than betray by word or sign the fiend who ruined her. I'll have him in my grasp before I die. He was an ass as well as ruffian to desert her; he'll never light on such another, that could be so true to him as she has been and will be."

This was a theme which possessed anything but charms for Jasper, and, therefore, with a few more words respecting the assistance he was to have to get Florence again in his power, he bade him good night and departed. He lingered as Churleigh fastened the bars across the cottage door, said a few words to Grinder to keep him from making acquaintance with his throat, and then looked anxiously up at the window of Joan's chamber. It was closed; there was no light, and the most perfect stillness reigned around. He pressed his hat firmly over his brows, muttered something, and retracing his steps over the stones, he made the best of his way along the lane, until he reached the patch of trees. He was passing through them at an increased pace, when he felt a hand laid firmly upon his shoulder. He turned swiftly round—it was Joan! Her name fell from his lips; her white face and bright eyes looking almost unearthly in their brilliancy, startled him.

"How came you here?" he stammered.

"Do not speak to me, but hear me," she exclaimed, hardly able to pronounce distinctly the words she uttered, from intense excitement. Do not speak to me, for your voice sounds like a demon's in my ears."

"Joan, what means this?" he cried, hastily.

"Speak not," she half shrieked, pressing her fingers in her ears; "speak not—I will not hear a word from thee."

He shrugged his shoulders, and remained silent.

"Wretch!" she cried, speaking in her throat and compressing her teeth with violence together; "monster! base, remorseless, treacherous, heartless ruffian, hear the last words I shall ever utter in your ear. Hold! not a word," she cried, pointing her finger menacingly at him as he was about to speak, "dare not speak to ME—to me, villain, whom you have driven to the wildest despair God ever visited upon human being. You have confessed that your love for me was base artifice. You said you never loved until your heart was given to her whom you seek to destroy. Liar, miserable liar, have you not unasked called upon God to witness that you loved me truly and sincerely— that you never did and never could love another so devotedly as you did me, and yet you have made the boast that you cared for me so far only as I served the villanous purpose for which you sought me. Worthless hound! you caused my destruction. I was fool, weak idiot enough to believe there was truth in what you swore to me. I thought you little less than a god, I have found you worse than a demon—but though I should have scorned and loathed you, I could have forgiven you if you had spared my child."

"Joan!" interrupted Jasper, loudly, "Joan, hear me,"

"Liar! I will not listen to a word," she cried, with terrible energy. "I have been too fearfully deceived, too monstrously, infamously betrayed to credit even the most tremendous oath you could force through your lips. I have torn you from my heart; I would rend every fibre of it to shreds if I thought you still retained the smallest hold upon any part of it. I loathe you, wretch, loathe you, and hate you more fiercely than I loathe you. You have made me a wreck. I think what I might have been; I feel what I am; it is your work. Still, I might have forgiven this, and passed, unbidden, to my Maker's presence to forget my troubles, but by the death of my little babe, whose future happiness I had prayed to God to grant night and morning— though I never raised a prayer for myself—you have crushed my heart with an iron hand to powder. Ruthless, cold-blooded fiend! murderer of your own

child and mine, mark me! I am not mad, though your villany might have destroyed a stronger brain than mine; but I am not mad, and utter not a promise
I will not strive to go through with, whatever the result, so help me God! I
have been your victim: I have been the sufferer as yet. You, you villain,
have suffered nothing, but have even made my agony the subject of your
jests. What I have heard fall from your lips this night has made me swear
to live, though the misery of late years had made me resolve on death; but
I will not die, I will not quit you—ah! start and place your hand upon your
pistol, you dare not destroy me. I stand alone with you, I threaten you
—you dare not murder me as well as your child, for even then I would never
quit you; turn which way you would you should see me. In the dead of the
night, in the broad glare of day, in the twilight, the halls of the mirthful, in
the solitude of your chamber, or the mountain top, still should you see me.
And now, Jasper Chough, thou proud of birth, thou descendant of a noble
house, thou reckless murderer, BEWARE!—Beware of ME! There is not
a hope on which you may set your heart I will not frustrate. I will be ever
at your elbow, but you shall not see me: you shall feel that I [am at
hand, yet not know where to watch for my coming. You may bar your
chamber door, but in the dead of night I will glare upon you; from the
agony of frightful dreams my voice shall rouse you to a worse horror than
you suffer in your broken and disturbed sleep. Your schemes of villany
cunningly devised and artfully planned as they may be, shall still be to you
a source of dread anxiety and uncertainty, for you shall never know
the moment my hand will not stretch forth to sweep them away, and
leave you the prey of defeated hopes, of the racking torments of wild
despair. Turn where you will you shall feel that my eye is upon you, and
it shall make you tremble, whether you be alone or in the midst of ruffians
equal in villany to yourself. There is not the place under heaven where you
can go shall free you from my visitation. I will haunt you until I have
brought you to the grave; but your death shall not be sudden or soon; you
shall be murdered by inches; despair and horror shall wear you to a shred;
you shall flee from what you dare not meet, and yet not escape. Your death
shall be as terrible as your life; you shall die a thousand times in the fear of
what is to come; and, though the agony of suspense shall be frightful, it
shall not reach in its terror and torments the torture which shall tear and
rend your soul when you are hurled to perdition. Mark me! still Jasper
Chough, I will not tell my father the name of him who has crushed my happiness to dust, and made him wear a heart of molten lead, until a fitting
time; then, Jasper Chough, I will speak the words which shall set him on
your track like a starved tiger. He shall hunt you from place to place—he
will do it—you know and feel that he will; you will have to penetrate a
thousand disguises to discover him, and save yourself from destruction which
shall hover over you like a bird of prey over carrion. I will lead him on;
every path you take you shall find me before you to turn you despairingly to
seek another—"

" Damned croaking jezabel! I will stop your projects," roared Jasper, who
had cowered, and still did cower, beneath her stern, searching look, and im-

passioned words. "Do your worst if you escape this," so saying, in a paroxysm of rage, he drew a pistol from his pocket, and fired at her. She moved not an inch; when the report died away, her clear loud laugh, scornful, taunting, and bitter in every tone, rung in his ear; his rage redoubled, he discharged his second pistol at her, with an oath, with no better success than the first. At this moment the moon, which had been obscured by heavy clouds, slowly emerged, and a long stream of its cold green light pouring through an opening in the trees fell upon her, displaying every lineament of her face, and every particle of her dress. Her long black hair was streaming in the wind; her face, pale naturally, whiter now with the fearful excitement under which she laboured, looked a ghastly hue in the moonlight. She looked like a phantom, so deadly and lifeless was her aspect, save her fiery eyes, which flashed as they turned upon him, with an unearthly glare. She laughed again, but it was so cold and hollow it might have proceeded from a corpse; it made him shudder.

"It was the deed of one who rightly guessed your treachery to draw the teeth of your weapons, while you supped, miserable hound," she exclaimed slowly, with cutting irony; "but had they been crammed to the muzzle with bullets, the unsteady eye and wavering hand of a murderer like thee would have made my life secure." Then she raised her hand like lightning, pointing her finger at him as she saw he was about to spring upon her. "Stand back! advance not a step, ruffian, the time has not come for your death, or mine," she cried, with a tone which rung in his ears like the voice of fate, "or I have that with me which should end all between us ere another word could quit your lips or mine. You have struck the first blow—as you ever did— towards our future career. Away! you shall pray for a death you dare not take; you shall quiver with horrid expectation every hour you are awake; you shall writhe in agony every hour you sleep; you shall find the hand of friendship nowhere; the hatred of your kind following you while you exist. And now, thou heartless, kindless wretch, let my last words to thee be written in words of fire upon thy brain. I hate thee, hate thee with a bitter, vindictive, revengeful hate; I curse thee, and call upon the Almighty to hear and ratify my curse. May it cling to thee like a scorching flame, wither thee to the bone, eat into thy flesh, thy very marrow, so that it may make thee howl with its consuming torture; thy parents shall execrate the shedder of his brother's blood—my little child, the pure and innocent, shall rise up in judgment aganst the father who murdered it; you shall see it in your dreams, you shall think of it with agony, when thoughts fearful and paralysing crowd thick upon you. Jasper Chough, the curse of a broken heart is upon thee— escape if thou canst, and now look upon me, and say whether I am life or death! Look on me and answer."

Her words had chained him to the spot; they had rushed through his brain as if every single one had impressed itself with a heat that seared it; he had not the power to move, yet knew not why. He felt a cold crawling of horror steal over him, as if his blood was curdling into ice, as the bitter curse she cast on him entered his ears; and when she put the last extraordinary question to him, his every nerve thrilled with horror. His eyes fastened

on her face with a facination so powerful, though it created the most intense
pain, closely allied to terror, he could not withdraw them; her aspect was
most unearthly, her face and lips were ashy, her eyes, though they gleamed,
yet had a deadly look; her face had frightfully changed since he had seen
her in the cottage; her voice was so hollow, and her whole appearance in the
pale moonlight so spectral, coupled with the firm belief that he had entertained of her being in bed when he quitted the hut, that when she put the
startling question to him, a shock, most tremendous in its nature, shook his
frame, and he fell back several steps, with the conviction that he was conversing with, and had attempted to murder the spirit of her whose happiness he had so wantonly destroyed. Every nerve in his body quivered with
actual terror; a cold sweat broke out over him, his teeth chattered, his hair
slowly lifted up, and he stood trembling, the most abject wretch conceivable.
Her features, which were stern and rigid as though they were formed of marble, now broke into a smile of contempt; she advanced close to him: he had
not power to move, had she inflicted death upon him, and he aware she was
about to give the blow.

"I have asked thee that which thou canst not answer—which thou durst
not, nor shalt thou know until the last breath is speeding from thy body."
She placed her fingers upon his forehead, and he felt as if his brain had been
pierced with bolts of ice: he stired not; a power he could not define rivitted
him immoveably to the spot. "My curse is on thee," she exclaimed, "Go
thy way, murderer; turn where thou wilt it will cling to thee, and thou
shalt know no redemption but death—death, which shall be denied until thou
hast suffered the agony you have made me bear. Go, thou accursed! in
sickness and in health, in wealth and in poverty, in solitude and in crowds,
in the silence of the desert, in the roar of conflict, alone or amid multitudes,
my curse shall be on thy heart like a case of burning steel. Go! thou
shalt not find one thou canst trust, thou shalt not see a smile of kindness
turned upon thee, or hear a word of sympathy; the world shall spurn thee
as thou hast spurned its laws; in misery and hopeless despair thou shalt
wear out thy existence; the curse and torment of thyself as of others. Away!
I look in thine eyes and see my curse has begun its work—thy doom is fixed.
Go—think of me and dispair."

He felt her fingers leave his brow, when their icy coldness had changed to
a burning, such as liquid fire would have caused: he saw her recede, or rather
glide, noiselessly from him: his eyes grew dim, his brain reeled, his knees
would no longer support him, and with a heavy groan, he fell senscless upon
the ground.

When he recovered, the moon had sunk, the stars were shining brightly,
and the mountain reared itself like a huge dark mass against the sky. He
was some time ere he could remember how he came in the position in which
he had discovered himself, but at length it burst upon him with full force, and
he cast his eyes shudderingly around, expecting to see her start from behind
one of the trees by which he was surrounded, but it was a fear which he
soon found was a vain one. He stooped to pick up his hat, which had fallen
from him when he sunk into a state of insensibility, and in searching for it,

discovered his pistols: they were as they had fallen from his hands, with the pans open, as he had discharged them. He remembered then the purpose with which he had fired them, and felt glad that he had failed in executing his project, though in his heart he cursed her as heartily as she had done him; he returned them to his pockets, recovered his hat, and took his way up the mountain to his hiding-place. He felt sick and faint, and though naturally strong minded, there had been something so awful in his interview with Joan, that he could not divest himself of the apprehension that she was hovering about his footsteps, and would again appear to him ere he reached his abiding place. But once more he entered, and was unmolested; he cast himself upon the floor, and tried to rid himself of a strange sensation of loneliness which was upon him—a loneliness which seemed as if it would be broken by the entrance of some ghastly thing which would wither his sight. He essayed to sleep, but for a time it was denied to him, and every effort to shake off this terrible feeling was unsuccessful. As morning drew near, his mind wearied by the excitement of the past, sunk into sleep, but not to rest; for dreams the wildest and most horrible tormented him until nature herself sought relief in waking: he passed the day there, and in the evening, when the sun was down, and before the moon had risen, he heard a footstep without, and a private signal followed its approach; he opened the door, and Churleigh stood before him. Jasper had a strange misgiving when he saw him, and instinctively grasped the stock of one of his pistols; his had pondered the whole day upon what had passed between him and Joan, and he reflections were anything but of an agreeable nature; there was a stern, remorseless vindictiveness in Churleigh's disposition which he knew never was satisfied but with the blood of any one whom he imagined had deeply wronged him; and he had so often expressed the determination of having a terrific revenge upon Joan's betrayer if ever he crossed him, that Jasper could hope for no mercy when he discovered him,

Perhaps it may be as well here to state that the reason why the old man had no clue to him was that his visits were only paid during his absence, when there was never any one in the hut but Joan, and as the hovel itself had obtained an evil name, few ever approached it. When Jasper did, it was in disguise, and under a false name; thus Joan, having with immovable fidelity preserved her secret, Churleigh was unable even to imagine any one upon whom to fix as the author of her misery. Jasper had been to the hut so seldom when Churleigh was at home, and knowing as the old man did, that he was of a good family, it never entered his head that he could be the person; and he was therefore safe from his resentment. He had cajoled Joan to part with her infant to him, persuading her that it would be far better provided for when away; and pretending to have discovered the child by accident, to Churleigh, he wormed, with much address, out of him the story, effecting surprise and wonder at what he knew too well had happened, and in a frank, rough, but kindly manner, offered to take the child away and place it where it would be well taken care of. As the sight of the child was a sort of eyesore to the old man, he consented, and Jasper obtained possession of it; he was villain enough to dispose of it in the manner he had related to Churleigh' and felt no compunctious visitings of remorse at thus destroying his own off-spring, brought into the world through his baseness, but who, he fancied, might be in future times a troublesome remembrancer of the past.

When Churleigh entered, Jasper eyed him with a fear that Joan had revealed all, and had sought him for the purpose of putting into execution the vengeance he had so often sworn to inflict; but Churleigh, instead of using fierce looks or harsh words, stretched out his hand and shook Jasper's in a friendly manner, and seated himself upon one of the rough benches the place contained; there seemed a thoughtfulness, even a melancholy about him which Jasper noticed, and at once connected it with himself and Joan, and consequently did not like to mention it. There was a silence between them which continued a little while. Churleigh at length broke it—

"How does your scheme go on ?" he said.

"I have done little towards it," replied Jasper; "it rests principally on your shoulders."

"Well, let me know what it is that I have to do," said Churleigh, "and I will set about it at once."

"This is my scheme," exclaimed Jasper, almost with a sigh of relief as he perceived in Churleigh no indication of Joan's having betrayed him; "you must habit yourself in the dress of a common sailor, and hang about the hal until you get sight of one of the maids, a black-eyed girl, something of a smart merry cast, named Martha."

"Suppose I don't get sight of her for several hours ?" interrupted Churleigh.

"That's unlikely," returned Jasper; "but if you should not, ask for Martha Bell, and say you have news for her from the West Indies. She has a cousin, a sailor, a sweetheart, I think, who has gone there; that will bring her out—then tell her anything you like about the fellow you pretend to bring a message from."

"What's his name ?" asked Churleigh.

"I don't know," replied Jasper, impatiently; "but that, by a little management, you may easily obtain from her first, when you have managed that tell her to whisper in the ear of her young mistress that you have news for her from Lieutenant Prior."

"Who's he ?" asked Churleigh, abruptly.

"That's of no consequnce," said Jasper: "it is sufficient to unkennel her Name the grove of sycamores as the place to meet her; name to-morrow night for the time, and the hour, twelve—bid her come alone."

"But will she?" inquired Churlegh, with a laugh.

"Never doubt it," replied Jasper, returning his grin; "the news she expects to hear through you must be received in secret, she knows well enough—trust me, she will not fail. I will be there in readiness with the pony; we will gag her to drown any screams she may take a fancy to give, and see if we can't place twenty-miles between us and the Hall by six o'clock in the morning."

"Where do you purpose going, Geoffrey, when you have got so far?" asked Churleigh.

"I suppose it is a matter of indifferance to you," exclaimed Jasper.

"What do you mean by that sneer? cried Churleigh, rather fiercely.

"I meant it as no sneer," cried Jasper, quickly; "my only meaning was that if you did not particularly wish to know, I would not tell yon, because I wish no one, in case of accidents, to have a clue to the path I shall take when I quit you."

"Do you fear I should betray you?" asked Churleigh, looking fixedly at him.

"No, no," he hastily exclaimed, "you shall know all, if you wish it."

"No, never mind," retured Churleigh, "keep your intentions to yourself— it may perhaps be for the best; I care nothing about knowing. You have a dress here that will suit me—I'll take it with me to-night, and to-morrow afternoon I will put it on and masquerade for you. What do you mean to give me for my work?"

"What do you expect?" inquired Jasper.

"Its rather hazardous," mused Churleigh. "I think it's worth fifty guineas."

No. 19

"They shall be yours," exclaimed Jasper at once.

"It's a bargain then," said Churleigh; "now, if you will hand me over a little brandy, I'll thank you."

"With all my heart," answered Jasper; "but excuse me, I don't think it's the first time you've been drinking to day."

"No; nor I don't think it will be the last either." he replied, seizing the flask which Jasper tendered him, and drinking a long draught.

"What ails you, Churleigh?" asked Jasper, "you seem dull."

"And so I am—damnably in the dumps," he replied.

"What has happened?" inquired Jasper, looking earnestly at him.

"Quite enough, qnite enough to make me doubly so, if possible," he answered; "I ain't quite sure whether I ought to look on you as a friend or foe."

"What do you mean, Churleigh?" cried Jasper, hastily, not exactly liking the turn the conversation appeared to be taking.

"I mean that Joan has fled from the hut," cried Churleigh, with sudden vehemence; "fled from me! gone! gone!" he added, striking his knee with considerable force.

"Fled! gone!" echoed Jasper, with an alarmed countenance.

"Yes, gone from me! fled in the night, I suppose," exclaimed Churleigh, evidently suffering great anguish of mind.

"Where has she gone? What has become of her?" asked Jasper, not a little interested in the reply.

"How should I know?" roared Churleigh, passionately. "What a cursedly stupid question. Do you suppose, Geoffrey Smith, I should be such an old ass as to be sitting quietly in this den if I knew where she had gone? Have you turned fool?"

"When did you discover her flight?" he inquired anxiously, without replying to the sneer.

"Not till this morning, late this morning," he replied. "I drank more brandy, as ill luck would have it, last night than usual, and just because I ought to have been up before the lark, I slept till the sun had marked ten on the dial. I leaped out of bed, and dressing myself, sung out for Joan to row her for letting me lay so late, but she made no answer to my call. I searched the place around, every nook and cranny, but there was no trace of her. She's taken nothing with her, not a rag. There hang her things where she herself placed them, untouched. Nothing is missing but her; all the rest might have gone to hell if she had staid, but there they are, and she is gone."

The last word seemed to stick in his throat, he rested his head on his hand, and leaned his elbows upon his knees; his frame seemed convulsed with strong emotion, while Jasper, remembering all that had passed between him and Joan, was oppressed with a sense of dread, which made him tremble and think of the future with painful apprehensions. So strong was this sensation upon him that he was obliged to clear his throat before he could make his words audible, in saying to the old man—

"Can you form no idea what has become of her?"

"Yes," cried Churleigh, fiercely, and starting to his feet, "and it's that idea which makes me feel inclined to dig my fingers into your throat and twist the life out of you, it is."

Jasper sprung to his feet on hearing this, his guilty conscience always inducing him to believe Churleigh was aware of his villany to Joan; he clapped his hand to his pistol, as an exclamation burst from his lips, for the old man to explain his meaning.

"You shall have it," roared Churleigh, "you shall have it in full; it's my belief that the girl overheard you tell me the way you had disposed of her child, and in the misery of her heart, has flung herself into the lake—"

Jasper started—not with horror, but with a hope that it was so, until he heard Churleigh's rejoinder.

"Ay, you may start—you have cause; for if I find she has, by the discovery of her body, you shall follow in the same wake, I don't want to hear anything, and I won't; my mind's made up to that. You killed the babby without knowing or asking whether it would be agreeable, and you must take the consequences. I'll be revenged on somebody;" he added, with glowing eyes, and vehement gestures, "I'll not suffer all this misery without retaliating; if I can't on one, I will on another; so look you out, Geoffrey, if she's dead your life will be short."

"This is nonsense," exclaimed Jasper, warmly; "what I did was for the best, and you agreed last night it was; it's not my fault if she has made away with herself. How are you to know whether she did overhear what I told you, or whether she hadn't made up her mind to do it before? You didn't behave over kindly to her; girls will make slips; nature's nature, you should have remembered she had no female companions or mother to teach her right from wrong."

"She knew it without teaching," shouted Churleigh, passionately; "besides, she was taught—she had a lady's learning, aye, a fine lady's learning, but it wasn't that she was cozened by, some damned smooth-tongued hound—oh, if I should ever lay hands on him, if I ever should, I'll tear him limb from limb. I'll hack him to pieces; he shall pay for it with blood—with blood, though the next instant I walk to the gallows."

"But am I to be punished for his fault?" said Jasper, with an affected appeal to justice, though he shuddered at the bitter animosity which was conveyed in the words of the old man, which, working his hands convulsively, he ground through his teeth. "You have something to blame in your own harshness to her," he added.

"I know I have, I know it, I feel it," cried Churleigh, stricking his breast; "but don't you taunt me with it. I feel like a wolf; I thirst for blood; a word will bring my knife out. Don't tempt me."

Jasper shrugged his shoulders and remained silent. Churleigh paced up and down the cave for a few minutes, and then said abruptly—

"I've searched through the village for her, but have had no trace of her; I have wandered up the stream from its shallowest to its deepest part; I have walked round the lake, but without finding a sign of her I will go now and hunt round for miles; it may be some freak of her—she may yet come back."

"I hope she may," said Jasper, coolly uttering a lie; in his heart he hoped no tidings might ever be heard of her again.

"It will be all the better for you if she does," said Churleigh. Jasper thought differently, but said nothing. The old man continued, "let me have the disguise, and to-morrow at sunset I will meet you at my hut."

"No, no, not there," said Jasper, hastily.

"Why not?" asked Churleigh.

"Because—because I have something to do at Keswick," he returned, evasively. "I wil meet you in the glen, Sour Milk Gill, at sunset; it will suit me best."

"As you please," returned Churleigh. "I will be there."

Jasper then gave him the dress of a common sailor, from the chest which had contained the disguise he then wore, and the old man with another deep draught of brandy, quitted him.

The next evening, at the time appointed, Jasper not having once quitted his hiding-place since Churleigh left him, made for Sour Milk Gill, a glen down which a stream, flowing from Easdale Tarn falls, and from the whiteness of its water has obtained its singular appellation.   When he reached it, he found Churleigh waiting for him, looking, in his disguise, as much an old weather-beaten tar as any in the service.   His intelligence was not altogether satisfactory, for he had ascertained that Florence was too ill to leave her chamber; it was impossible, therefore, to put the scheme into execution, and it was necessarily deferred for a few days until her restoration to health should give the opportunity for its accomplishment. Jasper was annoyed and vexed—time was everything to him; but he had no alternative—wait he must. There were still no tidings of his brother Frank, and that was a source of uneasiness to him; but Churleigh, with some glee, told him he had news of Joan.   The darkness of the place prevented the old man perceiving the change in Jasper's features as he mentioned this, or he might have entertained some suspicion which would have rendered his situation embarassing. The old man pulled forth a piece of paper.

"I found this upon the table," he said, "when I went home after leaving you; it is Joan's handwriting.   The words are few, but they have made me more satisfied, though I don't exactly understand what she means.   Read it, see if you can make it out."

"The place is too dark," replied Jasper, straining his eyes to decipher the writing, most anxious to know its contents.

"Never mind, I can tell you," replied the old man, taking the paper from his hand, "for I have read it again and again, until I know every word. She says, " Dear father, be not uneasy at my sudden absence; I am safe. I have quitted your roof to carry out a determination I have sworn to fulfil. My motive is just, and I will accomplish it, or perish in the effort. You shall see me soon. I shall be always near you. Let no consideration for me keep you in the hut. I repeat, I am safe, and you can perform your duties as usual. God bless you!' That's all, but its enough for me.   I don't know how the paper got there—it was not there when I went out. The fastenings were untouched when I went back, yet there it lay; it doesn't matter how it come so that it did come."

Thus the whole of the intelligence Churleigh had to communicate was dis" satisfactory, though Jasper dared not shew that he felt it so; he, however, pursued the conversation but little further, and making an agreement to meet in the same spot, at the same hour on the fourth evening from that time, they separated.

Jasper that evening quitted Grasmere, and did not return until the sun was fast declining on the appointed evening for the execution of his villanous project. Upon reaching Sour Milk Gill he found Churleigh had not arrived; he waited impatiently for some time, imagining the worst, tormenting himself with a thousand apprehensions, a fear of Churleigh's vengeance being the greatest. He devised numberless schemes to murder him, and thus rid himself of an anxiety which gnawed upon his heart as if 'it would eat its way through and destroy it. In the midst of one of these speculations Churleigh arrived.

" What success?" cried Jasper, impatiently.

" The best," returned Churleigh, with a laugh. " I run foul of the maid servant by accident, and quickly found out her lover's name—one John Andrews. I thought the girl would have kissed me when I told her I had brought tidings of him."

" You gave her the message to Florence ?" interrupted Jasper, anxiously.

" I did," he replied.

" And what said she ?" he demanded, rapidly.

" Give me a little breath," cried Churleigh, and stopped 'to wipe the perspiration from his brow. " I've walked fast," he said.

" Yes, yes, I see," exclaimed Jasper, and continued urgently, " what said Florence to the message ?"

" You shall hear," answered Churleigh. " The girl bore the message to her mistress, and was not long before she brought me back word that she would be at the place appointed, and alone."

" Then she shall be mine," cried Jasper, with a loud laugh of triumph, "and this time she shall not escape me."

A slight laugh followed his words. He turned quickly to Churleigh, and said, rather sternly—

" Why do you laugh ?"

" I laugh !" cried Churleigh, with surprise—" I laughed not : I thought it was you who laughed."

" We are overheard—there is a spy upon us," almost shouted Jasper.

" If there is, let him say his prayers," cried Churleigh, and proceeded to search the place around: but though he and Jasper scrutinized every spot closely, no one was discovered by them, and concluding it must be fancy, they gave up the search, and separated to meet again at midnight.

Florence, in the mean time, almost recovered in body from the shock she had received, though melancholy in mind at the loss of Frank, and witnessing the grief into which his parents had been plunged, was, by the message which Martha Bell had brought her, plunged into the deepest agitation. News of Eustace Prior was the dearest wish of her heart, and all that she had recently undergone, was forgotten in that one delightful anticipation; she had readily fallen into the trap which had been set for her, and was too happy at the thoughts of knowing something, however little, of one whom she dearly loved, to hesitate for a second in acquiescing to this clandestine meeting. She knew her aunt, as she believed Mistress Chough to be, had been set against him, and had been forbidden to suffer her receiving any communication from him through any channel; therefore she was compelled to indulge in this secret mode of getting information, or go without it, which, gentle as she was, there would have been some trouble to make her. Every hour was passed by her with an impatient longing for its departure; every moment was counted anxiously, making the time appear long and dreary, and midnight seem as though it never would arrive. The better to manage quitting the Hall at the time she had appointed to meet Churleigh, she had taken her station in a small chamber upon what might have been termed the ground floor, for it was raised but a few feet above it, the flooring forming a portion of the roof of a range of kitchens which were beneath. It was a favourite apartment of her's, because it was small, compact, secluded, and possessed a full view of a garden well stocked with flowers, and, by the care of an old gardener, kept in the best order. She stood at the open window watching the rising of the moon, and almost praying for the hour of twelve to come. She was attended by Martha Bell, who perceiving the agitation of her young mistress, sought to dispel it by talking to her. If talking could have accomplished it, Martha would not have had cause to complain of a want of success; she chattered incessantly, and as she knew that love matters were the principal cause of the excitement Florence displayed, she thought she could not do better than enlarge upon the topic; she fancied, too, the opportunity was so good she should be neglecting her duty if she did not take advantage and make the most of it. The same man—one and the same man—had brought her and her mistress news of their lovers; for Churleigh, the more to interest the romantic mind of the girl in her mistress's behalf, had told her that Mr. Prior was her lover, and unconsciously told her truth—and only to think they were both sailors! It was very droll, to be sure, but wasn't it delightful? So Martha thought; and in the full career of chattering, she did not hesitate to say so, at the same time giving a history of all the lovers she had ever had, from the time she toddled about at the age of five, when it was her fortune to be blest with a little curly, white-headed, ragged-tailed little clod, no bigger than herself, up to the present specimen of a sweetheart, by name John Andrew, and in everything else a duck. Whether she was a goose for thinking so was her affair; she had no suspicion, at least, that she was. She had gabbled and chattered, rattled and tattled on without stopping, not in the least tired; on the contrary, quite fresh, with an immense stock still on hand to dispose of, for she had only arrived at the dismissal of the swains previous to her first interview with the aforesaid John Andrew, clearing them away "at one fell swoop" with the declaration that she cared "nothin' for none of 'em;" she did not stop to see whether Florence attended to her—in truth, she had not heard a word, for her thoughts were upon him who was far away—from whom she had been separated by force, and of whom she so shortly expected to hear. Martha, however, unconscious of this, paused not but to clear her voice, which had got a little husky with constant exercise: that being done, she went on full sail again, chattering away at a furious rate, until she suddenly stopped short, and with a face pale as death, pointed to something in the shadow of a clump of trees in the garden, and cried—

" Gracious heavens, Miss! what's that ?"

" What !" exclaimed Florence, startled out of her reverie by her abrupt question.

" That, Miss! there, there !" she cried; "do you not see ?"

" See what ?" inquired Florence, moved by the alarm Martha displayed.

"Look there, Miss, in the shadow of those trees to the right there," she cried, affrightedly pointing to the same spot as before. " There, don't you see it now ? it's a ghost, Miss—a ghost. Oh, Lord have mercy upon us. 'Our father which art—"

" Hush, you foolish girl," exclaimed Florence, half frightened herself; " it's but a reflection of the moon upon the trees.''

" Oh, no, Miss! oh, no! only look at it ?" she groaned, clasping her hands together.

" Mercy upon us !" cried Florence, in accents of terror as she gazed attentively ; " it is a figure—it is the figure of a woman."

" It is a ghost, Miss! it's a ghost," half shrieked Martha, " somebody's been murdered there, and that's the ghost. Oh, lord : it's coming towards us. Oh, lord save us. Lighten our darkness—"

Overcome by horror she buried her face in her hands, and sunk upon her knees. At the same moment the figure which had given them so much fright advanced rapidly, until it stood beneath the window. Though equally affected by fear, Florence did not, like Martha, sink upon the ground, but stood rooted to the spot until she heard the voice of the woman break upon her ear, and then in a great degree her apprehensions vanished.

" You have an appointment at midnight," exclaimed the woman in low tones, but earnestly ; it is in vain to deny it, I know you have !" she exclaimed impetuously; and then continued, in milder, but sad tones, as she saw Florence shrink back, " be not alarmed at me—I will not harm you—I am your friend. Now mark my words! as you value the heart of him you love—as you value your own honour and happiness here and hereafter, keep not this appointment." She was suddenly interrupted by footsteps, which sounded as if advancing, she turned her head quickly in the direction, and paused, then exclaimed rapidly and with singular energy, " obey the warning if you would not be driven to despair and madness.

The next moment she glided round the house and disappeared ; the footsteps which had caused the interruption also ceased, and then all was silent again. After a minute's lapse Martha lifted her head up gently and glanced terrifiedly round; she then rose, and drawing near to Florence, she whispered with a shudder—

"Is she gone?"

"She is, Martha," replied Florence, breaking from a fit of musing into which the woman's singular warning had thrown her. "Did you hear what she said?" she inquired, a little sternly.

"Oh no, Miss, I put my fingers in my ears, and covered up my eyes, that I did," returned the girl, still trembling; "oh dear! Miss Florence, I can't a-bear ghosts, that I can't; only to think I should have seen one—ugh?" A cold shudder ran through her as she spoke.

"It was no ghost, Martha," exclaimed Florence, gravely, "and I am afraid that you know it was not; she spoke of my appointment to-night, which unless you have disclosed it to some one, she could not have known—"

"Miss—I—Lord, Miss Florence!" interrupted the girl in undisguised astonishment.

"It must be so," said Florence, "therefore do not add to your unkindness, not to say your deceit, by denying it, you have told my aunt or uncle, and they have invented this to prevent my going : you are a cruel girl, Martha, very cruel. I thought you were kind and attached to me, but I find you are like the rest, and do what you can to make me weary of my life."

"Dont'ee say that, Miss—dont'ee, dont'ee, dear Florence," cried Martha bursting into a paroxysm of tears. "I love you better than my own sister, that I do, and would sooner die than betray you. I haven't said a word, Miss, I'll give you my oath, to a living soul but you, as I hope to go to heaven when I die—and I wouldn't, though old master and missus went down on their knees to me, or stood over me with knives to cut me into slivers, that I wouldn't. Dont'ee say I be ungrateful and cruel to you, Miss: you'll break my heart, Miss, if you do, that you will. Dont'ee say I'm deceitful, Miss, I'd tear my heart out rather than deceive you, that I would. I'd do anything for you, Miss, I'd follow you anywhere, over sea even: I'd give up all the world for you, even John An—an—an—drew—Mi—Mi—Miss—and—all—that I would, only dont'ee say I'm un—un—gra—ate—ful—and—and cruel, and—and de—de—ce—eit—ful—dont'ee—do—o—o—o—"

Her crying became sobbing, and her sobbing was fast merging into something little short of a howl; Florence, therefore, thought it time to put a stop to it—she placed her hand kindly upon her neck, and said, gently—

"Don't cry so, Martha, there's a good girl. Hush! you will alarm the house. I believe you are faithful, and very kind and good; there, there, dry your tears—I am sorry I doubted you, and beg your pardon for it."

"Dont'ee beg my pardon, Miss—" exclaimed Martha, still sobbing.

"Hush! Martha," said Florence, placing her hand upon her lips, " we shall have my aunt coming to know what we are about here, if you cry so loud. I believe you have not told any one but me, so wipe your eyes and answer me as quietly as you can. When the sailor who gave you the message to me was talking to you, do you think any one overheard you?"

"No, Miss, not a soul," replied Martha, drying her eyes, and giving one or two quivering sighs by way of a wind up to her fit of weeping; "I'm

sure they didn't, for the sailor looked about as well as I, but nobody was about."

"It is very strange," murmured Florence; "the woman was evidently acquainted with the proposed meeting, and if she did not overhear, she must have been told, and then who could have told her? Can the sailor be false?"

"Not he, Miss," said Martha, quickly, "oh, no, he didn't look like a man who would try to deceive a girl; he was tall and dark, and rather glumpy; he frowned when he smiled; he wasn't a bit like John Andrew, not a morsel, for he was very ugly. Ah! but then I know why John Andrew sent the likes of him—"

"Why?" asked Florence, rather earnestly.

"Because he knew there was no chance of my falling in love with him; he

No. 20.

wouldn't send a handsome one, because he feared it might be dangerous— ha, ha, ha!" She laughed with much glee as she said this; and then checking herself, repeated in tones of great fondness, "but he needn't have feared that—no, no; for I should never love anybody else, even if he had sent to me the Pope of Rome, who, Mary Flannigan, the Irish dairy-maid, says is the loveliest and beautifulest of all the men on earth."

Florence turned away with disappointment, before Martha had half concluded her speech, and pondered upon the singular warning she had received. The strange energy the woman had displayed, her impassioned gestures, and the strong language which she had used, made a strong impression on her mind, and led her to believe that there might be truth in it; still, what had she to fear in meeting the sailor—probably a simple unsophisticated man— in all likelihood the same she had before seen in London, and whom she knew was devoted to Eustace Prior, he would himself defend her in case of danger from Jasper. And there was, too, the stranger who had rescued her; he had told her to rest there without fear, for there would always be a friend watching over her there, until her destiny changed, and caused her removal. In what way, then, could simply meeting a faithful, honest, though humble man, to learn tidings she would peril life itself to gain, of one she cherished in her heart of hearts as the " dearest, best, and brightest," drive her to madness and despair. Yet the woman's soul seemed poured forth in those words—she wrung her hands convulsively as she uttered them, and spoke as imploringly, as if begging for her own life. There was something very mysterious, look at it in what light she would; and her spirits were affected by it, more than even she liked to acknowledge to herself. Several times she resolved not to keep the appointment, and even told Martha as much, bidding her meet the sailor, and appoint the morning or the afternoon of the following day; but Martha told her the sailor had particularly stated midnight to be the only time he could see her, that he left Grasmere before daybreak. and if she did not come at the time appointed, she could neither see him afterwards, or learn what he had to communicate; and after some little further speculation upon the matter, she determined upon keeping it. To hear of Eustace, to know where he was, to know that he was well, and still kept her in his heart as she kept him, pure and bright as ever—to be able to send him word she was unchanged, and would never change, come what might, was to her of vital importance, was worthy of any hazard; it would be a source of joy, that for a long weary time had been denied to her, and she could not forego the chance of obtaining it, because a woman, of whom she knew nothing, had warned her in words which she could see little prospect of being prophetic if she disobeyed them. Her prejudices were upon the side of disobedience to the warning, and therefore, after the first surprise was over, she resolved to go, let the consequences be what they might, although she would not entirely despise the caution. It had been the sailor's express command that she should come alone to meet him; it was not her intention to disobey him, there being, as she thought, scarcely a necessity, as the distance of the meeting place was so short, that in case of any violence, which the woman's words seemed to prognosticate, her voice could easily be heard by the inmates of the Hall, and assistance rendered immediately; however, she bade Martha follow her a few minutes after her departure, and creep unseen as near to her as she could, that her voice and aid might be added to any required demand for assistance. While making these arrangements, the clock chimed three quarters after eleven; all the inhabitants, save themselves, had retired to slumber, and Florence, now with sick anxiety, awaited the hour of midnight, to receive the promised and so much desired communication.

The hour at length arrived, the last stroke of twelve was struck, and repeating her commands to Martha, Florence, with a beating heart, prepared to quit the Hall for the Grove of Sycamores. She drew a scarf hastily over her head, and pressing Martha's hand, set out. She trod noiselessly; as she walked swiftly along, she felt the cold night air play upon her face, and she shivered with it and a little apprehension which she could not define. A stillness so great prevailed, that of itself it lent something of a fearfulness to the scene, and she could not help turning her head nervously right and left, as she advanced, affected by some strange idea, that in each of the little coverts she was passing, lurked some unknown enemy. She, however reached the Grove of Sycamores unmolested, and as she entered it, and proceeded along it, she started, and almost screamed as she came suddenly upon Churleigh, in the garb of the foremost man, reclining thoughtfully against the trunk of the tree. He instantly changed his attitude as he perceived her, and said, quickly—

"Don't fear, it's all right, Miss; you keep your time well."

"You come from Mr. Prior," she exclaimed, quickly, yet timidly; "is not your name Gasket?"

"Not Gasket, but Grab'em," he said, with a slight laugh.

At the same instant a cloak was thrown over her head, and drawn tightly round, almost enough to suffocate her, and quite sufficient to smother any cries she might have made. She was lifted from the ground, placed upon the back of a small horse, and held firmly on; she felt the horse impelled suddenly forward, and with fright and agony became almost insensible.

Martha, after waiting a few minutes, followed her young mistress's directions, and crept very cautiously in the direction which she had taken, and when she had reached as far as she thought she dared without being discovered, she ensconced herself beneath a bush, and waited patiently, until she should hear her mistress's footsteps returning. She soon began to direct her thoughts to her lover, little thinking the perils he had undergone during his absence— and as one thought brought another, she became speedily lost in thought; nor was this the worst, for having risen at daybreak, the preceding morning, the late hours rendered her drowsy; the quiet and pleasing character of her thoughts assisted the workings of nature, and before she had been in her hiding-place half an hour, she was fast asleep, and filled the Grove with the mournful cadences which her nose, under the influence of strong slumber, poured forth. Here she remained until between two and three in the morning, when in the very heart of a dream she believed herself swimming with John Andrew "in a wide, wide sea;" the water was intolerably cold, she fancied, and John Andrew, in a spirit of mischief, must needs fit her arm

with a bracelet of ice—the intense coldness went to the bone, and she awoke
The first things her eyes caught sight of were the stars and sky, and though
awake, she still believed the swimming to continue, until the increasing coldness on her wrist and arm made her lift it up, for it had dropped beside her
and there she found a snake coiled round it; it was a harmless field snake,
but she thought not of that; she screamed, and with desperate action, dragged
it from her arm, flung it away, and sprung to her feet. She gazed affrightedly
round her, and pressing her hands over her eyes, tried to collect her senses;
in a minute she remembered all—she rushed hastily through the Grove, but
her mistress was nowhere to be seen. She retraced her steps, fancying
Florence must have returned, and was perhaps waiting her return in the
chamber in which they had sat during the evening; she flew to it, it was
empty—everything remained as she had left it. She sought her sleeping
apartment—it was in a like condition, nothing was disturbed, but she was not
there. Once more she returned to the Grove, half distracted, almost calling
down curses upon her head, for suffering sleep to get the better of her. It
was in vain that she searched every nook and corner, that she visited every
part of the garden, and left no spot unexplored. The poor girl

> " Sought wildly, but found her not."

Her mind was crowded with apprehensions the most vague, but wildest; she
was half choked with emotion, she wrung her hands, and burst in a passion
of tears.

" Miss Florence !" she screamed out, " Miss Florence ! dear Miss Florence !
Where are you?—where are you? Speak, for God's sake ! Miss—speak—
speak." She literally shrieked the last words, and while calling, she felt her
hand grasped; suddenly she turned round—it was the woman who had uttered the warning to Florence, and whom she had fervently believed to be a
ghost. She screamed louder than ever, on discovering who had hold of
her, and sunk upon her knees, almost insensible from fright.

" Did your mistress keep the appointment ?" exclaimed the woman in
strong stern tones, bending her mouth to the ear of the terrified girl.

" She did ! she did ! Oh, what has become of her !" gasped forth Martha.

" God help her—then she is lost !" exclaimed the woman, and releasing
the girl's hand dashed among trees and disappeared.

Martha redoubled her screams, went into hysterics, and fell her full length
fainting upon the ground. Her shrieks, however, alarmed the inmates of
the Hall, and the servants, half-dressed, hastened to the spot, and they were
soon followed by Squire Chough. Martha was raised from the ground and
carried into the Hall by the surprised servants, and means used to recover
her; it was long, however, before they were successful, but when they were,
and obtained from her the cause of her having been found in the condition
in which they discovered her, it was to be filled with fresh alarm. The
squire was nearly mad on learning the loss of Florence; he despatched the
men in all directions, bidding them arouse others to assist them in the search,
and offering a handsome reward to the first who brought tidings of her.

The men hastened away, and, before the sun rose there were between twenty and thirty of them stretching over the country round Grasmere, in strict search.

Florence, during this time, had been hurried forward at a rapid pace. A mile was passed over before the cloak which covered her head and shoulders was removed, and then her death-like stillness induced Churleigh to uncover her, though he had his huge hand ready to place over her mouth if she screamed; but she was in a swoon, and would never have awakened from it again if the cloak had remained much longer wrapped round her head; with the aid of some brandy and the cool night air she was restored. At the first tokens of returning animation, the pace of the horse, which had been slackened, was increased, and again they pushed forward rapidly. It was some time before Florence could properly understand her situation, but when her eyes lighted upon Jasper, who was leading the pony by his head, she saw at once she had been made the victim of a base stratagem; she shrieked wildly, and tried to fling herself from the horse to the ground, but she was held by Churleigh as if in a vice; he covered her mouth with his hand, and said in a harsh gruff voice—

" You had better keep quiet—it's no good making a hubbub, for you can't get away; there isn't a soul but us within five miles of you, and if there was, they're too fond of their bread and butter to interfere. Keep still—take my advice; you've no help for your situation, so make up your mind to it, and be happy and comfortable.''

Florence wrung her hands appealingly, despairingly, but it was to those who had hearts harder than stone—to those who could only feel for themselves without caring a jot what misery happened to others; several times she essayed to speak, but Churleigh would not remove his hand, and half stifled, with a heart bursting with grief and agony, she ceased her efforts, and remained passive. They proceeded some distance in silence; at length Jasper muttered a few words to Churleigh, and he replied—

" She would be better if the cloak was over her shoulders; she shivers and trembles with the cold dew, like one with the ague, and her hair is quite wet. Hadn't you better tie on the hat as well ?''

Jasper muttered as if afraid of suffering his voice to be heard, and Churleigh favoured him with an oath, requesting to know why he swallowed his words in that fashion, and surmising at the same time, that if he spoke as usual, he, Churleigh, must be deaf—only he used a very strong adjective to expresss the amount of deafness, which it is not thought necessary here to give. Jasper uttered a hearty pshaw! and repeated his words, at the same time stopping the pony and unstrapping a small bundle which had been buckled on the hind quarters of the horse; he drew forth a straw hat, such as is usually worn by the peasantry, and passed it to Churleigh, who, before he took it, said to Florence—

" If you want to be well treated you must keep your tongue still; a scream from you may bring you anything but help, so be warned. We can be very tender, but if you provoke us we can be uncommon rough."

He concluded his speech by slowly withdrawing his hand from her mouth, and prepared with force to replace it if she disobeyed his injunction ; but she, poor girl, felt herself so utterly helpless that she merely drooped her head silently, and uttered a deep sigh of anguish. Churleigh waited a moment to see whether she would follow his advice, and finding that she did, commended her prudence with an oath. Jasper gave him the hat, and he placed it on her head, bidding her tie the strings under her chin ; she obeyed him, and then, with the assistance of Jasper, the cloak was fastened round her, and she could not but feel a slight addition of comfort in the warmth it communicated, althongh her mind was in a great degree reduced to a despairing recklessness of whatever might injure her frame in the grief she felt at her abstraction. Again they proceeded, and the pony was urged almost to a trot.

"I wonder you didn't have a couple of horses, and make the most of your time," growled Churleigh, a little out of breath, and waxing warm, after he had traversed a couple of miles, subsequent to habiting Florence in the cloak and hat. "I wonder you, the cunning, long-sighted Geoffrey Smith, who can see further than most people, who have telescopes instead of eyes, didn't think of that."

He laughed at his own wit, as he esteemed it, although he was getting out of a temper, not the least too amiable at the best of times, because of his long walk, for he thought every now and then of the going back, which multiplied every mile into two. Jasper bit his lip at the sneer, and returned, in a tone twice as bitter, if it were possihle—

"It is because I can see farther than your would-be sharp-sighted friends' that I have not done as you fancy I ought. If I had been as blind as them or you, I should have done what you seem to think the best plan in the world, and have left a wide track for the greatest dunderhead in Grasmere to follow on my heels. No, in these disguises, and taking the most unfrequented paths, I shall make my way to a place, where all identity will be lost, and those in pursuit will never think of asking for two persons dressed and travelling in the manner which I and my companion are."

Churleigh conld not but confess that Jasper stood a better chance of success by pnrsuing the plan he had adopted ; but he did not like the terms in which the detail was couched, and would not, therefore, assent to it,

" Ah, you may think it very snug," he said, curling his upper lip.

" I dare say you do, remarakably cunning—but, if had to track you, I'd scent you out, for all your deep contrivance."

"But it isn't every one who is so sharp on a scent as you," replied Jasper, sneeringly ; it wouldn't do ; the world would be at an end if they were. I wonder you are not employed to find foxes when they've stole away ; you could, I am sure."

" Yes," roared Churleigh, and, " and bite if any one throws me out—will you try it ?"

Jasper instantly declined, and turned the conversation with a laugh. He knew he was in no condition to play with edge tools at that time, and Churleigh was one of the sharpest he knew ; he, therefore, prudently conciliated him, and thus they proceeded, until about four in the morning ; and then arriving at a broad piece of moor land, which extended three or four miles in length, Jasper stopped, and told Churleigh he would now release him from accompany him further. He gave him ten guineas, promising the remaining forty when next they met, an appointment for which was made then and there. Florence had the reins placed in her hands, and was bid keep her seat; Jasper still kept at the head of the pony to lead him, and shaking hands with Churleigh, they parted. Churleigh started swiftly on his way back pausing at one spot to watch Jasper and his prisoner across the moor, to note the direction they took, and remained until he was sure of it, and then proceeded on his way to Grasmere.

Jasper continued his progress across the moor, until he had passed it. He then turned down a narrow path without speaking, at rather a slower pace than he had used while Churleigh was in his company, but displayed great care in directing the progress of the pony, seeing that it did not stumble, and keeping it where the ruggedness of the road was not great enough to tire it before it reached the distance he had meditated upon gaining ere he rested nd fed it. He had not as yet addressed a single word to Florence; he had never once raised his eyes to her face; he could not, he knew not why—he knew only that he was unable to meet her gaze, and he studiously avoided it.

There was some strange alteration in him; he was not the same boisterous, reckless, rude being he had been but a few days since. Then he was apparently without feelings but such as his passions dictated; was uncouth, harsh, and quite careless, in his rough behaviour and speech, whether he offended or not. Now he was sullen and stern, silent where he had been noisy, and gloomy where he would have uttered coarse jests and unlicensed ribaldry. His face was pale and haggard; his eyes appeared red, and exhibited an appearance of restlessness and perturbed anxiety of mind; his brows hung over his eyelids in a perpetual frown; his teeth were set, and he glanced uneasily around him at every step he took. There was not a recess in the lane in deep shadow which he did not peer down. There was not a spot which could have formed a hiding-place he did not dart his eye into and penetrate its farthest corner, nor seemed satisfied until he had passed it without any person starting from it. Nervously did he ever and anon look back to see whether he was followed, and uttered what was little less than a sigh of relief when he perceived there was not a living thing save themselves and a few birds in sight. At length the lane terminated in a coach road extending both ways a considerable distance; its broad dusty path looking as though a wide roll of canvas had been extended along a carpet of green. This Jasper pursued until he came upon a plantation of firs, then he led the pony from the road, pushed open a long cross-barred gate, green with moss and age, and wound his way among the trees. The plantation extended some miles, and he seemed as if he intended to pass it before he stopped. Three miles had been left behind and their progress was uninterrupted. At last Jasper stopped; it was a wider opening than any he had seen, and he determined to make it the first resting-place. He satisfied himself that there was no one in the vicinity, and then he lifted Florence from the saddle. She

shuddered as he touched her—he felt that she did, but he made no remark.
He seated her upon a small knoll beneath a tree, and then stripped the
pony of the best part of the harness, rubbed him down, led him to drink at
a little brook which meandered through the plantation, and then turned him
to feed upon the grass. When he had completed this labour he took a
basket which he had brought with him, which was stored with a cold fowl,
ham, a bottle of sherry, and some bread. He brought these forth and
spread them on a cloth before Florence; he carved the fowl, placing the
choicest pieces in a small plate before her; he poured out some sherry into
a horn and offered it to her: without speaking she turned away; he took
the plate and placed it upon her knees—she laid it upon the cloth again. As
yet he had never raised his eyes to hers, nor trusted his tongue to speak a
word; he did not again offer the fowl, or the wine, but busied himself in
making a meal, apparently quite unaffected by her refusal; he took up the
horn containing the sherry, and flung the wine out of it, but drew a flask of
brandy from his pocket and filled the horn to the brim with it. He drank
half its contents at a draught, and before he finished his breakfast, he swol-
lowed the remainder. Once more he took a survey of the spot, searched as
if expecting to find some one concealed; but his search was not rewarded by
such a discovery, and, seemingly satisfied, he seated himself by the side of
Florence. He drew from his pocket a brace of pistols, examined the priming,
put a little fresh powder to them, closed the pans and restored them to his
pockets, and then laid himself back at full length. In this position he remained, between sleeping a waking, for about a couple of hours; then he
arose, harnessed the pony, gathered up the food and wine, and when all was
ready for departure he took Florence by the arm to lead her to the pony.
She refused to move, and clung to the tree; she did not speak, but there was
a convulsive agony of mind in her actions: it was disregarded by Jasper, he
seized her by the waist, dragged her from the tree, and lifted her in his arms
as if she had been a child. He carried her to the pony, placed her upon its
back, and for her own safety she was compelled to keep her seat, for he set
the beast in motion instantly. In all this he had not uttered a word; he
was afraid to trust his own voice; he asked himself, why—although he knew
too well, and he dreaded to think of an answer. What an abject wretch his
villany had made him even in his own eyes.

The day passed on, beautiful as nature could make it, but what a long,
miserable one to her. Once or twice during their progress he had offered
food to her, but she had silently rejected it. He made no comment, save to
utter an oath; but he pursued his plan of taking the most unfrequented paths
and by-roads, and had met no one save a little girl about twelve years old,
with a round red face, blue eyes, and nearly white hair, who stood and gazed
upon them with her hands behind her, until they were out sight, and then
ran home to tell what she had seen to her mother, who lived in a hut, stuck
in a corner where none but the man who built it would ever dream of
putting a cottage. Six o'clock in the evening came and found them still advancing, all very weary, the little pony not less tired than either of them.
They had reached a wide common—the sun was fast declining towards the

horizon, and as Jasper noticed it, although very tired, he urged the little horse to a faster pace, and struck across by a small path evidently used only foot passengers; it was a very extensive common, and looked, in his eyes, twice its length; his only solace appeared to be swearing at it, which he did at every spot, giving the pony, who limped with fatigue, a blow every now and then to hurry it to a faster pace than ever he could manage to walk. At last the termination of the common was reached, just as the sun sunk behind the distant hills. A wind of the road brought them to a changed character of country—tall trees sprung up and displayed the entrance to a small wood. Jasper led the pony past a short row of wooden rails and turned into the roadway leading through the wood; he had hardly rounded the corner and reached the shadow of a tree, when a man started from a bush, where he lay concealed, and for a short time previously had been watching their approach, and placing himself before the pony, stopped him short. Jasper sprung back, evidently much startled at this sudden and unexpected interruption; but a second glance showing him that it was not the person he in the first moment of alarm took the stranger for, he threw off his apprehension and looked with anger upon the intruder.

No. 21

"You travels werry late," exclaimed the stranger, whose garb showed him to be a gipsey, which, however, if it had not, might have been shrewdly guessed by the sight of a fire, two or three persons round it, and a gipsey tent close at hand. "You travels late," repeated the gipsey, laying his hand upon the pony's nose.

"And what the devil's that to you, if I do?" roared Jasper, passionately knocking away his hand. "Stand out of the way, or I'll fling you out of it."

"Oh, to be sure!" replied the gipsey, with a laugh; "you're Jack the Giant Killer, ain't you?" and, as he concluded, he seized the bridle with one hand, and elevated a crabtree cudgel with the other, grasping it tightly as if ready for instant use.

"Will you stand back?" shouted Jasper, fiercely.

"Will you cut off my nob, and carry it at your girdle as a token of victory, if I don't?" inquired the gipsey, with an insulting laugh.

"I'll spoil your laughing, you prowling gipsey thief," roared Jasper, "if you block up my path. Stand out of my way!"

"Perhaps you'll give me a penny," exclaimed the gipsey, his brown face glowing like scarlet, with rage at Jasper's words; "perhaps," he continued, with a sarcastic grin, "you'll give me a knife or a lock of your hair before yon go, to show my mates that I have had the honour of talking to Jack the Giant Killer; or perhaps you won't go at all," he added, in cool stern tones, "until we thinks proper to let you, Mr. Swallow-the-devil."

"Wot's the row, Slender?" asked a big, shaggy-looking fellow, who had approached, unperceived. "Wot is the row? Is the gen'l'man afraid he sharnt find the way to his crib?"

"Here's Sin' Paul's out for a walk," retorted his companion, "and turning rayther rusty because he's axed a civil question," he added, with a grin.

"Look you, my dusky duffers," cried Jasper, not at all cowed by the accession of strength on the gipsey side, "my path lies straight before me—your place is by yon fire, to munch the fowls and mutton you've stolen to-day. You take your way, and let me take mine, or you may repent it."

"You don't want for gab, my fresh'un." exclaimed the second gipsey; "you're rayther fast—rayther fast; Slender, isn't he?"

"Rather too fast," replied the gipsey addressed, whose name fitted him well, seeing the ratio of bone was very unequal to the flesh on his person.

"Fast or slow, you will do well not to stop me," cried Jasper, exasperated at the delay; "I'm not a boy to be frightened by an ugly mazzard or two, and if you don't stand out of the way, curse me if I don't knock you out of it."

"Perhaps you'd like a round or two?" exclaimed Slender, proceeding to tuck up his cuffs; "here's plenty of room for a ring; I don't think you can lick me, and I think I can you, though you are rayther bigger than me—but I've pluck enough to try, any vay. So, if you'll drop your stick, I'll accommodate you with a customer; it's a little dusky, but the moon will soon be up, and then we shall see better."

"Do you think I'm an ass?" roared Jasper.

"Vy, if I must speak the truth," replied Slender, quickly, "you approches werry near that vay."

Jasper suddenly threw down his stick, and drawing from his pockets his brace of pistols, he pointed them at the two fellows, who no sooner saw them than, and heard the sharp quick click of their being put on full cock, than they gave ground precipitately. Jasper grinned as he saw it, and exclaimed—

"Now, you sneaking, pullet-stealing, hedge-robbing vagabonds, give back, or I'll stretch you on the ground with a hole in your skulls. Let me see the fellow that offers to stop me, and if I don't send a bullet through him may I be—"

He was stopped by a hand being placed on his shoulder; he stepped back a few paces instantly, so that no advantage could be taken of him, and found it was an old woman, one of the tribe, who had stolen round during the hubbub.

"Don't be so violent, my dear," she exclaimed in a carneying voice, "there is nobody who wishes to hurt a hair of your head; if we wished, you have the means of protecting yourself. Why not wait and rest yourself? you need it, I can see, and if you will cross—"

"To hell with you, you old cat!" shouted Jasper, in a tremendous rage, "stand aside all of you, for if you stop me further, I'll blow you all to—"

"Hold, hold!" cried the woman, sternly, "you'll do nothing of the sort. If you won't stop, here's one here who must; if you would not carry home a corpse with you."

Her words startled Jasper, more so when he perceived her pointing to Florence, and then, without waiting for a reply, she advanced to her, and laying hold of her hand, lifted it; it fell heavily upon the pommel of the saddle, yet she retained her seat firmly.

"She's in a fit," continued the old woman; "her limbs are cold and rigid; if she is not waked out of it, she will perish ere an hour passes over her head."

Jasper cast his eyes doubtingly towards Florence, not believing that the woman could speak truth, and at the same instant his arms were suddenly and violently pinioned from behind, two terrific blows delivered on the arms, near the wrists, so as to render them powerless, and cause the pistols to fall from his hands. Slender and his companion then sprung upon him, he was forced to the ground, his feet were bound together, and his arms likewise; he was gagged, and then he was set upright; in this condition he was dragged to the fire-side. Florence was lifted off, and delivered to the care of two young women, with handsome faces, much sunburnt, and black eyes, which, even in that dim light, looked brilliant. The old woman directed them what

to do, while she foraged in a tent for an infallible panacea of her own com-
position.   The means employed to restore Florence were simple and un-
tiringly persevered in until they proved successful; a cordial was then administered to her, which revived her wonderfully; she was then borne tenderly to a tent, and laid upon a rude bed; the old woman bade her not
speak, as she muttered something, told her she was with friends, and drawing the curtains which covered the opening of the tent together, left her, and
resumed her seat by the fire.

The men who had watched, without speaking, the efforts of the girls to
restore Florence, now that she had been attended to, turned to Jasper, and
poured upon him the most bitter jokes, the girls adding their share, until he
writhed with rage.

His defeat had been accomplished by two of the gang, who had suddenly
arrived from levying contribntions upon some neighbouring farms, and laden
with spoils, had come up in time to see that a commotion, perhaps not of
an unusual nature, was going on between Jasper and their comrades, by his
keeping them at bay with his pistols.   In the excitement of the moment
their return had been unnoticed, and taking advantage of it, they crept
steathily behind Jasper and captured him at the moment his attention, which
was done purposely by the old woman, was drawn to Florence.   His powerful frame and great strenght availed him nothing with four tough and wiry
foes, and in less time than he could have believed it possible, he was made a
prisoner—a proceeding which the gipseys would not probable have reached,
but for his insolent bravado and ſdetermined opposition to them, added to a
shrewd surmise that he was not playing fair with the maiden in his possession,
and if it was as they suspected, there would be gain for them in stone, either
by befriending her, or furthering his designs, an object which they could only
obtain by keeping them both prisoners.   While their jeers were at their full
height, a member of their community arrived; he was a tall, thin man,
elderly, stern-looking, with a face like his people's, brown as a nut.   No
sooner had he made his appearance than Slender sprung to his feet, and in a
voice which he made closely resemble that of a touter of a wild beast show
in a fair, he cried—

"Hoy! hoy! hoy! vork up heere, vork up heere.   The greatest vonder
hof the fair, and no mistake.   Now's your time, my friends—Those has the
tin, shell out and see a vonder as never vos ekalled alive or dead, afore the
vorld began or since.   Hi-agh! hi-age! hi-agh! vork up heere, you shall
see vot you shall see, and vot you don't see you sharnt tell nobody nuffin on.
Hee'ars the fire eater from Afriky—"

A burst of laughter from the gang followed this description of Jasper, and
Slender, elated with their applause, proceeded with renewed vigour.

" The fire eater! the fire-eater! tork of you Salamanders, vy, it's all my
hi to a dead carrot! Ven he hopens his mouth, fire comes out on it; his
vords is cannon-balls, and his speeches is bombshells, and his langvedge is
made up a rockets and bullets, and thunder, and blaze, and bust.   He's fust
cousin to the devil, as is vell known, and has resided for some time in his
little snug back parlour; and that, my customers, as you know, is vorm

enough to frizzle vot nothen else'll melt. He'll swallow red hot pokers, vill breakfast off vite hot flat irons, and 'as no objection to a little biling lead to quench his thust; he's rayther fond of melted steel, but hif he has a preference, it's for dinner off a smelting furnace; he has no disgust for tin, nor as any on us as I know on, so fork out your ochre and see this vonder of vonders. If you're cold the sight on him'll vorm you, for verehever he is, it's as hot as 'ell."

"What the devil are you kicking up this row about," interrupted the new comer, with a countenance stern and unrelaxed by what he had heard, while the rest were in a perfect ecstacy of delight.

"Poetry is vasted on you, Badger, I sees," excaimed Slender, with a little touch of the indignant; "you've himagination; look there," he added pointing to Jasper, who sat furious with rage by the fireside, "there's a firey serpent trussed. You never seed a Bengal tiger—a African—such a blessed hot 'un to meddle with; he'd made up his mind to swollow all of us at a mouthful, but ve'd rayther not—and so ve packed him up and put him by the fire to cool."

This reply was not exactly the explanation which was desired by the last comer, to whom Slender had given the soubriquet of Badger, and therefore muttering a hasty "Pshaw!" he turned to another of the tribe and put the question—an answer to which he received in a detail of all that had taken place. He listened attentively and then advanced to Jasper, and as soon as his eyes lighted upon his features, he started and exclaimed—

"I know him! unbind him at once."

"And vy!" inquired Slender, with a tone which implied that he had no intention that anything of the sort should be done, at least yet awhile.

"Because he's a friend!" replied Badger, immediately.

"It vasn't very friendly on him to clap the muzzle of a barking iron to my nob, and promise to send me to kingdom come if I didn't let him have the whole of the road to hisself," exclaimed Slender, emphatically.

"He didn't know you, nor you him," returned Badger; "that's the reason."

"I ain't hambitious of the acquaintance neither, I can tell you," said Slender.

"That's nothing to do with it," persisted Badger; "unfasten him, or if you don't, I will."

"Ven vos Badger's vord made law?" cried Slender with a sneer. "I don't remember; perhaps some of you do, though my memory is so queer."

A laugh from his comrades emboldened him to proceed.

We doesn't see at all vy ve should untwist the cull," he continued; though you does; and it's my opinion ve ain't a going to do it, neither; and if ve don't, vy you von't—that I suppose you knows."

Badger walked quietly up to Slender until he nearly touched him, and then said, in a stern tone, cuttingly sarcastic—

"Your memory is queer, or else you would remember, two years ago, that you thought fit to oppose me upon a certain point with as much reason as a jackass, and that I licked you so soundly you was led about for six weeks by the girls on a Jerusalem pony, like a monkey on the back of a cur. Now, if you wag your red rag at me too frothily, I'm damned if I don't give you hotter sauce to it than ever you supped."

The laugh was now on the other side, and Slender, enraged by what had previously delighted him, roared out with more wrath than prudence—

"You can't! it isn't in you. You licked me two years ago because I vos a young'un, green, and know'd nothing; but I knows a little better now how to use my mauleys, and can spill a handsomer mug than yours, my chirruping cockolorum."

"Let's see, then, what you do know," exclaimed Badger, delivering a tremendous blow between Slender's eyes, which levelled him to the ground as if he had been shot. He lay stunned and bleeding copiously from the nose without moving.

"When you get up, I'm ready for you," said Badger, cooly to him; and then turned to the others, who looked a little surprised at the sudden and easy disposal of their favourite comrade.

"You've ill used our best friend," he exclaimed; "this is Geoffrey Smith; you all know Geoffrey Smith! he's managed more hauls safely for us than anybody else, and this is the return he gets for what he's done."

The fellows repeated the name quickly, and instantly removing the cords and gag from Jasper, raised him to his feet. He was not conscious of the reason why he had been set free, and no sooner found himself at liberty than he seized a stout cudgel that lay near him and hit the nearest gipsey a terrific whack upon the head, which sent him flying to the ground as speedily as Badger's blow had Slender. He flourished his stick, and was proceeding to attack the rest when his arm was arrested by Badger, who, in a loud voice, uttered an exclamation which Jasper imediately acknowledged by staring him hard in the face, and replying with a similar one, and n another minute he was shaking hands with the fellow he had just intended to cuff about the head with his cudgel. The gipsey who had been felled by him rose at the same instant with Slender, and both made a rush at their respective antagonists—Slender at Badger, and the other gipsey at Jasper.

"Stand off!" thundered Badger. "Stand off, both of you, or I'll make you remember it the longest day you have to live."

A couple of gipseys kept their companion from Jasper, while Badger caught Slender by the throat, as he rushed on, regardless of the warning he gave him, and held him with an iron grip.

"Fool!" he roared; "haven't you had enough to satisfy you? Do you want to be licked to a stand still? If you do, say so, and we'll soon have a ring."

The old woman and young ones now interfered, and drew Slender away, swearing and raging fiercely, vowing he would fight, and yet in his heart quite glad that he was prevented, for the blow he had received had cowed the little spirit which in reality he possessed. The man whom Jasper had struck down was pacified, though not without difficulty, for his head smarted and throbbed with the violent blow he had received and incited him at every pang to retaliate in some way. The offer of gold as a salve, however, had the effect of taking away the pain, and when the excitement had subsided and a conversation entered into, they all seated themselves snugly round the fire, and smoked, save the woman, who prepared to cook the food, which had been casually picked up, for supper. When it was ready, there was no one backward in partaking of it, and during the meal, Jasper, confessed to Badger, that he was taking his female companion upon a journey not exactly with her consent; but he said he hoped to persuade her, before they reached their journey's end, to be a willing fellow-traveller. The way in which he spoke of persuading her left no doubt upon the minds of his listeners of the diabolical meaning he attached to it, and he requested their assistance to help him to bring so desired a consummation to pass. He reminded them that he had often done them service, and he now expected it returned. The old woman replied to him before Badger could return an answer.

"You ask of us," she exclaimed, impressively, "that which we cannot grant, even if we would. We have laws which govern us as strongly as you in society have, and it is our pride as well as policy to abide by them. We have extended the hand of faith and hospitality to the maiden, we have acted the part of the good Samaritan to the wounded stranger, we will not now harm her, aid to do it, or see it done."

"This is all cursed cant," roared Jasper, indignantly.

"She speaks truth," returned Badger. "If we can serve you in any other way, we will; but you require what we cannot do."

"Will not, you mean," cried Jasper, grinding his teeth.

"If you like it better, certainly," replied Badger; "but you can go when you please, and take the girl with you; we shall neither prevent or molest you, or remember seeing you, if we are asked."

"Humph!" growled Jasper; "that's better than nothing. Well, get my pony ready, and let me be off."

"You had better wait until daybreak," said Badger; "the pony will be fresh, and the girl, if I understand our old woman right, will be able to start without knocking up on the road."

"That I won't say," interrupted the old woman; "but she will be well enough to go further on the road in the morning, though an hour's journey further to-night would have been her death."

"She is in bed, beneath one of our tents," replied the old woman.

"Let me see her," he said, as if he doubted her word.

"You need not fear," replied the old woman, quickly, "We shall be more tender of her than you, I warrant me—follow me."

She lit a torch of pine wood by the fire, as she spoke, and led the way to the small tent in which Florence lay, she pulled the curtains of the tent on one side, and elevating the torch, let its light fall upon the face of the maiden. She lay with one cheek upon the pillow, in deep slumber; her long hair hung loose upon her neck, which was partly uncovered; her mouth was slightly open; her eyelids looked wet with tears recently shed. There was a slight flush upon her cheek, which made her face look lovely. A smile passed over her features as they gazed upon her, as though some happy dream was passing through her brain. Jasper looked on with eyes of eager admiration; he stooped down, and would have kissed her, but the old woman stopped him.

"It is the sleep of innocence," she exclaimed; "it will be broken soon enough, and by you, if the stars permit you to have your will. Do not disturb her now."

"Pshaw!" cried Jasper, turning away and striding to the fire. He stood there thoughtfully a few minutes, and then lifting up his head and looking upon the old woman with an air of scorn, he said—

"You have gulled many thousands in your life with foretelling the future and reading the stars, and such humbug; did you ever succeed in gulling yourself into a belief that you told truth at any time?"

"You are a scorner of all things," replied the woman, drawing herself up with a dignity which was somewhat surprising in a woman of her class; "yet, scorner as you are, I can tell you that which will make you believe my art is not one of guess only. To us, as a people, is given the power of divining the future, of reading the paths of mankind by the symbols which they bear on their own persons; we have born this power from time immemorial and shall bear it until the world ceases. Lend me your hand: if I tell you not that which in your heart you know to be true, however you may disguise it, scoff at me for an impostor as you will."

"Here," cried Jasper, with a derisive laugh, holding out his hand, "here it is, and now let me know what the stars have in store for me. Stop!" he exclaimed, drawing it back: "I suppose I must cross your hand with a coin first; that's the rule, I believe."

"As you please," said the woman, quietly.

"There," he cried, giving her half-a-guinea, "there's gold; now give me plenty of good luck."

The old woman took the gold and his hand also—she perused the lines upon the latter attentively, and then, while the gang looked on interestingly as though their fame was at stake, she said—

"Your hand says but little of the future; there's the blood of one near to you upon it; it clouds the lines and hides them—"

"Blood!" cried Jasper, fiercely, with a hasty start, and drew his hand abruptly away. He looked upon it, and muttered something, and then, perceiving that he was eyed closely by the gipsies, he forced a laugh—

"You begin bad enough for the credit of your art; you have told me of that which is not true. Besides, I want to know of the future, not of the past."

"I have spoken truth," said the woman, with a piercing glance at him; "let me have your hand again."

"Not I," replied Jasper; "I have had enough of that; tell me without."

"It is impossible!" exclaimed the old woman, "unless by cards."

"Then by cards be it," said Jasper.

The old woman drew from her pocket a dirty pack of cards, seated herself upon the ground, and after performing a few manœuvres, she spread them out and commenced: after musing over them for some time, she said—

"They predict you a singular and stormy fate; you will be a pursuer and pursued; there are many enemies and a few friends: there's a strange mingling of success and ill-luck; your destiny draws you after a fair maiden whom you catch, but retain not; for there is a dark woman who steps between you and your wish constantly; this dark woman has been wronged by you—she seeks revenge—she clings to your footsteps—'

"Pshaw!" cried Jasper, with an oath. "This is the mere cant and babble of your tribe. I've had enough to satisfy me of the imposture."

"Enough! you mean that it is not so. You feel it's truth, and dare not hear further," exclaimed the old woman, energetically, her brilliant eye piercing him through. Jasper did not reply, but turned away; he held a short communication with Badger, unheeding the dissatisfied look which the gipsies generally regarded him, and then retired to the resting-place they had made for him, and threw himself upon it. He was soon asleep, but not long to remain so; he awoke groaning and struggling as if he was in the grasp of some horrid phantom. He sought repose again, cursing

No. 22

bitterly the terrible dreams that disturbed his sleep—but once more he awoke with horror at believing himself in the embrace of a fleshless skeleton whose eyeless and grinning skull bore a hedious resemblance to Joan, and the impression was so strongly upon him that he started from his rude bed and rushed from the tent. The moon was still shining—the cool air refreshed him, and enabled him to collect his thoughts. He looked around him; four of the sturdiest gipsies were sleeping round the fire which still blazed brightly, having been replenished ere they went to sleep; the short narrow tents were disposed in a picturesque fashion, a short distance from the fire; a small cart was standing at the back of the tents, and close to them Jasper's pony and another were feeding quietly. He surveyed the scene in silence a short time, then he strolled round the outside of the tents, looked carefully among the bushes and trees that grew near, and gradually returned to the spot from which he had started.

"She's not here," he muttered; "she's not here; 'twas only a trick to frighten me and keep me from making Florence mine—nothing more. She has not kept her word or I should have seen her before this; she's not dead —no—no such luck—yet why ask me with that ghastly face whether she was life or death? God! she looked a spectre then; but she said she would not die, she would not quit me—where is she now?"

This was muttered with a laugh, yet he shuddered and turned his head hastily over his shoulder, almost expecting to see her. Was she not with him, could he rid his brain of her for one moment! was there not a fear upon him, turn which way he would, he should meet her? If she was not present bodily, she was mentally, and that was to him, although he would not even to himself acknowledge it, worse than had she actually stood before him; some such thought crossed him, but he dismissed it with an oath, and determined not to be cowed by all she had threatened, or all she would try to do. Once more his eyes glanced round upon the sleepers and the tents; they singled out the one which contained Florence; he gazed thoughtfully upon it; gradually his brow lowered, his teeth compressed, and with an air of stern determination he crept stealthily towards it; he reached it and raised slowly the curtain before it. While in the act, the old woman rose up before him from the ground so closely as to disloge his arm from the folds of the curtain, and said in a low tone—

"Return to your tent, you have no business here; HER sleep shall not be broken that she may wake in fright while with us. We are acting as your friends—make us not your bitter foes, or the hand that is extended in amity towards you shall seek your breast armed with a knife—away! At daybreak she is yours to lead hence. She is ours now, and shall not have a rude finger laid upon her. Be wise and take my advice," she added, as she saw Jasper lingering; "an outcry from me would awaken yon sleepers, and a single word would cause your death—not even Badger, much your friend as he is, could save you. Go!"

The woman spoke in tones that induced Jasper to believe she uttered truth, and following her advice he quitted the spot, and entered his tent to try and obtain a little sleep ere he departed with his prize, even if it was to be broken by some such fearful dreams as had before haunted him.

He was sleeping soundly, when a hand placed upon his shoulder awoke him, he started, and sprung to his feet, as the voice of Slender broke on his ear—

"Come, Fire-eater," he exclaimed, "do you mean to lay here all day, or shall I vork off with the young voman myself?"

Jasper gave him a scowl, as he glanced round, and saw the sun above the horizon, and daylight reigning in undisputed possession of the place around.

"Ve should ha' called you afore to blow on our kettle to bile it, but the fire vasn't out, so ve vouldn't trouble you. Come, stir yourself, my Hafrikin sun, if you vants to put any vittles into your bread-basket, look sharp, cos ve vants to cut our luckeys, and your young voman 'as been hanxious to lammas hever so long."

Jasper looked fiercely at him, as if to revenge the insult his language conveyed, but he saw that he had a tremendous pair of black eyes, the gift of Badger's fist; he therefore only laughed and moved away. Slender read his thoughts in a single glance, and followed him.

"My peepers is in mourning, I knows," he said rather savagely, "but the fight isn't taken out of me no how, and I'm ready for a turn-up with you for anything, from a guinea to a hold bakky box." Jasper returned him no answer, and he continued—" If you von't fight, vy don't grin at my misforten, that's all." He paused a moment, and then added, with rather a good-natured laugh—"Shall ve make yonr grub red hot afore you has it—if it's only biling hot it'll make your teeth chatter vith cold, I s'pose."

"Come, Slender, stow your chaffing," exclaimed Badger, advancing and overhearing the last few words. He then said to Jasper—"you will have something to eat before you start, of course, but you had better be quick about it—the girl is ready, and we wish to be off also."

Jasper assented to the proposition, partook hastily of a rude breakfast and when he had finished, conferred apart with Badger. As soon as their conference ceased, he advanced to where Florence, seated upon the pony, awaited his coming; she was listening attentively to something which the old woman was rapidly uttering in an under tone, and which she concluded ere he arrived. He looked suspiciously at them both, and exclaimed, sternly—

"More fortune-telling, I suppose! What do you see in the stars for her, dame?" As he uttered the words he bent his eyes upon her as if he would read her through, but he looked on one whom no gaze of his could embarrass.

"She has a clearer hand than thine," she returned, readily and coolly, "and it tells of a better and quieter fate. The eagle is often struck with the hunter's shaft, while the dove is made a household thing to love and cherish."

"Spare your rant, mother, for the next fool you see," he interrupted.

"You've had your share, you think," she exclaimed, with a bitter laugh; "but mark me, scoffer, your fate will surely come, though you disdain to hear it."

"Well, let it, returned Jasper, with a grim smile, "it will find me pre_pared. But we've had enough of this rubbish," he added, hastily; "the sun is too high already to linger here.   Farewell, old dame, when I need your predictions I'll seek you out and purchase favourable ones from you.   For what you have done I will pay you anon; I shall see Badger shortly, and he shall be the bearer of my remuneration.   Good morrow to ye all," he concluded, turning to the people who had congregated around them.

"Good morrow," cried the old woman, adding her voice to those of her companions, " may it be a good morrow to you, may you profit by it: and a good morrow to you, maiden," she said, addressing Florence, and speaking significantly; " the stars speak fair that it should.   Trust and fear not."

Jasper was about to make a comment upon what he heard, but the old woman turned away; the rest of the tribe followed her example, and instantly set to work striking their tents.   Finding no further notice was taken of him, Jasper seized the bridle of the pony and commenced his march.   The country was varied in its aspect as he progressed—now bleak and barren, then fertile and cultivated; occasionally mountainous or hilly, then level in the form of moors and dreary looking wastes.   He journied on the whole day, stopping only for a short time in two or three secluded places to rest himself and steed, and to take refreshment.   Once or twice, after much hesitation and clearing of his throat, he spoke a few words to Florence, but she returned him no answer, and he relapsed into his previous taciturnity. She ate very sparingly, at the close of the day, of some food which he persisted in proffering her, though he spoke not in desiring her to accept it.   She was very pale, appeared dreadfully weak and fatigued, and the expression of her features was one of hopeless despair.   It seemed that she knew it was vain to appeal to him to restore her from whence he had stolen her, and she could only trust in Heaven for deliverance.   Night came, and still they toiled on.   Before them lay a large moor, which appeared to embrace miles ere its termination could be reached, and yet Jasper led the horse across it directing his footsteps towards the farthest point.   It had been a long, dreary day to her, and but that she thought of Eustace, she would have prayed it, might have terminated with her death; but for his sake she endeavoured to keep up, and to watch with the most persevering minuteness for the smallest chance of release, determining to use it at every hazard as soon as it should appear.

The path was evidently well known to Jasper; for though the darkness fast increased, aided by dark and angry clouds, which rose up in huge masses, tokens of an approaching storm, and cast a gloomy shadow on their way, he unhesitatingly proceeded by a small, slightly-beaten track, which, though he could barely see, he unerringly kept.   As his eyes detected the evidences of rough weather, he quickened his steps, though footsore and weary, dragging rather than leading his brute servant, who was no less tired than himself.   An hour's march over that moor brought them to a small cottage hidden by a group of trees, and scarcely to be seen from any point until closely approached.   As he drew near he gave a signal, which was answered by a light being placed in a window.   He repeated his signal, and the door was immediately opened by a man, who, crossing the threshold, advanced and gave him a rough welcome.

"Everything is prepared as you desired." said the man. I expected you before this, by at least an hour."

"I lost the hour this morning in sleep, or I should have kept my time," returned Jasper.

"Ah, Trusty Tom's are snug lodgings," exclaimed the cottager.

"Probably; but I didn't try them," returned Jasper.

"No, how was that?" interrupted the man, slapping the pony's neck in a fond manner.

"Accident," replied Jasper; "but you shall know more by-and-bye, Hand this young lady in, and let's have a little rest and something to eat before we talk. I am tired and hungry."

"Ah, I dare say. How far have you come since morning?" he inquired, lifting Florence from the saddle.

"Covered thirty miles; but save your tongue and give us your labour," cried Jasper, pettishly. "Give this young lady a seat by your fire. I hope it's a good one, for it's cursedly chilly to night, and I'll see to the pony."

He turned and led the animal away as he spoke, and the cottager conducted Florence into his dwelling. There was an air of comfort in the interior, although it was so humble; the furniture was rude but had the merit of being clean; the floor was covered with small tiles well sanded over, and in a chimney blazed a wood fire of an inspiriting size; above it was an iron pot or cauldron, which, by the fragrant smell issuing from it, contained something good in the shape of food, and the cottager seemed to derive considerable satisfaction from a number of sniffs which he regaled himself with while passing it, and placing a small settle in the chimney corner. Everywhere the hand of woman was apparent, in the orderly arranged household, but she herself was nowhere to be seen. Florence gazed around in the hope of perceiving one of her own sex; but she sighed as she saw there was none but herself and this man in the place, nor heard a sound which could tell her one was near. She looked in the man's face with some thought that if she appealed to him and told him how she had been torn away he would befriend her; but a glance was sufficient to tell her that in the features of low cunning, harsh, and sinister, there was no sympathy to be expected without a round sum extracted it, and, alas! she had but a few guineas in her purse, which by accident she had in her pocket when she was seized, quite insufficient to tempt the sordid wretch he appeared. She clapsed her hands in despair, and seated herself by the fire, where he had placed the settle. The man observed the look she gave him, but scarcely understood it, though he made somewhat of a shrewd guess at it.

"Miss looks fatigued, and wants her supper," he exclaimed, with something of a foreign accent.

"I am faint and tired, but not hungry," she replied. "You have a wife, my good man," she added, looking round at the bright platters which were neatly arranged upon a shelf.

"I had," replied the man, with a slight change passing over his features; "she was an angel—she is one now—she is dead."

Florence turned away her head and sighed.

"But she left me a daughter," he added.

"Where is she?" asked Florence, hastily.

"She is away from here on an errand," said the man, a little confusedly, almost startled by the sudden quickness with which she had asked the question. He then turned his back and continued to arrange the supper things.

"Has she gone far? Will she soon be back?" inquired Florence.

"She has gone too far to be back to-night," he replied briefly.

Florence sighed again, as she turned her eyes, filled with tears, to the fire. The man eyed her askance, he saw her heart was full, he saw that she was ill too, and knew enough to be aware a flood of tears would relieve her and make her feel better, if not more resigned to what he fully believed a hopeless case.

"Miss's face looks pale and fagged; a wash in cold water will restore its beauty. There is a chamber above, will Miss make use of it?" he exclaimed with a show of politeness, well assured, if she accepted it, she would, the instant she was alone, give way to a burst of grief, which, it was his opinion, would cure her despondency. He had had some experience with woman: it was his belief that tears were a great source of consolation to them, as well as rendering them more accesssible—more inclined to be tender, if caressed while the tears were yet wet upon their cheek. It was this belief that made him deem it policy to give her the chance of being alone for a short time, in order to bring about with greater facility a deed which he knew it was Jasper's intention to commit. Florence hesitated to accept the offer, but she heard the footstep of Jasper approaching, and glad of any chance of ridding herself of his presence, she seized a little lamp which stood upon the table, and hurried up the stairs to a small chamber, the door of which stood open. She entered, shut the door, and drew a small wooden bolt across which fastened it; she approached the window and opened it. It did not seem a very great height. Fatigued as she was, she believed by the aid of a sheet from a clean neat little bed which stood in the corner, she might be able to descend and get some distance across the common ere her flight was discovered, and then she would put her whole trust in Heaven to escape. She knew that she had not a moment to lose, as her whole hope of getting away rested upon the time she could gain ere it was known she had fled. She looked at the sky—it was dark and threatening; large drops of rain were beginning to descend; the wind howled and moaned as it swept across the moor in rude gusts, and a distant peel of thunder which broke upon her ears left her no doubt that a fierce storm would shortly burst over the spot. For a moment she hesitated at the frightful situation in which she would be placed—she, a gentle timid thing, alone on a wild moor at night, in the midst of a howling storm, with the fear of pursuit upon her, and utterly unconscious which way to turn for friends or shelter. But to remain was worse than death; better to die in the storm upon the moor, without a soul near her—no eye upon her save God's—than remain, far better. She muttered a short, fervent prayer, for support in her trial, to Heaven, and turned away from the casement to put her resolution into practice. At that moment a slight hand was placed upon her shoulder; she screamed; a flash of lightning filled the chamber, it was succeeded by a terrific crash of thunder, and the wind and rain howled and dashed furiously against the cottage. The sudden uproar of the elements drowned her cry as it was uttered, and as she turned, affrighted with both occurences, she beheld the slight form of a young girl, about fourteen, standing before her, and raising her finger with a low exclamation of warning.

"Don't be frightened," whispered the girl, putting her arm kindly round Florence's waist; "pray don't be frightened, I thought you would fancy I was a ghost, but indeed, I ain't; I am Letty Nehemie."

Florence gazed upon her a moment without speaking, the girl pressed her affectionately to her side, and then, scarcely recovered from her fright, Florence faltered out—

"Are you the daughter of the man below ?"

"Hush !" whispered the girl; "father's ears are as quick as the eye of a rook. He doesn't know I'm at home, and he mustn't either—he would murder me if he did—but I heard him talking to a man about you this morning. So when he sent me away this afternoon, I walked until it grew dark, and crept back again. I watched and waited about until he walked across the moor about an hour ago, and then stole in and hid myself here."

"What did you hear about me ?" asked Florence, hastily.

"Only whisper, if we are heard it will be bad for both," utterered the girl, in so low a tone, Florence could barely catch the words. "I heard but little," she continued, in reply to the question; "father said he expected a friend with a girl, then they whispered—then the man said 'But she'll scream and make a rare noise, won't she ?' Father laughed, and said, 'Let her, there'll be nobody to hear her; I shall send Letty far enough off, and I will be out of the way myself; he will then have the hut, the moor, and the girl, and no one else for companions.' And then they both laughed in a horrid way; it made my blood run cold, so I thought I would stop and see who you were, and if I thought you were good, I would put you on your guard that they shouldn't murder you."

"Murder me !" exclaimed Florence, with surprise.

"Yes. What else could they mean ?" replied the girl innocently. "Ah, they meant that, and so I thought you shouldn't die alone, for I am very wretched here, very indeed, and should be happy to die too," and the large tears rolled down the poor girl's cheeks as she spoke.

"Is Miss ready for her supper ?" cried the voice of the cottager from the foot of the stairs; both started, but neither made a reply, until Letty exclaimed hurriedly—

"That's father's voice—answer 'yes,' and go down: I'll hide myself here. You can make any excuse to come up when you have finished your supper; and then when father's gone, we'll fasten the door and hide here till morning, and then creep out of the window, and run away together."

"Is Miss ready for her supper ?" cried Nehemie, advancing up the stairs, until he stood at the door. Letty grasped her hard by the arm, and placed her mouth to her ear—

"Go down," she whispered, "or he'll break in, and drag you down by the hair of your head; he would me, so I am quite sure he would you."

She raised her finger, and crept noiselessly beneath the bed.

"Will not Miss answer me?" exclaimed Nehemie, impatiently.

"I do not want anything to eat," murmured Florence, with a beating heart.

"But your frame does," returned the man. "Be wise, take some; do not fight against what is sure to conquer you—the appetite is a sore combatant"

"Descend, I will follow you," said Florence in as firm a tone as she could use. He tried the door and found it fast.

"Miss will keep her word? I shall not have to break open the door and carry her down, shall I?"

"No," was Florence's reply.

The man descended—she waited until she heard him speaking to Jasper, and then unfastening the bolt and trembling with apprehension, she moved slowly down the stairs. As she appeared, Jasper jumped to his feet and obsequiously placed a settle by the side of the table, upon which was placed viands, simple but cleanly. Florence took the seat placed for her, and remembering the chance of flight Letty had held out, did not reject the food put before her; she knew flight was not successfully to be accomplished with a frame weakened by fasting, and under such impression made, to Jasper's satisfation, a hearty meal, When it was over, Nehemie hastily cleared the things away, and muttering a few words in Jasper's ear, he went quickly out of the cottage with a brief good night on his lips. The door was drawn harshly after him, and then Jasper and Florence were alone. He sat with his eyes fixed thoughtfully on the fire, and she rose from her seat; quietly and noiselessly she moved from the table, and had already gained the stairs ere he noticed her movement—then he sprang to his feet, seized her by the waist, and drew her to the fire-side again.

"I wish to have a few words with you, he exclaimed. "Listen to me, and heed well all I say. You are again in my power; this time more surely than before; turn which way you will, rend the air with shrieks as you may, there is none near hear to help you. You are with me alone."

"And God!" exclaimed Florence, in a firm impressive voice.

He had expected no reply—hers startled him; it was but for a moment. He laughed, and said with a sneer—

"He may hear, but will he help you?"

"I put trust in him," she replied.

"Rather trust yourself," he returned; "live for yourself—be not a fool; take the path which will lead to the best gratification of self—I do."

"I believe it," she replied, laconically.

"Ay!" he exclaimed, "it's the best plan; we should enjoy ourselves while we have the chance. Youth is the only time for enjoyment; old age comes on fast—the relish for pleasures fly with youth. The man's a fool who plods on in his earliest and best days for the sake of enjoyment in his old age; it is impossible then to enjoy that for which you have no desire, or if you had, be

cursed with a natural inability.   I'm not much of a reasoner, but that's my opinion.   Now, to plain fact.   You know, Florence, I love you—madly love you.   I would not, if I could help it, but it's out of my power to prevent it; and, therefore, I have given myself up to it.   I have told you my happiness depends upon you, and if you are not mine there is not that on earth which could give me joy.   I am not so weak as not to see that I am distasteful to you—more than distasteful.   I think I have seen enough of woman to know they will not suffer themselves to be compelled to love any man let his acquirements and personal advantages be as great as they may; but they are to be led and persuaded to it.   Why will you not give me the chance of trying to make you love me?   I have told you I can be gentle and kind to you I can be a slave to your wish, anything you can desire, if you will but turn your eyes kindly upon me.   I have been harsh—I have done rude acts, but for you they have been done; it is for you I have cast away the home of my birth; for you I have sacrificed father, mother, and brother; for you I have robbed my bosom of peace and made it the abode of the most fearful emotions, and for you I would be an outcast from the world itself."

"Jasper, it is vain you speak thus to me," interrupted Florence; " you cannot make me change the opinion of you which I hold.

No. 23.

" And that is deadly hate," he cried, fiercely.

"It is more fear than hate, Jasper," she returned, speaking with a firmness that almost surprised herself. "I regret most sincerely that I should have inspired you with a passion I cannot requite, and for that consideration I can forgive where I should loathe. I never can love you—I told you so when you first broached your passion to me, and from that hour you have done everything which could put to flight the smallest kindly feeling ever entertained for you."

"It was the work of despair," exclaimed Jasper, quickly, "the deeds of one who was driven by your refusal to frenzy and desperation. Give me bnt one smile of tenderness, one hope that you will be mine, and I will repair every sad or bitter moment I have made you feel with years of devotion."

"It is useless," replied Florence, gravely and with decision; "ere I came to Grasmere my heart was given to another."

"Ay !" shonted Jasper, excitedly. "Ay, my mother told me so but a few days since. Ay, that which you deny to me you have give to one who is a worthless libertine, a dissipated debauchee, a graceless scourge of a family, a wild gambler, a vagabond—"

"Hold !" cried Florence, in a tone as loud and excited as his own. "It is false—it is a base, wicked calmuny; he is noble, generous manly. He would have scorned even to have thought of the deeds you have done, and blushed for his race to hear of them; there is not an attribute that makes man Godlike which is not his. He is as brave as you are base and cowardly; his soul is bright, and unsullied by one such stain as the thousands which encrust thine; and had he been near me, you would have trembled and grown white with fear ere you had dared to lay a rude finger upon me."

Jasper's countenance worked fearfully with emotions of rage as she uttered her scornful words; but he struggled hard to repress them, and appear calm. As she concluded, he smiled, and with a sneer, said—

"He has a warm friend in you. Doubtless you would, though thy family hold him up to contempt and execration, go with him through the world, cherish him in your heart, and share his fortunes, be they evil or good."

"I would ! I would !" she exclaimed fervently.

Jasper drew a long breath : his heart felt sick at her reply, and though rage was in his bosom, yet there was a bitter sorrow with it that kept it down and made him feel more disposed to abject pleading than the application of harsh words or ruder acts. There was no doubt that he felt strongly and bitterly; the anguish of his features exhibited it, and the pain he felt was added to by an inward consciousness that he had no remedy. He knew that no brutal violence or tender persuasions, however earnestly they might be made, could make her love him, or look upon him with any other eye than aversion. She was a gentle fragile thing that even as he touched he was afraid of hurting; he knew he could destroy her as easily as he could a bird or a butterfly; but, though it would rob his rival of her, he should also be the loser to as great an extent—in his own heart he thought greater—than Eustace Prior. He could not bear to think of her dead; it seemed so completely the destruction of the only object worth living for, that he banished it from his mind as soon as it entered. It was not that he was villian sufficient, but he was too selfish, and wanted the courage to bear the remembrance of the deed afterwards as well as the decided aversion to remove from his grasp the prize for which he had hazarded so much. He could have struck her down for the fervency with which she acknowledged her readiness to partake the fortunes of Eustace Prior, but was witheld by a power that made him feel almost womanish. He had turned from her as she spoke, and paced agitatedly in front of the fire, but in a minute he stopped, and said, in tones of earnest entreaty—

"Florence, dear, dear Florence, if you knew how your scorn of me scorched my heart with a fire that blasts as it burns, you would pity me—you would pardon me for what I have done, and look with a gentler eye upon me. Ah, Florence, it is still in your power to make me honourable and worthy ; do not cast me from you so that I shall sink deeper and deeper in the toils of the fiend who has already ensnared me : you can restore me, a word will do it, or yours will be the hand that flings me to a perdition from which there is no redemption. Florence, hear me ; do not be too ready to decide against me. Him you have loved is of the sea ; I am so too, though few know it. I have a vessel at my command which is like a bird upon the waters, a sweet craft, so trim, so sweetly shaped, so swift it skims the surface of the sea leaping and glancing from wave to wave, when the fastes wood and iron in his Majesty's service labours through the water. It is all my own, and there are spirits on board rude, but free-hearted souls, aye, and staunch and true, and with courage like tried steel, who are at my beck, and will worship thee if I bid them. Come with me, Florence, and you shall be its mistress ; you shall rule with despotic sway over those who scorn rule. We will to one of the bright islands in the Spanish Main, where clouds never come, where there is a wild luxuriance of the fruit and of the flowers you so love ; there you shall be a queen, surrounded by every dainty the heart can desire. The most gorgeous jewels and dresses shall be thine ; luxuries shall be lavished on thee, and everything that can chase away a shadow of gloom, or discontent, or sorrow, and keep thy brow all smiles, shall be bestowed on thee. Oh, Florence, try but to love me, you will make my life an entire happiness, and that life shall be passed in striving to ensure thine unclouded—"

"Stay, Jasper," exclaimed Florence, interrupting him, as he was proceeding still more energetically to urge her to consent to become his. "Stay, and answer me this question ere you proceed. Is love, true, pure, REAL love, of such a nature that it can be removed at will from one object to another ? is it of that character, that after loving one tenderly and dearly it may be transferred to another ?"

"You think, Florence," said Jasper, eagerly, that though I love you now, I may change ; that in a few years I may grow weary of you, and seek for another. Oh ! no, have no such fear, I love you truly ; and true love can never change. As I love you now, so I shall to the hour of my death ; nothing in the world could make me swerve from thee—no temptations, no allurements ever move me: true love can be shaken by nothing. I am yours in life and death."

"I am answered," she exclaimed, fervently, casting her eyes heavenwards, clasping her hands with energy, and almost repeating Jasper's words, "true love knows no change; it can never change; I love thee, Eustace, truly! Nothing in the world shall make me swerve from thee—no temptations, no allurements ever move me. True love can be shaken by nothing—I am yours in life and death!"

To describe Jasper's convulsive passion as her words burst upon his ears would be impossible: he grew white and clenched his hands fiercely, while he ground his teeth hard together. He had been delighting himself with the fond anticipation that he had removed her obduracy towards him, and should succeed in persuading her to become his. In his eagerness to strengthen his cause he had quite overlooked the fact that putting his own fidelity in such strong terms he was using the most powerful arguments against himself; and, therefore, when he found he had put words in her mouth to strengthen her determination never to become his, his rage knew no bounds. He sprung towards her, and seized both her hands with a grasp of iron, before she had the power to resist him.

"Will you promise to be mine?" he shouted, fiercely.

"Have mercy!" she shrieked.

"Not a grain," he cried; "mine you shall be, by consent or force. Answer will you be mine?"

"God help me!" frantically scream the terrified girl. "Spare me, Jasper, spare me."

"Yes or no—I hear nothing else. Fool! we are alone on a wide heath, miles from a living soul—what will avail your struggles against my strength?

Once more I give you the alternative—will you be mine? Answer quickly and let your reply be a consent, or this instant shall see you a miserable dishonoured creature."

"Oh! Jasper, if you have any pity, if you really love me, let me free, for the sake of all you hold dear on earth, spare me," she cried, energetically.

"Will you be mine?" he roared.

"I cannot, I cannot!" she ejaculated, hysterically.

"It's a lie—a weak subterfuge—you can and shall," he growled passionately, and passed his arm swiftly round her waist. She screamed franticly, struggled with all the strength nature had given her; but she was but as a child in his powerful grasp. As long as she possessed an atom of strength she strove to extricate herself, screaming madly; but at length she grew exhausted, all power left her; she found she could struggle no longer; her reason seemed almost to be leaving her, and in the agony of the moment she screamed—

"Release me, Jasper—I will be yours, I will be yours."

"Ha! ha! ha!" laughed Jasper, with a loud shout of triumph; "mine, you will be mine! say it again, my bonny love—mine in life and death—say it, swear it!"

He pressed her to his breast as he spoke, and strove to print his loathsome kisses upon her fair face, white with horror; but as " God tempers the wind to the shorn lamb," so does he at desperate moments lend the strength of a giant to the gentle and fragile. Florence, urged to madness by his hateful carresses, once more struggled with the agony of despair, and, by a sudden and unexpected movement, liberated herself from his grasp. She darted from him like lightning, and with a fierce oath he pursued her, She took but a few steps when her eyes lighted upon Jasper's pistols lying on the table; she sprung upon them as a lioness would on its prey, and seizing one, turned round and presented it at her relentless foe. The muzzle touched his forehead ere he ascertained she was armed with a power superior to his own. He recoiled a short distance, and regarded her with fear as well as astonishment; she stood erect, her head thrown back, her right arm extended, with the pistol grasped firmly in her hand, and her finger upon the trigger.

" Stand back; she shrieked, " stand off, monster, or your blood be upon your own head. This weapon carries death. You carefully placed the means within it to ensure it, and by the Almighty power which looks down upon us now, I will send you to perdition if you advance one step, or seek to place a finger upon me."

Jasper could scarcely believe the slight timid girl should have thus suddenly changed into the bold firm woman; her eyes, usually soft and dreamy, now flashed with brilliancy, and as he gazed upon her, an uneasy thought of Joan crossed him, and assisted in making him less cool than was requisite to gain him any advantage in the position in which he was placed. Conciliation appeared to him his only chance, and drawing himself up he smothered his voice, and trying a smile, he said in a voice, which he tried to make appear calm—

" Florence, Florence, put down the pistol; I will not touch you—I had no intention of harming you. It was a foollsh wish to terrify you for sport's sake, which made me seize you; put down the weapon and retire to the chamber above, and I give you my word yon shall not be molested."

" I will relinquish this weapon only with my life," cried Florence, firmly, " your death or mine shall follow the smallest attempt to deprive me of it."

" Nay, believe me, I do not mean to harm you," he said, earnestly, advancing a step.

" It is false! base, kindless wretch," she cried, retreating as he advanced. .' Stand where you are, my finger is upon the trigger, my eye is firm, and my hand steady; your blood shall surely follow the first movement you make towards me. Do not doubt it—do not, for God will pardon me an act which I will assuredly commit in defence of that which to me is dearer than life itself."

Jasper fixed his eye keenly upon her; in the bent brow, the quivering lip, the flashing eyes, and the flushed cheeks, he saw the evidences of a determination which it would be fatal to attempt to surmount by an act of sudden force. The power was hers now, and he must trust to art to recover the advantage which the possession of the pistols had given her. He therefore folded his arms quietly, and said—

" Florence, were I bent upon dishonouring you, not the puny weapon you

hold, or one thrice its calibre, would stop me.   I would spring upon you now'
though in my leap the swift messenger of death from your hand sent me a
ghastly corpse to the ground.   From the first moment I got you in my
power, even previous to it, I proffered honourable love.   I have sought to
make you my wife, not my mistress.   I have given you many proofs of devotion in hazarding life and name for you, which him whom you profess to
love would start back from, and sacrifice you a thousand times ere he would
do one."

"Base calumniator," exclaimed Florence.   "He has none but honourable
thoughts, no deeds but what are honourable, and he would not have subjected me to half the misery, or a tithe of what you have; he would have
perished an hundred fold first.   Your love is a blithe, a pestilence, which
destroys those on whom it lights; tell me rather yon hate me, and have
persecuted me thus rather out of your extreme hatred than for any love you
may have for me, remorseless, iron-hearted man."

"Teach me how to gain your love, and let the task be the hardest human
invention ever devised, I will accomplish it," he cried, energetically.   "Let
me know a path by which I may reach your heart—point out to me a mode—

"It is useless to pursue this subject," interrupted Florence, speaking with
firmness.   "It is not in my power to bestow that which is not mine any
longer; and your harsh conduct to me, your insults, your violence, your base
abduction of me from a roof where I was, at least, safe and respected, has removed all chance that I could look upon you with any other eyes than ab-
horrence."

"I will never give you up," he cried passionately, "though the most terrible death be the result of my detaining you; I will be torn piece-meal ere I
part with you."

"I am not in your power," exclaimed Florence, energetically.

"Not!" he cried, with a laugh of derision. "Do you think weak girl,
that pistol though pointed at my brain, makes you less in my power?"

"Aye!" she returned; "for ere you could renew your villanous outrage
upon me, I would fall a corpse at your feet.   My hand might tremble in discharging this weapon at you—it would not at myself.   I could find it easier
to die than even to become your wife."

There is a firm determination, however expressed, a something—in look,
in tone, in manner—which carries conviction with it.   Florence made it plain
by a species of calmness which, in her, was a true symbol that she would
fulfil her promise if he proceeded further in his villany,.   Jasper, who was
not much skilled in reading countenances or in detecting intentions from ex-
pressions of features, his own impetuous passions and nature not allowing him
to cool enough for such inspection, was yet struck by the manner with which
she conveyed her resolution.   There was no hesitation, no appearance
of timidity or dread at the thought of her own death in it.   It
seemed the stern but decided choice of the alternative which would
avoid her dishonour.   There existed not the shadow of a doubt by
any indication, however small, that she would not adopt it, and Jasper, unable to detect any wavering, any sign that at the last extremity

she would hold her hand and yield it to him, felt but too satisfied that if he attempted to seize her in his arms he would clasp a corpse—indeed, he was almost afraid that she would proceed at once to carry out her terrible resolve, as the speediest way of delivering herself from his clutches; and as her death was anything but what he desired, he saw he must act with caution to prevent her accomplishing it.   He was puzzled what to do, but thought affecting indifference would be the best plan of proceeding. He looked at her a moments her beauty, in the red light of the wood fire, seemed more exquisite than ever; her disordered hair, her white skin, flushed cheeks, and the look of excitement which still brightened her eyes far beyond their usual character, appeared in his eyes to render her more lovely than he had ever beheld her, and make her a prize too great to be lightly parted with. His heart glowed like fire as he gazed upon her, and he swore inwardly that she should be his if art, or even force, if nothing else, after every effort had been made, could affect it.   At present he sobered down his intense look of admiration, and picking up a stool which had been flung down in the struggle, he seated himself upon it in front of the fire, and leaning his elbows on his knees, he turned his head from her, and said—

"You had better retire to your chamber, you must be overcome with fatigue; sleep is necessary to all, it must be particularly so to you, who have undergone so much since yesterday morning, and so unused to it as you are You need not hesitate, Florence," he added, perceiving that she still stood in the same position, looking like a statue. "Your sleep shall be unbroken by me or any one else. I will take an oath, if you doubt my word. You shall be unmolested, I swear. Lay down the pistol, retire to bed, and close your eyes with the full confidence of security. I swear by heaven I will not approach your chamber, and the slumber of the infant shall not be more secure or sacred than thine."

"I take you at your word, Jasper," said Florence quickly: "but I shall also take this weapon with me ; and remember, if you break your promise I shall keep mine."

Without another word she sprung up the stairs and entered the little chamber where Letty Nehemie, in a state of fright, was waiting for her, and every moment praying most fervently for her appearance.

Jasper watched her disappear, and then turned his eyes upon the fire moodily ; he sat for a few moments gazing abstractedly, and then raising himself to his feet, he gathered a few logs together which he found heaped in a corner, threw them upon the fire, and then mixing a quantity of brandy which Nehemie had left him, in a wooden bowl, with water and a lemon, he seated himself in front of the fire, and after casting his eyes anxiously round, he drank a long draught. When he removed the bowl from his lips, he sat down and raked the wood embers together until they blazed up brightly and threw out a light which filled every corner of the apartment; he seemed more at ease when this was accomplished, and after peering into one or two dark corners which the light could not reach, he stretched out his feet before the fire, and leaning towards it, he muttered

" She could not track me here ; she's sharp witted, but she could not track me here.   No, no, my road was too well chosen for that, unless she be a spirit.   Pshaw ! I'm an ass to think such a thing—yet I have seen some of those ruffians on board the Lightning, who feared neither man or devil, turn white as they have told of the ghosts of those who fell by their hands, who have started up in their path at the dead hour of night in lonely places.   I wish I had never seen her damned face, or had seen Florence first—but that's useless now ; I must make the best of it.   I don't think Frank is dead—I don't think he is, or he would have been heard of before this.   It is strange there is no trace of him.   Could Churleigh—no, he would have soon told me if he had picked him up—he would not let so long a time pass without asking gold for silence.   It is strange ; no matter, let it go ; let what will turn up, I will fall on my feet if I must fall.   If it was not for the fear of this cursed Joan dogging my steps, I would not care, but I know her devil's nature ; she will hunt me if she can to the death, and if she once sets the old ruffian on my trail, I must double and double again to avoid the knife or bullet of the bloody-minded old villain.   Curse her a thousand fold, for her curse is upon me.   I dare not sleep for the horrible dreams that haunt me, and if I am awake at night, I cannot feel alone ; I expect her to start up in some spot and fix that eagle's eye of hers upon me.   Well let her come,' he said suddenly, almost aloud ; " let her come : if she be life or death, I will send a bullet at her—she shall not daunt me.   If she be life, I shall be rid of her—ha ! ha ! free from her for ever ; and if death, I am but where I was."

. Once more he drank the brandy copiously, and then the fire, added to his fatigue, drew him gradually off to sleep : he slept soundly and for a considerable time, but how long he had he could not tell, when he was awakened by a rude grasp upon his shoulder.   So profound was his slumber that it took a considerable effort to arouse him, and for a few moments he could not understand where he was ; he rubbed his eyes hard and stared around him ; the place was filled with smoke from the wood upon the hearth, which not even the bright glare could penetrate, though it dazzled his eyes to gaze upon it.   At first he fancied that he had awakened from some casual effort of nature ; but he happened to cast his eyes upwards, and there, standing towering over him, looking in the murky atmosphere, like a spectre, stood Joan.   He started horrified, and would have leapt from his seat but she witheld him, and in a strong bitter voice, cried—

" See, I am with the again.   Thou hast expected me ; thy broken and disturbed slumber, thy dreams of horror have told me that ; but thou didst not expect me HERE, yet I am with thee.   There is not a spot on earth, how-e'er remote, which thou mayest seek, where thou wilt not find me by thy side, to curse thee for thy villany—to taunt thee for the miserable failures of thy designs on one whose simplicity and innocence equals the dove's, whom, vulture as thou art, hast not been able to strike to the dust as thou hast me, and, mark me, thou shalt not. Already is she beyond thy power, but should she again fall into it, ere thou hast gained thy object I will be by to thwart thee ; I will start up between thee and thy prey, and, saving her, thrust thee into the hell of defeat, where thou hadst made most sure of

triumph.   Had she been less pure, less guileless—had she hated thee less than she does.   I would have been her foe as I am thine; the same devouring, insatiable thirst for revenge upon her would parch my heart as it now does for thee, thou reptile. O, thou mighty in talk, thou villain in deed, thou paltry wretch, of little courage and no honour, thou quailer before men, thou boaster in the presence of weak women, thou trembler to the strong, thou swelled boaster to the weak and timid, where is thy victim? where thy slight fragile prey, she who is a timid creature, even to the faint hearted, she whom thou couldst not conquer, where is she?   Oh, thou cunning deviser, I will tell the—she has escaped; let me shout it in thy ears—she has escaped, and is far away from this—"

"Woman or devil, witch, spirit, life or death, whate'er thou art," roared Jasper, springing to his feet, and roused by her words from the paralysed

No 24.

state into which the sudden discovery of her had thrown him, I would know the worst or best of what is to come. If you are a spirit, this cannot harm you; if living, I am rid of you for ever."

He grasped his pistol as he spoke, and with a steadiness, which, in his excited state, might scarcely have been expected from him, he aimed the deadly weapon at her head, and discharged it. The report was loud, and the smoke of the powder filled the space between him and her so densely as to prevent him perceiving what effect his fire had taken, but it cleared rapidly away, and he saw her standing before him unhurt, and with the same fierce, yet ghastly smile upon her as before. He sunk upon his seat, the pistol fell from his hand and he groaned bitterly as he muttered—

" I am a doomed man."

" Aye, Jasper Chough, thou art doomed, now and for ever," cried Joan pointing one finger at him, and extending her right hand clenched in the, same direction. " No mercy did'st thou show to me, none shalt thou have from; from this moment until we again meet thou shalt look for me in every place that has a shadow—you shall not say one minute, ' she is not here,' without expecting to see me next. I will give thee counsel and infor_mation, but such only as shall add to thy misery and incertitude. Listen to me, and believe I speak nought but truth. Beware of meeting with my father—he is now your foe, and more than ever he was your friend; there is another also on your track, and his gold is more powerful than a gipsey's honour, a golden key has unlocked a chest more strongly secured than a gipsey's tongue, and he who buys his information has a quick wit to take a path pointed out to him, though he comes not in search of the lost one; but there are others who look for the lost maiden, who have keen eyes and are swift of foot—they will not sleep or rest until they have unkennelled thee, and if they do fall in with thee, my revenge might have a feebler satisfaction than in knowing the fate that would ensue thy capture. On all sides are you hunted, and all seek thy life, with nought else will they be satisfied. Escape as you can, I have yet to fill up my measure of bitterness for you. YOUR BROTHER IS FOUND! but where, by whom, or in what condition, I leave time to discover to you. Florence has escaped, and you are here alone with me—and now what devils are busy at your heart—nay, move not, you have no power over me, or your pistol would not have failed you. You are a doomed man, Jasper, and I will shout your doom in your ears when the hour arrives for its fulfilment."

She drew nearer to him as she concluded. He was not naturally superstitious, but his inkling religion had made him so, and the circumstances which were attached to Joan, made him believe she was a spirit permitted to visit him after death for the villany to her, and he shrunk back with horror as she approached. She placed her hand—it was like ice—upon his forehead, which burned with feverish excitement, and it produced the same effect it had previously done on the night when she uttered her fearful curse upon him. All perception quitted him in the horror she excited, and he sunk back insensible.

An hour passed away and he recovered from his swoon. He was alone, the sun was shining brightly in at the cottage window; he rose and found himself weak, and with a depression upon his spirits for which he could scarcely account, until he remembered his appalling visitant; then he remembered all she had said, and not the least remembered was the intelligence of Florence's escape. He rushed up stairs and tried her chamber door—it was fast, he pushed against it with great force, but it did not yield, he called her by name—she did not answer, he exerted all his strength, he threw himself against the door and it flew open, he searched the chamber, but she was not there; he entered the adjoining apartment, it was vacant, he returned to the chamber in which he supposed her to have reposed, and noticed that the casement was open, to the upright bar, which divided it into two was a rope attached, fastened in an awkward manner with half a dozen more knots than were at all necessary; this hung outside the window, and by this, to the girls difficult and dangerous mode, it was obvious the escape had been effected. Jasper looked eagerly right and left along the moor, but could not discover the slightest trace of the fugitives, and descended to the ground floor uttering the bitterest curses and oaths. He looked about for Nehemie; he shouted his name, but received no answer, save in the echo of his own voice. He paused for some little time, uncertain what to do, but Joan's information respecting those who were in search of him, decided upon not remaining at the cottage, so saddling the pony, he led it forth, and providing himself with such things in the shape of eatables as he thought he should require, he quitted the cottage, closed the door, mounted the pony, and guided him in the direction he deemed it most probable for Florence to have chosen in her flight.

Florence, upon quitting Jasper in the lower apartment of the cottage, had hastened to the room in which she had left Letty Nehemie, and upon gaining it, instantly secured the door upon the inside. Her little friend appeared from her hiding-place the moment this feat was accomplished, and after a short consultation, it was agreed that Letty was to keep watch while Florence laid down for an hour, and endeavour to sleep off some of the fatigue which she laboured under. and thus fit her better for that which she had yet to undergo. Kissing her kind little companion, she threw herself upon the bed, and recommending herself to Heaven, was soon lost in the blissful unconsciousness of deep and innocent slumber. Letty sat at the foot of the bed and gazed upon her face earnestly while she slept, and it might have been that there were painful remembrances crossed her mind as she watched the flushed and feverish face of the sleeper, and listened to her short, quick breathings, for the tears would steal down her cheeks. and her bosom heave with deep sighs, though she strove hard to repress them. Once she crept softly to her, and bending over her, kissed her, and then knelt down and buried her face in the bed clothes to stifle the sobs, which, in spite of every exertion, would burst forth; but when the passionate ebullition of grief had had its way, she rose up again, and stationed herself in her old place at the bed s foot, and sat and watched patiently.

Three hours passed away, still Florence slept profoundly. Letty suffered her to slumber on undisturbedly until there were signs of the day beginning to dawn, when she unfastened the door noiselessly, and crept down the stairs to see if it were possible to escape that way unperceived. When she reached the kitchen, she saw that Jasper was seated asleep in front of the fire, with his head turned to the stairs. He was moaning, groaning, twisting, and writhing in his sleep, and, to Letty's apprehensive imagination, appeared every instant as if he would awake and spring upon her. His gnashing teeth, his clenched hands, and rapid succession of groans frightened her into the belief that it would be impossible to pass him without awaking him, and she therefore crept back again to her chamber to contrive some other mode of escape. It quickly recurred to her memory that three or four times, when some strange men had come to the cottage and inquired for her father, he had bid her tell them he was away, and that, by means of a rope, which he kept for the purpose, he had lowered himself from her chamber window, and secreted himself near the spot until they were gone. This rope was always kept in the chamber, and she at once resolved to use it in the same manner as her father had done. The time having arrived for their departure, she awoke Florence, and told her of the only means by which they could hope to get free. Florence threw no obstacles in the way, and they proceeded to fasten the rope round the upright bar which divided the casement into two parts, and then to attempt the descent. Florence attired herself in the cloak and hat which Jasper had provided her with, and Letty in her own. The pistol, which had been of such service to her, Florence resolved not to part with, and accordingly carried it with her. The descent, which was attended with some difficulty as well as danger, they accomplished safely; and once upon the earth, they both ran forward at the top of their speed until their breath failed them and then they slackened their pace to a rapid walk. Letty pointed out their way, and Florence, with a shudder, looked back upon the place she had quitted, and its much dreaded inmate. The sun at this moment appeared on the horizon, sending up its rays behind the cottage, tinging its roof and the neighbouring trees with its glittering golden hues. She hailed it as a good omen, and proceeded with fresh spirit. A moment after, on passing a large mass of gorse bushes, they were both terribly startled by the sudden appearance of a woman, who rose up from the ground and stood before them as though she had been a phantom; they both screamed, and would have fled, but she stayed them with a voice which had more sadness than aught else in its tone.

Fear me not," she exclaimed. "I am not your foe."

Florence recognised the voice instantly and stopped. She looked earnestly at the woman; she was the same person who had warned her not to keep the appointment which led to her abduction. Her gaze was returned tenfold by the stranger, who eyed her most scrutinizingly, perusing every feature with the most intense curiosity. Florence cowered beneath her bright black eyes, and said, timidly—

"It was you who warned me on the night I was torn from my friends."

"Aye," said the woman, heaving a deep sigh as she spoke, and rousing herself as if from deep abstraction; "and had you obeyed me you would have been spared much pain. It is vain to talk of that ; you have suffered the penalty, but you have escaped?" she added quickly, interrogatively.

"I have," replied Florence.

"And HE," she said, through her teeth.

"Is there," replied Florence, pointing to the cottage.

"Asleep, and groaning and talking in it dreadfully," observed Letty, a little recovered from the fright into which the sudden appearance of the stranger had thrown them. The woman laughed bitterly as she listened to Letty's speech, and then said, rapidly—

"Away ! Before you are far you will be pursued. Let no foolish fancies of fatigue stop your flight if you wish to escape. Rest not, pause not, until you are miles from here, and then sit not down until there are those near you who can protect you, if HE should overtake you."

"Which way shall we take?" asked Florence, eagerly.

"You would return to Grasmere?" said the woman.

"I would," replied Florence.

"Then follow this path until you reach the road. Keep along the road to the right, until you arrive at a small wood ; you will find a beaten track in it—follow the track wherever it leads, until you meet with those who can and will direct you, and let not the advice of the gipsey be lost upon you."

"I will not fail, and thank you heartily for your kindness to me," said Florence.

"You may well thank me," responded the woman. "I feel that I deserve it, for it is hard to be kind to those who have caused one the misery which you have me."

"I cause you misery !" reiterated Florence, with astonishment. "How ? In what manner ? Heaven knows if I have, it was unconsciously."

"It is true," she returned, "it is unconscious on your part ; but the misery is not the less acute. And if I knew not that you hated him, as I am sure you do," she added with vehemence, "you would find me a far bitterer foe than he is, but let it pass," she continued mournfully, almost soliloquizing. "It is a face that might have enslaved a harder heart than his. I might have forgiven him, after looking upon such beauty : but my child, my helpless innocent, the little smiling, sinless thing, rises up in judgment against him, and drowns every emotion of pity or forgiveness the iron barb of revenge alone remains, and in this heart shall it be buried."

She paused a minute in deep thought, but her features in their convulsive workings showed how bitter the remembrances were which thronged through her brain ; but they passed away, and addressing Florence, she said, in tones which were deep from their earnestness.

"Farewell, and if you have a prayer to bestow upon a wretch who is destitute of every happiness, who cannot look forward to one minute of joy— who, even in the grave, scarcely expects to meet the rest and peace which others enjoy when they quit the earth for ever—think of me, couple my name with your the prayer, and you shall have my blessing."

"I will, I will, indeed I will !" exclaimed Florence, fervently.

"Enough ! we may meet again : if we should, you shall know all that

now seems a mystery to you.   Away! time is always precious to the fugitive.
Follow my counsel—pause not; remember every step increases the distance
between you and your enemy, and let not weariness, or heat, or any trifling
cause, induce you to lessen your speed, or arrest your progress.   Farewell!
God bless you, and bestow upon you the happiness which I may never know."
Waving her hand she quitted them, and made towards the cottage with singular speed. They watched her a moment, and then following her advice,
they pursued their own path as rapidly as possible, wondering who this
strange woman, whom the reader has easily recognised to be Joan Churleigh
could be.

They obeyed Joan's injunction to the letter, respecting the path, and found
she had correctly directed them ; they gained the road, and hurried along
it until the perspiration stood like pearls upon their foreheads. They stopped
for ten minutes at the cottage after they had been walking about three hours
and obtained a draught of milk, for which Florence offered to pay, but the
woman cried—

"Lard a massey, bless the child, I never take nothen for what costs
nothen.

And so, with thanks, they went their way.   They walked on without
meeting with any one, beguiling the time with saying kind and affectionate
things to each other to support them under their fatigue, until ten o'clock in
the morning, when they began to feel both hungry and fatigued ; and perceiving another cottage they made their way to it, and Florence purchased,
from one less scrupulous in taking money, some refreshments, which were
placed in a little basket, for which also she paid, and without stopping to
partake of any, fearing to be overtaken, they carried them with them, and
went on, determining to stay at some cool shady place and rest themselves
there, and obtain rest and refreshment at the same time. It was extraordinary to see with what perseverance they proceeded, nearly overcome
with heat, footsore and weary, not a cloud or a tree to shade them from
the bright hot sun, nor a breath of wind to cool their almost burning faces ;
yet they did not slacken their pace—the dread of being captured was
stronger than the disheartening effects of fatigue.   They looked many
times behind them and it was somewhat encouraging to them to see that no
one was upon their track.   Anxiously did they watch for the appearance of
the wood, and every wind in the road seemed to be THE wind that hid the
expected place from their sight, but they turned it to find themselves mistaken.   They had now been walking nearly eight hours ; they had passed
twenty miles with only one short rest, and were ready to drop with their
exertions : much farther it seemed impossible to go, when the little wood
gladdened their eyes with the cool green umbrageousness. As the wearied
and parched traveller in the desert, almost at the last extremity, sees afar
off the spring of cool sparkling water which is to endow him with new life,
makes fresh exertions and feels a renewed vigour pervading his limbs to
enable him to reach it, so did our two feeble travellers, with sparkling eyes
and smiles on their jaded countenances, press forward to their long-looked-
for resting place. They soon reached it, and without waiting to penetrate

far into its intricacies, they seated themselves by the side of a little pebbly brook. that, like a piece of silver tape, found itself a tuneful, sinuous path through the wood. They divested themselves of their cloaks and hats, and brought forth the eatables, and with appetites, which Florence, at least, seldom felt, proceeded to clear the basket of its contents. When they had finished their meal, and were cool—the shadowy trees which waved over them, lending a wonderous assistance—they bathed their faces and hands, and endeavoured to fit themselves for the continuance of their journey.

" We will rest ourselves here, Letty, for a little while longer," said Florence to her companion. " and then we will walk on again until we can meet with some conveyance which will carry us to Grasmere."

" I'll do anything you tell me," replied Letty. " I used to be obliged to do so for father, but I will gladly do it for you, for you speak so kindly and gentle to me; and you will take me to your home, won't you? and if father wants me back again you will not let him have me, will you ?"

" Why do you dislike your father so much, Letty?" enquired ,Florence, after replying affirmatively to her question.

" Because he is always so cross, and speaks so roughly to me, and makes me go into the village and tell stories, and say he is so poor, when I know he is not, because I often see him with a great many golden guineas, and silks, and laces, and barrels of brandy ; and then I have to carry parcels to ladies, and I get beaten if I do not say exactly what he tells me—and they are all stories he bids me say."

" Your father then is a smuggler ?" said Florence.

"I don't know what that means," replied Letty ; " but since mother's death he has never been kind to me—always calling me dreadful names, and telling me all mother told me about God and Heaven, and right and wrong, all foolery ; and if I cried to hear him speak so of my dear, dear mother, who was so kind to me, he would strike me with his fist, and utter such horrible oaths. It is only a little while since that a horrid man, like him who brought you to our cottage, asked my father to let him have me to live with him ; and father said if he would give him a lot of golden guineas he should— and he agreed to it. And then he caught hold of me, and pulled me on his knee, and kissed me, and asked me how I should like to have him for a sweetheart. I struggled and screamed until he let me go, as I ran away crying, I heard him say he knew the way to tame a wilder colt than I—and then both father and he laughed. I got my hat and cloak and went over to the village; I ran all the way there, and I went to a cottage where somebody I know lives ; and though father came to fetch me, he could not make me go back until he had promised me that I should never see that man again ; and I never would have gone back if—"

" You will go back now, then. I think," exclaimed a rough voice, with a rude laugh.

They both looked up in a fright, and there stood Nehemie, coolly surveying them. A scream burst from each ; they were on their feet in an instant, and would have fled, but he seized Letty by the hand, and picking up the pistol, which Florence had placed upon the grass by her side, he pointed it at her, and, in a voice of thunder, bade her come back or he would shoot her dead upon the spot. She obeyed him, and sinking against a tree, covered her face with her hands and gave herself up to despair. Letty sunk upon her knees, and implored her father to set them free. He would not listen to her, but in a stern voice told Florence she must accompany him back to the cottage. It was in vain that Letty entreated, prayed and exhorted of him not to detain them. It was without effect that she frantically wept, burying her face upon his hand, and saturating it with her tears. He made no reply, but pointing with the pistol in the direction which they had come, he commanded Florence to attire herself in her cloak and hat, and accompany him. When Letty found he was immoveable she sprung to her feet, and looking him with flashing eyes in the face, said, as she broke from his grasp.

"I'll not go home—I'll never go home any more."

'Won't you?' said Nehemie, quietly. "I think you will, and I would advise you, my lady, to go quietly, too, or your bones will be sore before you reach it—mind that."

"I don't care for that," cried the girl passionately. "I don't care. If you do take me home you shall have to carry me home dead. I will never go alive—never."

"Then stop away," replied Nehemie; "you are worth nothing—this damsel is. You may go and starve, for what I care; but if you stop behind, I'll make sure Miss, here, don't."

As he finished, he seized Florence roughly, and bade her instantly don the hat and cloak, and return with him. To refuse was useless; she was in his power, and nothing was left her but to obey him. When Letty found Florence was compelled to accompany her father, and that if she stayed behind it must be alone, she burst into a new flood of tears, and placing her arm affectionately round the neck of her gentle companion, she told her she would go with her, even if she broke her heart in doing it. Nehemie laughed scornfully at her words; but Florence, who felt it some consolation to have a companion in her painful situation, gladly took her at her word, and thanked her earnestly for the sacrifice which, for her sake, she was making. Nehemie interrupted any further colloquy between them by urging them to depart, and with sad hearts they obeyed him. They retraced their steps along the path which they had pursued in coming, but with feelings far different. In the morning their hearts were buoyed up with hope, and in the desire for escape they felt not the fatigue of walking a distance neither of them had ever before attempted; but now, their hopes destroyed, cast down with despair and oppressing forebodings of the future, the weariness, which their spirits and perseverance had enabled them to keep off, pressed upon them with a heavy hand. Their limbs ached; their feet were swollen and blistered; and they dragged along, dejected and worn out with fatigue. Their imaginations, bright and expectant in their flight, had lightened and shortened the way; but now, every yard was converted by them into a dozen and every mile a six.

Nehemie, depositing the pistol in h s coat pocket, took a hand of each, and

dragged them along, unheeding the appeals for a slower progress, replying
only to their requests by saying it served them right for coming and chuckling at the same time at a lucky accident, which, in the morning before he
returned to his cottage, gave him imformation of their flight and the path
they had taken—which lucky accident consisted of a sight of the fugitives
being obtained by a labourer, who, an hour or two afterwards, encountering
Nehemie, mentioned it to him; his first object was to return to his cottage,
and doing so, found it empty. Jasper, Florence, Letty, all gone, and no clue
left to ascertain how, or the cause of their disappearance. In an instant he
conjectured Florence had escaped, and his daughter—how, he knew not—had
aided her, and Jasper had gone in pursuit. Taking the intelligence of the
labourer as certain, he at once followed the route he had pointed out, and

No. 25

the result was to find his information correct, and the object of his journey successful. It was his intention to make the best of his way back to the cottage and there keep Florence a close prisoner until he had an opportunity of conveying to Jasper the intelligence that he was in his power. He took no notice of the pale haggard faces of his two prisoners, or that they hung heavily on his hands; for nearly two hours he pulled them along without pausing, until at length Letty fell upon her knees and sobbed out her inability to proceed farther. Nehemie swore a tremendous oath at her, and lifted her up in his arms. He carried her for some distance, until at last, Florence, exhausted and tired to death, refused to proceed until she had rested. Nehemie who began also to feel weary of his burden, consented, and they seated themselves by the way-side, upon a little green knoll, beneath a tall hedgerow, but the noise of an approaching vehicle made Nehemie resolve upon changing his position; and commanding the two to follow him, he passed through a small opening in the hedge, and entered a field. Once more beneath the hedge, only on the opposite side, they took their seats and ere they had been a couple of minutes there, a party of gipseys made their appearance through the same opening, with the evident intention of pitching their camp on or about the very spot on which our travellers reposed themselves. No sooner did the eyes of Florence perceive the garb and character of the new comers, than grasping the hand of Letty, she whispered in her ear, rapidly—

" Now, Letty, if there is any truth in the word of these people, we are saved."

" What do you whisper," muttered Nehemie, savagely.

Florence remained silent, and he continued—

"If you tell a word about yourselves, or ask for help, I'll murder you both."

He received a slap upon his shoulder, and a rough voice, exclaimed—

" Good afternoon to you, friend ; you are sitting here out of the heat and dust, I suppose—eh ?"

" *Comment vous portez-vous ? Monsieur Bohemien,*" exclaimed Nehemie, quickly, with a shrug of the shoulders, and a smiling face.

" I don't understand the lingo," replied the man; " don't you speak English ?"

" Oh ! *oui, Monsieur,* a leetle," answered Nehemie.

" That's right," responded the man, who was now surrounded by three or four men, and as many women, all regarding Nehemie and his companions with eyes of curiosity. " Them gals with you seems very tired; you have come a long way, haven't you."

" *Oui,* Monsieur, ve have come a verra long vay," returned Nehemie, with a glance at Florence and Letty

" Well, I dessay you're very peckish, and, if you like, you shall have some of our grub ; we shall cook it directly."

" *Non ; je vous suis tres-oblige, je ne peux m'arreter a present,* exclaimed Nehemie, hastily.

The man stared at him a moment with surprise, and then said—

" Vy don't you talk sense, like a man.   " Who's to know vot you mean by that gibberidge ?"

" He says he would rather not," exclaimed Florence, with rapidity ; " but we will, if you please."

" And so you shall, my lass," said the man, " and welcome, too."

Nehemie scowled dreadfully at her, but she did not heed his looks.   She was desperate ; she believed there was a chance of getting out of his clutches and at every hazard she resolved to try it.   Nehemie made several remonstrances, but was overruled by the tribe ; and having assumed the character of a Frenchman who knew but little English, he could not well prevent the unpromising turn which the affair was taking.   He persisted in saying he wanted to go, but they would not listen to him.

" The gals say they want to stop," said the man who had spoken before : " and says, too, there's no occasion to hurry.   They look fagged, and are, I daresay ; therefoie, Mounseer, you may as well make yourself comfortable, and see how pleasantly we gipseys live."

" You are very ple-sant," said Nehemie, with a grim smile, and observed almost with feelings of distraction, a woman of the tribe approach Florence and Letty, speak a few words to them and lead them away to a spot where a few of the gipseys were busy pitching a tent.   If he dared, he would have prevented them moving ; but no excuse offered, and they left him a prey to gnawing anxiety.   There was no extricating himself from the dilemma into which he had unexpectedly fallen, but by remaining quiet, and trusting to a feeble hope that his threat of murder to Florence, if she betrayed him, would keep her tongue still and enable him still to retain her in his possession until Jasper claimed her from him.   When out of necessity, he arrived at this determination he affected the possession of much enjoyment, which he was far from feeling, and from time to time eyed with a jealous eye and a beating heart an animated conversation which, accompanied by earnest gestures, was taking place between Florence and the gipsey woman.

CHAPTER XI.

" Moments there are, and this was one,
   Snatch'd like a minute's gleam of sun,
   Amid the black Simoom's eclipse;
      Or, like those verdant spots that bloom
   Around the crater's burning lips,
      Sweetening the very edge of doom !
   The past, the future—all that Fate
   Can bring of dark or desperate
   Around such hours, but makes them cast
   Intenser radiance while they last.
                                          T. MOORE,

Father's have flinty hearts.
                                          MOUNTAINEERS.

Injurious time now, with a robber's haste.
   Crams his rich thievery up, he knows not how :
As many farewells as be stars in heaven,
With distinct breath, and consigned kisses to them,
He fumbles up into a loose adieu ;
And scants us with a single famish'd kiss ;
Distasted with the salt of broken tears.
                                          SHAKSPERE.

The hero of this novel, if it has a hero, which it is possible may be doubted
seeing that the incidents are as yet more than equally shared by other characters—however, he that should be the hero of this work, John Paul, has
been for a long while left swinging in his hammock in deep slumber.   Let
us now wake him out of it.   Suppose a few days to have transpired, and the
smart Wildfire ploughing her way with a very fair-wind rapidly towards old
England ; let us suppose him, through the instrumentality of Mr. Prior, upon
the quarter deck, leaning over the side, looking with a vacant eye upon the
sea, which is belted with a zone of lustrous silver from the light of the moon.
His brain is thronging with thoughts, and he is all unconscious that he is on
board his Majesty's frigate, the Wildfire, homeward bound.   The dash of the
spray, as it leaps on each side of the cut-water, the whistle of the wind through
the blocks and cordage, the strain of the sails as the breeze bellies them out,
are all unheard ; the regular tread of the watch pacing to and fro, and the
motion of the vessel, as it bounds from billow to billow, are unnoticed, and
fall upon an ear which has no space to receive their sound ; at length, he is
aroused from his deep abstraction, there is a hand placed upon his shoulder,
and a voice murmurs in his ear—

"Paul ! Paul ! will you not look upon me ?"

As swift as an arrow he turned round to the speaker.

" Alice !" he exclaimed, quickly, and in tones of astonishment.

" Even her, Paul," she replied, rising her finger to repress the loudness of
his speech.   " To find you here," she continued, speaking in a low voice, but
fervently, " has given me much happiness ; it has made me feel that all my

perils are at an end; for where you are I know that I am safe. Oh! Paul since last we parted I have undergone such trials, that, but for the remembrance of you, I should have died ere I had gone through half I have endured.

"It gives me pain to think you should have suffered one unhappy hour," replied Paul, taking her proffered hand and pressing it; "the more especially when I know that, in a certain degree, I am the occasion of it."

"Say not so, say not so," hurriedly exclaimed Alice. "How are you to blame for my father's tyranny and harshness? Why condemn yourself for his iron heart and cold selfishness? No, Paul, it is I who have forgiveness to ask of you for the indignities you have received at his hands, after having saved his life and mine—for the taunts and insults which you have borne quietly for my sake. I know, I feel that I am the unhappy occasion of your sacrificing the noblest feelings of your nature, and suffering your name to be impugned, to be covered with the reproaches—"

"Say no more, Alice—let it pass," interrupted Paul, "a time may come—and I will perish but it shall come—when I may claim you in a manner which shall make him proud to acknowledge me as his son. It is here, Alice," he cried, striking his breast, "and I wait but for the time to bring it forth. I will WIN you, Alice, as you deserve to be won, or my head shall lie so low it shall never rise again."

"Talk not of death, Paul," exclaimed Alice. "I have been on its threshold since we met. I thought of you at the time when the world was fading from my senses, and that thought brought me again among the living. To be where you were not bore an agony greater than any death could possess: and to be here, if you were in another world, Paul, would be to send a life of incessant prayer for the hour that consigned me to the tomb. Talk not of of death, Paul; it is terrible to seperate and live, to be far apart and exist: but to be divided by a power which renders re-union, save in heaven, impossible, is to me a reflection that carries madness with it. It overpowers me. Do not talk of dying."

"Death has but one terror to me, Alice," said Paul, with a mournful smile. "It is that it may come before you are mine—it may rob me of all chance of wearing you, the spirit of my dreams, the tutelary angel that first roused my soul to action, that made me pant for glory. Oh, Alice, when in that of my boyhood which determined my future career I saw your face, I felt my heart glow as it received the impression which was never to be effaced. I felt the desire to accomplish good deeds run through my frame, and make my blood course through my veins like liquid fire, and when rescuing you from the waters, of Loch Lomond, my eyes fell upon your features, discovering to me the lineaments of the angel of my dreams, that same glow warmed my heart, my blood tingled and thrilled with emotion, and I said unto myself, ' here is the being upon whom my fate rests."

"I am humble, Alice—I am poor; but there is not a man from the hand of God who has a spirit freer than mine, who has a soul and honour more unsulled than mine. There lives not him who can, with truth, point out one stain, one spot upon my name; and all the attributes which make one man little less than a God, and the want of them in his fellow a worthless slave, I feel dwell within me, waiting but the opportunity to spread forth and make me what my ambition bids me hope to be—one who may look down from a towering height upon thy parent, proud noble though he be, and claim thy hand, a prize he will gladly yield with smiles and honied words, where now he spurns and rejects my suit, at least he fears will be my suit; but let him not be afraid; I would not seek you, so peerless as you are, without I had some equivalent to offer for the priceless gift of thy heart and hand. At least, Alice, you shall be offered an honourable name, one which shall in men's mouths be great and praiseworthy; or you shall for me, retain your own. I would not insult you by hinting at my adoration for you, I did not feel sure that day would come, when, with the honours of a king, the flattery of nobles—which, though I despise, my ambition will receive as its due—and the homage of a people, I could ask you to be mine without subjecting you to the sneering remark of the ignorant fools of fortune, or to the tyranny of a father, who makes his own aggrandizement superior to that of his child."

"There is much wild romance in your expectations," said Alice, thoughtfully; "but the romance of our connection has been more singular, more wild and fanciful, than your expectations. To me, Paul, you can never be different, even if invested with the honours you dream of. Your worth will never be raised in my estimation, because the world suddenly discovers you to be what I have long known you to be. I love, you Paul; I have cause to do so. You have deserved it of me, and, but that in a weak moment I swore an oath to my father never to marry without his consent, I would offer you my hand now."

"I would not wrong your generosity so much as to accept it," exclaimed Paul, earnestly; "although there is not on earth one wish, one hope, I so fervently desire accomplished. I will, in name, be worthy of you, Alice, or I will never ask your hand. You shall not be told you have thrown yourself away upon a beggar; you shall know a father's house whose doors is closed to you; I would not doom you to one such uneasy thought, to realise all the happiness which the possession of you would give me."

"The closed doors of a father who cast me off because I preferred your happiness and my own to the furtherance of his avarice, would never create one pang in my bosom, Paul," returned Alice, calmly; "and the sneers of those whose good or ill word would not touch me, would not lessen the happiness of a home, however, humble, where you were. You have my heart, you shall have my hand, or never shall it be given in wedlock."

"You but strengthen the proud thoughts within me, Alice," said Paul, with energy; "I should take shame to myself if I took advantage of the nobleness of your nature, and made you mine without laying some laurels at your feet. No, Alice, I have said I will WIN you, and I WILL! Had your father calmly listened to me, he would have known I would never have attempted to enter his family clandestinely. I am to proud to stoop to such an act—had he studied me a little more, he might have known it. Upon the day when we first discovered we loved each other—when, in the midst of a sweet communion of bright thoughts and hopes we pictured a time when we should be side by side, passing through life smilingly and happily together, ministering to each others joys, softening each other's cares, smothing the clouded brow, chasing away the gloomy thought, and dressing the face with unalloyed peacefulness and contentment of the heart, he, overhearing our colloquy, burst in upon our fairy visions, like some evil spirit, to blast all our hopes, at the moment when, though habited in the garb of a common seaman, I stood before him with unspotted honour, the preserver of his life—he heaped upon me execrations, stinging reproaches, called me dog and slave, when, shaking his fist in my face, he would have struck me but that his passion had not so blinded him but he saw danger in such an act written in my glittering eye—when, Alice, I was goaded almost to madness by his unmanly reproaches to me, his sarcastic and villanous insinuations against your spotless fame, I could have sprung upon him and torn him limb from limb, my eyes encountered your white but calm countenance; its expression of firmness, which not all his intemperate language could shake, your single look of agony for the torments he made me endure in his unjust and untrue virulence, cooled me down to ice though the moment previous my breast was scorching, and had I been a rock his words could not have fallen on me more unheeded. I waited for a pause in the ebullition of his mad rage to tell him the determination I had formed ; to swear to him I would never ask your hand, or seek to persuade you to bestow it upon me, until I had made myself worthy, in pocket, in his eyes, and in glorious fame in yours. I let him rage on; his words were lost on me : I looked upon you ; you were then as I saw the glorious figure in my dream ; every lineament the same—the expression, the look, all, all, the same. In that moment I swore to myself that I would never rest until I had worked myself into a glorious position. I had it on my lips to tell him so, to bid him know that, if poor, I was as proud as he, and I loved you too well to disgrace you by an alliance with one who could not boast a line of noble ancestry, or supply the want with some fair equivalent. But let us speak no more of this: the struggle is over ; the heartburnings and rankling feelings raised by scornful taunts have passed away, and left but the clear flame of ambition burning within my breast. I know not how my hopes are to be realized, the path is yet hidden from me; but I feel that the veil will be lifted, and raised too ere long—when it is, Alice, I will but breath thy name to my soul, and it must be a strong hand indeed that will stay me in my onward career.

"I will not wrong you by supposing that, though years may separate us while I am striving to obtain the means of claiming you, you will forget me, or find in another qualities which may induce you to withdraw your heart from me to place in his keeping. I know you to be too noble, too single-minded. I know that, were we not to meet again until the frost of age was upon our temples, I should find you the same true, unsulled being you are now."

" Why do you speak thus ?" interrupted Alice, fixing her large clear, dark eyes upon him with an air of interest; the tenour of your speech is such as to lead me to believe you deem our parting will be immediate."

" It will," replied Paul, dropping his eyes sadly.

" Immediate !   Why ?   How ! speak Paul, what mean you !" she inquired hurriedly.

He raised his eyes to hers, and replied in a low tone—

" You have not to learn that Captain Pearson is an old friend and school-follow of your father's,"

" True ; he has told me so," she returned ; " and has fully supported the character of his kindness to me ; but how is that to effect our separation ?"

" He has obtained from me a history of our acquaintance," answered Paul, " a casual remark from John Andrew made him aware that we were known to each other.   He sent for me, and questioned me.   I saw no reason for disguise ; indeed, feared to compromise your name by silence, for the disparity of our situations in life might give rise to suspicions which a few words would dispel, and related as much as I deemed necessary. But, again, John Andrew stepped in with a simple remark ; which was enough, however, to make Captain Pearson understand the enmity your father bore to our affection, and command me not seek to hold communication or converse with you while you were on board.   I am in a kings ship, and opposition to the command of him, whose slightest word is law, would be utterly useless, and perhaps be bringing you into the disgrace which would fall upon me for disobedience of orders.   This opportunity, though in opposition to his command, is therefore not likely to occur again, and I wish to take advantage of it by—"

A rapid footstep behind them interrupted him, and a quick voice, which he instantly recognised as the Captain's, exclaimed, hastily and sternly—

" How now, sir ! what do you do here ?"

" I am here by Mr. Prior's orders," replied Paul instantly.

" What does he want with you ?" he asked.

" I cannot say," returned Paul ; " he sent for me aft, and I wait his commands."

" Where is he ?" inquired the Captain sharply.

" In his berth, I believe, sir," replied our hero.

" Um !" ejaculated the Captain ; and then called aloud to a seaman stationed close to the wheel—" Quartermaster !"

" Sir," was the instant reply.

" Send some one to Mr. Prior's birth ; if he is there, say I wish to speak with him."

The second lieutenant, whose watch it was, approached the Captain, having overheard the colloquy between him and Paul, and said respectfully—

" If you require any confirmation, of Paul's statement, I can give it you. I was by when Mr. Prior sent for him, and when he bid him remain until he came upon deck again."

" I do not require you interference just now," returned the captain quickly ; " when I do, I'll send for you ; for the present, perhaps you will favour me by keeping a little to windward,"

The lieutenant bit his lips with a mortified air, bowed, and crossed to the weather side. The captain watched him until he was out of hearing, and then said, in a low tone—

"Your presence here is accounted for ; yet I scarcely believe this meeting to be accidental. You knew my express command upon this matter ; you have violated it ; you must be prepared to take the consequences."

"You are premature, Captain Pearson," exclaimed Alice, with much dignity of manner. You assume a disobedience of orders without knowing that it really is so, and would, without waiting for proof, act upon your assumption as if it had been proved. You are mistaken, the meeting was accidental, at least upon the part of Paul. If there is blame to be attached to

No 26

any one, it is to me; I accosted him, I held the conversation, and I have yet to learn that you have the power to prevent me speaking to whom I choose."

"You are well aware, Miss," replied the captain, a little tartly, "that your father is entirely averse to your holding communication to this young man. When I met with him in Porto Rico, I promised him, if I succeeded in recovering you from the hands of the pirates, I would supply his place. I conceive I should not be fulfilling the duty I have undertaken to perform, if I did not to the best of my ability prevent all communication between you and this young man during the time you are beneath my care. When we reach England, and I am able to place you in your father's hands as safely as when I received you, then I consider my duty will cease, and, as far as I am concerned, you can of course act as you please. As for you Paul," he added, addressing him sternly, "you know my—I will not say my commands, but wishes; you acknowledged the justice of them, and promised me they should be obeyed. At the very first opportunity I find you break your word, violate my order—

"Stay, listen to me for one moment, Captain Pearson," exclaimed Alice interrupting him.

"I beg your pardon, Miss," answered the captain, "another time—at present—"

"I will be heard, sir," she cried, almost vehemently. The captain looked at her a little astonished, and she unheeding his looks, proceeded—"I cannot suffer your base surmises to be used as facts. Captain Pearson, I acknowledge warmly and thankfully the services you have rendered me, in saving me from a terrible fate. I acknowledge with every sentiment of gratitude the kindness and attentions, which, since I have been in this vessel, have been paid me, and which have succeeded in restoring me from a miserable condition to comparative health; and this, sir, merits and receives my most incere gratefulness, and if there is any way consistent with my knowledge of what is due to myself' by which I can show you my strong sense of it, I shall feel but too proud and happy to do it—"

"My dear Miss, there is no occasion for this," interrupted the captain, impatiently; "this has nothing to do with the subject—"

"You mistake, sir," replied Alice, not allowing him to proceed.

"Hear me out, and you will see that it has; thus far, at least, it has to do with it; it gives you a certain power over me, which I neither will attempt to deny or shake off; but, permit me to say, it does not render me so subject to your will that you may at pleasure prevent me from speaking to whom I please."

"It is only with this person; and while you are in this vessel," exclaimed the Captain, quickly, "that I would forbid communication."

"And he, Captain Pearson, is the very person for whom I feel bound even to throw aside the services you have rendered me, and be exposed to the charge from you of ingratitude," she exclaimed spiritedly. "I owe my life to him—my father owes his life to him; he has borne persecution, misrepre-

sentation, insults, and flagrant injustice for my sake, and I would scorn myself for ever, if the prayers, entreaties, or even positive commands of any one
made me avert my face, or treat him with silence or coolness. I feel it but
justice to myself to make you understand this, and in justice to him I
assure you, by the honour of one whose word was never broken, whose
truth was never impeached, that I sought the interview, that I addressed him
that he acquainted me of your commands, and thus has not infringed your
orders or rendered himself amendable for punishment; and you have yourself
had disinterested evidence to prove that his presence here—if the spot is interdicted to all in his station—was the result of his obedience to an order,
which to have disobeyed would have ensured him severe punishment."

"Words are poor offerings for the deep feelings of the heart," said Paul to
Alice; "but in the best terms that my soul is capable of finding expression I
thank you for the earnest endeavour you have made to screen me from the
resentment of Captain Pearson, and remove from me all the blame to attach
it to yourself; it would be unworthy of me," he added proudly, "were I
quietly to permit this, and creep out of the liability I have incurred, through
your kindness. I feel that I should do shame to your most friendly interest
for me, were I to act thus meanly ; and feeling equally as grateful as though
your kindness had gained its desired object, I do not hesitate to tell Captain
Pearson I was a participator in the conversation, freely and without con-
straint; that I held communication not merely by replies, but by questions
also; and I am fully prepared to undergo whatever punishment he may
deem necessary to inflict upon me; at the same time, I wish it understood,
Sir," he continued, addressing the Captain particularly, "that when the
promise was made to you, it was with the idea that I should not have an
opportunity of meeting with the young lady while on board, unless I sought
to gain an interview with her, and conceiving that, as it was against your
commands, if I attempted it I might cause her uneasiness and discomfort, I
readily promised what I knew would be a hard task for me to perform,
but what I fully believed would ensure the lady the absence of care and
anxiety. When I found an opportunity within my power, placed there
without the smallest effort of mine, a meeting which was as accidental as
unexpected, I confess I was regardless of what might ensue with respect to
myself, and gladly availed myself of the chance of exchanging a few words
with one whose friendship I esteem as the brightest gem in my existence.
I do not consider that I have broken my word, for however greatly desired
and gladly seized the interview was, it was unsought. You, sir, may have
a different view of it. I am in your power completely; act as you please,
I must submit; but shall not flinch, whatever your determination may be."

Mr. Prior at this moment appeared, and advancing to the captain begged
to know his commands.

"You sent for John Paul aft, I understand?" said the captain, sharply.

"I did," was the reply, given in as quick a tone as the question.

"May I enquire the duty you required the man to perform?" asked the
captain, rather sarcastically.

"I had a private communication to make to him, sir," replied Prior stifly.

"Private communication!" echoed the captain, with unaffected astonishment, and looking rapidly from one to another; "I was not aware, Mr. Prior, that you were such friends with a common man."

Paul's face glowed liked a furnace; and Mr. Prior, knitting his brow, said hautily—

"Paul, sir, is no common man, though on the forecastle. You have had occasion to admire his skill, and have yourself made the remark that he was born to be an officer."

Paul said nothing, but he fixed his clear bright eye upon the captain, and thought a day might come when he would compel him to acknowledge him no common man. The captain turned his head impatiently away at Prior's speech and, paced a few steps; he, however, returned and said hastily—

"I thought, Mr. Prior, you had been long enough in a king's ship to know that the quarter-deck is no place for loungers and idlers from the waist or forecastle, you should have asked the man to your cabin, if you had a PRIVATE communication to make to him."

"So I should have done, sir," replied Mr. Prior, "but that I was finishing some papers, and was not ready to receive him."

"Hem! Then you should have deferred your communication until the morning," said the captain, "a man who has been on deck, save at meal times, since day-break, would rather be in his hammock than kicking his heels upon the quarter deck, waiting for your private communications. You will, perhaps, remember this, Mr. Prior—Hem!"

As he concluded, he waved his hand for the lieutenant to retire, who, bended slightly, obeyed him, he then turned to Paul, and said, somewhat sternly—

"You have some strong advocates in your behalf, and the evidence I have received induces me to believe that your disobedience was unpremeditated, and, to a certain degree, done unconsciously; taking that view of the case, I acquit you. To your berth, sir, and do not run the hazard of being placed again in the same situation; you may find me less disposed to be lenient."

"Am I to understand, Captain Pearson," exclaimed Alice, quickly, as Paul attempted to depart, "that you forbid Paul to speak to me?"

"As long as you are on board, certainly," he replied.

"I suppose your interdiction does not extend to his listening if I see fit to speak to him; for you will please to remember that I do not acknowledge the power which, as one of your company, he is compelled to do."

"I have little doubt, Miss, that you will view me as a stern tyrant," said the captain; "I cannot help it if you do; a time may perhaps come when you will think otherwise. At present, whatever, your thoughts, I shall perform what I deem my duty. I forbid John Paul, upon pain of being severely flogged, holding communication of any description with you, as long as you remain on board; and if you would not desire to see him suffer, you will abstain from speaking to him, or acting in any way which will bring punishment upon him. I hope you both now thoroughly understand me."

" I understand only that I am to consider myself a prisoner," said Alice, indignantly.

"Whatever you please, Miss," returned the captain sarcastically; "you know my determination. Paul, to your berth. Mr. Prior will not make his PRIVATE communication to-night, I have no doubt."

Paul, who knew the madness of attempting to disobey him whose very power was absolute, turned to Alice, and said—

" Farewell! we shall meet again, and in happier times, until then, believe me—"

"As true as the needle to the pole," interrupted the captain, hastily. "No more of this nonsense, sir; to your hammock at once, or you may perhaps have the assistance of a few of the people to show you the way to the lower hold, and put you in irons."

"I go, sir," said Paul; "but I take back my promise not to hold communication with this young lady : I know the penalty, and if I see fit I shall not hesitate to incur it, or shrink from receiving it if detected."

"A little more respect to your captain, and less of your insubordinate remarks would be more prudent—begone! Miss, allow me to attend you to your cabin."

Before Alice could speak the Captain took her hand, and Paul, bowing to her, retired slowly to his hammock, while the captain led Alice to the cabin he had placed at her disposal, and left her to endanger her restoration to health by weeping the night through.

A few words may be necessary to explain how her meeting with Paul originated. John Andrew, who, having been her faithful companion in such heavy trials, was much attached to her, and fond of speaking about her. The interview which had taken place between himself, the captain, and John Paul, had been faithfully and accurately narrated to Gasket, and by Gasket to Mr. Prior. The latter, having several times seen Alice, when so far recovered as to quit her berth, took an opportunity to mention Paul's name to her, and, at her express wish, contrived their meeting in the manner that had been seen. The lieutenant was much stung by the captain's sarcasm, and resolved, notwithstanding he could perceive how determined the captain was against it, to contrive another meeting, and take all the blame upon himself.

A few days passed away; the vessel still held her course for England, and as the wind held also, the passage bid fair to be a favourable one. A couple of seamen one morning, who were in the main-top, were holding a discourse as to the merits of John Paul, quite unconscious that a stealthy foot had brought the captain, who sometimes indulged in a visit, there. As he heard the name of our hero coupled with that of Alice, he paused, and, although it was not a very gentlemanly act, he felt so interested in what was transpiring to hesitate listening without discovering himself.

"I tell you, John," said one of the speakers, "when the devil gets to windward of him there's only another, and that's himself, and that, you see, wouldn't be a easy job—for though a man may get to windward of himself when he's three sheets in the wind, he's much too apt to fall to leeward when he's sober; but, howsomdever, that's not much to the purpose.   She may be richer and handsomer than he, but that's not enough to make her better than him; for I tell you its my opinion, that there isn't a king's daughter of them all that's above him in worth, and if I was a princess, which I ain't—and, for the matter o' that, not a bit like one—I should say to him if he asked me to marry, here's my fin and may I be damned, but I stick true blue to you till I drop my peak to grim death.   Ah, John, if this girl be a lady—a real, right down lady—it's my belief she won't look at her family tree, if it be even as long as the fore-topmast-stay, but splice with him, in spite of the devil.   I'm sure she will, and battle the watch with a hundred fathers or captains of any craft to get speech with him."

"She'd wish to do it, in her heart," said the other seaman; "but I'm afraid she's too gentle—she wants pluck."

"Does she?" retorted the first speaker.   "Did you find her scream and hollow when you thought you were both going to Davy Jones?"

"No," replied his companion; "she was very quiet, and said all manner of comforting things to me, to keep from looking as if a week's grog had been stopped."

"Very well, then," triumphantly exclaimed the first speaker, "she don't want courage to do it.   I tell you I'm sure she's a noble girl, or else he wouldn't strike his colours to her : and, besides, do you think she'd have talked to him as she did the night afore last after the captain had turned in."

The captain opened his ears, a little wider, approached a little nearer, and listened a little more attentively.

"She did," said the second seaman, in surprise.

"Aye!" replied the first; "though she knowed the captain swore blue murder to the first as talked to the other.   He told Johnny Paul that he'd run him up to the yard-arm, and would keel haul the young lady, if he run athwart them speaking by word of mouth or talking with bunting ; and when you knows as much of the captain as I knows on him, you'll know there's no mistake about his keeping a promise if he makes it. If he says to you, my man, I'll give you a dozen, you may be as sure of your dozen as if you had it, and there ain't nobody as can turn him to mercy either, you'll have your dozen. Paul knows this as well as I, and yet he never cared half a sheave about it ; it wouldn't stop him when he had made up his mind to see the girl. He takes no account of life when he's boused up for a service, so, taking the for and by, he lays a plan to outwit the captain and see the lady and lay out for a yarn. Well, and I tell you how he does it." Here he lowered his voice a little, and proceeded; "he waits till the hammocks are piped down and—wheugh!"

The last sound was a long and protracted whistle; his arm was pinched by his companion rather sharply while he was speaking, and a slight gesture with a thumb disclosed to him the presence of the captain. The two speakers were Gasket and John Andrew, and the latter, having accidently cast his eyes round when Gasket, as a precautionary measure, lowered his voice, saw the captain listening eagerly to their conversation: he communicated by a pinch his discovery, and as a matter of course the conversation as instantly ceased. Immediately the captain found he was detected, he smiled with an appearance of good nature upon them both, and said affably to Gasket—

"Don't stop, my man. Go on, go on with your story."

Gasket, however, was to his feet in a moment, and his example was speedily followed by John Andrew; he looked at the captain with an expression of astonishment and embarrassment which would have been ludicrous, but that the matter he was telling was too interesting to allow of mirth. He scratched his head and with an open mouth stood staring, but did not utter a word. The captain waited a moment, and then said, testily—

"Do you hear me, man? What's the matter with thee? don't stand gaping at me like a shark looking for prey—go on with your story."

"What story, sir?" said Gasket, recovering himself a little.

"What story!" repeated the captain, sternly; "why the one you were telling when you perceived me at your elbow; finish it, sir; finish it at once."

"Oh!" said Gasket, affecting suddenly to recollect. "Oh, I know what your honour means now—oh, I had just finished it as you came up, your honour."

"Oh! you'd just finished it, had you?" said the captain.

Yes, your honour, that was the end of it," returned Gasket, assuming a most innocent expression.

"Um," grunted the captain, as if he rather more than doubted it. "I don't think it will be the end of it—perhaps you will oblige me by repeating it to me."

"Ay, ay, sir," said Gasket, touching his forehead respectfully; "I am not much of a hand at a yarn, and if I should fall overboard in working my ship, your honour will perhaps heave me a rope."

"You shall have a rope, my man," said the captain, sternly; "but I would advise you to keep a good reckoning, or you may not perhaps approve of my method of bestowing it. Proceed, sir."

"Your honour knows," commenced Gasket, clearing his throat, and displaying some little embarrassment of matter, although he strove to hide it. "Your honour knows that spinning a yarn twice in one bell is like chanting a stave twice over in one breath, one don't seem the same—"

"Never mind your feelings," interrupted the captain hastily; "go on with your story."

Gasket looked at Andrew, as much as to ask for a helping hand, and went on."

Your honour perhaps does not know that afore I was in the Howdacious I was a topman in the Snarler, eighteen-gun sloop—such a craft to walk through the water—"

"I want to know nothing about the Snarler, or where you happened to be before the present moment," interrupted the captain, impatiently, and frowning angrily at the perplexed seaman; "your yarn was respecting John Paul you will tell me that, if you please, and quickly."

"I know no yarn about John Paul, sir," said Gasket, rather doggedly.

"Don't you," returned the captain.   "I think you do; I'll refresh your memory with the cat, if you don't recollect at once what you said about him as I approached you."

"Your honour can do what you please," said Gasket; "but the cat wouldn't make me remember what I know nothing about."

"I suppose you remember what you were telling to this man," exclaimed the captain, grinding his teeth with anger, as he pointed to Andrew.

"Oh, yes, your honour," returned Gasket, quickly; "that's the yarn I was going to tell your honour when you stopped me."

"Well, tell it me," said the captain, speaking emphatically; "and remember I overheard part of it.   Now, if you attempt to deceive me in what you are about to tell me, as sure as my name is Pearson, you shall be seized up to a grating.   Understand that and proceed."

Gasket shrugged his shoulders, and then looking at the tips of his nails, with a half closed hand, as if something important to his story was there situated, he began—

"I told your honour that I was a topman on board the Snarler sloop of war.   We had a lieutenant on board who was first cousin to the captain; at least so I heard; he might have been, and he might not—but as that's werry little to do with the story, it's no matter; though, now I remembers, it had to do with the story, because it was about the relationship that there was such a splutter.   He was a midshipman when I first went, and afterwards a lieutenant, which as your honour knows, is right and proper, because a lieutenant must be a mid before he can get his wash boards——"

"I see what you will get shortly," cried the captain; "what the devil's all this to do with John Paul."

"With John Paul!" echoed Gasket; "Lord love your honour—nothing.'

"Nothing!" repeated the captain, furiously.

"No, your honour; I was speaking of the lieutenant, Paul Patterson, who we used always to call Paul, and the yarn is about his falling in love, and splicing a young lady that his uncle, a Admiral, swore he shouldn't have; but he'd smuggled her aboard the Snarler, and I was telling John Andrews of a rig he used to get to talk with her, because you see, sir, nobody knowed but he and one or two others that she was aboard—not even the captain himself.   He was a commander then; I dare say your honour knows—"

"That you are telling me an infernal lie," roared the captain; a vile subterfuge to deceive me.   Follow me to the quarter deck, both of you; I will see if cannot work a little of the truth out of you."

He descended the ratlins as he spoke, and the two prepared to follow him; but ere they departed, Gasket clutched Andrew by the arm and whispered, rapidly—

"I'll stick to John Paul until I drop my peak. You'll not betray him or the young lady, will you?"

"They shall run me up to the yard arm, and then I won't," replied Andrew.

Gasket squeezed his hand, and they both were upon the quarter-deck as soon as the captain had reached it. The latter lost no time in pursuing the subject he had sprung, and once more interrogated Gasket closely, but failed in eliciting anything from him. He then turned to John Andrew, and asked him to repeat all that Gasket had said to him in the maintop. Andrew shook his head slowly, and complained of a defective memory.

"You suffered from no want of memory when relating the occurrences transpiring after your departure from Porto Rico until you were picked up by my people," exclaimed the captain, angrily.

No. 27

"Aye, sir; but if you recollects, they was all acts and deeds. What Gasket said was only talking. I can remember what I see and do better than what I hear," he replied readily.

The captain grew furious. All his catechising and questioning, cross-examination and threats, were unable to get from either Gasket or Andrew the confirmation of the suspicions which were aroused within him. From what he had overheard, he felt sure that Paul had contrived another interview in defiance of his threats and vigilance; and enraged at being directly disobeyed, he determined to punish him severely if he could bring it home to him; but that was a matter more desired than easy of accomplishment.

It will be as well to state that the interview had been accomplished by Paul's ingenuity, slightly aided by Mr. Prior, who conveyed to Alice a note containing the time and place of meeting—which was at her cabin window Paul, at the time appointed, had gone aft as far as he could without attracting attention, and then with a rope which he fastened round his body, the other end of which had been made fast to the taffrail by the negro, who could get there without exciting suspicion, and whom Paul knew to be one he could trust. He then lowered himself over the side, and suffering himself to fall in the water, he was towed in the wake of the vessel, and drew himself close under the stern; and then avoiding the windows of the captain's cabin, he climbed up the wet and slippery rope, and reached the cabin of Alice, and there held a long converse with her in a tone not above a whisper; quitted her, and clambering up to the gunwale, he held it with his fingers, and glided round the side by the aid of his knees and toes until he reached the mizen chains; crawled along the gangway and contrived to get to his berth un-noticed by any one but Gasket, who had the larboard watch, and would not see his friend on any account.

The captain had overheard quite enough to make him guess all that had passed, but before he could punish he must have proofs, and to get these proofs was the difficulty. He had some hopes that the sight of the cat might have an effect on both Gasket and Andrew, and, therefore, instantly ordered a grating to be prepared, and the boatswain and his mate to be in readiness to exercise their unpleasant duty. As he gave the order he looked sharply at both, but neither showed the smallest indication of alarm, or care for the punishment they were likely to undergo. He had mistaken his men; they were not easily intimidated. The captain now inquired who had the watch aft on the evening previous to the last, and on being told, he sent for him. It was the third lieutenant. He was asked to remember who he had seen aft that night during his watch. He instantly replied that he had seen no one but the negro, and he did not notice what he did. The black was sent for, and the captain questioned him quickly and sternly. The black scratched his head and grinned.

"What brought you aft the night before last?" roared the captain in a passion. The black grinned again.

"'Im legs, sar; 'em crew no say da berra hansum, but 'em sarb a turn, massa."

"Quartermaster," shouted the captain to a seaman close at hand.

" Sir," cried the man.

" Take a rope's end in your fist and stand by this black fellow, and when I tell you, give the rascal the bight of it over his shoulders," exclaimed the captain. " Now, sir," he added, " perhaps you will be careful how you speak."

The black rolled his eyes and looked wistfully at the quartermaster, who obeyed the captain immediately, and stood by his side ready to use the rope the moment he was bid, as coolly as if he had been ordered to beat the dust out of a jacket.

" 'I no fist at talking, sar," exclaimed the black, with a whining voice " he berra sorry if he affront you—he berra glad to—"

" Now tell me," said the captain, " for what purpose you came aft; the lieutenant of the watch says he saw you at the taffrail. What business had you there ?"

" He no business there, sar," replied the black, with a trembling aspect.

" Then, what the devil did you go there for ?" roared the captain.

"He go there for noting," said the negro, shrinking as if he expected the blow to arrive every instant.

" You scoundrel," passionately cried the captain. " Do you mean to say you leant over the taffrail without an object."

" He no objek wid him, sar," murmured the black. " A chaplain say da nigger, poor dark objek, hab no soul—so, sar, he berra dark and want lighten- ing."

" Give him the rope," roared the captain to the quatermaster.

The man obeyed him, and the poor fellow leaped with pain from the blows ; when he had received half a-dozen cuts, the captain cried.

"Hold on !" and the man ceased his flaggellation.

"Now, sir," exclaimed the captain, "can you tell me who induced you to come to the traffrail, who asked you, and what they asked you to do ?"

" Massa flog a nigger's heart out of he body if he tell him," exclaimed the black, pretending to cry very hard.

"No, no—I'll reward you instead," cried the captain, rapidly, beginning to fancy there was some prospect at last of coming to the truth.

" And no hab him seized up to grating an gib him two dozen, sar ?" in- quired the black.

" No, no. I tell you," returned the captain, impatiently. " You shall have a double allowance of grog and a guinea, if you tell me the truth".

" Then him tell all, s'ep him gorra mighty," said the black.

"Ha, ha," chuckled the captain, with a look at Gasket and Andrew, as much as to say, " I have you now." They both trembled for Paul ; and the black pushed the quartermaster, who held the rope, a little further from him, wiped his eyes, and said—

" Massa promise him he no flog when he tell."

" You have my word, you black scoundrel," cried the captain ; " isn't that sufficient."

"Iss massa, den here go," said the black. "You see, massa, a shirk follow us for some time, and nobody see'em but me, sar. Well, a' ear Dick Stretchout say dat wonderful ting in a shirk belly—hanspik, sar, a topmast, and a cock hat sar, an a sword, an a man, sar—one Jonah—who lib tree day and tree night in a belly, an a'come out libe and well, sar, and so 'em tink 'em catch a first shirk he see and cut him open and try; cos, sar, da shirk which John Paul kill was hove overboard in a gale afore he open—so a make lump a' junk fass to a piece o' line, and take a turn with oder end roun a taffrail, sar, an tow'em beef a starn to catch a shirk—dat's all, sar."

"That's all, is it?" said the captain, lowering on the black an awfully ominous frown.

"Dat all, sar," cried the black, placing his hand upon his breast and performing a low bow.

"You will take your oath to it, I suppose?" exclaimed the captain drily.

"He blast he soul to de dibbil, but he say true," replied the negro in-stantly.

"Give the rascal another taste of the rope," shouted the captain to the quartermaster, the moment the oath left the negro's lips. The seaman, who stood ready with the rope, gave a flourish with it, and aimed a smart blow at the black, but he dexterously darted from him. dodged him round the captain, screaming and jibbering like a monkey.

"He speak a trute—he dam to hell but he speak a trute; belay de rope—massa pass him word he no flog him if he tell him trute. Avast, Massa Sheathing; hold on, sar—cap'en gib his honour he no floggee"

"But, you rascal, you have not told me the truth," cried the captain; "you shall be soundly lashed, you black monkey, for lying."

"He no lie, sar—s'ep him gorra, sar, he no lie. He speak a trute; he wish he may be cussed for ebber, but he speak a trute. Massa say he no floggee—massa no lie, he sure o' dat; he gib a nigger 'he word. Massa Sheathing, sheer off, sar—like your dam imperence, sar, to make a cap'en tell lie to a nigger—avast with the rope end."

The captain though much enraged, could not help laughing at the antics of the negro to escape the quartermaster, and finding that he was not likely to come at the truth of his suspicions, even by flogging the fellow, he said to the quartermaster—

"Start the nigger forward, and then let him be."

The man answered with the brief "Ay, ay, sir!" and sprung at the black, but he was to nimble for him; he twisted about like an eel every blow that was made at him, crying as he ran from the quarter-deck.

"Way, 'nuff Massa Sheathing—way, 'nuff, sar, wid the rope."

Just as the words left his lips, the quartermaster, a smart seaman, who was delighted with the fun, caught him with the bight of the rope over the part of the frame which sailors denominate the stern, and which polite landsmen designate the seat of honour. Nature had been bountiful to the negro in quantity, but had been sparing in the thickness of skin, and the effects of the blow, given with a strong arm, was to make him leap three or four feet in the air, and scream out—

"Avast, you dam tief—gorra mighty! you hurt a nigger cussedly—oof—ah, cuss him, he cut him to de bone. Hold on, sar—hold on: look out for your beef, sar; he be dam but he spoil a taste for him afore he leave the galley fire. He no know him for beef, he cuss if he do. Avast you lob-lolly—you pawder monkey's mate's minister—you Tom Coxe—he for'ard now, so hold on wid the rope and be dam to you."

By this time the black had reached the forecastle, having raced through the waist at the top of his speed, roaring out the foregoing exclamations, all the while accompanied by the laughter and jeers of the people, who all enjoyed the discipline of the negro with the most exquisite delight, each wishing they had the starting of him. As the quartermaster quitted the black to return to his duty by the quarter deck, the black shouted after him—

"Look out for your beef, sar, a dam'fishus, imperant rascal. Look out for your grub—he cuss if he don't make him 'member starting a nigger. Oh, oh how 'em burn, oof—him smart like a debbil."

And rubbing the part affected, he went grumbling and swearing to the galley fire. As soon as he had disappeared from the quarter deck, the captain turned to Gasket and Andrew, and again sharply interrogated them respect. ing the conversation which made him feel satisfied Paul had seen Alice against his express command : but with all the tact and ingenuity he could exercise, he failed in drawing the smallest admission from either which would give him fair grounds of proceeding against Paul. He lost his temper dreadfully during the interrogation, and while he was in his most wrathful fit, the boatswain made his appearance, and touched his head respectfully, said—

"All ready with the grating, sir."

"Tie this fellow up," he replied, quickly, pointing to Gasket. "We will see if the cat will bring the truth out of him. Strip, sir," he continued, addressing Gasket. "Strip, sir, and quickly. As for you," he exclaimed, turning to Andrew, "I shall not punish you, because I heard enough to tell me you are unacquainted with the whole trick which I wish to discover and punish the author of, and your silence of what you do know arises from a natural desire to screen your messmate; but you shall see his punishment, and it will prove, perhaps, a warning to you to speak the truth when it is required of you."

"I beg your pardon for speaking, sir," exclaimed Andrew, when the captain ceased ; "but, by your leave, I will say a word or two. I ain't been in the ship with you, sir, very long, but since I have, I have found you very kind and just, and I have the same to say of my messmate here; we never saw each other till I came on board, but he's done me many a turn, tho' I was a stranger to him, and this I have to say, that when a messmate holds out his hand for you, why keel-hauling's too good for you if you don't do the same for him when the time comes. Your honour knows, when first I came on board the Wildfire, I was howdacious bad—my breast bone was athwart hawse of my back bone. I was thin enough to hide and never be seen under the lee of a rope yarn. I was little better than a sheer hulk—my life lines were all but unrove.   Now there stands the man, who, with John Paul, stuck to me like true blues, as they are, till I got fat and strong as you see me now. If I'd been their sick babby and they my mothers, they couldn't have been more tenderer and kinder than they was; they did me more good than the doctor, they were never aweary of bringing me little things as I could take, and never left off till I had a clean bill of health.   Now, saving your honour's presence, if I forget it may I be damned, and so your honour a back can't make any difference to you so as it is a back, and here's mine; let me take the lashes you intend to give my mate—here's nobody knows much of me aboard, all the crew know him well, and knows he don't deserve the cat I can bear the disgrace—"

" It's useless, my man," said the captain, interrupting him, " he has incurred, the punishment, not you. I might as well run you up to the yard-arm for a murder which you never committed. No, no, my man, stand aside."

Gasket turned to Andrew as he was led away, and said in a cheerful tone

"Don't put on such a long figure head, John: let the cat come—I don t care—it's no disgrace when you haven't deserved it."

" Silence! there," cried the captain.   " Tie him up."

Gasket was instantly led to the waist, where the punishment was to be given, and fastened to the grating. Paul all this while was upon duty on the forecastle, and could only gather a little of what was going on from the broken sentences of the black, and without open insubordination could not leave his post. He could only learn that Gasket was to be flogged for telling lies to the captain: but what the lies were, or when they were told, his informants were unable to acquaint him with, and in a state of the greatest anxiety he waited for some further enlightening on the matter. cursing the power which withheld him from approaching the scene of action, and ascertaining for himself the real state of the case. He knew the value and necessity of discipline, and would not so openly set it aside.

. When Gasket was fastened to the grating, and the boatswain and his mate stood on each side holding the cat, and a large proportion of the crew stood around wondering, the captain said—

" Now, my man, you see I mean to keep my word, it is not too late to confess.   Speak, will you tell me now?"

" Captain Pearson," said Gasket, speaking excitedly, " I've stood too often by my guns in hot actions, without sheering an inch, to be afraid of the cat, if it wasn't for the disgrace it brings on a man's name.   You see my back, sir, there's not the scar of a single lash upon it, and I can swear that a rope's-end has never crossed it in the way of punishment since I was a youngster, and then, sir, I only had it by way of sharpening me, sir, and merely for sky-larking: never, upon the honour of a man, because I was on the black list: and now, sir, I ask you one thing, which I know you will be just enough to answer truly—was I ever reported to you for not doing my duty, for drunken_ ness, or any other misconduct."

" No," replied the captain.

" Excepting Paul, he's the smartest hand we have in this ship," said the second lieutenant, touching his hat to the captain.

" And I'll stake my life for his truth and honesty," cried Prior, warmly his face flushed with indignation at the treatment the simple-hearted fellow was about to undergo.

The Captain waved his hand.

" Gentlemen," he said, " wait until I inquire your opinion of the man's merits, than I will thank you for it—but not until then."

" I am much obliged to you, gentlemen, for your goodness," said Gasket, speaking in his throat, "it will make the cat fall the lighter and the shame all the less : and now, bo'sen, did you ever find me in the waist when my duty called me on the jib-boom ? was I ever playing Tom Coxe's traverse when I was wanted to lay out on a yard or reef to'gaunt sails ? was I ever among the idlers when a blue jacket was wanted aloft ? was I ever the first to leave the deck in a gale, or the last to tumble up the main hatchway ? was I ever a skulker ? did you ever have occasion at any time to report me for not doing my duty ?"

" Only once," said the boatswain.

" Once !" echoed Gasket, quickly, almost fiercely, "when—out with it— when ?"

" Why when we were in a gale off San Domingo," he replied, " you was put in the main chains with the lead, and the ship gave a lee lurch, and Mr. Freeling, the midshipman, fetched away overboard : you sung out for somebody to take the lead and jumped after him. You broke your duty, but you saved his life—that's all I know agen you."

A murmur of approbation passed through the crew when he finished, and Gasket, with a gratified smile, turned with thanks to him, and then addressing the crew, he exclaimed, in something of a proud tone—,

" Is there any among ye. lads, who can say I have not been a true messmate ? Is there any on you who can say I was never fair and aboveboard— that I carried false colours, or took any man's share of ease to let him have my work ? Is there any of the crew that can say I sneaked for favour or topped the sea-officer over them ? How many among ye is there would think the Wildfire the better for my being out of her ? Is there ary here who can step for'ard and pint me out as one who deserves the cat ? If I have done wrong to any of you—if you have found me a lubberly vagabone, come for'ard and tell the Captain ; but if you have nothing to bring agen me, and have always found me what I have tried to be—a honest friend and true mate, why give me a cheer, boys."

A long and loud cheer, though rather against the rules, replied to him : it was given by all heartily and unequivocally. Gasket gave a chuckle of gratified pride, and said—

" Now, bo'sen, I'm ready, lay on, I shan't think the worse of you for doing your duty."

Just as the boatswain raised his hand to give the first blow, Mr. Prior stepped forward and cried—

"Hold!"   The boatswain obeyed, and he said earnestly to the captain, " Let me intercede for him, Captain Pearson, a better or a kinder creature never existed. He may be mistaken in his preseverance in the present instance but it is from a honest, good hearted motive.   Grant me his release, and if you can point out any way in which I can repay the favour, you will find me but too happy to do it."

" I have passed my word, Mr. Prior," said the captain, half relenting his severity in receiving such unequivocal testimony of Gasket's good character. " I cannot break it, the punishment must proceed."

"I hope you'll pardon me for stepping for'ard agen, sir," said Andrew, approaching the captain respectfully, " but if you will allow me I will go as far as to say you never said you would flog Gasket."

"Did I not?" said the captain, with a slight jeering laugh.

'No, sir," replied Andrew, " you said you would have him seized up to a grating, but you never said you would flog him.   You have kept your word sir, for he is seized up to the grating, and won't be r unning 'thaw't hawse of your conscience if you order him to be taken down."

The captain looked steadily at him for a minute, and then paced to and fro, while the people all preserved the greatest silence. Presently he stopped short, and said to the boatswain—

"Take him down, and mind, sir," he added, addressing Gasket sternly, " when I ask you for truth again, tell it me. Mr. Prior, the wind seems lulling, we'll have a little more sail on the ship : set the royals and studding sails."

"Ay, ay, sir," replied the lieutenant quickly, with a cheerful countenance and then gave the necessary orders to the boatswain, whose shrill whistle was immediately heard, followed by his hoarsely shouting a repetition of the lieutenant's commands. In an instant the topmen were seen scrambling up the rigging, and not the least merry among them were John Andrew and Gasket, rejoicing at the narrow escape the latter had from receiving severe punishment.

The incidents of the remainder of the voyage home were few and uninteresting. The fair wind still held, and the frigate being a swift sailer, bounded merrily and rapidly before it, making the distance between her and old England considerably less every hour. The course was shaped for Spithead, and ere long ran up the channel at a spanking rate, in a shorter period than the most sanguine on board expected, the frigate entered the road and dropped her anchor. The captain after the affair with Gasket, which had satisfied him an interview against his strict commands had taken place between Alice and Paul, kept a most vigilant eye upon both to prevent a recurrence of it. He so far succeeded, that, by keeping Paul constantly on duty forward, and Alice to her cabin, he gave them no chance of meeting by ACCIDENT, and he looked out too sharply to prevent their meeting by private agreement. It cost him much trouble and broken rest to accomplish this ; but he might have spared himself all the labour and inconvenience if he had known that they had mutually agreed at their secret meeting not to attempt another interview while on board, but had concerted measures

to obtain one when both were removed beyond his power. The anchor had scarcely bit the ground when, with considerable satisfaction that his duty respecting Alice had ceased, the captain entered her cabin. He found her seated in an attitude of melancholy thought which, however, she instantly shook off the moment she perceived him, and rose to her feet.

"Be seated, miss, I beg," he exclaimed, assuming a smiling countenance; "we are once more on the shore of England, and ere long it will be my pleasing office to place you in a father's arms; I have sought you that I may learn where to forward to him information of your safe arrival, after many dangers, great enough to have destroyed weaker minds than your's, and to express to my old friend the unbounded satisfaction I feel in being the instrument of your deliverance."

Alice bowed with dignity, and replied in a tone of coldness—

"My father will be no less happy to thank you, Captain Pearson, for restoring me to him than you in being the restorer. He will find words, sir, to express his sense of the obligation, a task to which I find myself

No 28

inadequate ; not, sir, but I feel deeply your kindness, and shall remember it gratefully." The captain bowed. "When I parted from my father at Porto Rico," she added, " it was agreed that when the vessel in which I embarked whose destination was London—reached the Downs, I should be landed at Deal, and he would be there to meet me. The time of my expected arrival has long elapsed, and it is impossible therefore for me to say whether it is likely he may be found at Deal. With your permission, captain, I will land here, take up my abode at an hotel, and write to a near relative to receive me until I can ascertain where my father is sojourning."

"I can save you the trouble, my dear young lady, of landing here," replied the Captain." After transacting some business here, I shall have to carry the frigate to Sheerness. I can land you at Deal and if your father should not be there, you can then proceed to Dover, which is but a short distance, and there put in practice all that you intended doing here. "

" I am at your command, sir," answered Alice, coolly.

The captain seemed stung by her iciness of manner ; he bit his lip and was silent for a minute, At length he said, with some warmth—

" You regard me with looks of coldness and dislike, Alice ; you look upon me with the aversion you would show your greatest enemy. I feel hurt that you should, for I would not have the child of one whom I ever esteemed with the greatest friendship hold me in such unpleasant estimation. I have done my best to make you comfortable and happy during your stay in this vessel, I assure you ; if I have failed, it has not been from the absence of a desire to see you so, or the effort to make you so ; and if it had not been for one unpleasant occurence I strongly believe you would have been so. "

" Captain Pearson, I have been as happy as it is in your power to make me," returned Alice. " I have already expressed my thanks for it. I have also been as unhappy as it is in your power to make me, and you will pardon me, I trust, if, in feeling that the unhappiness you have occasioned me overbalance the kindness I have received, I should not look upon you with the same sentiments of esteem and regard I should have possessed for you if you had not made the unpleaant occurrence to which you allude."

" I perceive it is in vain to reason with you upon that point," exclaimed the captain, shrugging his shoulders ; " it is perhaps natural we should view such an affair with very different eyes ; still I would have you believe that it is far from my wish to do any thing to pain you, and the conduct I have already displayed respecting this—this—matter has been reluctantly pursued. Think as you please of me, miss. I feel that I have done my duty, and it will be a consolation to me to know that although I may have incurred your hatred I have not departed from the strict path of my honour and faith with your father, or what I deem due to your own fame and happiness."

" My own fame, Captain Pearson," said Alice, with a flushed brow, " will never suffer by being entrusted to my own keeping, and I am willing to risk my happiness by choosing for myself the path which may lead to it. I do not hate any one, sir, nor could I, unless they had once held a very high place in my estimation, and had acted in such a manner as to fall entirely from it. Our connection, and the circumstances it entails are not sufficien to place either high in the other's estimation, and therefore your charge of hatred falls to the ground: we hate not where we are indifferent; but, sir, though you flatter yourself you have not departed from your honour and faith with my father, I cannot understand how you can reconcile your honourable feelings with the fact of having obtained surrepticiously certain information from one whose soul is without a stain, humble as his position may be, and hen using your knowledge in the most ungenerous fashion."

"You misconceive the facts," cried the Captain, hastily; "all I obtained from Paul was done fairly and openly; his answers were candid and honest, for as much I give him credit. It then rested with me, understanding fully your father's objections to your romantic attachment, to shew him the friendship I have always possessed for him, I chose the course I intended to take; I have, to the best of my ability, pursued it, and so long as you are an inmate of the Wildfire so long shall I exercise the prerogative I assume to be mine in this affair, Think of me as you will, I act as a friend to your father and, in my own sincere opinion, to you."

"And as an enemy to one who never gave you cause for the slightest ill will or harsh treatment," exclaimed Alice, warmly. "John Paul has, by the testimony of every man in the ship, officers included, performed his duty as few of the men under your command have been able to equal—none to excel; he has received frequently your highest commendations, and now without having done aught to rob himself of the good opinion he has earned, you would treat him as an unworthy slave, as one who is debased in mind and degraded by his conduct. Is this just, sir? Is this preserving honour and faith with your own conscience?"

"Beyond what restrictions I may deem necessary to place upon John Paul with regard to you, Alice," returned the captain, " he will suffer nothing. I am not the less inclined now than I have ever been to acknowledge that he is the cleverest hand under my command, and that if he has the opportunity, he will make an extraordinary man. I shall not treat him differently to what I have hitherto done, unless he disobeys the command I have given him. If you think me a tyrant, at least do me justice to believe I am above inflicting punishment, or otherwise degrading a man for doing that for which he cannot be blamed; nay, rather have his taste praised," he added, with as slight bow. "You must understand that discipline on board a ship is carried to its furthest limits—no monarch's sway is so absolute as mine over my crew, and wilful disobedience of order is punished severely. So long as Paul continues his duty, which includes implicit obedience, he will be treated as well as heretofore; and to show you that I will keep my word, indeed that I will not give myself the chance of breaking it by entertaining a prejudice, I will, when we arrive at Sheerness write to the Admiralty for his discharge from the service."

Alice eyed him earnestly as he spoke, and when he concluded, she held out her hand to him, and said in an altered tone to the one she had as yet used towards him—

Captain Pearson, I believe you act conscientiously. I have felt aggrieved by your conduct to me, I confess ; for the future I will consider that what you have done has been done from a good motive, and from no wanton exercise of a tyrannical power. I have been mistaken in you, as I am certain you are deceived in me, and in the course I firmly determine to pursue. But let all that has transpired sink into oblivion. I will accompany you to the Downs, and cheerfully subscribe to the continuance of the line of conduct you have hitherto followed, and I give you my word that neither myself nor John Paul will attempt to remove the bar you have placed upon our communication with each other. I will answer for him, sir, as myself."

"You have given me great pleasure by your promise," exclaimed the captain, in a gratified tone. " I had intended to question you both respecting an interview which I more than suspect has taken place between you since I so strongly interdicted it, when we met upon the quarter-deck ; but I say with you, let all that has transpired be buried in oblivion. I must now leave you to give some orders. We shall weigh anchor with the dawn, and twelve or thirteen hours, if the wind holds, will bring us to the Downs."

With a few more words, the captain quitted her and went on shore ; his stay was short, and when he returned he visited her once more with, as he said, " the pleasing intelligence," that her father had arrived in England, had left a message for him (the captain), to be given instantly upon his arrival, the purport of which was, that if he had gained any tidings respecting Alice, he was to forward it to Dover, where he was staying, anxiously awaiting the arrival of every ship from the West Indies, in hope that it would bring him some intelligence of his daughter. The captain told Alice he had written a few lines, and despatched a messenger to him across the country with it, communicating her safety, and telling him that she would be off. Deal the next evening or the succeeding morning, so that he might be prepared to meet her. Alice received his information with a mixture of pleasure and sadness ; for although she naturally felt glad at the prospect of being restored to her father, from whom she had so nearly been sundered for ever, yet the restoration involved the separation from Paul, which, in the natural order of events, was likely to be for years ; and therefore, whatever gladness she might have felt in one case, was counterbalanced by her sorrow in the other. The captain was rather surprised that she did not display more joy at his news ; but he new little of women, and he only came to the conclusion that they possessed an uncommon cold manner of receiving agreeable intelligence : so he left her, rather congratulating himself that he had no daughter.

As the Captain had promised with the dawn the order was given " all hands unmoor ; " the anchor was weighed, the courses, top, and top-gallant sails set, and once more the saucy Wildfire ploughed her way through the heaving waves ; but as the wind did not hold, and gradually died away to a soft summer breeze, the Downs were not reached until the night had set in. The anchor was cast and the sails were furled to there respective yards, everything was made snug alow and aloft, for a strong sou'wester was seen approaching, and it failed not to come a few minutes after the men had ceased their labour, and glided down the rigging like so many strange shadows to the deck. All night it blew a gale, and in the morning, although the wind dropped, the swell was too heavy, and the surf which broke on the beach too great to admit of a boat landing. Towards the afternoon, however, the swell subsided, and though there was a clouded atmosphere, and gulls were flying here and there, screaming and wheeling about in every variety of evolution, the sea became as calm as a lake. The captain, upon ascertaining this, ordered his gig to be " tossed out," and quitted the deck with the intention of acquainting Alice that the time had arrived for her to go ashore. In descending, his foot slipped and he was precipitated down the companion-ladder with considerable violence ; in his fall he sprained his ancle severely, besides inflicting a contusion upon his forehead, which produced blood and rendered him insensible. The noise he made in falling brought the stewart to his aid ; the doctor was instantly summoned, and he was carried to his cabin, where every attention being paid to him, he shortly recovered his senses. His brain racked with agony and his ancle pained him terribly, but he treated the matter lightly. He sent to Alice a message by Mr. Prior, expressing his sorrow that he was unable, in consequence of the accident, to attend her ashore as he had intended, but begged that she would convey his warmest remembrances to her father, and request him, if he could spare an hour in the next six, to come aboard and crack a joke with him.

"Mr. Prior," continued the captain, " see that the gig is manned by her crew in proper trim, and that they make her skip over the water ; put one of the gentlemen* in the stern sheets, and see that all is ship shape."

" Ay, ay, sir !" returned the lieutenant, bowing ; and, as he quitted the captain, he laughed in his sleeve to think he should fulfil his commands to the letter, but not exactly to his wishes.

John Paul was the captain's coxswain, and Gasket was the strokesman , and both of them took their places in the gig which was to bear Alice to the shore, a proceeding which the captain would have interfered with if he had been able to carry out his intention of accompanying her ; but the agony his accident occasioned him made him forget who was cockswain, and Alice took her station in the boat with Paul close behind her, and a midshipman, scarcely fourteen years of age, by her side. The parting between her and John Andrew was warm and almost affecting ; she made him a handsome present for his services, and wrung him kindly by the hand, and bade him at any time he needed a friend to apply to her or her father, and he would, be sure to meet with one. The water stood in his eyes as she thus acknowledged his devoted conduct to her, and it was with a husky voice that he told her he thought he deserved no thanks or presents for what he had done ; and that when she was thinking of old times, if she could find a kind thought for him among them he would be more satisfied.

"We shall meet again," she replied ; " and when we do you shall find that I have neither forgotten you or your noble services. Farewell, my kind

* Midshipmen in the navy bear the appellation on board of the " gentlemen."

friend. I may hereafter meet with persons higher in rank, in wealth, and in birth than thee, but never with one possessing more worth."

"God bless you, miss!" said Andrew, with a gulp, "God bless you! May you get spliced to the lad of your heart, and as long as you live carry the red flag of happiness at the fore."

Alice smiled, shook him once more by the hand, and the next minute was seated in the gig; they pushed off, the order was given to "give way," and the boat shot from the vessel's side with great rapidity. The shore was soon gained and Alice was landed. A couple of servants were in waiting for her, but her father was not their; he had expected the arrival of the vessel on the preceding day and waited until he grew weary, but as she did not arrive until late he returned to Dover. The next morning he was there and saw, the frigate at anchor; but although he made handsome offers to the Deal boatmen, who at that time as now were famed for their intrepidity, they refused even to attempt to take him on board, the sea running so high as to render it impracticable. He waited with the hope of the swell going down, but his impatience made him deem it unlikely to take place until evening or the next day; he therefore left two servants in case his daughter, by any remote chance, landed, to receive her, and made his way back to the hotel at Dover, where he was residing, to fret and fume, and irritate himself with the thouegts that it might take a week to render the sea smooth enough to suffer a boat to land—an idea which was not dissipated after making an inquiry respecting it of the waiter, who assured his honour that he had known it in heavy weather to be three weeks before a boat could land or put off, for which information nothing but a celerity of movement saved him from being kicked out of the room. The servants who were waiting for Alice received the luggage belonging to her which had been saved from the wreck, and were sent forward with it; while Paul, who had assisted her to land, walked with her up the beach, and then Alice suddenly stopped. Hitherto their progress had been made in deep silence, and now she boke it by requesting him to seat himself by her side and utter the few words which were all that were to pass between them for an indefinite period. Paul obeyed her, and side by side they sat on a huge clump of chalk, and gazed upon the sea, each with swelling bosoms, but with tongue which could find no language to express their deep emotion. At length Paul took the hand of Alice, gently, and pressing it, said—

"You are sad, Alice—very sad; and the change in your features since we met upon the quarter-deck tells me you have indulged in forebodings of evils in futurity which have depressed your spirits, and made your happiness a thing only of remembrance or of dreams. I, too, feel a weight upon my heart heavier than I have ever known it, and yet I would wish to be cheerful, for I have the strong hope that the time is not far distant when I shall make a bold and successful essay for the elevation that will entitle me to claim your hand. It is no light matter, Alice, to part with you as I shall part with you now—to separate for a period which will involve years in it—one which will be stormy and perilous, though it lead to glory, to fame—to you. It is not at the danger or peril that I cast a thought of care or anxiety, but that I know you will be sickening in suspense and doubt until you learn that the actions which bring me glory have not taken my life. You have a strong mind, Alice; I know you to possess it. I know that you have a nature which is superior to a useless brooding over fears which may be never realised; and I intreat you to exert it while we are apart. Never believe me dead, or think that aught can deprive me of life, until you know that I am no more; but ever, for ever, wear in your heart the impression that each day brings our union nearer. Be cheerful and happy; look upon the future with a calm, firm eye; divest it of its uncertainty, and view it only with the bright hopes which, in some blissful moments, the fancy loves to indulge."

He paused, and regarded Alice with a look of deep fervency. He expected her to speak, but her head drooped, and she remained silent.

"You do not speak to me," he said. "Ah! Alice, did I not feel that our destinies are woven together, I could wish, for your sake, that we had never met; I have been the cause of much unhappi—"

"I will not hear you speak thus," she interrupted hastily; "it is not so; you have never caused me one moment's pain; you have ever been to me all the heart of women could wish, and if circumstances, over which neither you nor I have control, have rendered our wishes unavailable, you are not to blame. If I am unhappy, it is not you, Paul, who has occasioned it. I wish I could say that of one who ought to have made my happiness more his study than his avarice; but, alas! fate has denied it, and grievous as it is to bear, it must be born; for their is no way of obviating it. I should consider myself unworthy of you, Paul, if I weakly repined at that for which their was no remedy; you have done me justice in attributing to me more firmness of character; had I been of a weaker nature, your hold upon my heart might have been shaken by the efforts which have been made to accomplish it, but their exertions are vain; my heart has made its election, and it is not in their power to change it. We must part, Paul—it is too true, we must part—and as you have said, it is hard to part as we shall. To feed on hope, to live on expectation, to depend upon a futurity whose prospects, whatever the sanguine aspirations of an earnest heart may picture them, are clouded and hidden beneath an inpenetrable veil, is alas, a cheerless position. For your sake I will strengthen my heart against anticipations of sorrow, of destroyed hopes, of despair; I will strive to be firm; I will look my adverse condition in the face, and defy it to crush me beneath its withering power; I will hope only for the time the bright spot that may come in our lives, when our trials shall cease, and hand in hand we shall descend to the peaceful grave together."

"My noble-souled girl," exclaimed Paul, with enthusiasm, his eye lighting up as he spoke, "my heart glows to hear thee, and receives a new impulse for action at thy words; my soul is strengthened to bear this separation with less pain, now I know how you will regard my absence. Alice, I have hesitated till now to tell you my intentions respecting the path I shall take. England is no sphere of action for me; the path to honour and fame is inaccessible but through the door of interest—interest wihch I do not possess.

No, the new world is my road to glory and wealth, and I hasten to place my foot upon the ground which shall bear my tread as the wearer of a proud name, or shall receive me in its bosom lifeless. I know America; I know its capabilities, and I know its resources. I was not idle the short period of my stay there. I have a brother, whose intellect might be admired in a statesman, and from him I have received hints of which I shall fail not to avail myself. Many thousand miles will separate us, but in spirit we shall be together. We shall look upon the same sun, if we do not upon the same sky; the same moon will shed its soft rays over us, though we may not tread upon the same ground; and our thoughts, which no distance or climate can affect, will be with each other, though seas and mountains intervene. Alice, dear Alice, I know that I possess your love; too much have you sacrificed for me to hold a shadow of a doubt upon it. I know, too, you have no unworthy thought of me; if you had, your love would not be mine, and thus I feel there is little need to tell you, that the sun is not more true in its revolution than I will be faithful to you. To tell you I love you with the entire devotion of a heart which has never been touched or affected by other than yourself, is but to repeat what I have before uttered; but now that the last moment approaches, which for a long period we can pass in each other's presence—which perhaps may be, if such be the will of fate, the last time we may gaze on each other for ever. I swear that at no time since I have known and loved you has your image been for one instant weakened in my soul, or lives there the maiden who can say that she took your place in my heart in any moment of weakness, or under any circumstances of lightness of heart, when recollections are drowned in present pleasures. And, Alice, though we may never, never meet again, may God blight my dearest hopes, may every prospect of future happiness be utterly effaced, and I rendered the most abject, mean, contemptible wretch on earth, if I swerve in truth or love for thee—if the sweetest face united to the most bewitching graces make me turn aside, even in thought, thou beloved of my soul, from thee. No, Alice, thou'rt the shrine of my adoration; no knight of chivalry ever bore his mistress's image more truly, more honourably, more devotedly than I—and as I keep my oath, so God judge me hereafter."

"Oh, Paul, there was no need for this asseveration," exclaimed Alice, her eyes suffused with tears. "I know your truth and honour; I know your worthiness; I have no fear that you have at any time forgotten me, or will forget me, let the circumstances be what they may. I do not doubt you—I never did; I never shall, but I doubt the kindness of fate. I feel a strange foreboding that we shall never meet again; that we are now looking our last on each other; that we are now uttering the last words which our ears may receive from one another. I can bear your absence, Paul, even cheerfully, for I know that it is occasioned by the necessity of your undergoing a probation which must be passed through; but I cannot composedly think that the dangers in that probation are so imminent that to signalize yourself sufficiently to obtain your aim you are exposing yourself to death constantly. I cannot calmly think of the future

as holding out a bright and glorious vision of joy and peace and love, without feeling also that a hand of blood may distroy the vision and reduce me to utter despair. Oh, Paul, should this be our last interview—should we never— never meet again—I—I—"

Her heart was too full to utter more; she bowed her head and covered her eyes with her hand. Paul's heart was full too; his eyes glittered with tears, he clutched his neckerchief convulsively with his right hand, as though, loose as it was, it would choke him. He had not the power to speak, but he pressed the hand of Alice to reassure her, though his want of command over his own emotions was insufficient to enable him to find a tongue to utter consolation, and was therefore little calculated to restore her to equanimity. At several

No 29.

strong efforts he conquered the bitterness which had overpowered him, and clearing his voice, which sadness had rendered dry and hoarse, he said—

"You have drawn a gloomy picture, Alice, this is not looking upon coming events with the firm eye you have promised you would; to part is not to die, to sever is not be sundered for ever. Death comes when it will, there is no place which is beyond his reach; a strong man of gigantic form and limbs has been choked by a cherry stone, and a weak, feeble-looking creature, has passed through a stormy campaign, surrounded on all sides by blood and death, unscathed. Fortune favours the brave, Alice; the dame has been unkind to me in many instances; she may favour me in my future career—she will, I feel she will; therefore, sweetest Alice, dry your tears and let me, ere I depart, see thee calm and cheerful."

The sound of a ship's gun startled them both, and the quick eyes of Paul at once turned to the frigate, and instantly detected a change which had taken place on board. He saw the blue smoke of the discharged powder wreathing up in pale curling white vapours round the foremast, and he knew the gun had been fired for the instant return of the gig; he saw also the fore-topsail cut loose—which was the signal for sailing—and ere he turned his eyes away, he saw a boat which contained the pilot, a signal for whom had been flying, making the best of its way to the Wildfire. He knew the hour was come for parting, and in a few broken sentences he explained to Alice the painful intelligence. The remainder of their interview was passed in the utterance of fervent protestations of faith and truth. Alice sunk into Paul's arms, and as he passionately imprinted a burning kiss upon her cheek, he raised one hand to heaven and said—

"In life or death, Alice, I am thine—thine only."

The sound of approaching footsteps, caused them to disengage themselves, and one of the men servants who had taken charge of her luggage stood before them; immediately he saw Alice he stopped, and said, respectfully—

"Oh, if you please, Miss, I saw your father at a distance on horseback; he is coming this way, so I thought I would run and tell you.

"Thank you," replied Alice, turning deadly pale at his news, and then exclaimed, huriedly, "away, and meet him; stop him, tell him I have quitted the vessel and will be with her instantly—away!"

The man looked at her with some surprise, but immediately obeyed her; she then turned to Paul, and cried—

"Leave me, Paul. Dear Paul, lose not a moment; I would not have him see thee for a world's wealth, his interperate nature will lead him to insult thee with some cruel taunt—fly!"

"Fly, Alice," said Paul, proudly. "I fly from no man, let him be who he may."

"Oh, Paul, there is no display of fear in flying him, but policy! For my sake, for the pain and agony which I shall endure to hear thee unkindly reproached in the hour of separation—leave me, leave me, to shun him."

"For you, Alice, for you I go—I leave you to gain you," he exclaimed, fervently, as he once more enfolded her in his embrace and pressed her to his heart. " May the Almighty keep you in his grace, calmly and happily—may you never know annoy, but until we meet be ever placid and contented, no evil to ruffle the serenity of happy peacefulness, and for ever after be removed from all care and pain."

" God bless you, dear Paul!" sobbed Alice. " God blessed you, you have all my heart—I have no thought, hope, wish, but for you, and I will perish ere my living soul shall compel me to change from thee or forget thee. Farewell, God avert all evil from thee. God bless thee! God bless thee! we shall meet again, Paul, in Heaven, if not on earth. Heaven preserve you, and make you in all things happy. Farewell."

Paul strained her to his bosom, kissed her a thousand times, passionately, and then she tore herself from his arms, cried, her whole soul in the words, " God bless you!" again, and hurried sobbing from the spot. She waved her hand, and the next moment she was hidden from him, as it seemed for ever. He stood for a minute plunged in grief; she was gone, she was all the world to him—life, soul, everything—she was gone, perhaps, for ever; it was a moment of agony—he squeezed his hands crushingly together, and turning his face to the wall, he sobbed like an infant.

He had remained thus scarcely a minute when he head the step of one running towards him. Dashing the tears from his cheeks, he bent his brows sternly, and turned to meet the comer, it was Gasket.

" Didn't you hear the signal for the boat to return, John ?" he cried, quickly out of breath with his run, "and don't you see the foretopsail cast loose eh ?"

" I do," replied Paul, by a strong effort assuming a calm demeanour

" Well, you take it pretty quietly. Hows'ever, here's the young gentleman in the stern sheets swears, by thunder and lightning he'll report you to the first lieutenant for keeping the boat after the signal to go on board has been made."

Another gun was now fired from the bow of the frigate, and directly its distant " boom" struck upon Gasket's ear, be whistled and cried—

" Spanker, Driver, Ringtail ! but there'll be some quarter deck talking to some of us. Come, John, let's crowd sail for the boat, or the gentleman will shove off without us. I could hardly make the little swab let me come to hurry you."

" Stretch out," answered Paul, with an attempt to smile, " when we get in the gig we must make the people bend their backs to the work."

Gasket gave an assenting reply and darted off at a good speed, followed, closely by Paul. The former easily perceived in our hero's countenance traces of the suffering his spirit had endured in parting with Alice; but with the delicacy which not unfrequently dwells in the minds of men of primitive education, he would not notice it, feeling sure that any observation he might make respecting it would only add to the distress instead of alleviating it. A gave time elapsed ere they were once more in their respective stations, and the middy, with a squeaking voice, cried out—

" Now, you sirs, where have you been playing at Tom Coxe's traverse?

You've been bowsing up your jib-stay at some grog shop, I'll be a best bower to a marl'spik.   I tell you what it is, my fine fellows, if you don't get a taste of the Captain's red bunting and the boatswain's wife, I'm damned.   The lieutenant will ask me WHAT kept the boat, and I shall tell him WHO; so look out.   If you don't get a starting and your grog stopped besides, why I'll confess to the mess I'am a Tom Bowers of a fellow: Come, step out, lads, we shall have another black Betsy else to quicken us."

" Give way my lads," cried the clear toned voice of Paul, taking the tiller-lines in his hand, while the little midshipman screwed himself up in a boat cloak; " bend your backs and pull with a will men," continued Paul, " make her jump out of the water, lads."

A cheerful ay, ay! responded to his commands, and the men plied their oars with great strength, giving the man-of-war roll with the most perfect precision.   The boat flew over the water swiftly, and before the midshipman could get to sleep, which he tried hard to do, the nose (the boat's not the boy's) grated [the ship's side; the crew leaped on board and the boat was hauled up.   They had not much time to spare, for the anchor was weighed, and fold after fold of the canvass was dropped, until she was covered from heel to truck, and with a breeze which had just sprung, up, stood out of the Downs for Sheerness.   To the surprise of all the gig's crew, the first lieutenant, after simply chiding them for not returning at the first gun, said no more and although they made every inquiry of their messmates for the reason of their sudden departure, when it was expected they would have remained some hours longer in the Downs, no one could satisfy them; but the truth of the matter was, that the Captain all of a moment remembered who was his coxswain—it was some time after the departure of the boat—he recollected also that he had not forbidden him to take his usual post in the gig, although he had told Mr. Prior to put one of the gentlemen in the stern sheets.   It no sooner struck him that it was possible Paul might have accompanied Alice than he summoned Mr. Prior, and found that he had.   He was in a towering rage but he could not help himself; he could not punish Paul for doing his duty—he could not quarrel with the first lieutenant for not doing what he was not ordered to do; and turn the matter which way he would nothing presented itself to take hold of as a handle by which he might punish our hero; it struck him also that he had sent an invitation to her father to come on board! and as it occurred to him that it was not all impossible the companionship of Paul and Alice might be discovered by him, the probabilities were that the enraged father might come aboard, and instead of cracking a joke, crake his head.   At all events it was most likely there would be much recrimination, fending and proving, and as he was remarkably averse anything of the sort, especially upon a matter which was of no interest to him, he being really quite indifferent whether Alice married Paul or Pope Pius the Seventh, he thought the best thing he could do was to " cut and run."   There was no necessity to remain, the pilot had answered the sig-nal made for him by putting off from the shore, and the wind was fair; he therefore ordered a gun to be fired to recall the boat the moment he thought it had reached the shore, and as no notice appeared to be taken of the first, he ordered the second to be fired, making up his mind that a third gun should carry with it a round dozen for every "rascal" of the gigs crew; he was the more impatient for its return, as he was not quite satisfied that Alice's father would not take the opportunity of coming on board in the gig. He was considerably relieved by the report of the return of the boat and the people, particularly when he found the expected, but somewhat unwelcome guest, whose fiery nature he well knew, was not included in it.

The frigate was not long ere she rounded the Foreland, glided with stately bearing round Ramsgate and Margate, and when night again spread "it's dusky mantle o'er the skies," she was riding at anchor off Sheerness. In a few days she was paid off. The captain keeping his promise, applied to the Admiralty for the discharge of Paul, and obtained it; he presented it to him, at the same time made an acknowledgment of his services on board, by the present of a ring, and requested him to bury the harshness he had latterly shewn him in oblivion, or, if he did not think of it, to view it as a matter of duty only, and so pass it over. He likewise expressed his best wishes for his unqualified success, now that he was free to quit the service, in whatever path he might choose for his future career. Paul could not but feel affected by his generosity, and returned his acknowledgments of it as warmly as lay in his power; so with a mutual good feeling they parted.

Eustace Prior, who had never for one moment wavered in his determination of seeking Florence immediately upon his return to England, had, in accordance with the superstitious feeling which his dream respecting Paul had raised within him, insisted upon his fulfillling his promise to assist him in the search for his beloved, and so carried him to London with him, accompanied by Gasket, over whom he held a sort of protective right; and there for the present we must leave them, and return to John Andrew, who, when the Wildfire was paid off, which she was immediately after her arrival, went also to London to the owners of the Penelope, to acquaint them with her capture by pirates, and also with the loss of the brig which had received him and Alice from the Andromache. His communication was attested by the passenger who was rescued with with him and his fair companion from the wreck of the brig by the crew of the Wildfire, whose dangerous hurt was yet uncured. The owners, who were insured to the full value of both vessels, received the intelligence with a calmness which they might not have shewn if the destruction of the vessels, with their cargoes had proaed a dead loss to them; they therefore paid John Andrews his full amount of wages, and presented him with a handsome sum by way of compensation for the loss of all his property in the "Pen-ne-lopee." The passenger, too, a man of considerable property, also made him a present of twenty guineas, for the services he had rendered him when the brig was deserted by the crew, which services had prevented him from perishing miserably. Thus, what with his pay from the Wildfire, the Penelope, his presents from Alice, from Paul—who reiterated his thanks most warmly ere he parted with him, for his noble behavionr to Alice—from the passenger, and from Captain Pearson, who also was a donor after hearing his relation of the events occuring to him from his departure from Porto Rico to his appearance on board the Wildfire, he was possessed of a good round sum, a sort of miniature fortune, the value of which he was not precisely acquainted with, but had a good general notion. He was surrounded, like the rest of the people of the Wildfire, when she was paid off at Sheerness, by a number of crimps, who all protested they knew him well, and professed the greatest friendship and delight at seeing him once more in the land of his birth, and hinted in the gentlest manner possible what infinite gratification it would afford them if he would settle the SMALL account which he was NOT indebted to them, although they took the most tremendous oaths that he was; but he answered their demands with his fist, and after thrashing two or three, and ducking one, they found out they were mistaken, and had no such name on the debit side of their books as John Andrew. They expressed their sorrow at their SINGULAR error, and at once clapped the amount which they demanded of him on that of two or three other seamen who did owe them about a thirtieth or fortieth part of what they claimed. Andrew had once been stripped in this way of all his money, and was compelled to make another voyage before he could return home to see his friends: it was a lesson he did not forget. He had a widowed mother who was very poor, living on his half-pay, and now a little sweetheart; he therefore steered clear of his messmates, who were making their money fly like the name of their vessel, and took his place in a coach for Leeds, from thence through Yorkshire towards Westmoreland. The facilities of travelling to remote parts of England were very different fifty years since to what they were fifteen years ago, and John Andrew found out that in taking different stages here and there, every office swearing that their vehicle went within a short distance of Grasmere, he succeeded in arriving at Richmond, from whence a conveyance went to Appleby, he found that no vehicle of any description which could take him to the desired place, unless he hired especially hired a post-chaise for the purpose—a proceeding he would as soon thought of pursuing as setting up a carriage and four; he, therefore, determined to trust to nature's mode of travelling, and foot it. His luggage consisted only of what a pocket-handkerchief would contain, which, with his money carefully folded up in it, was appended to a stick and placed over his shoulder, and he set forth from the inn determined to make the time between meeting with his mother and Martha Bell as short as possible.

It is not necessary to follow him in all his turnings, windings, and the mistakes of the way which befel him during his progress, but we will suppose him fairly on the high road — HIGH enough it was — to Grasmere. It was getting towards four in the afternoon, a fine sunny day it had been, and still remained. He wound his way up a steep hill, and after gaining some distance he came upon a sharp turn in the path; he rounded it, and started as he perceived a man in a sitting posture fast asleep: by his side lay his hat, his right hand grasped the stock of a gun, while the barrel crossed his body and rested upon his left arm; he was moving his head uneasily from side to side, as though his slumber was disturbed by painful dreams. Andrew bent over him and regarded him with some attention ; the face, which was pale and haggard, was overrun with long straggling locks of dark hair, of which the sleeper possessed a profusion. It struck him that he had seen the man before, but where or when he was unable to remember. While yet gazing upon him, the uneasy contortions of the dreamer increased unto such a degree of evident agony, that Andrew shook him by the shoulder and awoke him. Before he was conscious who had broken his slumber he leaped to his feet, and leveling his gun, roared out—

"Fiend! hell-cat! will nothing rid me of thee?"

He pulled the trigger, but fortunately for Andrew it missed fire, and ere it could be re-cocked he threw down his bundle, and seizing it, wrested it from the man's hands.

"Avast, messmate," he cried, when he had obtained possession of it. "What's in the wind that you want to stop my grog in the turning of a glass, without looking to see whether I am friend or foe, eh? Why, how you stare! what do you take me for? one of the wild savages from South Ameriky? or a flying dolphin from the Chaney seas?"

The man, who by this time had somewhat recovered his self-possession, scrutinised the seaman from head to foot with an earnestness which led him to inquire the cause of such a searching gaze in the terms given above, but he received no reply, and in his turn looked very hard at the stranger; at length he said with a significant nod—

"I rather think I've seen you afore."

"I'm sure you've not," the man replied, surlily, and at the same time averted his head.

"Ah, but I have," persisted Andrew; "I can't exactly overhaul the bearings to tell me the whereaway, but we've been in the same latitude, and spoke each other, or my name's not—"

"What?" asked the man, eagerly.

"The same as my father's," replied Andrew, instantly, with a chuckle.

The stranger's brow lowered gloomily, and he uttered a contemptuous "Pshaw!" which as soon as Andrew heard and saw the expression accompanying it, he struck his thigh, and exclaimed in a confident tone—

"I have seen you, I know I have, and you know it too."

"Where?" said the man, with a rude laugh. "Tell me where and I'll tell you if your memory serves you correctly."

"My memory serves me as a ship's log would the captain if it was cut in half and he had only one half of it," returned Andrew, "he gets an idea of the day's work, but he wants the other half to make it plain sailing. My memory is a one sided one—I know I've seen you, but the latitude is torn out of the log and lost; besides, when we were along side of each other you was more bluff about the bows, your figure head didn't show so much service—but now you're all ribs and trucks, like a sheer hulk, and looks howdaciously like a picter of the Flying Dutchman which one of the topmen had pricked on his arm when I was aboard the Pen-ne-lopee."

This by no means flattering personal description of the stranger seemed rather to displease him, for still regarding the open hearted sailor with a stern countenance, he said gruffly—

"You've missed stays in your reckoning, my man, and you'll be wrecked on the shoals of ignorance; you never came athwart me before, and I don't care how soon we part company now."

"Oh, you've a little blue water talk, have you," said Andrew, "yet your rig is not very ship shape and Bristol fashion; tho', for the matter of that, now-a-days, it aint always the rig of a vessel that tells the nater of her service. You've smelt salt water, friend, I suppose."

"Ay, and tasted it too," he replied. "I know a forefoot from a stern post, a dead-eye from a topsail-sheet block, a spanker from a sky-scraper, a jib-boom from a royal-mast, a backstay from a bowline, a cathead from a capstan, a cable from a signal-haliard—"

"And the cat from a rope's end—both of which you have tasted, I'd wager a week's allowance of grog," exclaimed Andrew, interrupting him, and laughing at his own conceit. "In what ship was you flogged last, eh, mate?"

"In neither of the last five that you were catted and rope's ended in for idling and lubberly conduct, and keel-hauled for stealing your messmate's grog and slops," he returned, hastily and angrily.

Andrew laughed, and gave him the retort again with a piece of sea wit, which made him writhe with rage; he, however, did not continue the exercise of his smart faculties, but, holding out his hand, exclaimed—

"You are too clever for my company—you shall have a wide offing. I'll trouble you for that gun."

"Will you?" replied Andrew; "I don't think you will. It's my belief I am not the gull you fancy me—once hit, twice shy. You have had one pop at me—at least it wasn't your fault that the flint and steel didn't do their duty: I'll take care you don't have another chance. I sha'n't give up the gun.

"You won't!" exclaimed his companion, fiercely.

"I won't," he returned, coolly; "nor no frown nor growl of yours will make me hand it over, either; so, if you want to haul your wind, why 'bout ship and sheer off."

"You'll give up the gun," exclaimed the man, grinding his teeth.

"When I gets to Grasmere I've no objection," answered Andrew; "but unless you shows me good cause that I should, if I do before then, why may I be cobbed."

"Grasmere! are you going to Grasmere?" asked the man, with considerable rapidity; "you know some people there? your friends live there?"

"That they do, I hope; they did afore I left England, and unless there's been some awful change, they does still," responded Andrew.

"Have you many friends there?" interrogated the stranger, with an air of interest.

"Friends!" repeated Andrew, "very few people has many friends

anywhere; friends is a scarce commodity, especially when the locker runs empty of shot; but I know two or three good folks there. And as for relations, I've a old mother, if the old gal's soul hasn't gone aloft; and there's another that isn't a relation that I hopes to see, without she's spliced, and if she has—; but that's neither here nor there. Do you know anything about Grasmere, that makes you ask me so anxiously?"

"No, no;—oh, no!" hurriedly replied his companion, with some confusion of manner; "that is, I—I—know the place, but none of the people.''

"Then what made you ask me in such a anxious manner about it?" inquired Andrew, with a searching glance.

"Nothing particular," replied the man, assuming a cool, indifferent air; "only that I was going there myself, and I thought if you knew

No. 30.

many people you might gather a little information for me that I wish to obtain, and which may cost me much trouble to get, as I know nobody there."

"Oh!" exclaimed Andrew, somewhat doubtfully, " then I suppose you will range up alongside of me, and we shall run for the port together?"

"If you've no objection," was the reply.

" Not I, man," returned Andrew, "though I might be seen in better company without making much exertion for a mate; but this gun belongs to you, I dare say. I've got it, and I mean to keep it until I get home, so I don't mind your keeping company with me till it's time to receive your property; then I shall expect you to haul off."

The stranger laughed contemptuously

"You may laugh if you like," observed Andrew, composedly, "but you ain't exactly the sort of build and rig of a Christian to go yard-arm and yard-arm home with. The old woman would think I had served with rovers and smugglers, and other piratical miscreants."

The man started and frowned angrily, but Andrew took no notice of it.

" Now, mate, my foretopsail's loose," he added; " so if you're bound for Grasmere, get under weigh. Do you know the path across these highways and byways, eh?"

"I do," returned his companion, quickly; "I'll lead you there safe enough and by the shortest road."

" That's well," said Andrew; "but mark me, no foul play; I ain't of a cantankerous nater, but if I'm roused up, my play isn't child's play."

" You needn't fear me," exclaimed the man, with a smile.

"Fear you!" echoed Andrew; "oh, no, I don't fear you; if you run away with that idea, you'll soon get to the end of your line. I don't fear you—I doubt you, that's all. I think your natur can't be good to send a bullet at a fellow's head because he waked you up when you were making ugly faces in a dream.'"

" I confess I was hasty," uttered the man, apologetically.

" And so was I," returned Andrew, or the old woman wouldn't ha' seen me agin."

" It was a very unpleasant dream," said the man, with some little embarrassment.

" Ah, that it must have been," replied Andrew, "for you called me fiend and hell-cat, and so forth, and wanted to get rid of me. Was you dreaming of a woman?"

"Yes—no—it was nothing. Come, the sun is dropping; we have a long way to traverse; we can talk as we walk. Let us move forward," said the man, confusedly.

" Ay, ay," cried Andrew, taking up his bundle and stick, and beginning to move forward.

" I'll carry the gun," said the man, stretching forth his hand to take it. Andrew drew back.

"No you won't," he exclaimed; "not at present. I'll see a little more of you first; by-and-bye you may, but not now—exactly."

His companion muttered an oath, and led the way without another word. Andrew followed, whistling " Come all you jolly sailors bold." They walked a quarter of a mile without exchanging a sentence ; then the man turned abruptly and said—

" You have come from the West Indies ?"

" I have ; from Port Rico," was the reply.

" In the merchant service ?" interrogated his companion.

" I left the Indies in a merchant brig, but our vessel was captured by pirates and burnt by them. A few of us were taken aboard their vessel, and soon afterwards—not a month—the people nearly all died of fever, the vessel sprung a leak and went down, and I and another were saved on a raft. We were picked up by a frigate outward-bound, but her captain put us aboard an homeward-bound merchantman, and she was wrecked in as heavy a gale as ever I was in. We were once more picked up, and brought to England by a clipper of a frigate, and— here I am."

" Rather a diversified voyage ; full of incidents and quite romantic," observed his companion, something like a sneer curling his upper lip. " What was the frigate's name that brought you home ?"

" The Wildfire, Captain Pearson," returned Andrew.

" Did you ever hear anything of a master's mate, or midshipman, or lieutenant——"

" You'd better go through the compliment of a frigate at once," cried Andrew, interrupting him, jeeringly.

" The man I mean is an officer, that is if he is not kicked out of the service before this," said his companion.

" What is his name ?" enquired Andrew.

" Prior—Eustace Prior," he replied.

Andrew gave a whistle, then his brown face had a bright tinge of red in it, and with a more angry aspect than he had hitherto shown, he looked his companion in the eyes with a steadfast gaze, exclaiming—

" Kicked out of the service ! What do you mean by kicked out of the service, eh ?"

" Isn't that plain enough?" retorted the man, roughly. " Don't you understand what kicking out of the service means ? Do you know him ?"

" I do—but I'm damned if you do, or you would never have asked that question," returned Andrew, with a ruffled visage. " Do you know what licking means ? I should think you do by the cut of your jib—that's plain enough. Now, if you pay out any lingo disrespectful of Mr. Prior afore me, keep a wide berth of my fist—do you understand that ?"

" Two can play at that sport," returned his companion, unmoved by the threat. " I don't know this Prior," he added. with an indifferent tone, " but I have heard that he bears a particularly bad character."

" I wish I could come athwart those as pitched such a lying yarn to you," exclaimed Andrew, clenching his fist, " I'd make him sing small, as the bo'sen's-mate did the boy of the lieutenant's mess when he shoved him over-

board for singing out while he payed him over the shoulders with a bight of
a topsail-sheet. I tell you what it is, mate—never give a man a character
when you knows nothing of him; be sure of all that's down in his log before
you talk for or agin him, or you may be brought up all standing when you
don't expect it."

"Did you sail with him?" inquired his companion, disregarding the tenor
of Andrew's speech.

"Yes—I came to England with him," he replied; "he was first lieutenant
of the Wildfire, and a better officer or gentleman, or a kinder man to the
people under him, never trod the deck of a ship."

"Then he is not a blackguard, a swearer, and drunkard?" inquired the
man, anxiously.

"No," shouted Andrew, excitedly, "he's a gentleman from heel to truck
—aye, and a handsomer figure-head he has than any man I ever clapped
toplights on. Lord love ye! his eyes would rake a woman's heart fore and
aft; the prettiest she on the 'arth, let her build be the cleanest or carry
what sail she may, driver and ringtail, skyscrapers and all other dandy duck,
if she didn't strike her colours to him, jack, ensign, and pendant! my
name's not—"

He paused again, the man looked at him, and then said, with a feeble
attempt at a laugh—

"What!"

"What I just ain't a going to tell you," replied Andrew.

"It's immaterial to me—I know it," exclaimed his companion.

Andrew looked at him with surprise, and then laughing, said—

"What is it? out with it? I'll tell you if you're right."

"It begins with a J, follows with an A, and ends with a W," answered his comrade; "and when put together makes JAW. Whatever
other name you have I don't know; I see the initials J. A. on the back of
your hand, and I knew it only wanted the W to make the name perfect,"
concluded the man.

There was something too near the truth of his real name for the
seaman to easily credit this explanation, and he was about to make an
observation respecting it, when he was interrupted by his associate, who
exclaimed—

"You say Mr. Prior was lieutenant of the ship which brought you
to England; do you know whether he is likely to remain long in this
country?"

"My JAW seems to run foul of your liking," replied Andrew, rather
offended by the allusion to his previous communicativeness; "I'll clap a
stopper on it. You seem to be a fist at guessing—guess what you want me
to answer."

His companion laughed and tried to remove the conceit Andrew had taken,
but he was unable to succeed. The sailor walked on, and neither replied to
any questions put to him, or made any remark, but followed the path which
the man led in perfect silence. After a few more efforts to draw him into
conversation, his companion also ceased speaking and sunk into a deep fit of

abstraction; two hour or more elapsed and the silence was unbroken by either, each seemed to be fully occupied with his own thoughts, and progressed without noting anything in their path or the decrease of daylight, until the twilight was merging into night, and the path was becoming difficult to discern in the faint, misty light that remained. Then Andrew turned abruptly to his companion, and said—

" This place seems wild and lonely—are you sure you know the way?"

The man started, as though a ghost had sprung up before him, and stared wildly round him. A second glance recovered him, and upon Andrew repeating his question, he answered hastily—

"I know every inch of it. Just beyond that turn in the road you see before you, there is a steep descent; half-way down it, by the road side, stands a cottage—we must pass the night there."

" Pass the night!" echoed Andrew, " why I thought we were close to Grasmere."

" We are a good twenty miles from it," returned his companion.

".Twenty miles!" cried he astonished; " why the landlord of the public house where I had my dinner, told me it was only thirteen or fourteen miles further."

" Thirty or forty, he meant," exclaimed the man. " Come, we are both hungry—at least I can answer for myself; let us push on, we shall soon be safely housed, and in the morning we shall make our way to Grasmere, fresh and lightly; we shall reach it by noon."

Andrew gave rather a dissatisfied assent, and followed his companion, muttered something very like oaths at the disappointment he experienced in being so far away from his destination when he expected to have been within a mile of it, but there was no help for it, and he resigned himself to it with the best grace he could. No farther conversation took place between them during their progress to the little cottage of which his companion had spoken. A few lusty knocks brought forth a man, with by no means a pleasing exterior. He was tall, rough-looking, and possessed a voice whose tone was sufficient to stamp him as ferocious and forbidding in his nature. He appeared to recognise Andrew's companion instantly, and grinned a rude welcome. He stared hard at Andrew, but no comment.

" I didn't expect to see you to-night, Geoffrey," he exclaimed; " are you going to stop?"

" I am," replied Geoffrey, " and my friend here with me; we shall sleep here. We can have beds I suppose, Tom?"

" Ay, to be sure," returned he; " come in."

They both entered, and found a room, which was rude in all its bearings. smelt very strongly of tobacco-smoke, and appeared to be the resort of only the roughest and wildest characters.

" I've nothing ready for supper," said Tom, " but I'll soon prepare you something fit for an emperor, and give you a glass of grog into the bargain, such as you don't often drink—real heart, body, and soul warmer.'

They seated themselves and began talking. Andrew expressed his intention of being away by daybreak, and taking the shortest path to Grasmere.

" Grasmere !" echoed the owner of the hovel with surprise, and was about to make a remark respecting it, but a sign from Geoffrey—or, as the reader must be aware, Jasper Chough—silenced him, and changing the subject, he made a number of inquiries of Andrew respecting his voyage, and by a judicious leading of questions, a tact for which no one, to have looked upon him, would have given him credit, he obtained from him the whole history of his voyage, up to his journey to Grasmere. Jasper paid no attention to the relation, and sat before the fire plunged in deep thought.

"Your voyage, then, which bid fair to put an end to you, turned out fortunate after all," said Tom to him, when they had supped, and sat drinking some grog.

"Why pretty well so," returned Andrew; " I've got more rhino by a pretty round sum than if I had made a fair run from Port Rico home."

" Have you sent your money home ?" asked Tom, carelessly.

"Sent it home !" returned Andrew, "not I—I carry it with me."

"What loose in your pockets ?" exclaimed Tom, with affected astonishment.

" Not exactly. They wanted me to take paper, and said it was the same as money," said Andrew ; "but gold is gold—eh! mate—so I had it all in golden guineas; and just but a few that I carry to pay my passage home with, I had it all sewed fast into a canvass bag, which I carries in this bandanna."

" Oh, in this bandanna," observed Tom, placing his hand upon it and lifting it up. "It's heavy," he added, "your friends were generous."

" Ay, that they were," Andrew answered ; and unceremoniously pressing the hand of Tom, he continued—" I'm sleepy—I should like to tnrn in; show me to my berth, will you ?"

Tom obeyed, and with a brief " good night" to Jasper, Andrew was shewn into a small miserable looking room, with little furniture in it, and that not of the newest or best manufacture. Tom set down a small taper, which he carried in his hand, upon the table, and wishing him a good repose, left him. Unlike the thoughtless acts of seaman in general, instead of divesting himself of his garments, Andrew made a careful survey of the room ; he fastened the door as well as the bolts would permit him, and then threw off his coat, waistcoat, and shoes, blew out the light, and placing the bundle containing his money by his pillow, he made one end of the handkerchief fast to his pigtail, which was somewhat of the longest, and resigned himself to sleep. A few minutes sufficed apparently to steep his senses in utter oblivion.

Tom, in the mean time, descended to Jasper, whom he aroused from his reverie.

" Have you had any tidings of the girl yet ?" he inquired, when Jasper was aware of his presence.

"No," replied he, "not any. Nehemie is away in search, and I have some hope that his shrewdness will bring success with it. She is not at the hall yet, that I have learned."

" You'll get her yet," said Tom, " when you do, make sure of her," he added significantly.   What made you bring this tar here with you?' he inquired.

"Why I fell in by chance with him," he returned ; " an accident made me acquainted that he was going to Grasmere ; and then it cost no trouble to guess that this was the very fellow that Churleigh personated when he helped me to carry off the girl. I found out, in the course of conversation, that he brought tidings of the lieutenant she is in love with. Now it does not answer my purpose that his arrival in England should be known ; therefore I have purposely led him out of the path to Grasmere down here, to keep him out of the way. He trusted himself to my guidance, not knowing his road, and a rare dance over the hills I've led him."

" What d'ye want done with him ?" asked Tom, with a laugh.

" I don't care what—anything, so that he don't intrude where he's not wanted," replied Jasper. You have earned the name of Trusty Tom, to your care I leave him—I shall trust in you."

" He shan't trouble you, I'll warrant, exclaimed Tom with a laugh which almost chilled Jasper's blood.   " Are you away again ?" he added, as he observed Jasper make for the door.

" Yes," he answered, " Badger's tribe is somewhere in the neighbourhood: I want to see them. If they have fallen in with the girl I shall hear of it. You will see me soon again—good night.' '

" Good night," responded Trusty Tom, fastening the door after him when he quitted ; and drawing a stool in front of the fire, " Let me see," he solilloquised, stretching his legs on each side of the glowing embers, " I should think there's from two to three hundred golden shiners in that bundle, judging by the weight ; that will be a pleasant swag to finger all to my own cheek. Cutting throats is pleasant work when one gets well paid for it ; three hundred guineas down, I'd cut a couple of king's wizens, or a brace of common ones for half the money.   I'll have a good stiff glass of grog, see that my knife's in good twig, wait for about an hour, until he's sound asleep, and then I'll make mutton of him."

He rose up and lit a pipe, which he had filled with tobacco during his soliloquy, mixed his grog and sharpened a butcher's large knife until its edge was nearly as keen as that of a razor, and then sat himself down to enjoy his liquor, waiting coolly for the hour to pass away. By the time his grog had all gone, and his pipe was finished, he judged it time to commence his work. He drew off his boots, trimmed his lamp afresh. and taking the knife in his hand, he crept stealthily up the stairs ; no cat in the act of committing a robbery could have crawled along more silently or soundly than he. He gained the door, and tried it gently—it was fast. He was not at all disconcerted— he descended the stairs to the ground floor—he drew from a corner a slight ladder—he shouldered it and returned up stairs with it.   Immediately over the door was a window ; for what purpose placed there it was difficult to define, unless to afford admission in the manner now about to be attempted, and to prevent suspicion of the use made of such an entrance.   To this window Tom placed the ladder and mounting, ascended with lightness until he reached it, and then opening it, like the door of a cupboard, he inserted his ungainly person through the aperture, and dropped to the ground, where for a minute he lay, holding his breath, and listening whether his victim had been awakened by his movements ; but the regular breathing and unmoving frame of the sailor assured him that he remained undisturbed. It was his object to perpetrate the deed before Andrew was conscious of his presence, for though he had little doubt that if a struggle took place he should prove the victor, yet there was something in the brawny limbs of the seaman, and in the glance of his eye, that made him appear a dangerous subject to contest with, and in a matter of life and death the weak obtain a strength which at any other time they cannot display. Tom's reasoning went scarcely so far as this, but he knew it was best done quietly, and he resolved to do it so. He unfastened the door, and taking up the light, he shaded it with his hand until he gained the bedside, and then he turned the light full upon John Andrew. He lay upon his back, seemingly in profound slumber ; his throat was bare, and his face appeared flushed beyond its usual clear reddish brown, but he lay still and calm, his chest heaving at regular intervals, like that of one whose slumber was deep and happy. Tom grasped his knife firmly, and placed his lamp upon the floor while he did the deed. He rose up and bent over the bed, and lifting up the knife was about to draw it rapidly across the naked throat of Andrew, when a violent and sudden knocking at the outer door startled him. It was repeated with vehemence, and muttering a tremendous oath, he took up the light and rushed out of the room. As he quitted it he encountered the ladder ; he struck his head against it with terrific force—the light was dashed out of his hand by the concussion, and he fell prostrate with great violence upon the ground, inflicting severe blows upon his shins in his fall. But for his proximity to Andrew he could have roared out a string of oaths; he, however, restrained himself and raised himself up quickly, notwithstanding his pain, for the knocking was continued with more vigour than ever, and a voice called him repeatedly by name. He descended, and opening the door Jasper rushed in pale and haggard.

"Shut the door," he cried, rapidly and urgently ; "shut it—fasten it—bolt it. Quick, quick."

And without waiting for Trusty Tom to obey him he closed it himself, placing the fastenings with frantic haste. When he had completed his task he staggered to the fire-place and exclaimed—

"Give me some water ; quick ; my throat scorches as if a fire was consuming it. Water, Tom, water."

"Here's some brandy," replied Tom, offering him a bottle.

"No, no ; water," he cried, and buried his head in his hands, rocking himself to and fro, as if undergoing excessive agony of mind or body.

Tom brought him some water in a pitcher, and he drank eagerly a huge draught. Tom watched him in a sort of stupor of surprise, and at length said—

"What, in the devil's name is the matter? You look as white as a ghost, and your eyes glare like an owl's in the dark. What the devil has turned you into a milkfaced booby ?"

Jasper raised his head up and seized Trusty Tom by the arm with a convulsive grip, and staring him wildly in the face, cried—

"You know that grisly old tiger, Jack Churleigh, he has a daughter.—"

"And a fine handsome angel oi a gal she is too," replied Tom.

"I seduced her."

"You!" exclaimed Tom, opening his eyes widely, and staggering back.

"Yes, I. She had a child by me. I had it thrown into the sea, and for
that she has sworn to be my ruin ; she has followed me like a bloodhound on
a track. To-night, when I left here, I made my way to Badger's tent, just
ere I reached it I felt my arm seized firmly. I turned—it was Joan. Joan,
the witch, who will blast my life. She whispered in my ear. A word—a
whisper, will bring you certain death—follow me. She led me unresistingly—

No 31.

for I was paralysed to meet her thus unexpectedly—to a clump of trees.
Here I came upon Badger and her father in conversation. I was the subject
of their talk. Churleigh had got an inkling that I was his girl's destroyer
He knew I had deserted her for another, and I heard him swear that he would
hunt me down—that he would pluck me from the heart of an army, but he
would have his revenge. He said he knew I was near at hand, and he
would tear me limb from joint. Damn it, Tom, I am no coward—I never was ;
but there was something in the old man's words, and in the glaring eyes who
held me with the grip of a vice by the wrist, that made me tremble like an
aspen leaf. Scarce knowing what I did, I broke from her and fled hither."

His head again sunk in his hands, and Tom stood staring upon him as
though he was thunder stricken. At last Tom said—

"Well, you have got the best of me for a decent while. Phew ! but this
is a go! I know old Churleigh, and so do a few others, who swears he lapped
blood when a babby, instead of milk. Why, he'll carve you into bits if he
catches you, and will growl and swear over you like a cat over stolen meat.
I tell you what you must do."

"What, what," eagerly cried Jasper, "tell me, for curse me if I can think,
my brain is in such a whirl."

"Why you must keep out of his way for a little while," he returned, "find
out where he is lurking about, and dodge him until you can quietly put a
bullet through his lug ; and as for the girl, though it's a pity to kill such a
fine creature as she, you must meet her, coax her into a lonely place, and
twist her neck, that's the only thing you can do. But, first and formost, you
must get away from here."

"Yes ; now," cried Jasper, rising.

"No, not yet," said Tom, staying him ; "you might run foul of Churleigh
wait till daybreak and then out."

"It is best as you say," answered Jasper, seating himself. "Where's the
sailor ?" he inquired, after a moment's thought.

Above in bed," returned Tom. "Your knocking saved his bacon ; my
knife was at his throat as you kicked up that devil of a row at the door

"That's right ; I'm glad of that," said Jasper ; "he shall depart with me
in the morning ; he will be company."

"But I can't let his gold go," said Tom ; "he must leave that behind."

"That will never do," returned Jasper ; "He's not the fellow to do that
quietly, and I want his company,   I tell you what, Tom, I will lead him to
Sour Milk Gill, by a roundabout path, and you can meet me there ; I will
then leave him to you.   Will that suit you?"

"That'll do, so that I get the shiners," exclaimed Tom. "But wait a
moment, I will just go up stairs and look about, I kicked up such a noise in
coming down to let you in that I must have waked him. If he's overheard
our confab we must settle him here."

He took the lamp as he spoke, and returned up stairs ; everything was as he
left it ; he raised up the ladder and placed it against the wall, he pushed open
the door and stole into the room, he advanced cautiously to the bed, and
saw Andrew nearly in the same posture as before, and apparently as fast

asleep: hewas satisfied with his scrutiny and returned to Jasper. They sat drinking and talking until daybreak, when Tom went and roused Andrew, who rose, washed and dressed himself, partook heartily of some breakfast which Tom placed before him, and was ready to depart as soon as Jasper, whose nervous impatience to start made him leave the food nearly untouched. No money was taken of Andrew for what he had received, although he desired to pay; and when the little altercation respecting it was at an end, Jasper armed himself with a gun, and he started. They walked on briskly for a few hours, now on eminences, now declivities, and then levels; at length a small woody spot presented itself, and they entered it; a small stream, which fell down from a rocky height, and rambled murmuringly along, displayed such attractions to Andrew that he must needs stop, hang his hat on a bough of a young tree, and take a draught, and then seat himself upon a bank for a rest. Jasper followed his example, and drank copiously of the pure liquid. On raising his head from his draught he was not a little surprised to find Andrew presenting a pistol at his head, and had got his two feet firmly planted upon his gun, which he had laid down while he drank of the water—one arm rested upon his knee, while the other was raised before him. Andrew enjoyed the astonishment Jasper exhibited without uttering a word, but Jasper broke the silence by observing—

"What do you mean by presenting that weapon at me?"

"I'll tell you," answered Andrew. "It isn't your fault that I'm here now alive and kicking. Two to one's long odds placed as I was, or, dam'me, but instead of being friendly with you, I'd had a shy at both of you."

"I don't understand you," exclaimed Jasper.

"Don't you," replied Andrew, "then I'll just make it all clear to you—smooth and plain, like the captain's looking-glass. You see, when that shindy was kicked up by some thief hammering at the door, I woke up and jumped out of bed. I walked to the head of the companion, and overheard you tell that pretty story about getting to wind'ard of a young girl and shoving her youngster into salt water—a pretty damnable devil's babby you are; and then I heard your mate tell you how near he had sent me to Davy Jones's locker, and be damned to him; then I heard you plan that nice little bit of villainy to lead me to Sour Milk Gill, or Gull, or whatever it is, to ease me of my money. Now, curse me! but for half a sheave, I'd make a Sour Milk Gill of you, you white-livered, black-muzzled, ugly-looking miscreant. D'ye see this pistol? well, I have a brace here; I stumbled on them after that thief of a mate of yours had been eyeing me to see if I had heard his and your villainy; they are both loaded with ball, and well primed. Now, mark me, you haven't a weapon, for I've your gun under my feet, and a hand of yours stretched out to reach it would bring a bullet through your head-rails. I know you've misdirected and are running me right out of my course; now you shall convoy me correctly, for if I find by the first one I meet, be it man, woman, or child, that you are not steering true, damme, if I don't scuttle your nob. Jump up and lead on, I am not to be played with like a ooy; I should think it a vartue in me to shoot you, so don't tempt me. Lead on, and remember, if I find that you have led me out of my course, I'll bring you down as I would a rat, or any other vermin. Lead on, you gallows-looking, piratical, half-hung serpent. I wish I had you seized up to a grating, and was the bo'sen's mate to give you three out of six dozen; I'd make you know where the cat scratched. Lead on, don't stand staring there like the figure-head of the Shirk sloop of war, all eyes and mouth; come, bear a hand and show the true way, or look out for a blue pill. Heave ahead;"

Jasper's astonishment as well as rage was unbounded. He clenched his fists and ground his teeth, as on his knees he remained, staring Andrew in the face; but to help himself was out of his power. Within a foot of his head was a pistol; his gun was out of his reach, and there was that steady air of determination in the seaman's countenance, which told him plainly that he would keep his word if any attempt was made to resist his commands.

It is extraordinary how circumstances will change the character of human beings. The wildest, most reckless, and daring have been placed in positions which, despite their brute absence of fear, have reduced them to tame led-at-will creatures. Jasper, originally courageous, of a daring nature, impatient of control, had from boyhood passed a life of adventure and peril of his own seeking, in defiance of the prayers and entreaties of his mother and the commands of his father. Until his first abduction of Florence, all had gone, if not smoothly, at least fortunately with him. He had by bold impulses and reckless conduct passed unscathed through perils which might have daunted the stoutest heart, and he believed himself, from repeated successes, invulnerable. He had ever followed the path which his passions had led, and the exercise of a ferocious determination had borne him safely and successfully along; but it was to have a check. It has been seen that repeated reverses ensued his vile conduct to the gentle Florence and his heartless villainy to Joan. Whatever scheme he laid—however he tried to carry it into execution—he was foiled and defeated as well as made a prey to the gnawing bitterness which disappointment and ill success in one of his dearest projects would have upon such a fierce, ruthless nature as his. His anxiety and great exertions had weakened his frame; the frustration of his plans against the honour of Florence, the curse of Joan, and the indefinable dread respecting her which hung over him, and which he could not, try as he would, shake off, considerably weakened his strength of mind, and went far to reduce him to the level of those who were inferior in strength, capacity, and daring.

In the present instance he was cowed and subjected, something to his own surprise, for had the incident occurred in the full tide of wild success, he would have regarded the pistol with contempt, and sprung upon Andrew with tiger-like ferocity, risking life and limb to have punished the insult which he would have deemed had been offered him: even now he might have gone far to have had a struggle for mastery, but there was a crawling horror upon him that the sound arising from a deadly struggle might fill the air and wake up the echoes of the lonely spot they were in, and so bring down he of all men to be avoided—Churleigh—upon them, and this reflection decided him to yield quietly to the honest sailor, who, he fancied, in case of encountering the "grisly tiger," would prove a kind of protection to him. It was impossible to deny the truth of what Andrew advanced as having overheard; indeed he was more of a bold than an artful villain, and the idea of disavowing it never crossed him, nor did it enter his head to endeavour to remove the impression against him by conciliation; he was conscious what his thoughts would have been of one acting as he had done, and assumed, therefore, the opinion Andrew had formed of him to be the same; so when the repeated commands of Andrew to lead the way, and that correctly, were given, he rose up with a sullen gloom and advanced; while Andrew, finding the gun likely to encumber him, discharged it, and then threw it into the stream. The report was a loud one, and was repeated by the echoes a hundred times.

"What the devil did you do that for?" exclaimed Jasper, angrily, when Andrew fired the gun.

"Because it was in my way, and I didn't choose it to be in yours," replied the sailor; "these pops will do for me, and—"

A loud hollo interrupted him; it proceeded from a distant part of the wood, and Andrew immediately answered it with a loud and clear throat.

"Hell and fury!" roared Jasper, "what are you about? Are you mad?"

"Mad! not quite," replied he; "I don't take your word for Bible truth, and I mean to ask a question for myself. Ship ahoy!" he roared with stentorian strength: his hail was answered, and the form of a man appeared among the distant trees. No sooner did Jasper's eyes light on his form, than almost shrieking—

"Damnation! it is he

He darted in an opposite direction past Andrew, and fled at the top of his speed. The sailor was so taken by surprise that he had not power to stop him, and he was beyond the range of pistol shot before he thought of sending a bullet after him; he amused himself by bawling a volley of invective, and then waited with some little anxiety the arrival of the stranger, whose appearance had produced such an effect on Jasper. He was not kept long in suspense; the man rapidly advanced, and when he got near enough to exchange words, Andrew cried,

"Hoy; the ship ahoy!"

"Hollea!" replied the man, with something of a professional tone.

"A word or two with you, brother," exclaimed Andrew, and with a nod of assent the man stopped as soon as he reached him. Jasper's suspicions were correct, the man was Jack Churleigh.

"I want you to give me the bearings to a place, either no'thard or west'ard of this place, called Grasmere," observed Andrew.

"You're running away from it," returned Churleigh; "you must bear away to the left, and make for the Rydal water by a cross road, which yon path will lead you to; you ascend the hill over High-close, on the way to Longdale, until you see a road which runs to the west'ard, that's the road you must take, and it will lead you down the side of the lake to Grasmere."

"You ain't getting to wind'ard of me, are you?" asked Andrew, with a slight expression of doubt playing over his features.

"What makes you think that?" replied Churleigh, with a surly look.

"Why because a damned thief whom I fell in with yesterday offered to convoy me to the village, and instead of doing it run me right out of my course did his share towards cutting my life-lines adrift, and but for this persuader," he continued, holding up the pistol, "he was going to carry me to Sour Milk Gill, and there intended, with the help of another vagerbone, as great a rascal as himself, to clear out my lockers; hows'ever, he didn't like the open mouth of this small talker, and we were beating up for Grasmere when you hove in sight."

Churleigh listened to him with great attention, and when he had finished he exclaimed, hastily—

"Was it you who fired the gun?"

"Ay, ay!" replied Andrew; "the gun was his'n; but I didn't see fit to let him have it to drop shot into me when he fell into my wake. Yes, it was I who fired the gun and answered your hail. Lord love you, as soon as he clapped eyes on you he sung out an oath, and says, says he, 'it's he,' and under press of sail, bowled along like bells."

"Ha!" cried Churleigh, with a start, and asked, rapidly, "what sort of a man was he? what was his dress? Quick; speak, man."

"He was something of the same build as yourself," returned Andrew; "though you've been off the stocks longer than him; a white ghostly figure-head, with enough hair to take a sheep-shank in. He had bent a coat large enough for the Spanker of a seventy-four——"

"Brown, with a scarlet waistcoat and large riding boots," interrupted Churleigh, rapidly—"his name Geoffrey Smith?"

"Now you have it as plain as if you 'saw it down in a log," answered Andrew.

"Which path did he take?" eagerly inquired Churleigh.

"Why he bore hard away for that point," he replied, extending his finger in the direction which Jasper had taken, "and stood for it the moment you hove in sight."

"Then I have him," exclaimed Churleigh, with a tremendous oath: he then said quickly to Andrew, "I've told you correctly the road which you must take for Grasmere, and if your name be Andrew, and you know anything of one Martha Bell, you will bear a hand, nor slacken sail until you run alongside of her. Heave ahead, and thankee for your news."

As he concluded he darted off with, considering his age, surpassing agility along the path which Andrew had pointed out as the one pursued by Jasper, and left the simple-minded seaman perfectly astounded with the knowledge which people of whom he knew nothing seemed to have of him and those belonging to him. He looked after Churleigh until he was out of sight, and then he muttered something about there being unaccountable people in these parts, while shouldering his bundle. He followed the advice he had just received from the old man, and taking the road he had shown him, made the best of his way to the village of Grasmere.

The last words of Churleigh had an ominous sound to him. The reference to Martha Bell—his own pretty, sweet little craft, that had hung upon him and wept so when he went away, and of whom during his absence he had built up such fond and charming fabrics—staggered him and made him feel uncomfortable. He thought of a thousand evils. Had she forgotten him and made the port of matrimony with another, or was she about to do it? was she ill, and like to slip her cable for another world? A thousand painful conjectures crossed his mind, and rendered him uneasy enough to be almost miserable. He certainly obeyed Churleigh's injunction, and went a-head in style. He wound up the steep ascent to High-close, after pursuing the cross road by the foot of the Rydal—disregarding the exquisite scenery as well as his fatigue. It was with no little joy he reached the road which wound down the westward side of the lake, and showed him in the distance, down in the beautiful vale, about a quarter of a mile from the high road, the port for which he was bound. He knew every spot well now, though not his native place, and crossed the fields to the village as rapidly as though the earlier he arrived he should be able to fend off some evil which might be about to happen to his sweetheart. It was afternoon ere he reached it, and on coming to the last style, which was between him and the village, his heart throbbed violently; he felt sick with anticipation; he felt almost afraid to advance for fear he should come to the knowledge of disastrous events that would carry all his happiness by the board; he could not muster courage to proceed; and so seated himself upon the stile, leaned his back against a tree, and gazed earnestly upon the spot which contained either the realization of his hopes and future happiness, or the black doom of misery and despair. He perspired as much with his thoughts as with his long and rapidly accomplished walk, and he removed his round straw hat from his head to cool it, and let the gentle afternoon breeze fan his heated forehead. There he sat, his bundle placed upon his knees, clasped by his hands; his round hat depending from them, his stick by his side and his head turned homewards; his eyes bent earnestly upon the spot in the village where stood his dear mother's humble cot, his heart beat fast as his eyes picked out the dwelling, and he would have given all he possessed, cheerfully, to have known for certain that the inmates he had left when he departed were still there, and well and happy. Five minutes' walk would decide the matter, it was true, and had he not have met with the incidents narrated during his progress hither, he would not have paused or waited for one moment to consider what changes might have occured, but gone at once boldly—thoughtlessly, rather—and have seen all that had; but Jasper's knowledge of him, the successful attempt to lead him out of the way, and the unsuccessful one upon his life, Churleigh's advice and acquaintance with his name and that of Martha Bell's, all united, stirred up within him a mass of reflections and anticipations of a nature painful, and, to a certain extent distressing. The sight of his home increased the turbulence, and it was a matter of difficulty for him to persuade himself to go home before he had met with some one belonging to the village who could inform him of all he desired to know. So deep was he wrapped in his meditations that he heard not the light step of a female who had followed the same path he had taken a short time after him, and who had now reached the stile which he occupied, with the intention of crossing it. His garb attracted her attention, but his face being partly turned from her, she was unable to tell whether the sudden fancy which shot across her was to be realized. The female was Martha Bell, and her imagination conceived but one sailor in the world, and that one John Andrew The form of the young man upon the stile was that of her John's, but hang. it, she couldn't see his face ; but the hair and whiskers were the same, and if it wasn't John, who could it be ? Yet if it was not John, and he, a stranger, was to turn round and find her staring at him " with all her eyes," he might seize her by the waist, talk nonsense to her, or try, and prove otherwise " howdacious." She was a pretty smart looking little piece of goods, and she, knew it—most girls, when they are so, do, as well as anybody, and so did Martha ; but to do her justice, she had no desire to be kissed by anybody else but John, and she wouldn't have kissed anybody else but John, and she wouldn't have kissed anybody else but his mother or her own for all the world, " she would die sooner, that she would." Therefore, if this clean built tar who looked so like John was not John, she would do her best to get out of the way as soon as she could. As she arrived at this conclusion, she caught a glimpse of his nose and profile—she burst into a loud laugh of joy.

" Ha ! ha !" she laughed, " it must be he, that it must ; that nose is John's and nobody else's. John—Johnny, it be you, bain't it ? It is ! Oh, John—Johnny, my own dear Johnny, ha ! ha ! ha ! thou bees't come back to me at last, that you be, ha ! ha ! ha ! I shall die with joy. Oh, John, dear—dear John, ha ! ha ! ha ! ha !"

Her laugh ended with hysterics, the case with most young ladies in a like situation. The first sound of her voice had made Andrew turn his head like, lightning ; the next instant his bundle, hat, and stick were upon the ground he leaped from his seat and caught her in his arms, squeezing her to his breast with a vigour worthy of the delight he felt in beholding her. He kissed her cheeks, her eyes, her lips, not a bit to her dissatisfaction, and mumbled a few words which were so detained in the throat that they were indistinguishable, save that the name of Martha, coupled with a few nautical phrases expressive of his ecstacy, escaped from the fate of the others. After he had squeezed her passionately, and kissed her " a score and more," and called her a foolish little thing for working the pumps, though he confessed the water poured from his scuppers as it does from decks washed in hot climates, he asked, hesitatingly, after the " old woman," and learning she was quite well and very comfortable, principally through Martha's agency, though that she did not tell him, he owned he was the happiest fellow in the world.

" And you, Martha—Lord love that darling face—ain't you happy, too, lass, eh ?" he exclaimed, with fervour.

"Oh, John, I am indeed happy, so happy I hardly know what to do; and if it was not for my young mistress I should be happier than any ten in Christendom, let the other be who she may," returned Martha, smiling through her tears.

"And what of your young mistress?" inquired her lover. "I hope she doesn't behave ill to you?"

"Lord bless you, John, what put that into your head?" replied Martha, quickly; "she behave ill to me—the saints preserve her! No, no, John, she's the kindest, goodest, dearest soul under heaven; she's been spirited away, master says, by evil-minded ruffians, even his own son, Jasper, Andrew!— you remember Jasper, you saw him come in the night we danced at the wedding of Mary Mills with Joe Green?—if you recollect, you said you didn't like him, he looked such a how—"

"Phew!" interrupted Andrew, slapping his thigh hard, and elevating his eyebrows, as if a new light had suddenly broken in upon him. "Now I remembers where I saw that ugly vagabond's figure-head. To be sure. I know'd I'd seen his dam—"

No. 32.

"Andrew!" half screamed Martha, as the oath was leaving her lover's l.ps, "don'tee say them words; they don't make your speech stronger, and they do make it uglier."

"Well, well, Martha, whatever you like," returned Andrew, fondly; "but it's pleasant to fling a word like that at such half-cobbed-marine's-mate's-cook's-minister's swab. I know'd I'd clapped eyes on him afore; I know'd I had the minute I saw him, snoring away like a captain's tea-kettle on a galley fire."

"What are you talking about, John?" asked Martha.

"Never mind now, Matty—you heave ahead," said Andrew; "pay out your story if you have it coiled like a cable, fake over fake, and when you're brought up by the end of your hawse, pass the word to me."

"Can't you talk sensible English, John?" said Martha, rather perplexed—"I don't understand half what you have said."

"Sensible English!" repeated Andrew, with surprise—"Lord ha mercy, how ignorant you are in these inland parts—I have spoken your true lingo, which it's proper for a seafaring man who's all fair and above board and no lubber, to talk, and you don't read the bunting. Well, I s'pose it's all natural and proper, 'long-shore people talk 'long-shore talk, and sea people speak in the fashion of those whose craft is their home, and the deep sea their country. To speak in your country's manner, I means this: tell me all you knows about your mistress and this here Jasper as I saw at the dance afore I went my last voyage."

"I can do that in a dozen words," cried Martha, eagerly.

"Sway away, then" answered Andrew; "that's the way I likes to hear yarns."

"You never saw my young mistress," began Martha, quite ready to run through her story as glibly as possible.

"No," returned Andrew. "Who was she?"

"Oh! it's all come out since she has disappeared; everybody has been told who she is, why she came here, and all about it," rattled forth Martha. "You must know that she was called here Miss Florence Ranklyn, but that was not her name—no, her name is Stanley, and she is nearly related to Earl Derby. Well, she's got a lover who is a sailor—none the worse for being that, I'm sure, though it's said he was. Oh, Andrew, they say he is a wicked, dreadful man, full of such oaths, and drinking, and swearing, and winning young girls' hearts and then leaving 'em to die of broken hearts, like many other false, parjured swains; and he, by his sly cunning and witchcraft, made Miss Florence in love with him, but her friends wouldn't let her have him, and as the pretty song says—

> "Her father proved to her most cruel,
>   And to sea he sent her swain,
> And vowed there should be no renewal
>   Of their tender vows again;
> 'But,' cried she, when they was parted,
>   'When o'er the wild wide seas you roam,
> 'Think of her, who, broken-hearted,
>   'Mourns her sailor far from home.'"

" Now, that's what I call a proper fine song," exclaimed Andrew, with a burst of enthusiasm : " I should like to hear that again, Matty."

" Oh, you shall hear it all by and bye," she replied, " it is a pretty song, and many's the time I used to sing it when you was far away, and we never heard from you, and never knew whether you would come back any more." The tears sprung in her eyes, and her tongue faltered at the last words. Andrew kissed her, and blessed her sweet figure-head, which he swore never a vessel in the navy or merchant-service could equal; no, not even the Fairy schooner nor the Angel frigate. A little love passage, of no immediate importance to the reader, followed this, and Martha proceeded, relating, after her own style, all the events which had occurred to Florence, coming under her cognizance, not forgetting the contrivance by which Martha was deceived, for which Andrew promised the masquerader a sound rope's-ending whenever he came athwart him. At length the name of Prior transpired, coupled with a long string of harsh appellatives, which John Audrew cut short very quickly as soon as he discovered that it was the first lieutenant of the Wildfire in question; and, in contradiction, gave him such a character that Martha began wonderfully to alter the opinion which, in common with everybody else connected with Florence, she had been led to entertain respecting him, and to think that Florence, so far from being misled in maintaining her love for him, had acted as a girl of spirit ought to do who loved one who was worth loving, whether he was rich or not.

" And I tell you what, Andrew," she exclaimed, earnestly, " I think it's right and proper that he should be made acquainted with all that's taken place concerning her, and you shall send up a letter to London to him at once, and tell him how she has been carried away for near three weeks or a month, by either a ghost or by that wretch Mr. Jasper—which master says he thinks is the fact, for he has kept away; and there's poor Master Frank, who went away the same day, and we've never heard of him since. Master thinks he's murdered, but he doesn't say what makes him think so; but it's a strange matter altogether. I know that I've cried my eyes out for poor Miss Florence, besides being laid up in bed for nearly a week with a cold which I caught when I fell asleep in the garden. Ah! if I had not dropped off into a dream, I'd have torn the eyes out of the wretches that carried off my sweet young mistress before they should have taken her away."

" What was she taken away for ?" inquired Andrew.

" That's where all the mystery is," returned Martha; " that's why I think it's a ghost which came in the shape of a tall dark woman, who came up from the ground before Miss Florence went to see the monster that pretended to come from you and Mr. Prior, and appeared to me after she had been taken away. ' She is lost,' she said to me, in such a ghost-like tone, and then vanished. I'm sure, John, she spirited her away."

" I'm afraid, Matty, that will do for the marines," said Andrew with a laugh; " it's more than I can quite hoist in. What does your master think of it ?"

"Oh, he said at first it was Mr. Prior that had carried her away," replied Martha, " until little Mat Meadows came and told us a long story about finding Jasper in a cave, bound hand and foot; how he unfastened him, and how Jasper, when he set him free, made him promise, upon the pain of being drowned in the lake, not to tell that he had seen him; but that a strange man, who said he had set Miss Florence at liberty from Jasper's clutches, and fired a shot at Jasper as he ran away from the cave, came to him, and told him that he had a warrant to capture Jasper for piracy and smuggling, and that it should go hard, but he would have him : and after asking a few questions, he had set off in chase of him. So master has made up his mind that Jasper has murdered his brother Frank."

" What," cried Andrew, with a start, " murdered his brother?"

"Yes," returned Martha, "such a good, kind, sweet-spoken young gentleman as he was, too. And besides that villany, he suspects that Jasper is in love with Miss Florence, and has carried her off to make her his wife. Oh, there has been such trouble—such a to-do. Her family—that is, her father and brother, have been down here, and all our people have been on the search, but we have not heard anything of her, and I am afeard we shall not." Martha burst out crying as she concluded ; and Andrew, pressing her gently to his breast, said—

" Don't take on, Matty—don't take on, girl ; we shall have fair weather yet. I think I know something of this affair, and can point out the latitude where this Jasper is cruising. I'll go and have a bit of a jaw with the old woman, and then we'll see what is to be done. If I fall in with master Jasper, I'll clap dead on him, and I'll take care we don't part company until he has belayed about the young lady. I'll make him spell out where he has stowed her, and then I'd rather be keel-hauled every day for a week than stand the racket he will catch. Come, Matty, dry your eyes ; give us a kiss and let's away to the old woman—there's a little duck. When did a fairy ever have such head-rails, such toplights?" and imprinting a kiss upon her lips, and giving her an extra hug, they wended their way to the cottage in Grasmere, which contained his mother.

CHAPTER XII.

" Pol.—What follows then, my lord ?
Ham.—Why,
   ' As by lot, God wot,'
And then you know,
   ' It came to pass, as most like it was.'
The first row of the pious Chanson will show you
more ; for look, where my abridgments come."
                         SHAKSPERE.

There is a secret sympathy, no matter what the respective situations may be, in woman, for those of their sex who have been wronged or ill treated. The humblest will view with commiseration the wrongs of her whose station may be far above their own or on a level with it; and, vice-versa; the rich, whatever may be said of them, do feel grieved for the sufferings of those females who are inferior in birth and rank to themselves, and hence the thousands of cases of private charity, which, though they never meet the public eye, are, nevertheless, known to exist, and are, in fact, more estimable and more genuine offerings of the heart. It is beautifully ordained by nature that to be the victim of oppressions and injuries is to create friends in the worthy and honourable. The undeserved wrongs of a subject, however humble, when known, has aroused his fellow-countrymen to arms; and a public wrong to a Queen was received by the women of England as an insult to their sex. Those females who have been pressed down unjustly to the lowest depths of poverty, but who have preserved their self-respect, have found that there were plenty of their own sex, who, if they could not effectually relieve them, have shown their sympathy in a thousand little delicate ways. To put a familiar case, if a man ill-uses his wife, do not all her female friends and acquaintances unite in dubbing the husband a brute and monster, unworthy to live, while, they hold up the wife as an example of an injured saint, "if ever there was one;" and if this conduct is not precisely guided by reason and justice—always supposing there may be some faults on the lady's side—is it not delightful to see that the best feelings are aroused in behalf of one of their own kind who has been as "a stricken deer?" This feeling, or to call it by its better name, this sympathy, is more often displayed in women than men. Women will stand up in defence of women, will argue boldly and warmly in their favour, will at 'un again, Jan," until they have done their service, if they have not succeeded in carrying their point, where men similarly situated with their fellow men would be indifferent and callous to the result, even if the event affected in an indirect manner their own taste. If this were not the case, and men were less selfish, more regardful of the happiness of each other, the miseries of the people would be as a mote in the eye to what they now are. The possession of this kindly feeling towards their sisterhood is one of the best and noblest additions to the many sweet attributes which make woman so lovely, so loved.

The state in which Jasper brought Florence to the tribe of gipseys, which he designated as the tribe of Badger, had created in the women a feeling of sympathy for her helplessness, which might have been doubted to exist in such people; but, nevertheless, did find a place in their bosoms. The discovery of Jasper's character and connection with them, by Badger, had prevented them displaying this feeling to its fullest extent, by delivering her from his power, which it was their first intention to do, but they did their best to restore her strength, and gave her a pass-word to any tribe she might fall in with, who would upon hearing it, protect her and restore her to her friends. Thankfully did Florence listen to it, and treasure it up in her memory resolving the first opportunity to make use of it. It had not been her fortune to meet with any of the tribe until she encountered those who came up to the spot where she was seated with Nehemie and his daughter Letty. The prospect of release at once presented itself before her with gladsome aspect, and the first use she made of her tongue, when a woman of the tribe led her beyond the hearing of Nehemie, was to give the pass-word and beg for succour. The woman listened with some little surprise, and obtained from her a brief outline of the circumstances which had placed her in this position. Her attenuated frame, and the lines of care and fatigue marked upon her otherwise beautiful face, was strong attestations of the truth of her story and the woman, who was addressed by her companions by the name of Bridget, bade her be of good cheer, for all that could be done in her service should be. Rescuing her from Nehemie was a matter easily accomplished, but returning her to her friends was not so easy, because to ensure it they must not part with her until close to Chough Hall, and some recent acts of Badger and his tribe, in the shape of smuggling, had made the vicinity rather dangerous to any of the fraternity to approach it; for the officers, having been apprised of it, were on the alert, and as there was not that nice discrimination in the tribes which would separate the innocent from the guilty existing in the perceptive powers of the men of law, it was possible that the first community they came across, clothed in the careless garb of this class of Egyptians or Bohemians, they would seize *vi et armis*, and consign to the safe custody of four stone walls, and a Cerberus to guard the door. The old woman did not exactly enter into this explanation, but told Florence if she would not mind staying a few days with them, enduring the inconveniences resulting from their mode of living, she would pledge her soul she should be as safe as in her father's house, and at the same time every effort should be made to render her return to Grasmere as early as possible.

"I am sure you will not deceive me," said Florence in reply; "I feel that whatever prejudice may exist against you, your word, passed as you have given me yours, is sacred, and may be depended on as such."

"It may," said the woman emphatically.

"Then I will remain with you," she concluded, "and patiently abide the time which will bring me deliverance ; for I had rather die then return with this man to the greater villain who has employed him."

"And I will stay, too," said Letty, quickly ; " you will let me stay, won't you?" she cried, addressing the woman. "I'll do anything you ask me only let me stay."

"If the young lady wishes it, my dear, you may," rejoined the woman.

"Oh, thank you, a thousand times," exclaimed Letty, "she wishes it, I know she does ; don't you ?" she inquired of Florence.

"I do, my kind little friend," returned Florence, "with all my heart ; but will your father suffer you to remain ? will he leave you behind ?"

"Oh, yes ; you must make him," she uttered, anxiously ; "you must send him away without me. I will not go with him. I would sooner kneel down for any one here to kill me than go back. You said you would take me with you, and I should live with you. You will not desert me ? If you do I shall break my heart ; I shall drown myself or go mad. Oh, let me go with you. Pray, pray do !"

"Hush !" exclaimed Bridget. "The keen eyes of the Frenchman are upon us ; stratagem must be used against stratagem ; remain thou here with my daughters while I talk with one who has the power, if I can create within him the will, to aid you. Should he consent to befriend you, it must be by a potency and subtlety stronger than any possessed by yon shuffling, grinning trickster, or his employer, that he will be prevented keeping his faith with you. Make yourselves happy, at least for the present, for while with us you remain, no harm can or shall come to you."

As she concluded she quitted them. Letty, with an affectionate smile, wound her arms round the waist of Florence, and said, as she looked wistfully in her face—

"Oh ! if we get to your home, and I live with you, there will be nobody in the world so happy as I."

Florence imprinted on her soft cheek a kind kiss, wiped the tears, which strong and earnest feeling brought to her eyes, from her lids, and promised her that so long as it was in her power to befriend her she would not desert her, an assurance which yielded the child infinite delight.

The daughters of the gipsey woman, two fine dark-eyed, handsome featured girls, with raven hair and nut-brown skins, now addressed the two fugitives. They requested them to seat themselves by their sides, ann with laudable kindness did their best to amuse them during the absence of their mother, by telling them wonders about the stars, fates and destinies, strongly tinctured with the cant of their calling, shewing how a dairy maid came to be a countess, and a farmer's daughter, one patient Griselda, to be a Queen—how the influence of the planets had brought relief to the distressed and succour to the oppressed, and how they possessed the power to read the signs and symbols exhibited in the heavens in the hands of the human race, and displayed in the conjunction of the stars, fortelling the future happiness or misery of the inquirer. The mysteries of fate were made plain to them and the destinies of lovers, their positions, situations, trades and professions, their truth or falsity, the time of their appearance, the day, the hour they would send a love letter, whether they would proffer marriage or prove base deluders, whether carriages were in the ascendant, or whether marrow bones were to be the mode of conveyance for life; whether one or three husbands were to be the number their lot was to be blessed with, and a pigeon's pair or two and twenty sweetners of human life, the family which was to felicitate their union. All these desirable communications, and others, too numerous to mention, but not less important and interesting, were in the province of their power of prediction.

Florence listened to their almost solemnly uttered disclosure of their skill in divination with an incredulous smile; but Letty heard them with open mouth, frequently expressed astonishment, and had ready upon her lips a string of questions to be resolved. When the old woman Bridget returned there was an evident expression of pleasure upon her countenance, and she said, with emphasis—

" I have been successful ; you have a friend in one who can make a bitter foe ; he has given his word to protect you to the furthest extent of his power. You shall see, maiden, how a despised and contemned race can keep faith. The hospitality of our tribe is sacred—the recommendation from one body of our people to another is no less so. Deem yourself safe till it is the will of Him before whom the proudest potentate must bow, to restore you, through our means, to the bosom of your friends. Yon Frenchman returns empty handed to his dwelling, or he never returns ; rest with us in contentment— we are rude and uncouth in our manners, we are simple in our mode of living, but we know how to respect those whose situation requires it. We can be rough to the brawler, but gentle to the timid and helpless. You shall find, maiden, that on your bed of down, surrounded by relations and friends, guarded by domestics, and shielded from cold or care, you cannot be more secure or more tenderly treated than by a 'a gang of gipseys.' "

" I believe you, firmly and fully," replied Florence, with fervour; "there is a candour in your manner which looks not like deceit ; but even were you inclined to play me false, there is so little to be gained in making me, help- less as I am, a victim, that I should still, without your promise, trust in for safety, for it is rare even that the worst disposed will do evil without a strong consideration, and no consideration have you to do evil unto me. But your protestations to return me to my friends, and your promise that I shall not be subjected to any insults or oppressions, make me feel contented and secure. I can, while with you, sleep in peace and wake, if not happily, at least with a sense that I have much to be thankful for; and, though I may look forward to my return to my friends with anxiety, I shall feel comparatively at ease in your society. You shall find me grateful for your aid, and my friends will be bountiful to you for your services to me. I rely firmly upon your truth ; but let you keep your faith as you may, I would rather trust to you and die in doing it, than return with that man."

" Maiden, as there is a heaven above us, our faith with you shall not be broken," exclaimed the old woman, earnestly.

Florence repeated her thanks warmly, and Letty chimed in, determined, as far as prayers and protestations would go in aiding her stay with Florence,

not to be backward in using them.   The gipseys, who were not exactly cognizant of the origin of her connection with Florence, or the circumstances attendant upon it, readily included her in their promises of protection; and with a lighter heart than she had that day had she partook of a simple meal, placed before her and her companion by the girls, who joined them in the repast, and looked forward to her deliverance from her father as the greatest blessing heave u could grant her.

Nehemie, in the mean time, was in that frame of mind which has been so powerfully illustrated by some ancient author depicting a person *sans culotte* seated upon a cushion composed of briars, hawthorn bushes, and other prickly vegetation; or, as some more modern, but perhaps more familiar, not to say vulgar writer has expressed it—he felt as comfortable as a cat on hot bricks. And to say the truth, his position was about as enviable; he had to support a conversation in broken English with two or three of the gipsey men, whose frames were more powerful than his own, and to bear that colloquy with the appearance of frank good humour, he had also to keep a sharp eye upon Florence and Letty, and discover, if possible, by their gestures and the expression of

No. 33

their features, the nature of their communication to old Bridget. His daughter's face displayed to him all she felt, and her gestures were sufficient to shew that she was not keeping her feelings and wishes pent up in her own breast.   A torrent of bitter rage rushed through him, and mentally he promised her three fourths of the blade of a long knife, when he had her securely in his power.   Still he had the power of preserving a composed and even gratified expression of features which would have deceived most persons, save such as those by whom he was surrounded, whose lives and skilfulness were exercised in reading the countenance of those with whom they came in contact, and, with all his cunning, they could detect the anxiety he felt in the occasional glances he directed to the females, and the lines and twitches of his mouth—a feature which displays the workings of the mind perhaps more rapidly than any other—but, as if they enjoyed the nervous irritation under which they knew he was labouring, they kept him in conversation upon the most indifferent as well as tedious subjects they could devise, and certainly far removed from the tenor of his thoughts.   It was with no little anxiety he watched Bridget leave Florence and summon the gipsey who had first accosted him, and who seemed to possess considerable influence over the tribe. He watched them retire to a spot where not a word could reach his ear or a movement his eyes, and swore at fate ten thousand times for placing him in so cursed a predicament.   The return of the gipsey, however, he hoped, would afford him some clue to the nature of the conference ; but he was mistaken, for when the man again appeared it was with a countenance as unembarassed and as unconcerued as before ; he went on with the conversation which had been interrupted by his departure with the air of one who had heard nothing in his absence to surprise him, or create an angry or unpleasant feeling towards him who felt himself to have been the subject of the conference, and was as humorous and chatty as before. Several times Nehemie determined to ask him the reason the woman called him away, but he could not find a pretext, and he scarcely liked to venture for fear of its being taken as an insult and resented accordingly. There was something in the glancing eyes of jet belonging to the men who rolled lazily round him that made him think twice before he spoke once.   When a man is in the company of those he estimates as wolves or tigers, he is usually circumspect in his conduct, and prudent in his conversation.   Such was the case with Nehemie, and though his breast was being gnawed as if he had a vulture there, by restless longings and anticipations not of the most agreeable decription, he preserved a shew of courtesy and indifference to what was transpiring with a stoicism almost to be admired He was, as Bulwer would say, a shrewd man, that Frenchman.

Evening drew on apace.   Nehemie watched the sun sinking and redden as if he was blushing modestly at the idea that every one in this quarter of the globe knew he was going to bed : he saw, as the bashful luminary drew the curtains of night around him—his bed-curtains of course—that daylight was becoming a thing that had been ; and with the decline of day he saw a favourable opportunity of disclosing his desire to depart, express his delight at the pleasant life gipseys lived, and trouble them to deliver the two damsels once more to his charge, and he would, with many thanks, wend his way homeward. The gipseys heard him with a silence which struck him as a little ominous, and he reiterated his thanks for their hospitality, accompanied by remarks incidental to the charms of being a gipsey, but still they heard him in silence. At length when he put the question directly, with an annoying presentiment that he should be thwarted in his wish, the elder gipsey, whose sobriquet was Tom Cooper—this being one of the Cooper tribes, the most numerous in England—returned in reply, that he could not be rested enough, to which Nehemie answered, he was as fresh as if he had not walked at all.

"But them two young creturs ain't," returned Tom Cooper, "and I've just heerd that they means to stop with us to-night. If you're in a hurry, Mounseer, you can go, if you likes—but the young 'uns don't."

"I must take them with me," exclaimed Nehemie, a little nervously.

"Must you," returned Tom, rather doubtfully; "well, I tell you what," he added, "they can't go to-night, there's no mistake about that. Young gals like they, who have walked a matter of twenty-five or thirty mile, ain't so free and lithe of limb a'ter it as a long-legged, gridiron-looking French mounseer like you. I've promised the old 'un that they stops with us, and that nobody molests, or insults, or wags an imperdent tongue at 'em while they're with us; and those as don't want the pinted part of a long knife looking into their wittling office to see how things is going on, will mind what I says, for I'll keep my word with them, or I never kept it with nobody; and that I HAVE kept it, Mounseer, here's one or two here 'as had pretty decent proof on it."

He looked around at his fellows with an air of triumphant appeal, and the slight grin which the men uttered in token of assent, was sufficient to assure Nehemie that he had spoken the truth. Still the "Frenchman" urged his departure, which Cooper told him again and again he might take, but it must be alone, and to that Nehemia would not consent. At length he said, when he found that the gipsey was immoveable upon that point, that he would himself stop the night and depart in the morning. Tom grinned as he heard him, and consented to the arrangement; a place was yielded to him by the fire, where he could lay down and sleep; and as the night was calm and mild, he made no objection, or found any inconvenience from it. When the morning came, although his sleep had not been continued, yet, when he awoke, the gipseys were up and about; breakfast was made and eaten; both Florence and Letty were partakers of it in his company, and his language to both was mild, conciliatory, and by those unacquainted with his previous conduct or his wishes would have been termed affectionate; but all there knew how to appreciate it,. and though managed and conducted with considerable skill, it was, unfortunately for him, a failure. He was rather surprised, when the meal was finished, and he expressed himself ready to depart, that he again met with a rebuff from Cooper, tinctured more strongly of a flat refusal than before.

"Our gals has taken a fancy to them," said Cooper, "and they has taken a fancy to our gals. Our gals have invited them to stop a day with them and they've agreed; now don't you step in to spoil comfort—I say, don't do it, cos it ain't friendly on you, and may make me ride rusty; and ven I'm that vay inclined, I'm like a rusty knife : a cut from me is rather dangerous— do you mind me ?"

It was in vain that Nehemie uttered a thousand reasons why it was most essential that he should depart, accompanied by the girls; the gipsey was inexorable, and at last coupled his refusal with an intimation that danger would follow any further importunities. Nehemie perceived that there would be danger too, and raging inwardly like a tiger, was compelled to consent to t he arrangement, adding that it really was impossible they could stop longer than to-morrow.   Cooper laughed.

"You says 'we,'" he exclaimed, "*we*' can't stop longer than to-morrow; now it's without my knowledge if any of the gals asked you to stay with us : I don't think one of my pals have, and I'm sure I haven't; if you does stop, it's agin our invitation, and by your own—for you see, though you may be a good sort of a fellow in your way, we doesn't see nothing so very agree- able in a French mounseer as to want his company for a week; however, if you will stop, why you may, but look ye, not longer than that sun shows his face over the hills. In the morning, as soon as he comes, you go—you under- stand that ?"

"*Parfaitement!*" replied Nehemie.   "*Je sais bien ce que vous voulez dire.*"

"What ?" cried Tom, elevating his eyebrows.

"I say I know vell vat dis you mean," answered Nehemie, gesticulating his words.

"Oh, that's all right, replied Tom, "and since you knows what' I mean you vill know wot to do, that's all."

The tents were struck and packed up; all traces, save the burnt and ashy spot where their fire had been made, were removed, and they took their de- parture from the place, just in the opposite direction to that where lay Nehemie's dwelling.   He failed not to express his sense of it, and was cut short in the midst of his broken English by the laconic but decided remark of Cooper, who said, as he regarded him with a look which he intended should render his reply all sufficient—

"It's our vay, Mounseer."

And instantly busying himself with the departure of the tribe, rendered remonstrances useless. It was so contrived that during the day he had no opportunity of addressing Florence or Letty alone, and their progress, which had been slow, and by unfrequented paths, afforded him no opportunity of expressing the dissatisfaction he felt. Night came, the tents were pitched upon high ground, and commanded a beautiful view. The evening's meal was partaken of, being provided by some of the men, who, having been absent some hours, returned with materials for a dainty supper. The same mode of keeping Nehemie and the two maidens apart was persevered in, and when the former stretched himself once more before the fire to sleep, he racked his brain to invent a scheme by which he might get Florence in his power. He devised a number, but before he had decided upon one, he fell asleep. When he awoke the day was breaking, the sun had not yet appeared above the distant hills, although his beams were to be seen shooting up into the sky, heralds of his approach. He gazed around him; those gipseys who kept him company round the fire were still buried in deep slumber, and the deep stillness which reigned, gave him assurance that all who occupied the tents were in slumber as deep as those around him; he determined to creep to the tent which contained Florence and Letty, and promise them both the most dreadful fate if they did not return with him that morning to his cottage. As he was about to fulfil his intention, he found one of the gipseys was laying on a part of one of the broad skirts of his coat. To remove it was to awaken the man; he therefore took it off, and left it, while he crawled stealthily to the tent which he had seen the two girls enter the night previous. He listened, and could scarcely hear sufficient to tell him that any one living was beneath that small arched covering, so placid and calm was the slumber of those within; he placed his ear close to the ground, not daring to remove the curtain for fear of being mistaken in the tent, and tried to catch the smallest sound which might give him an indication that he was right. Presently he heard a slight moan, and he whispered, in a voice he was in the habit of using towards his daughter—

"Letty!"

"Yes, father," replied the low voice of the child instantly.

"Listen to me," he muttered through his teeth; "if you do not return with me this morning, and make your companion do so, I'll murder you—I'll cut you to pieces—I'll tear you limb from limb; there shall be no one that ever died by frightful torture shall suffer such dreadful agonies as I will inflict on you, if you do not as I tell you. Remember, you come with me; if you come quietly and readily, I'll make you as happy as a queen, and do no harm to miss—but if you say nay, or hang back even, dread—"

He was interrupted by feeling himself powerfully seized by the neck of his waistcoat, and by a single exertion raised to his feet: he struggled to get free, and succeeded; he turned round and found himself confronted by Tom Cooper.

"That's mighty good English for a French mounseer," exclaimed the gipsey in a low tone, with a bitter laugh, "but it's werry bad sentiment to talk to a child; say as much to me when I says they sha'n't go with you—say as much to me, you peeked-nozzled, swallow your whiskers, ugly-phizzed vagabond, and curse me if I don't ram those glass bottle grinders down your throat—say as much to me, if you're a man, which I don't think you are, or you wouldn't be a Frenchman."

"*Il me semble que vous avez tort,*" ejaculated Nehemie, in somewhat of a deprecating manner.

"Don't talk that stuff to me," roared Tom; "you can speak English well enough to talk about murdering and cutting to pieces, to a little gal who'd be afraid of the wink of a eye-lash; and you can, if you like, speak English to me, and you shall. Mark me, you white-livered, half-hung, gallows bird, I know why you want the gals, but you won't have 'em at all. Ah, you may start and frown, that won't frighten nobody—I'll make you start more afore I've done with you. Look here," he added, extending his fist towards him, "there's a good handful there; now if you doesn't be off at once I'll lay it about your mazzard to a tune that shall make you dance quicker than any fiddle, and show the colour of your blood in the twinkling of a bedpost."

Nehemie was furious—his prudence at these taunts was lost sight of; he ground his teeth as though he would reduce them to powder, and in a paroxysm of passion, ere the last word had left Cooper's lips, he aimed a terrific blow at him, which, alighting on the unexpected gipsey's forehead, despatched him to the ground with the same celerity with which a cannon ball would have performed the same operation. Most persons are astonished once in their lives—it is doubtful whether Cooper ever had been to such a degree as now he was, and it was unlikely whether he ever would be so much as long as he lived. He lay stunned for a second, and then scrambled up; he rushed at the Frenchman, but received another terrific blow on the ear, which staggered him. He found the man could fight, and caution was necessary: shaking off, therefore, the effects of the hit, he sparred to gain a little wind, made a feint, which deceived Nehemie, who threw up his arm, and received instantly a violent blow in the body, and a tremendous one on the face. He went staggering back, Cooper sprung upon him, seized him by the hips, and threw him a terrific cross buttock, which bid fair to shake all the breath out of his body. Before he could rise, the gipseys, awakened by the noise, congregated round the spot in evident surprise at the scene which was being acted. By the directions of Cooper two of the longest and strongest raised Nehemie to his feet, and then Tom exclaimed—

"Now, Nat and Phil, you two are the longest-winded and longest-legged—hold the Frenchman tight, and run him four miles. Show him how gipseys run, and when you've passed the four mile, make him go on, and pelt him with the largest bolders you can find till he's out o' sight. Now, Mounseer," he added, addressing Nehemia, who was struggling in the grasp of the two men, "now, you vagabond, off with you, and thank your stars you hav'n't had me stand over you with a oak towel like that," he pointed to a thick cudgel in one of the gipsey's hands, "and wipe you down with it till you know'd what rubbing maant. Off with you, and don't let me catch you prowling about our whereabouts, cos if you does, mind, laying in a bed won't be agreeable to you for six months a'terwards. Cut along, lads, step out with him; the run will do you good."

The two gipseys, who laughed and seemed to delight in their task, seized him by the collar and by the waist near the small of his back, and putting out their strength, they started off down the hill at full speed. Nehemie resisted to the best of his ability, but he gained nothing by it, save a few falls, all three being down together, and with violence too; but the two gipseys were quickly up, picked up their prisoner, and galloped away with him. Occasionally their speed became frightful, their legs touching the ground only at long intervals, their strides being enormous, and their bounds resembling those of a deer, until they lost all control, and then a stumble on the part of Nehemie brought them all again with considerable force upon the ground. This was an exercise which was common with the gipseys—they were expert at it, and their falls were so managed as to bring them little or no damage, while Nehemie's breath was every time pretty well bumped out of his lungs. Bleeding from the nose and mouth, his face cut, bruised, and grimed with dirt, his last fall having been made with his head coming first to the ground, and his face acting the part of a spade, by shovelling out some earth, as though he had made up his mind to commence digging with his head Breathless and exhausted, Nehemie was once more hauled from the ground, firmly grasped by the two " vagrants," and borne along as swifty as before— it mattered not that his legs refused their office, he was forced on—so, with a faint groan of despair, he resigned himself to his fate, and run along with them as if it was an amicable affair, and abounded with pleasantry, he being the most delighted as well as most honoured of the three ; it is true the hill was long and the speed great—it was certain that running was not an exercise in which he was skilled—it was undeniable that his breath was short, and that altogether he was unfitted for locomotion of this description, though he was without his coat, and possessed a fasting stomach ; but despite all this, the truth that he could not help himself was stronger than all put together, and, therefore, with that species of desperate regardlessness of what may come next, which people, who are sea-sick to death feel, he gave himself up and bounded along with almost as much agility as his companions. The four miles were soon passed, though terrific that distance appeared to him. They accomplished it within thirty minutes, which was good running, only they had the advantage of a third of the way being down hill. To Nehemie it seemed two hours, and when they released him he was scarcely able to crawl ; but this the gipseys would not perceive. They fulfilled their instructions to the letter. They hallooed to him to keep on his run, and when he looked appealingly at them, they favoured him with a blow from a stone. He quickened his speed, though he was panting and blowing like a porpoise, and perspiring profusely. It was a sweating exercise that he had never anticipated. He deemed it cursedly unfortunate, to add to his other grievances, that the spot should abound in smal lumps of stone—large when they came to be flung at a person's head. There were lots of ammunition, and the gipseys were remarkably skilful in throwing. It was singular with what unerring precision they hit the mark, and not less unpleasantly strange the force with which they dispatched them. He was without a hat, and received a blow from one on the head, which produced, instanter, a lump as big as an egg, and strong with rage, he turned round, seized a stone from the ground, and flung it back with all his strength ; but it went wide of the mark, and receiving a couple in return, with more correctness in the aim than he had displayed, he found there was nothing left him to do but to give way to circumstances and trot on again. Away he started ; the stones came flying about his ears, and few missed him, until by an little extra extertion he contrived to get beyond their reach. The gipseys did not follow him, and smarting with pain and rage uttering the fiercest anathemas and promises of revenge, he pursued the road before him. His remorseless companions retracing their steps at the same time to the spot from whence they started. ;

By the time the two gipseys arrived at their late bivouac, the tents had been struck and the party were moved a couple of miles onward. They had left a track to show the path they had taken, which the men easily followed, and came up with them as they were finishing their breakfast. They related their success, and their recital was listened to with peals of laughter. " Their story being done," and the meal, too, they moved forward once more. It was a long distance to Grasmere, and the open ways were, from causes explained, debarred to them. The secret paths were longer, more intricate and involved much time in surmounting. A week, therefore, passed away and Florence found herself still far from Chough Hall : and during the time elapsed she found the gipseys honourably kept their faith with her. She was treated with the greatest respect and attention, the rude conduct, and rude sayings of a people ever living without the restraints of civilised society, were softened down ; and neither were her ears or eyes offended so far as a well-intentioned strict observance of propriety could prevent. She was presented with the choicest dainties of their board, and her couch was spread with more care and comfort than the rest; there was no insulting act to disturb her slumbers, which, though removed from the ground only by bedding of a very primitive character, were sound and peaceful. There were no coarse jests or remarks to make her regret or look with horror upon her situation; she could not but see the efforts made to render her as comfortable as the nature of the circumstances in which she was placed would permit, and drew from it so much content as to make her bear the inconveniences to which she saw subjected with fortitude. Upon the evening of the tenth day the tents were pitched high upon one of the numerous range of mountains in this county; the night was clear and bright, and with nearly a full moon gliding slowly up the heavens with its silvery smile, and the soft air as though it were its warm breath playing on the brow, proffered charms to Florence too great to be resisted. The view was lovely, and she who admired enthusiastically Nature in all its garbs, could not suffer so delightful an opportunity of gratifying her taste to pass unseized ; she resolved, therefore, to stroll a short distance from the camp, and with eager eyes devour the scene so exquisitely laid out before her. Letty would have accompanied her, but sweet community with her own thoughts—unseen, alone—was her desire, and persuading the warm-hearted girl to retire to rest, she walked gently away unaccompanied. An admonition from old Bridget not to proceed too far was acknowledged by a promise to obey, and she proceeded up the mountain. At first the scenery every step she took lifted her heart up with ecstasy, but as she gazed, thoughts rose up within her which soon banished the loveliness around her from her memory, and in deep abstraction she wandered on until a gloom around her caused her to look up —she found that she had entered a wild mountain pass, had even

proceeded some distance along it without noticing it, and judging by the altered character of the scenery, she believed that she must have strayed considerably farther than it was prudent to do, and resolved at once to return. She had scarce advanced a step in pursuance of this resolution when two men sprung from a place of concealment—a jutting piece of rock which she had a moment previously passed in her wandering, and caught her in their arms; before she had time to utter a sound, a silk handkerchief was passed across her mouth. She was lifted from her feet and borne swiftly away. She was overcome with horror, and it was completed to a loss of senses when she heard the voice of Nehemie exclaimed with a coarse laugh, echoed by his comrade—

"Miss may be witty and clever, but she will be cunning indeed if she escapes this time, eh? Trusty Tom."

It is, perhaps, a wise provision of nature, that in moments of excessive fright, such as the present, the faculties of the gentle and timid are for a time suspended; the capabilities for resistance in such a case are so small as to render their application quite out of the question, and probably, it is as well that much of the agony which the horror produces should thus be spared the victim. The swoon into which Florence had fallen continued for a long period; when she recovered, which was through the agency of means employed for the purpose, she turned her eyes round feebly, unconscious where she was—she appeared to have awaked from a long dream of happiness to find herself in the desolate cave of despair. A man, whose face she did not recognise, save that it belonged to the genus scoundrel, was leaning over her and bathing her temples with brandy; he was alone, and was grumbling aloud at the trouble given him to restore her. The place was a miserable looking one, and the fumes of spirit and tobacco declared plainly that it was not the temple of Diana; any person possessing a moderate share of sensitiveness in the lungs would have been suffocated at once, and it was with difficulty that Florence could draw her breath in so impure an atmosphere. As soon as the man discovered she breathed, though not over freely, and by her looks was recovered from her fainting fit, he held up a small lamp, and said in a rough, but careless voice—

"Now, miss, I'll show you to your room."

Florence turned to him, and wrung her hands.

"Why have I been brought here?" she exclaimed. "Why am I thus detained?"

"I thought you know'd," said the man, with a little surprise.

"I do not know," she returned hastily, "unless I was brought hither by Nehemie, and then I can, alas! too well guess."

"Then your guess has it, for you was brought here by he and I," observed the man, with a laugh. "But come, it's late, you'd better go to bed—you'll be fit for nothing in the morning, if you don't."

"Let me escape," cried Florence, earnestly. "Let me free; if you have any mercy or pity, suffer me to depart."

"Why that's agen orders," he returned, coolly. "My name's Trusty Tom, and this is my crib, which my pals prefer using to any other. My orders, miss, are to keep you here as safe as I would my nob on my shoulders till the gov'nor comes himself for you—and so it's no use in wasting time in asking me to let you go, cos I can't, and I won't, and that's all about it; so take your light and toddle up stairs, and don't talk no more, cos I shan't listen to you. The room is atop of the stairs straight afore you."

Florence felt her heart sink within her; she took the light from his hand and prepared, without uttering a word, to mount the stairs. As she reached the first step, Trusty Tom said—

"Stay, will you have any prog? anything to peck, I mean," he added, as he observed Florence look as though she did not understand him. "There's some nice wittles in the cupboard if you will, he continued; "I was told to use you tenderly and good naturedly, and so I will, and no gammon."

"I cannot eat," she replied, as he paused for her answer.

"Will you drink?" he inquired. "Some real nobby good stuff in the bottle."

She replied in the negative.

"Oh, very well," he responded; "I shan't press you; good night; the bed's comfortable and the room snug: good night, nobody'll come near you till morning."

With a heavy heart Florence moved up the stairs, and entered the room which was to receive her. Her first object would have been to fasten the door, but there was no fastening, and as the door opened outwardly there existed no means of making it secure—a simple latch was all the door possessed, and that was not available for the purpose required. She, therefore, determined not to retire to rest: she took her lamp and scrutinized the apartment, it was a mean one ; the window was in a recess, and the bed was in another, with a wretched curtain run on a string drawn before it to make it look decent. There was an oval table and one chair, a pitcher containing water, and there ends the inventory of the furniture. Though this was the cottage to which Andrew had been taken by Jasper, the room which Florence now occupied was not the one in which he slept, but one contiguous. The poor girl, when she had completed her survey of the apartment—a short time it took her—seated herself by the table, and with almost a broken heart reflected upon her situation—one to which she had been a second time brought through her own imprudence: in bitter agony of heart did she weep and implore heaven to release her from this strait, one which all the sins of her past life, and they were very few, did not entitle her to suffer: "those whom the Lord loveth he chasteneth," and thus it was why one so pure and good should be visited with affliction.

Her purpose of not retiring to bed she kept, and during the night she sat watching with a sorrow-stricken heart, the pain of which was augmented by a dreadful expectation that her solitude would be broken by the villain who had caused her all the anguish she had latterly endured, but she remained undisturbed till towards morning, when she heard a knocking at the door of the hut : it was repeated again and again ere it was answered. At length she heard the sound of a naked foot in the apartment beneath her, and the person demanding entrance was admitted. The voice of the new comer was gruff, and not sparingly exercised, and shortly after his arrival his voice and that of Trusty Tom sounded in high dispute. The word LIAR was repeated several times, accompanied by terrible oaths uttered vehemently, and ultimately a scuffle took place. She listened in affright: she heard the settles thrown down violently, muttered oaths and imprecations forced through gnashing teeth, the heavy clashing and scraping of feet backwards and forwards upon the floor, then she heard a groan—almost a shriek : it was followed by the fall of a heavy body upon the floor, and then all was still—the grave was not more silent. Her heart beat almost to suffocation : the stillness seemed more awful than the previous struggling. She listened intently, and with horror that chilled her blood, she fancied she heard a creeping step upon the stairs ; she held her breath to aid her hearing, and could detect the slow, stealthy foot of some person advancing slowly and almost noiselessly, resting upon each stair as it mounted, that its approach might not be heard. Her nerves thrilled with terror ; her blood seemed to coagulate, and every hair of her head to vibrate. She hid her face upon the table, encompassing it with her arms, to shut out from her eyes the object of her fright when it came. She clasped her hands in an agony of prayer for deliverance, and while in the midst of it, she heard the door creak as it gently opened, and she felt that she must die with excessive fear.

Through the opening of the partly unclosed door peered the face of a man, whose features were plainly exhibited by a light which he held in one hand and shadowed with the other, to prevent its rays being seen by the tenant of the room. The light being thus reflected upon himself, rendered his face clearly discernible, and disclosed it to be that of Churleigh. He looked anxiously into the apartment, and seemed surprised at seeing Florence there alone; he surveyed her attentively a moment, and then passed his eyes slowly but penetratingly round the apartment to discover if any recess held another; but his gaze not fulfilling his expectation, he dropped the stealthy cautiousness he had hitherto used, and entered the apartment with a heavy tread. He advanced towards Florence, who, as he approached, sprung from her seat and fled shrieking to the door; he followed her instantly, and seized her by the wrist. In spite of her struggles, he brought her back to the centre of the room.

"Make no noise," he exclaimed, "and don't be frightened; you shall find me a friend if you answer me correctly and truly. Don't shrink and tremble so; I shan't hurt you, girl, though I did lend a hand in carrying you off."

The sound of his voice being different to that which she expected, induced Florence to turn her averted head and eyes upon him. It was some relief to find that it was not Jasper who held her in his grasp, but little consolation to perceive that it was the same man who had carried her from the grove of sycamores in the grounds of Chough Hall and placed her in the power of Jasper; she turned her eyes away from him, and it was easy to percive her disgust and apprehension had subsided in a very small degree. Churleigh scarcely noticed it, save that she become more passive, and that being all that he required, he toned down his voice from its usual harshness, and said—

"I have a few questions to ask, which must be answered without equivocation; and 'if you, who can answer them, will do so with truth, you shall find me a firmer friend than ever I have been an enemy. It is true I helped to rob your friends of you, and place you in the power of one who has no mercy or pity. I put you in the hands of one who, though he said he was madly in love with you, and acted as if he was, would sacrifice you utterly without caring what misery or suffering he made you endure; once let him gratify his passion, and your destruction would become a matter of indifference to him. Now, girl, I don't say this that you may think me a saint, because I can't and don't wish to lay claim to the character. I am not too tender-hearted I know; those who have been much with me, companions in many deeds of daring enterprise, have, on the contrary, given me credit for a heart of iron and a hand of blood; how much of the character I really deserve is better known to myself then them, though it may suit my purpose to let them think as they do—but little as I aim to be thought tender, I would not destroy any one upon whom I set my heart. Jasper Chough is an infernal villain, and you must know it. I don't think you like him, whatever his love for you, and I do hope you hate him—hate him bitterly as I do. Now tell me, girl, where he is?"

Florence looked up in surprise; she had listened to the speech, wondering to what it tended, and having naturally conceived the man to be an agent of him he spoke thus harshly of, his request to know his locality was to her somewhat extraordinary, and she hesitated to reply.

"It is in vain to endeavour to conceal him," said Churleigh, sternly, on finding her remain silent. "I know that he must be in this neighbourhood; I have tracked him since yesterday, and your presence here is quite a sufficient proof that he is here, or near here, also."

"I hope he is far from here," exclaimed Florence, in a trembling voice; "no one can wish his absense more devoutly than I do, but where he is, I know not, although I fear he is near this spot."

"You fear!" repeated Churleigh, contemptuously; "you know it, you mean. Girl! girl! dost thou think because he has ruined thee; because thou hast fallen a victim to his strength, that thou should'st treat him as though thou loved'st him? No, rather look on him with horror; with the most devouring hate, and lose no opportunity to be revenged to the death upon him—you should regard him with no other feeling. Disclose to me his place of concealment, and I swear to repay the evil that he and I have done you with his heart's blood."

"It has pleased heaven to save me from his intended villany," returned Florence, with a flushed brow; "villain as he is, and miserable as he has rendered me, it has not been in his power to sully my honour."

"Can I believe this?" said Churleigh, eyeing her with an eagle's glance. "Jasper is not the man to sleep over a task he once determines upon executing."

"I have spoken truth," returned Florence, firmly, but calmly; it was stamped upon her brow, and Churleigh read it as he gazed upon her. He was convinced almost against his reason.

"It is strange!" he exclaimed, "you are the first to whom he has displayed so much lenity, but you will not be spared long; do not be misled, he affects this generosity but to make you more securely his—body and soul."

"I have not to thank his generosity for my escape," replied Florence. "The sudden possession of a pistol, which, had he persisted in his villany, should have sent him or myself to death, saved me once; escape from the cottage to which he had carried me, rescued me from his hands, until I was recaptured to again escape—"

"What is all this?" interrupted Churleigh, hastily: "repeat this, maiden—this is new to me, and of no little importance."

Florence hesitated, she had an indefined doubt of his object in requiring all this information; she had only known him as practising deception upon her: it was not likely she could place trust in him. He read the cause of her hesitation in her aspect.

" The evil men do cling to them like melting pitch to a dry hand," he muttered ; " I have deceived you once, maiden ; you cannot believe I can be well-disposed towards you because my first deed was to your hurt—but I was PAID for that ; it was from no inclination to do you harm—it was for GOLD. Now I would serve you to gratify my revenge on him : revenge, girl, is sweeter than gold—you should know that. Come, fear not to give me this history, it will not be used against you at least : I will swear to that, and if more be necessary, know that the injury he attempted to inflict on you he has accomplished on one dear to my heart—curses on him. Now are you satisfied ?"

There was a manner and tone of voice in what he said and did which made Florence inclined to believe him, and, a moment's hesitation, she gave him a brief relation of all that had occurred to her from the time he quitted her and Jasper up to the time of her being captured on the mountain, and brought by Nehemie and Trusty Tom to this hut. Churleigh listened to her without interruption, and when she had concluded, he mused for some time : at last he broke the silence, which, after she had finished her story, had taken place, by saying—

" I'm glad he has been thwarted thus : there's some little satisfaction in that. D'ye think Nehemie, knowing where to fall in with him, has gone to tell him of capturing you, and so will bring him here ?"

" I do believe as much," replied Florence, adding urgently, " if you will deliver me from hence, and place me safely again in the hands of my friends, I promise you most faithfully you shall be largely rewarded with gold."

" Two to one will be longish odds," muttered Churleigh, not heeding her appeal. " No, I can do better then that—I will make more sure of him : I wish he was unacquainted with my knowledge of his villany to Joan, I could then trap him with more certainty than a poacher snares a hare : no matter, I will have him yet. Like a moth about a candle, he will flutter round the flame which will cause his destruction. She shall with me to the island, he will be sure to follow—ha, ha ! there are gorges, ravines, and cliffs which will make a flight down them turn his blood to ice. Yes, it shall be so."

Florence overheard this audible soliloquy with apprehension she surmised that a portion of it related to her, and in terms of urgent entreaty, she once more begged of him to deliver her from this place, and restore her to her home.

" I will do so," he answered, with frankness, to her prayer for release. " I do not wish for gold or reward : it would be a poor return for the unhappiness I have assisted in occasioning you. When you are ready to depart, we will set forth."

" Now, now," she cried, eagerly, " this very minute—I am ready. I shall be too happy ; let us not lose a moment. Come, I can walk a long way, a very long distance : and if I should be tired or faint, I will not complain, but keep on with a good heart until we reach Grasmere."

Churleigh turned away his head, and muttered something which she did not catch, and then he exclaimed, hastily—

" It must be so, there's no help for it.   Come, put on a cloak and hat if you have them, and we will set forth at once."

" I am ready," she cried with delight, and seizing her round hat and cloak, which she had flung upon the bed on entering the room : she quickly put them on, descended the stairs after him to the room below, and turned sick with horror on suddenly perceiving Trusty Tom half-dressed lying before the fire, bleeding from a ghastly gash in his side. His wound was not so deadly that it deprived him of consciousness, and he lay groaning and muttering the most fearful imprecations at his disaster, and then at its perpetrator. She shuddered as in passing she had to approach him, but Churleigh looked upon him with the greatest unconcern, and walking up to him, whispered in a tone not loud enough for Florence to hear—

" If you had never played with edge tools you would not have got cut : you are a fool, you ought to have known better—you've got hurt, you see, and it serves you right—it will teach you better manners when next we meet. Now, mind me, you will have Nehemie and Geoffrey Smith here shortly when they come, you can tell Geoffrey the bird has flown, and if he wants to find its nest, he must look among the crags and crannies in the island for it. Tell him he needn't hang back, the bird will be there when he comes, and if the bird is worth having, it is worth while to beat the bush. Good bye, Tom, I hope you'll get well soon : mind you deliver my message."

Tom replied with a volley of oaths, which Churleigh answered with a coarse laugh; and joining Florence, who had reached the door, he followed her out, and swung the door to after him. The sound of their retreating footsteps speedily died away, and Trusty Tom was left alone bleeding and growing each minute faint to death, until he sunk into a swoon from loss of blood. .

An hour elapsed without a change having taken place in the state of affairs within the hut.   At the expiration of that time several hard blows were bestowed upon the door, which not, of course, being answered, were repeated : and at last the patience of the knocker, or man who knocked, being exhausted, he applied his shoulder to the door, making the application with a desperate exertion of strength, the effect of which, as the door was not fastened, was to cause it to fly open with amazing rapidity, and to induce the immediate entrance of Nehemie, who it was performed this operation, at a rattling speed into the centre of the apartment, coming with considerable force in contact with the table and the floor, while his companion, Jasper Chough, with a laugh at his accident, walked quietly in : but his laugh and placidity of demeanour was quickly changed when he discovered the state in which Tom was lying, and Nehemie, who was pouring forth anathemas with the volubility with which a termagant will approach her husband when she has something like cause, as instantly changed his tone and exclamations of wonder at the altered situation of Tom to that in which he had left him. They both instantly exerted themselves in his restoration, on discovering by the feeble beating of his heart that he still lived, and as he suffered only from a flesh wound and loss of blood, their efforts were successful.   By the aid of stimulants and stopping the discharge of blood, they recovered him so far as to enable him to speak, and then Jasper inquired the meaning of his being in this condition.

"It's all along of old Churleigh," he muttered feebly; "he came here, and whacked at the door until he nearly broke it in. As soon as I heard him, I turned out of my bab, half-togged myself as you see me now, and let him in. He asked for you, Geoffrey: I said you wasn't here. He said you was. I said you wasn't agin, and then he calls me a liar, for which I bid him be civil, as I was; I gave him the lie agin worse than he gave it me: well, he swore you was here, and wouldn't take no denial: he wanted to search the crib, but that I wouldn't stand, so we had a tuzzle for it. I whipped up my knife, which laid on the table, thinking to settle his business, but he twisted it out of my mauley, and dropped it into my ribs far enough for me to talk about kingdom come, I believe."

"Did he search the hut?" asked Jasper, quickly.

"Oh, yes," replied Tom, scarce able to speak from exhaustion: "he floored me, and then quietly took up my lamp, and went creeping and crawling about like a snake, until b'ine'by he comes down with the gal, with her walking toggery on, and whispers to me to tell you if you wants the bird he took away with him, you'll find its nest in the crags of the island—"

"In the island!" cried Jasper, quickly, "what in Man?"

"Of course he means there," said Tom, "but he didn't say no more but this, 'it the bird's worth having,' says he, 'the bush is worth beating,' or something of that sort, and then he and the gal went away; and now you have it all. Just carry me to bed, and let me have some water or some brandy by my side, for I feels infamous queer, that I do. I'm cold, and yet I sweats and trembles every bone and jint as if I was made o' jelly."

Both Jasper and Nehemie looked bewildered, but the latter seemed to let the surprise have least effect upon him, for he at once proceeded to obey the wish of the wounded man, and obtained the aid of Jasper to carry him to his bed; when that was done, he turned to Jasper, and said—

"Now, Smith, let us put out our speed; we shall soon be on their track."

"What would you do?" inquired Jasper, looking earnestly at him.

"What!" he reiterated, "why after Churleigh at once, and catch him before he has time to cross the water."

"Are you mad?" asked Jasper, with surprise.

"Are *you* mad to ask that question?" returned Nehemie. "Come, we lose time; let us away."

"Not to follow Churleigh," replied Jasper, recoiling at the idea.

"Why not?" asked Nehemie, with astonishment; "you will not let him get quietly off with the girl, will you?"

"You would not have me run into his arms, after he has sworn with most tremendous oaths to have my life, would you?" returned Jasper, with a sneer.

"Well," cried Nehemie, half savage, half laughing, "suppose he has, he's not obliged to take it if he has; your chance is as good as his."

"Pshaw!" cried Jasper, "who ever knew Churleigh vow a revenge he failed

to take?   I overheard him swear to murder me, and if he catches me, he'll keep his word.   I'm not the fool to run into his jaws."

"Is it the bold Geoffrey Smith talking thus?" cried Nehemie, with stinging sarcasm, determining for the sake of gratifying his own revenge upon Florence, for the discipline the gipseys had bestowed upon him, to induce Jasper to follow her.   "Is it the gallant Geoffrey," he continued, "who has boasted that he fears neither man nor devil, that so trembles at the threats of man who has neither his strength nor courage.   What would the saucy crew of the Scud say if I were to publish to them that there lived the man of whom their hardy captain was afraid—"

"Hold!" cried Jasper, with excitement; "don't talk thus to me, or I shall do murder on you.   Lead on; were he a hundred times the tiger he is, I would after him.   If I fall, it shall be life for life."

"I thought you wouldn't part with pretty Miss so easily," exclaimed Nehemie, with a cunning smile; "she is too precious an article to be hawked about among our people for inspection by such an old rat as Churleigh."

No. 35

"Lead on." roared Jasper; "though hell-fire yawned between him and me, I would leap the gulf and after him."

" It is still the bold Geoffrey, the darling of the crew," shouted Nehemie, as he rushed from the cot, followed by Jasper, whose every nerve quivered with excitement.

Nehemie led the way up the mountain, following the path he supposed Churleigh and Florence to have taken, and advanced at a speed which showed he was well acquainted with his road, and the method of surmounting it. Jasper kept pace with him, and his ardour was sustained by Nehemie, who kept dropping inuendoes respecting Florence, and the contempt which the crew of the Scud would exhibit if they knew he feared encountering Churleigh, which almost maddened him; and each moment his resolution to pursue him to the verge of destruction was strengthened, until all thoughts of hesitation or abandoning the pursuit were completely cast aside, and but one determination—to wrench Florence from his grasp—remained. In the midst of a whirl of thoughts which ran like fire through his brain, his progress was suddenly and unexpectedly checked. They had entered a defile. On each side of them the rocks ran irregularly to a considerable height, and the road seemed to be formed through a cleft made by some convulsion of nature: at a remote period it was serpentine, and the turns were at short intervals from each other. As they wound round one, a woman suddenly stood before them; they started, and Jasper, who instantly recognised the stranger to be Joan Churleigh, shrunk back with alarm. She was panting for breath, evidently having exercised great speed to obtain the spot she now occupied. As soon as they confronted her she bid them stop, and exclaimed, as well as her palpitating breath would permit—

"Villains, I know your cursed purpose; have ye to learn that walls have mouths as well as ears. Fools! when ye plot imfamous projects, you should know that there is not a breath of air to convey your base schemes to those whose greatest joy is to thwart and frustrate every machination upon which your heart is set. You go to the island in search of the weak girl you have laboured so hard, and so unsuccessfully—ha, ha! there is joy in that—so ineffectually, Jasper—to destroy. You go there to tear her from one whose fury when aroused is that of a whirlwind. Thou knowest what HE is; wilt thou still pursue thy purpose. Better hadst thou seek out a starving wolf, and tear meat from his famished jaws, than attempt to withdraw her from his power. An' thou wilt go, Jasper, mark me, there is a storm brewing there which will burst upon thy head with destroying fury; go not, if thou wouldst not be hurled to everlasting perdition at one blow: but stay HERE thou canst not, there are bloodhounds on thy track, Jasper, who scent thee—who will hunt thee down an' thou stayest; they are drawing nearer and nearer to thee every hour—thou wilt be soon encirled beyond the possibility of escape if thou dost remain, and know that a father leads on the hounds. He will hunt thee down, his own son, the believed murderer of his youngest and best beloved; to save thy wretched life thou must fly, but not the Scud—the crew are bold and bad men, but they will not have a fratricide for their leader, a run to the yard-arm will be your fate there, if thou dost attempt to regain the ascendancy which thou didst once hold over them. Away, wretch! thou must flee, but not to where thou'rt known by friend or acquaintance. Thou Cain, thou'rt 'cursed from the earth, which hath opened her mouth to receive thy brother's blood from thy hand—a fugitive and vagabond shalt thou be on the earth,' so saith God's holy word, so prophecy I, but wheresoever thou fleeth, there shalt thou find me hovering like an evil spirit over thee, thou slayer of my beloved child—of my eternal happiness. Away! despair is thine now and for ever."

As she concluded, she pointed warningly at him, and then retreated with a rapidity almost incredible. Her form was soon lost in the gloom which pervaded the place, and she had entirely disappeared ere either broke the silence which her absence had created. Her appearance had been so sudden, and so unexpected her denunciation, so singular, at least, to Nehemie, and to Jasper awful, that they had both stood fixed to the spot as if paralysed. She had spoken with such volubility, yet with such emphasis, and in a tone so deep, that even if the surprise at her appearance had not taken away their speech, it would have been accomplished by her rapid and strongly marked enunciation. When the wonder had somewhat subsided. principally through her disappearance, Nehemie drew a long breath, and said—

"If I believed in ghosts, I should have taken that witch for a foul spirit. Lord! what a white face and fiery eyes she has. Is she mad, Jasper? She knows you it seems pretty well; who and what is she? Come, never bury your face in your hands thus, man; what fearest thou?—not a lunatic."

"Do you not know HER?" groaned Jasper, with his hands pressed before his eyes; "do you not know HER?" he repeated, emphasising the last word with bitterness.

"I've seen her face before," replied Nehemie, "but cannot remember where; but what signifies, let her go to the devil, we waste time standing here; let's on."

"No, no," cried Jasper, shuddering; "heard you not what she said?"

"Yes, as well as you," he answered, impatiently, "but what of that, who cares?—I don't."

"But I do—I do," exclaimed Jasper, with almost anguish.

"You!" repeated Nehemie, "why should you heed the ravings of a mad woman?"

"She is not mad," roared Jasper, excitedly, "yet she must be; she must be; and I have made her, too; cursed, damned idiot that I was to sell myself thus. Nehemie, that was Joan! Joan Churleigh; it is for ruining her and destroying her child that her father has sworn my destruction, and she, as you heard, has registered an oath to haunt my footsteps till she drives me to hell inch by inch."

"Why don't you shoot her?" said Nehemie, coolly.

"I have tried it," he replied, quickly; "thrice have I fired at her, but bullets will not reach her."

"Pshaw!' said Nehemie, decisively, "your excitement made your hand unsteady. I'd wager my head I'd bring her down with one of my barking irons; be cooler nexttime you meet with her; keep your pop loaded and well primed, and then sight your pistol steadily; fire when you have brought it to bear on her head—always hit the head fair if you can, it will drop your object dead with more certainty. If you aim at the body, you only wing them, perhaps, without hitting a vital part: that will rid you of her, she's got no charms, I know, against a well-cast bullet. Come on; why, curse it, you will become worse than a babby, if you give up to a woman's croaking and an old man's threats like this. Come on, Jack's as good as his master till the game's told."

"Nehemie, there's not the creature on earth I fear but her—and Churleigh," exclaimed Jasper, earnestly.

"And why them?" said Nehemie, scornfully.

"I know not," he returned; "there seems a spell upon me with regard to them which I cannot master; I feel that they hold my fate in their hands, and the thought unnerves me—makes me worse than a coward."

"This is a weakness I could have sworn *you* would never have displayed," said Nehemie, sarcastically; "you, Geoffrey Smith, afraid of a woman! the hero of the iron heart, and the prowess of a giant, cowering to a woman's tongue! Pshaw! shake it off, man, we can but die once—we must all go once, but only once. Cast this fear to the devil, and one man is as good as another, save in expertness; and who excels Geoffrey Smith in the use of pistol and cutlass? Come on, Geoffrey, be the devil you have ever been. Make old Churleigh fear you—make his croaking raven of a daughter tremble at your glance, and be glad on her knees to propitiate you—*allons, mon brave*—you of the bold heart and eagle eye, come on, and show these chatterers you're still the reckless dare devil as of old."

"Nehemie, your words are fire to me," cried Jasper, his eye kindling and his heart inspirited by his address; "I am with you; I have trembled at naught until a strange dread of Churleigh and his daughter seized me, and perdition light on me! if I will not now shake it off with scorn, and to the island at once. I will tear Florence from the old tiger's grasp, or perish in the attempt. Come on, you shall find me now as willing as before I was backward—knife for knife—blood for blood."

"*Vive Geoffrey Smith!*" shouted Nehemie, and hastened forward, followed by Jasper, whose countenance seemed lighted up by a ferocity which rendered it scarcely human. With rapid steps they continued their progress, and were soon out of sight of the scene of their meeting with Joan Churleigh.

In the meanwhile Churleigh escorted Florence across the mountain in the direction, as he assured her, of Grasmere, and she walked contentedly along with him, in the hope that he was not misleading her. She was totally unacquainted with any of the mountain passes, and knew not one path from another; her progress was, therefore, conducted cheerfully by her as a matter of faith, and she even chatted with Churleigh in a spirit of hopefulness which touched even his rugged heart.

He had come to the determination of conveying her to the Isle of Man, which, at that day, was the haunt of smugglers and other disreputable characters. He was a smuggler himself, and carried on the practice, aided by several already mentioned in this work, to a considerable extent. The proximity of Cumberland and Westmoreland to the island rendered them convenient channels for the introduction of goods for which no duty had been paid to Government, and depots, in the shape of remote cottages and hovels, for the receipt of contraband articles, were stationed in various districts. The proprietors of these dens had been the instruments by which Jasper had worked to enable him to carry off Florence, and there were others in his path whom it was his intention to employ.

It may, perhaps, be a favourable opportunity to state here that Jasper—who, as described, was a youth of a wild uncontrollable nature—in one of his mountain wanderings when scarcely eighteen, discovered one of the secret depositories of the smuggled goods, and while in the act of gaining entrance was detected by a smuggler who was afterwards shot. After a short struggle, which promised to become a fiercer one, an explanation ensued, and the smuggler, instead of finding a spy as he expected, discovered a congenial spirit, carried him with him to Man, and subsequently took him several voyages in a schooner up the Mediterranean· The daring and free-hearted natures of the bold spirits Jasper met with agreed with his own, and he readily joined them, though of a family whose descent was noble, and whose character was irreproachable, His influence and comparative wealth rendered him an object of great importance to the free traders, and his reckless indifference of danger, his loose morality, and unbridled temper endeared him to them, and they unani · mously elected him captain of the craft when the conflict with revenue officers deprived their leader of life. The nature of the duties he undertook led him into frequent communication with Churleigh, and, consequently, with Joan, who was a fine handsome girl, high-spirited and generous-hearted. When he first saw her he was greatly attracted by her person, and quickly was his admiration strengthened by her liveliness and really sparkling wit. He believed himself in love with her ; he declared his attachment to her, wooed her passionately, and gained her heart; her ruin followed. The reader knows the rest.

Churleigh had resolved, as previously mentioned, to carry Florence to the island ; he flattered himself he knew enough of Jasper's nature to be sure he would follow him there, if he doated on Florence, as he had declared to him he did, in the cottage, upon the evening he had disclosed his monstrous brutality respecting Joan's offspring, and if, as he fully expected, he did come, he had devised a scheme [which should fully satisfy him respecting the truth of the more than strong suspicion he entertained of his being the villain who had crushed Joan's heart to powder, and ensure the accomplishment of the revenge he had sworn to have. He felt a commiseration for Florence's situation, but his desire for retaliation upon Jasper was stronger, and she for a time must be the victim of it, for by means of having her in his power he hoped to bring his foe face to face with him ; but, although resolved to carry Florence off, he determined that she should not suffer molestation or injury, and that her treatment should be as kind and tender as circumstances would permit. It was his intention also to return her safely to her friends a soon as he accomplished his object. He still kept her in the belief that she was journeying towards Grasmere, although he was making his way into Cumberland with the purpose of going to a creek near St. Bee's Head in Cumberland, and from thence returning in a lugger to Ramsey. They stopped at a humble cottage to have some breakfast, and Florence took an opportunity of whispering to a young woman to ask her if it was the way to Grasmere.

"Oh yes," replied the female; "you can go this way, but it be a mortal long way, surely."

Florence was satisfied, and thought not to ask in which direction the village lay. She little thought when she left it with a light heart filled with high hopes and fond anticipations, that she was leaving it far behind her each step she took. She walked on cheerfully, toiled up the mountain without a complaint, and though as they passed the bleak heights the wind blew with violence, she did not murmur or say she was tired or faint, or overcome with weariness. Churleigh had not expected her to behave half so bravely, and once when, after talking of the scenery, she told him how delighted her friends would be to receive her, he half determined to forego his intention, restore her to them, and seek some other method of drawing Jasper into his power, but a second thought wiped out the kind resolve, and he held his intention and way in the same direction. During one of the fearful gusts that swept across the mountain with a force and velocity which bid fair to throw them to the ground, Churleigh shielded her to the best of his ability from the blast, and then for the first time she murmured—

"Have we VERY much farther to go?"

"Aye, that have we," he returned; "a long, weary way; but cheer thee, girl, cheer thee; thy tender limbs shall not be made to ache much longer—not far from this is a resting place, and then two stout horses shall perform the rest of the journey for us."

Florence felt cheered by his words, and continued her efforts to proceed without another complaint. She was not insensible to the endeavours which her rough companion made to protect her from the sudden change in the weather, nor did she fail to draw satisfaction from the reflection that her conductor was an old man, and therefore one more likely to keep faith with her than if he had been a much younger one. Half an hour's walk brought them to a house, which had some pretensions to the title of inn, but only small pretensions. There was a landlord and landlady, who treated Churleigh with a respect which struck Florence as being rather singular, inasmuch as his costume was not of that attractive character which, upon personal inspection, would command polite attention to the wearer. They paid Florence also a species of civility of a description rather approaching homage, which, perhaps, was less singular in her case than in his. Once again, as a doubt of Churleigh's truth crossed her, she inquired whether she was in the direct route to Grasmere, and it struck her that there was some little reserve and embarrassment in the woman as she replied in the affirmative. The confirmation of her hopes, however, led her to pass it unheeded, and, if she did think of it, to believe it proceeded from some other cause. A few hours rest found her quite ready, and desirous to proceed, and when it was announced to her that the carriage that was to convey her to Chough Hall was ready, she descended and entered it with alacrity. Churleigh made an excuse for not entering with her by saying he had little doubt she would prefer her own company to his, and so fastened the door and took his seat by the driver. It was an old fashioned conveyance, in which the connection between passenger and driver was very remote; if the coachman happened to be deaf, and had a fancy to drive furiously, the passenger had nothing to do but resign himself to fate. He might bawl himself hoarse, but would gain no release, and could only cling to the desperate hope that if a frighful accident ensued he might escape with broken limbs, and would assuredly turn up somewhere. When the vehicle was put in motion Florence had no distrust, nor had she for some time, until she discovered that she was proceeding with amazing velocity. The windows in the hardly-worthy-the name-of postchaise were particularly dirty, and rendered a view of the scenery a matter of great difficulty; but she could see the dim forms of trees and shapes of stones flit by her with a rapidity most startling, and was jolted to such a degree from the wretched state of the springs and a horribly uneven road, that she began to conceive there was a motive for this unusual speed beyond the mere desire to return her to her friends. She tried to open the doors, but they would not yield: she attempted to pull down the window, but it was never intended to perform such an operation, or else it was immovably fast. She screamed, but no notice was taken of her cries, and, at length, with a certain and painful consciousness that there were fresh evils in store for her, she threw herself back in the corner of the chaise, and, with a heart full of misery, wept bitterly. The progress of the carriage continued unchecked during the day, save once, and then fresh horses were put to, but though she made every effort to force open the door, or make herself heard, no one came near her. Night drew on; the speed of the horses was kept up where the road would permit of it, and where they were so rugged as to prevent it the horses were still urged on at a pace beyond the usual course. Midnight arrived, and the carriage stopped. The door was opened, and with a cry of gladness she sprung towards it, but a mantle was cast over her head which drowned her cries and blinded her. She was lifted out of the coach by a strong man, carried a short distance, and then seated carefully upon a wooden bench. She was still held firmly, so that she could not remove the cloak which encircled her; a brief order, the rattle of cordage and blocks, and the rippling of water told her that she was upon water, and her heart died within her.

The shrewdness of Nehemie, aided by the knowledge of Jasper, enabled them to follow the track of Churleigh across the mountain with tolerable accuracy, and they hastened on at as swift a rate as the nature of the ground would enable them, with the hope that they should overtake him and his fragile companion before they reached the vessel which was to convey them to the Isle of Man. Churleigh's departure from the cottage where he and Florence had breakfasted had taken place but a short time when Jasper and his comrade arrived at it. An earnest inquiry respecting those they were chasing obtained for them a minute detail of a direction they were said to have taken, and after despatching a hasty meal, they started off again in pursuit. Unfortunately for them, the old man had anticipated their following him, and had given particular instructions to the people of the hut to set them upon a wrong scent, which with much talent they did, without creating a suspicion that they were misleading these pursuers. The mountain paths in the Cumberland and Westmoreland counties are very extensive and varied, at times bleak and cheerless, and again exquisite in loveliness. It was in one of the gloomiest passes they had yet traversed that they came unexpectedly upon three gipseys—one of them was Tom Cooper; he gave a shout of delight on perceiving them, whistled loudly and shrilly, and repeating a few words to his comrades he sprung at Nehemie, crying out—

"Where's the gal, you yaller-lugged dog? Where's the gal? give her up, or I'll twist your wizen like a barn-door cock's, I will—by the Lord I will. Where's the gal—tell me no lies—no lies, you French varmint. Where is she? speak, afore I stretch your gullet half a yard."

Nehemie did speak; but it was with a knife, observing, while struggling with Cooper, that he had a long sharp knife like a pruning knife stuck in a belt which he wore round his waist, under his coat and over his waistcoat; he made a clutch at it, drew it forth, and plunged it with all his force into his body. It glanced down the collar bone and buried itself in his chest, he gave a shriek, and roared out—

"He's done for me, the gallows Frenchman has spilt me. Lay hold on him, lads—lay hold on him."

Nehemie, who was about to repeat the blow, felt himself suddenly seized, the knife in an instant wrenched from his hands, and he himself flung with violence on the ground, and in as quick time as that evolution was performed, his arms were bound firmly to his side. Jasper had looked on at the whole affair with a surprise which, for the time being, had taken away his power of action, but now that he saw his companion bound, and preparations made to perform the same office for himself, he resisted and kept the two gipseys who attacked him at bay with comparative ease: but the sudden arrival of five or six men, summoned by Tom Cooper's whistle, speedily decided the matter, and, notwithstanding his great strength and determined resistance, he was captured and bound hand and foot. When this feat was accomplished the victors turned their attention to their wounded companion, from whom the blood was pouring like water: they raised him up and quickly divested him of his upper garments, and did their best to stanch the wound, but the hemorrhage was terrible, and bid fair to defy all their exertions to stop it, though their operations were conducted with a readiness and a skill few persons would have given them credit for possessing. At length temporarily succeeded, and replaced a portion of his vestments round the shivering

shoulders of the wounded man. When they had finished they were about to move him from the spot, but he checked them.

"Stay a bit," he whispered, hoarsely; "stay a bit; there's no hurry now my business is settled; the Frenchman's knife in my bread basket has cut my grub for ever. The game's up, lads, with me, and all you'll have to do will be to put me to bed with a spade, and say, if I deserves it, that you're sorry that I've cut my lucky."

"You ain't agoing to turn up your toes yet, Tom," exclaimed one of the gipseys, in a consolatory tone.

Tom shook his head.

No. 36

"I'm cooked," he returned; "I'm done, and you knows it. Well, what's the odds? the tribe, I dare say, will get on with out me, and if it don't, vy I can't help it, that's all. I ain't afeard to die: all as knows Tom Cooper knows he's game to the backbone, and now my pipe's put out I ain't agoing to dung it; damme, lads, I'll die game; if I don't, leave me for the crows to peek. There's one thing, lads, I wish you to do for me, and I shall take it as a favour if you do."

"Name it, Tom," cried one of his comrades readily.

"You'll promise me, lads, you'll do it," he said eagerly; "it's what you can do, and what I'd do for any of you."

"Out with it, Tom, we'll do it," rejoined his followers.

Tom's face, which had grown a ghastly hue, the natural dark yellow of his skin having changed to a pale stone colour—lighted up with a smile, or rather grin, that made it look horrible; he fixed his eyes, which were supernaturally bright, upon Nehemie, and slowly raising his hand, which had become of the same deathly tint as his face, he pointed to him and said, in a clearer voice than he had used since he had received his wound—

"Take the Frenchman and treat him to a dance upon nothing from that fine tree."

The men looked at him, at Nehemie, at each other, and a frightful silence ensued.

Tom turned his eyes from the object of his meditated vengeance to his companions, and perceiving their hesitation, he said, slowly—

"What you won't do it then? Well, I thought you'd ha' stood by me back and edge; I thought when you saw me stuck like a pig, you'd have had life for life. Well, it only shows me that pals is nothing, countrymen is nothing, tribes is nothing, and the world is nothing—but humbug, the whole lot on it. I should ha' died easier if I'd ha' known the French varmint hadn't had the best on me; but never mind, I can go to kingdom come like a brick, without no favours from nobody; take your mauleys off, I can cock my toe here as vell as any vere, so you may cut your sticks as soon as you likes. Off with the whole lot on you."

"Don't be too hard on us, Tom," said one of the men, "I'm ready to stick by you, and do wot you wishes done; I ain't a half-and-half pal, and if any von 'ull stand by me, why you shall see the tree turned into a nubbing chit afore you can tell a hundred."

"There ain't none of us going to cut you, Tom," said another; "tip us the word, and we'll turn him off as clean as Jack Ketch ever twisted off his man;" the remainder of the crew signified their unequivocal assent to the foregoing promise, and Tom's countenance once more displayed a smile.

"I thought you'd turn up trumps," he said, faintly; "wot's the use of being a gipsey if you can't have pals who would do more for you than you'd do for yourself? Now, lads, that vagerbone has bolted with the young gal I took a oath to pertect, and thereby has done me out of a small swag; he's also made you von less in number, and therefore it would be uncommon hard if von didn't retaliate on him in his own way; scripter says, a hye for a hye, a tooth for a tooth; he's sp'ilt me, now spile him. Never mind vot he says, drop him like a ripe plum from the tree—damn him, drop him, drop him."

The last words were uttered with a sort of growl, and were almost in-audible, from the faintness which his excessive loss of blood had produced. The gipseys proceeded to obey him. It was a frightful crisis for Nehemie, and the little courage he possessed fled before the evidently relentless deter-mination of the gipseys to hang him. He screamed for mercy when they seized him; he promised with tremendous oaths never to seek for Florence again, or in any degree molest her; he denied having her in his possession; he stated the real truth of the matter, and in distracted terms implored them to release him, but he might as well have prayed to stocks or stones. He was unheeded.

"Don't listen to his gab," cried Tom Cooper, with rancour, " he's a LIAR; I know him to be so, and even if he has told truth he has dropped me off my perch: blood for blood—up with him. Stay! look in his pockets, if he's got a silk handkercher hang him with it. When people finds him out they'll call him a suicide. Ha! ha! ha!"

With a shout the gipseys replied to Tom's directions; a silk handkerchief, large and of Indian manufacture was produced, and a noose was made in it, and then passed over Nehemie's head to his neck, and was adjusted as a hangman places the fatal rope round the neck of a condemned criminal. The shrieks and cries which the wretched man uttered were dreadful, and he was gagged to prevent their repetition. His struggles were terrific, but he was a child in the hands of half-a-dozen men, each equal in strength with himself. He was dragged to the tree; he was raised upon the shoulders of two of the men, while, supported as well by others, one of them mounted the tree to fasten the handkerchief to one of the stumps which projected from the trunk of the tree. He did his work strongly, and when he gave the signal, the gipseys who held Nehemie removed themselves from beneath him, and with a sudden dash he was launched into eternity, He had no covering over his face, and the contortions of his features were hideous to an awful degree, and the convulsions of his frame were equally horrible, but death soon put a stop to his struggles, and he waved to and fro in the wind a frightful specimen of a gipsey's vengeance.

Jasper viewed with intense horror the fate of Nehemie, a fate which he had no power to prevent, and which was brought about without his will or contri-vance. He would have felt lettle compunction in doing it; but not being a party to it, not having ordered it, caused it, or wished it, and coupled as it was with the probability of his being similarly disposed of, he was filled with terror and sickening apprehension, and was in that state of excitement a compound of fright and despair, that when an oath for the observance of secrecy was tendered to him he scarce knew what was said to him; he subscribed to it without understanding its purport, and when his bonds were withdrawn, he started off at the top of his speed, nor once looked back upon the horrible scene he had just witnessed.

The gipseys, on their part, lifted up their wounded leader, and carried him carefully to their camp which had been pitched at no very great distance from the spot, unknowing whether they bore in their arms life or death.

All that day the body of Nehemie presented the same ghastly spectacle in the bright sunlight, and when night came on it still swung to and fro in that desolate spot, the prey of carrion birds—an awful instance of a career of sin suddenly but effectually cut short for ever.

END OF THE FIRST VOLUME.